Shaw

Son of Eldar

SON OF ELDAR
by Shawn Lamb

Published by Allon Books
209 Hickory Way Court
Antioch, Tennessee 37013
www.allonbooks.com

Cover illustration by Andrea Fodor

Graphics by Robert Lamb

International Standard Book Number: 978-0-9964381-3-1

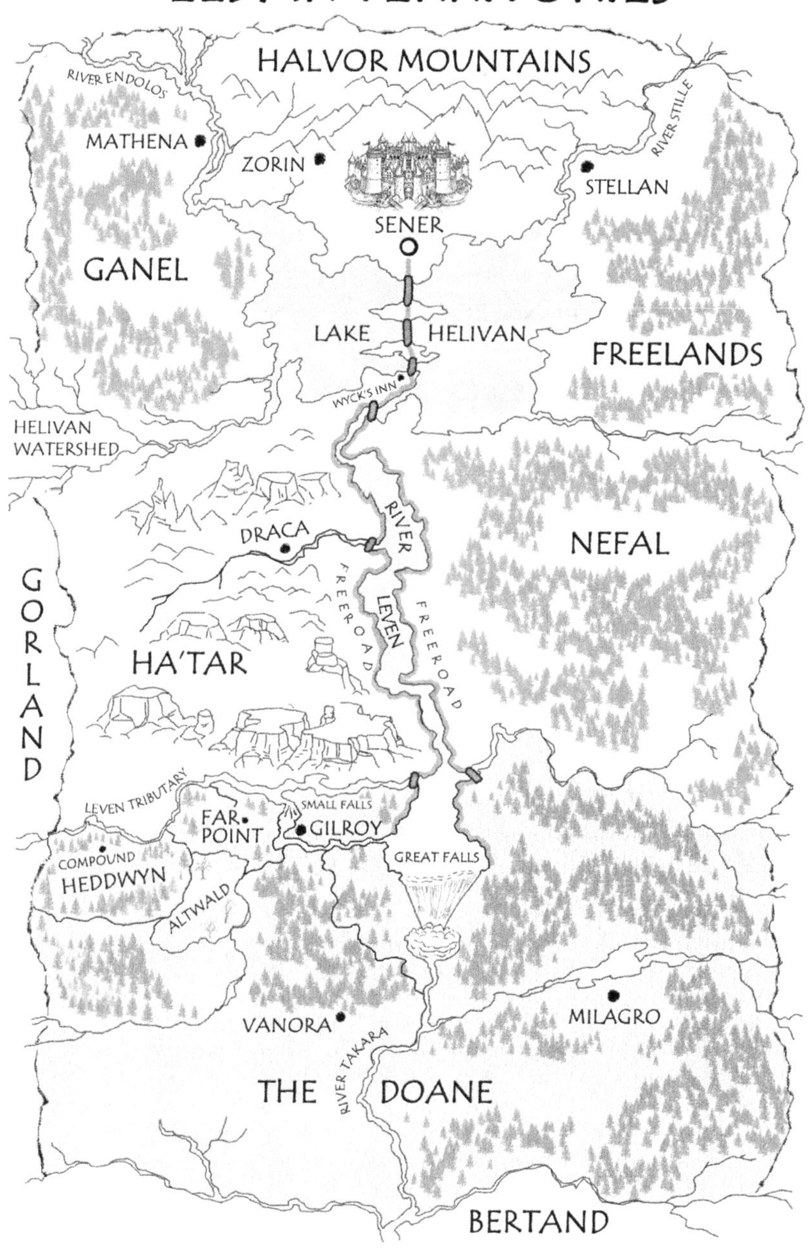
ELDAR TERRITORIES
HALVOR MOUNTAINS
RIVER ENDOLOS
RIVER STILLE
MATHENA
ZORIN
STELLAN
SENER
GANEL
LAKE
HELIVAN
FREELANDS
WYCK'S INN
HELIVAN
WATERSHED
RIVER
LEVEN
DRACA
NEFAL
FREEROAD
FREEROAD
GORLAND
HA'TAR
LEVEN TRIBUTARY
SMALL FALLS
FAR
POINT
GILROY
COMPOUND
HEDDWYN
GREAT FALLS
ALTWALD
MILAGRO
VANORA
RIVER TAKARA
THE
DOANE
BERTAND

Other Books by Shawn Lamb

Young Adult Fantasy Fiction

ALLON – BOOK 1 – STRUGGLE FOR ALLON
ALLON – BOOK 2 – INSURRECTION
ALLON – BOOK 3 – HEIR APPARENT
ALLON – BOOK 4 – A QUESTION OF SOVEREIGNTY
ALLON – BOOK 5 – GAUNTLET
ALLON – BOOK 6 – DILEMMA
ALLON – BOOK 7 – DANGEROUS DECEPTION
ALLON – BOOK 8 – DIVIDED
ALLON – BOOK 9 – IN PLAIN SIGHT

GUARDIANS OF ALLON – BOOK ONE – THE GREAT BATTLE
GUARDIANS OF ALLON – BOOK TWO – REPRIEVE
GUARDIANS OF ALLON – BOOK THREE – OVERTHROW

PARENT STUDY GUIDE FOR ALLON ~ BOOKS 1-9
THE ACTIVITY BOOK OF ALLON

For Young Readers – ages 8-10
Allon – The King's Children series

NECIE AND THE APPLES
TRISTINE'S DORGIRITH ADVENTURE
NIGEL'S BROKEN PROMISE

Historical Fiction

GLENCOE
THE HUGUENOT SWORD

Characters

Prince Axel, descendent of King Oleg
Sir Gunnar

Sener

Javan, Elector of Eldar
First Minister Dolus
Second Minister Beltran
Sylvan

Eldar's Six Territories

The Doane Territory

Nollen of Far Point
Ida, Nollen's sister
Magistrate Bernal
Hertz
Jonas, Innkeeper at Gilroy
Sharla, Jonas' wife
Abe and Bart, sons of Jonas
Destry, ferryman of Gilroy
Governor Ebert
Lady Blythe, Ebert's wife
Jabid

Heddwyn – inside The Doane

Arctander
Jarred
Bardolf, White Wolf alpha

Ha'tar Territory

Fod, leader of the Ha'tar
Gan, Fod's son
Kyn, advisor to Fod

Ganel Territory

Lord Ronan, governor of Ganel
Baron Irwin
Lord Cormac
Alfgar, Lord of the Unicorns
Othniel, Great White Lion of Eldar

Freelands Territory

Governor Gorman
Captain Mather

Nefal Territory

Lord Argus, Nefal chief
Dowid
Spoor

Halvor Mountains Territory

Artair, Eagle King
Ottlia, Artair's mate
Mayor Lorne, human governor of the Territory

Chapter 1

SHORTLY AFTER SUNRISE, HE DREW THE HORSE TO REIN ATOP THE plateau. He slipped back the cloak hood to take in the sweeping vista. The movement revealed a tall, strong man of thirty. Jet black hair reached his shoulders, while his beard closely trimmed. Despite the soil from lengthy travel, his clothes were made from fine material in shades of black and burgundy. The hood and shoulders of his cloak glistened with morning dew. He wore both sword and dagger.

Bright, almost clear, hazel eyes took in the magnificent view. The kingdom of Eldar stretched across the horizon. The early rays of sun shimmered across the mist rising from the late-autumn landscape. Large areas of bare trees and tall pines were broken by cleared pastureland and villages. Towns close to the border appeared fortified. Further in the distance, rose gentle foothills, the peaks bare of foliage.

With intense wonder, his eyes looked upon a place he had never seen. A place of his people. A place that drew him with a sense of purpose, of wonder, and of trepidation. Before today, he only heard stories told by those old enough to remember the last dispersion. Joined with what he read in The Ancient Manuscripts, his mind's eye envisioned what Eldar would look like. The real-life view surpassed anything he imagined and brought with it a whirlwind of emotions.

Beside him, another man sat upon an identical black steed. His head bare since the damp hood lay flat against the back of the cloak. A clean-shaven face showed a man fifteen years older. Grey invaded his auburn hair at the temples. He dressed similarly, though plainer in fabric.

Around his collar hung a gold-etched gorget, a sign of his position. Over the left breast of his doublet, an embroidered patch resembled the etching on the gorget. He shifted in the saddle, blue eyes vigilant in regard of the surroundings.

"Removing your hood is unwise, Highness. We may have avoided the border defenses, but Javan's spies are everywhere," he said with warning. He received no answer, as the Prince stared at the vista. "Did you hear me?" He reached over to touch the Prince's arm. "Axel?"

Axel didn't flinch at the touch, but did speak in a breathy, profound voice. "Do you feel it? A familiarity I didn't expect. Compelling, yet dark and hopeful at the same time." He turned to his companion. "Gunnar, is this what you remember of Eldar? An irresistible sensation?"

Gunnar sighed, as he shook his head. "*Irresistible* is not the word I'd use. Then again, I was ten when we were driven out." He turned to the vista. His lips snarled to curb rising anger. "The last of the Shining Ones fleeing for our lives. Death followed us to the border. Gott only knows how any of us survived."

Axel clapped Gunnar's shoulder. A soft encouraging smile appeared. "You know why. For Gott to use you now, for this moment."

Gunnar gazed with unwavering intent at Axel. "My use is nothing compared to what you must face, My Prince." He clasped the hilt of his sword. "Gott give me strength to help you through it."

Axel's smile changed to an expression of resolve. "You're wrong about being the last. Gathering the scattered is part of our task. Now, remember, no titles. Just call me Axel." He replaced the hood before he kicked his horse to descend from the plateau to the valley.

A mile away on a neighboring plateau, two men occupied an outlook shelter. A third man waited beside fully saddled horses. On the ground beside him, sat a cage with three birds inside. By their manner of dress, one was a nobleman while the others were soldiers. All were armed with swords.

The nobleman stooped slightly at the shoulders due to a deformity. His salt-and-pepper nut-brown hair was close-cropped. He held a leather-cased spyglass to this right eye. He chuckled with great pleasure, as he lowered the spyglass. He spoke to the soldier by the cage. "Send the message. He has crossed the border."

The soldier obeyed by releasing the birds from the cage.

"Should we follow him, Lord Dolus?" asked the other soldier.

A sardonic smile accompanied Dolus' answer. "No need to risk being seen." He collapsed the spy-glass and stepped out from under the shelter. He hooked it on the saddlebow before making a lengthy whistling call that echoed across the plateau.

The reverberation placed the soldiers on wary alert. Dolus noticed their reaction. "Be easy. *If* they heard anything, they will mistake it for a harpy."

At that moment, the screeching of a real harpy grew near. The bird's sharp talons extended, as the slate-black wings prepared to land on a tree limb. Once it settled on the branch, its double-crest rose, as a gesture meant to intimidate. With head stretched out, it screeched.

"Patience, Aras," Dolus spoke to the harpy. "You must follow him without being seen."

Aras rose tall on the branch, the double-crest at full spread with wings opened wide. The harpy's threatening posture made the soldiers retreat a step.

Annoyed, Dolus chided, "Enough, Aras! You will follow him until I say otherwise."

Aras settled back into a submissive posture with head lowered and the double-crest smoothed down.

"There now," said Dolus kindly. He stroked Aras' head. "The time will come for you to strike. Now, go, before he gets too far ahead." Dolus stepped back to allow Aras room to take flight. He watched until the harpy flew out of sight then said to the soldiers, "Our task is done. We return to Sener."

At the loud screech of a bird, Gunnar jerked in the saddle to look up. They rode in a short clearing between the plateau and forest.

"Quickly! We need to get under the trees!" Gunnar snapped the reins.

Axel's horse kept pace with Gunnar's mount. They reached the trees before another bird-cry sounded.

"Half-bare trees aren't much protection against an attack from above," said Axel in observation of the forest.

The pines grew straight and tall, but most deciduous trees were devoid of leaves. The pine branches provided some cover, but a good bit of sky could be seen through the bare limbs. A bird screeched again.

"It sounds like an eagle, so why are we running?"

"No, it's a harpy!" Gunnar chided. He watched for signs of the bird.

"I thought the eagles dominated the skies of Eldar."

"They did. A long time ago. The Nefal bred captured eagles with black vultures to create the harpys. When they had enough, they released them against the eagles …

"At the battle of Meder," said Axel.

"Aye. That battle drove the eagles from The Doane into the Halvor Mountain and helped the Nefal secure most of the eastern half of Eldar." Gunnar's face grew harsh with each word spoken.

Axel took notice of the reaction. "You're not old enough to remember Meder, so what disturbs you?"

Gunnar didn't immediately reply, rather kept a sharp lookout.

"Did the harpys or Nefal have anything to do with you fleeing Eldar?"

Gunnar's jowls tightened, as he nodded. Another bird's cry made him spy a harpy circling above the trees. "Burn that sound into your memory, for a harpy's cry is high-pitched compared to the deep resonance of an eagle."

Suddenly, smaller birds swooped through the trees to attack them. Short pecks with sharp beaks felt like stinging bites, drawing blood from both men and horses.

Gunnar pushed his horse into a gallop. Axel acted quickly to do the same. They recklessly weaved their mounts through the trees to avoid the birds.

Bursting into a clearing, Gunnar steered his horse toward a small lake. At full speed, he plunged his horse into the water. Axel came close behind. The depth of the water reached the horses' chest, but without any current. The small birds veered off in a steep climb to avoid the spray and splash caused by the violent entry.

Axel watched the agitated birds fly around the water's edge. "Why did they break off the attack?"

"Harpys don't like water."

"Those are harpys?"

"Fledglings. The older ones are too big to navigate a forest attack. That's why they drove us into the open." Gunnar drew his sword at sight of a full-grown harpy flying above the fledglings.

Drawing his sword, Axel placed the pummel in front of his face.

"No! Not yet," snapped Gunnar.

Axel lowered the sword to follow Gunnar's watch of the adult harpy. At two short cries from the adult, the fledglings headed back into the forest. The adult disappeared beyond the tree lined horizon. Axel glanced with guarded curiosity at Gunnar, who warily watched the sky. For several long moments, they waited in anticipation. Nothing.

"The purpose may have been to drive us into the open, so we can be easily spotted," said Gunnar.

"Well, there are more woods on the other side," said Axel.

Gunnar shook his head. "Until we are out of The Doane, the harpy will keep us from the forest." He surveyed the lake. "To the west, the Ha'tar. To the northeast, the Nefal."

"Sener is north. The place we are headed," said Axel with determination.

"You plan to swim up the Great Falls?" Gunnar dryly quipped.

"You said water will keep the harpys away." Axel flashed a wry grin. He turned his horse to cross the lake.

Gunnar grabbed the bridle of Axel's horse. "The Great Falls will take us out of The Doane but riding in the open is the most dangerous way to Sener."

"I can't avoid danger." Axel sheathed his sword.

Gunnar frowned in momentary thought. "If we travel along the shoreline until nightfall, we can avoid more harpy attacks. Going east or west is your choice. What does your heart tell you?" He put up his sword.

Axel took a deep breath and closed his eyes. His brow wrinkled then grew tightly knitted in concentration.

The expression concerned Gunnar. "Axel?"

With a loud exhale, Axel relaxed. He rubbed his eyes before speaking. "West. There is someone I must find."

Moving onto the shore, Axel headed in the stated direction. Gunnar stirred in the saddle. In one hand he held the reins, with the other, he gripped the hilt of his sword. For several hours, they traveled in silence. At midday, they ate some of the packed provision, while they continued to ride.

Shortly after eating, Axel noticed Gunnar's nervousness. "The harpy has returned and is following us, isn't it?" he said without glancing skyward.

"Aye," Gunnar grunted in reply.

Axel lowered his head with eyes shut. His lips moved, but no words spoken. The wind began to gust, followed by a crackle of thunder. Lightning streaked across the cloudless sky right in front of the harpy. The bird barely veered off to miss being struck, yet the force of the lightning knocked it sideways. It fought to right itself against the powerful wind. Another crash of thunder and bolt of lightning forced it from the sky, somewhere out of view.

Gunnar pulled his horse alongside Axel. "You must refrain from acting. It will only draw the enemy's attention!" he chided.

Axel looked along his shoulder at Gunnar. The clear hazel eyes steady in their regard. "Do you trust me?"

"Of course. I'm merely concerned for your welfare."

Axel smiled softly. "My welfare is not in question for this task. As for the enemy, he already knows I'm here." He motioned back in the direction of the harpy's disappearance.

Gunnar reluctantly muttered in agreement.

"Until I complete my task, I will use what powers Gott has made available to me. My only concern is how it will affect others. You included, old friend."

Gunnar straightened in the saddle, his shoulders square and head held high. "Be not troubled on my account. As Gott guides us, and aides us in our task, all will go as planned."

Axel fought back a tremor on his lips at Gunnar's declaration. He faced forward.

Around a bend in the river, they spied a gristmill. Two men worked outside, one older, one younger.

"Perhaps they know a place we can spend the night," Axel suggested.

"Let me speak with them." Gunnar took the lead. "Good day to you, friends." He spoke the familiar greeting with the accompanying hand gesture.

"A good day to you, friend," the older man replied with same hand gesture. He then grew a bit wary. "You sound Eldarian, but your clothes are foreign."

"A traveler newly returned home." Gunnar widely smiled.

"Ha!" the man scoffed a sarcastic laugh. "Who would want to return?"

"One who missed watching the mist rise from the Halvor Mountains and catching an abundance of fish from the Stille."

The man curiously eyed Gunnar. "You've been gone a long time if those are your memories. Nowadays, no man ventures into the Halvor, while the Stille is nearly devoid of fish, those worth eating anyway."

"Aye, those are the memories of youth," agreed Gunnar. "Tell me, friend, does hospitality remain or has that also changed?"

"Sadly, friend, much that was once free and easy is gone."

"Then perhaps, for a price, we can find a place to rest and food to eat?" Gunnar reached into a pouch on his belt and produced a coin. "Half a talent."

"Gold? Papa," said the young man with amazement.

The father shushed him, though the earlier wariness returned. "Gold is scarce, so you are either a robber or a cheat."

Gunnar raised in the saddle at the insult. "I am neither, friend! As I said, I'm returning from travels beyond the borders. I came by this from *honest* work."

"Whoever pays you in gold must be rich."

"Me," said Axel.

"And what would a foreigner want in Eldar?"

"I came to seek that which belongs to me."

Gunnar rolled his eyes in frustration at Axel's unguarded response.

"What would that be?"

"Not *what* rather *who.*"

Gunnar loudly cleared his throat to get Axel's attention. He then pressed the miller. "Do you want the gold in exchange for food and shelter or not?"

The miller hesitated with guarded consideration.

"Papa?" the son questioned, almost insistent.

His son's inquiry prompted an answer. "Food. I can't offer you shelter. The mill is only big enough for us, and I don't want jackals attracted by your presence."

Gunnar pulled his hand away when the miller reached for the coin. "Then oil and a lantern instead of shelter."

The miller nodded. "Done." He took the coin. "I'll fetch the food. Go to the shed for the lantern and oil," he told his son.

"You really need to be more careful!" Gunnar lowly chided Axel when the miller and his son left.

"Part of my task is to find the *brethren.* I can only do that if I probe. Or if Gott gives an unmistakable sign. Either way, we will know each other."

A few moments later, the miller and his son returned with the requested items. The miller handed the sack to Axel.

"Two-days rations is all we can spare."

"Thank you, friend."

The son gave an old lantern and oil flask to Gunnar, and asked, "Where are you heading?"

"West," replied Axel.

"Best go to Milagro for safety," began the miller. "There is nothing but hazardous wilderness to the west."

"Except Far Point," said the son, innocently. He received a scuff on the head from his father.

The reaction made Axel ask, "What is Far Point?"

In a begrudging tone, the miller answered. "A trading post at the furthest end of The Doane before Ha'tar territory. Only a fool would live there, much less trade."

"How many days journey from here to Far Point?"

"At least ten days. Take my advice, go to Milagro."

Axel's focus turned west. "No. We must go west." He turned his horse away from the river to continue the journey.

"Thank you, friend," Gunnar said to the miller.

"I think your *friend* is a bit daft."

Gunnar kept his eye on Axel yet asked the miller, "Is Milagro far?"

"Three days southwest, if you keep to the main road."

"Same direction as Far Point?"

"Generally. But—"

In his hurried departure to catch up to Axel, Gunnar didn't hear the objection. "We need to stop and rest before nightfall."

"We'll find shelter elsewhere. Don't want to endanger them with jackals."

"No, you intend to go to Far Point."

Axel didn't reply.

"Why?" insisted Gunnar.

"Because he named the place I need to go. I knew the signal came from our people in The Doane. When he mentioned *Far Point*, my spirit immediately recognized the answer."

"What he provided won't get us there. Milagro is three days ride on the main road. We can stretch the provisions and oil and obtain more supplies for a longer journey."

After brief consideration, Axel agreed, "Very well."

Gunnar glanced skyward through the trees. "Nightfall is coming. Harpys don't fly at night, but that is when jackals hunt." He let the reins fall to tend to the lantern. The horse continued to pick its way through the trees.

"What are you doing?"

"Trimming the lantern. When we stop for the night, this, and a good fire, will keep the jackals away. They hate light, and the brighter, the better."

Axel glanced around. "Which is best for travel, day or night?"

"It depends. Would you rather be attacked by birds or eaten by jackals?" Gunnar wryly countered.

Axel ignored the dry humor. "Are jackals also servants of the enemy?"

Gunner coaxed the flame for light, low since it was still twilight. "Not that I recall. Although much has changed."

"Then we travel at night and hide during the day yet keep the main road in sight."

"How did I know you were going to say that?" groused Gunnar in his normal dry-witted humor.

Gunnar removed a short pole from inside the bed roll. It measured almost four feet in length. He set one end of the pole in a sheath on the saddle pommel. The top of the poll had a four-inch-deep notch, and a strap attached a foot down from the notch. He set the lantern handle in the notch then used the strap to secure it to the pole for stability. This allowed him to ride without continuously holding the lantern and provided light for riding.

Chapter 2

BEING SUCH A VAST TERRITORY, THE DOANE HAD TWO MAJOR cities, Milagro in the east, and Vanora in the west. The River Takara served as a dividing point between the two halves of The Doane. The eastern part of the territory consisted of lush meadows, forest, and rolling hills. The western half experienced drier conditions, thus the barren lands stretched from Takara to cover the southernmost part of The Doane. Traveling further west, woodlands and meadows returned, fed by tributaries from the misty River Leven.

To ensure safe passage, a mile on either side of the main road to Milagro was cleared of forest and brush. This gave travelers time to sight dangers from harpys or jackals. Workers maintained the clearing for five miles to the last watering hole before the city. This stop provided much relief for those enduring the hazards of travels west to reach Milagro. For those heading east, it became a place to prepare to face the dangers.

Wrapped in a fur-lined cloak with raised hood, she sat on a bench outside the caretaker's hut. Beside her, a man impatiently paced. He anxiously watched the road. The late afternoon sun sank lower in the western sky. Most of the day's travelers had come and gone, leaving them alone to wait. Even the caretaker went inside to begin preparations for the evening.

"My lady, we must leave *now* if we are to return before the gates are shut," he urged.

"He will come," she calmly insisted.

"So, you have said all day. However, the danger grows the longer we remain. And not just from jackals," he spoke with strong emphasis.

She raised her head to look at him. "Are you afraid?"

"Not for myself."

She smiled. "My dear Deron, your concern is appreciated. However, I will not leave. I cannot, and you know why."

"Aye, my lady. I will speak to the caretaker about accommodations." He turned to go inside when she rose and grabbed his arm.

"He comes!" Her voice rose in excitement.

When they emerged from a path in the woods, Axel and Gunnar turned onto the main road a hundred yards from the watering hole.

She moved to stand in their way, just in front of the well. She lowered her hood to greet them. Her light brown hair showed signs of grey, but her face bright with a smile of expectation.

"My lord." She made a low courtesy to Axel. "Long have I waited for your coming."

"Indeed," said Axel, a bit guarded.

She took hold of the horse's bridle. Her voice lowered to speak privately. "Please, I realize my bold approach is unusual, but I beseech my lord, allow me to offer you accommodations." She slowly opened her gloved hand to reveal a medallion. "In the King's service."

Axel's eyes lifted from viewing the medallion to search the woman's eyes. "What is your name?"

"Blythe, my lord."

Axel smiled. "My Lady Blythe, I accept your hospitality."

Blythe beamed with joy. "Deron! Our horses."

Once mounted, Blythe moved beside Axel. "It is best any further conversation wait until we are safely home."

Axel nodded and motioned for Blythe to proceed.

From a window, the caretaker watched the departure.

They reached Milagro a few moments before the gates closed for the night. The gatekeeper and watchmen formally greeted Lady Blythe. To Axel and Gunnar, they simply nodded, visibly wary about the foreigners

"Visitors inquiring about trade," Blythe sternly answered the unspoken question.

"Of course, my lady," said the gatekeeper.

"Shut the gate, and be about your business," she ordered.

The men bowed when she, Axel and Gunnar entered town.

Blythe led them through the now deserted streets. At nightfall, even the citizens of Milagro moved inside. Few roamed the streets after dark, except for the lamplighters and night watch.

On the north side of the town square stood the territorial governor's residence. Blythe drew rein and waited for Deron to help her dismount.

"See their horses are well cared for," she told Deron.

Once inside, a maid and male servant promptly arrived.

"Welcome home, my lady. We became concerned." She took Blythe's cloak. The man took Axel and Gunnar's cloaks.

Blythe kindly smiled. "Riva. Food and drink for our guests."

"At once, my lady. A fire is prepared in the private salon."

Blythe escorted them to the mentioned room. "Please, warm yourselves while we wait."

Axel rubbed his hands over the flames. "This home belongs to ...?" He searched for an answer.

"My husband, Ebert. He is governor of The Doane."

"Is he home?" asked Gunnar, concerned.

"No. He is en route to Sener with the quarterly tribute. You need not fear us being interrupted." She flashed a sweet smile.

Axel turned his back to the hearth. "You said you were waiting for me. How is that possible?"

Blythe approached carrying two glasses. "Gorlander sherry. A rare treat in these parts." She handed them each a glass. "To answer your question, among *our* people I am considered a prophetess. A humble honor bestowed by Gott, for which I am truly grateful. Especially today."

She fetched a glass to raise a toast. Her smile trembled, as tears of joy filled her eyes. "To your blessed arrival, my *liege*."

Axel accepted the toast. He and Blythe drank.

Gunnar hesitated to join them. Instead, he spoke his concern. "You take a great risk bringing us here. And you for accepting," he said to Blythe and Axel respectively. His attitude a bit gruff.

The rough manner distressed Blythe, so Axel said, "Sir Gunnar, my loyal friend and bodyguard, speaks only with concern for our welfare."

Suddenly aware of his unintended offense, Gunnar hastily apologized. "Indeed. Please forgive my bluntness, my lady." He bowed to Blythe.

"Your concern is understandable. I assure you, Sir Gunnar, the servants I retained this evening are all brethren sworn to the Oath. I would not endanger the Son of Eldar."

Gunnar grinned and lifted his glass to drink.

"What of your husband, Lord Ebert?" asked Axel.

She grew timid, and weakly admitted, "Alas, he is not of the brethren. The nature of his position causes him to view everything with skepticism."

"Why did you marry him if he does not share your faith?"

"We married before he became governor. We were young, and a bit impulsive." She sat to continue her recollection. "Back then, Ebert was kind and gentle. He willingly listened, and on some points of faith, even agreed. Jabid, my brother, tried to warn me. He and Ebert have been best friends since childhood." She took a drink of sherry to recover her nerves at speaking on the subject. "Becoming governor changed him." She then looked at Axel with urgency. "But he has never been unkind to me. He allows me whatever freedom I ask."

"Then I renew my earlier objection about risk," said Gunnar. This time he maintained an even tone.

She soberly nodded. "Perhaps. Only I followed Gott's leading." She pointedly asked Gunnar, "Which would you do, take a risk to obey Gott, or face guilt for disobedience?"

A grin of approval spread across Gunnar's face. "A well-placed riposte, my lady."

"How much further to Far Point?" asked Axel.

The question caught Blythe off-guard. "Far Point? Oh, you mean the last outpost before Ha'tar." She shrugged in consideration. "A week or more. Much depends upon the weather, and other hazards," she added with warning.

Axel motioned to Gunnar. "Gunnar grew up in the Freelands thus familiar with harpys and jackals."

"We will need enough oil and provisions for the journey," Gunnar said to Blythe.

"You plan to night travel?" she asked, concerned.

Gunnar wryly smiled. "The lesser risk."

Riva, and two other servants, brought food, plates, and tankards. They quickly set the table."

"I ordered the guest room prepared, my lady," said Riva.

"Thank you."

The servants left. Blythe, Axel, and Gunnar sat to eat. She offered a simple, yet grateful prayer for the meal.

"Let us enjoy, and speak no more of risks," she sweetly said. "In the morning, I will send you on your way with whatever is required. My task was to welcome you, and tell you there are many ready to rise in service of our True King."

Axel patted her hand. "You have faithfully discharged your duty both to Gott, and me."

She suddenly shivered and paled.

"Lady Blythe?" Axel gripped her arm in support.

She fearfully stared at him. "Gott says, *Beware of Dolus!* Javan may hold the title of Elector, but Dolus' evil machinations rule through him."

Axel glanced curiously to Gunnar, to which Gunnar replied, "I've not heard his name before."

"He came to power ten years ago. His pact with the devil runs deep and infects Eldar like a plague. *He* ordered the slaughter of the priests!" Her eyes grew misty with grief. She fell back in the chair, exhausted.

"Riva!" Axel shouted. "Riva!"

The maid hurried in answer to the call. "My lord? My lady!" With great concern, she knelt beside Blythe's chair.

"Take her to her room, and see she is given a tonic of wine mixed chamomile and lemongrass to calm her nerves," Axel instructed.

"My lord," Blythe spoke in distress, unwilling to release Axel.

"All will be well, dear lady. Rest and recover." Axel helped Blythe stand and gave her to Riva.

As the women departed, Gunnar moved beside Axel. "What do you make of that?"

"A timely warning." Axel stared at the door in consideration. "We leave as soon as the gates open."

"And the supplies?"

Axel grinned. "Somehow I think we'll have everything we need by dawn." He nudged Gunnar's arm. "Let's finish eating."

Chapter 3

Deep in the forest that separated The Doane from the Ha'tar, majestic pines and massive ancient oaks formed a protected canopy under which they lived in seclusion. Although the current season meant no leaves on the oaks, the numerous limbs and branches provided ample shelter even during the harshest of winters.

Six huge oak trees formed a circle enclosing a half acre patch of ground. In a narrow gap between two of the oaks, they constructed a gate to appear as a natural barrier. The gap-gate opened wide enough to allow horses or a small wagon to pass single file.

Up in the sturdier branches, several structures were built in such a way as to appear natural outgrowth of the oaks. Branch bridges stretched between the structures. Two spiral stairways wound around the trunks leading to the ground.

In the middle of the ringed compound stood a finely crafted longhouse. A hive of activity happened inside and outside. At several outdoor fires, women prepared breakfast. Two saddled horses, and three pack mules stood tethered by the entrance to the longhouse. From the back of the saddles, hung small crossbows, and a quiver of darts attached by a leather strap.

Inside, people went about their daily chores. Children gathered in the circle on the floor where they listened with rapt attention to an old man. For being aged, his white hair remained full and supple, his voice strong and clear. With animated gestures, changing facial expressions and vocal tones, he captivated his young audience.

"Then! The sky will be filled with the sound of rushing wind, as the eagles swoop down. No harpy will be safe from the eagles' mighty attack. The unholy alliance between the Ha'tar, Nefal, and Elector—"

"But, when, Arctander?" a teenage boy impatiently interrupted.

"Aye, we've been waiting so long already," another teenager chimed in.

"Patience," began Arctander. "It won't be much longer. Signs of the True King's return are being fulfilled as we speak."

"We've heard nothing about the Six Treasures. Nor about Othniel. Have you even seen this great white lion of Eldar?" scoffed the first teen.

Arctander scowled in effort to maintain his temper. "Just because I have not seen Othniel does not negate his existence. I have not seen Gott, but I *know* he exists. And Othniel is Gott's spirit guardian of Eldar. The supreme of all beasts."

The teenagers huffed in dismissal, with one speaking in refute. "For all we really know, Gott's presence is as elusive as Othniel!"

Irate, Arctander stood to confront them. "Blasphemy during Zakar is outrageous. This is the time for us to remember what Gott has done, and what is promised! Are you two of such little faith that you scorn the Almighty?"

"We didn't mean that."

"Then what did you mean?" asked a new male voice in a tone of command.

The teens found themselves confronted by a tall, burly man of thirty-five with auburn hair and beard. He moved beside Arctander. He appeared every inch a woodland leader in his leather clothing of brown, tan, and black.

"Jarred!" the teen stammered. In hasty regret, he blurted out, "We meant no disrespect."

Not swayed by the excuse, Jarred folded his arms. "Questioning Arctander and scoffing at Gott sounds like disrespect to me." His gaze shifted between the boys. "You both will stand the night watch for a week." He motioned with his head for them to leave.

Without further protest, the teens withdrew.

"Impatience makes them edgy," said Arctander.

"They aren't the only ones," groused Jarred.

Nollen, a young man of twenty with brown hair and pale blue eyes, approached. He wore clothes different than the woodlanders, those of a merchant with grey wool trimmed in sturdy black leather. "That's the last of the supplies," he said.

Jarred's attitude changed to agreeable toward Nollen. "Good. Now, what news from the outside world?"

Nollen shrugged. "Nothing much to report. The Ha'tar are quiet for now. Though how much longer that will last is anyone's guess."

"What of the dragons?"

"As long as the Ha'tar aren't riled up, they remain content to stay in their territory."

Arctander studied Nollen. "Tell me, has Javan done anything out of the ordinary lately? Anything you can think of."

Nollen considered the question then shook his head. "No. Of course, he likes to throw around his edicts, and demand for tribute, but nothing that causes alarm. Why?" he asked when visible worry made Arctander sit.

"Something stirs." He motioned for Jarred and Nollen to sit beside him. He spoke in hushed tones. "Lately, I've been studying the old scrolls with a profound sense that change *is* coming." He seized Nollen's arm. "As our only contact with the outside world, you *must* keep your eyes and ears open, your sword sharp, and faith strong."

Nollen made a nervous laugh. "I can do everything but the sword."

"This is no laughing matter!" Arctander scolded. With a heavy hand on Nollen's shoulder, he continued with urgency. "We depend upon you and Ida."

Nollen's brief nervousness became replaced by solemnity. "I know. As Gott is witness between us, our people will survive."

Arctander embraced Nollen. "Go in Gott's peace, my beloved grandson." He kissed Nollen on the forehead.

Nollen gave Jarred a nod before he exited the longhouse. Outside, he found his sister, Ida, with another woman at one of the cooking fires. They chatted and laughed, ignorant of his approach. Older by ten years, she shared the same hair color, only darker eyes compared to him. She wore clothes identical with slits in her skirt to make riding astride easier.

"I'm afraid, we must be on our way," Nollen informed Ida.

"Not on empty stomachs," insisted the woman. She fetched two small loaves. "Fresh oatmeal honey bread. Ida already packed more provisions for later."

Nollen took a whiff of the bread and smile. "Smells wonderful. Thank you."

"No, thank you," said the woman sincerely. "Your provisions are Gott sent. May the Almighty guide you safely home." She embraced the siblings.

Ida followed Nollen to the horses. Relieved of their burdens, the pack mules trailed behind Ida's mount by way of a lead-line. They bid the others farewell and rode from the compound. Two men closed the gates behind them.

After a half-mile, Nollen stopped in a clearing. When Ida took the lead with the pack horses, he dismounted beside a large pine with a split trunk. He reached inside the trunk. With a snap, a net covered in leaves rose from the ground to meet the lowest branch of the pine. To the casual observer, the camouflage appeared so dense as to forbid passage between the pines.

Ida waited for Nollen. "Any instructions?"

"Grandfather told me something important." He popped a piece of bread in his mouth.

"What?" she eagerly asked when he paused to eat.

"According to the scrolls, change is coming … *soon.* He's worried in a way I've not seen before. Jarred heard him too."

Ida took a moment to digest Nollen's assessment. "What does he want us to do?"

"Watch for anything unusual. If change is coming, Javan might be quick to act." He ate more bread.

"Did Jarred say anything to you personally?" she asked with a certain probing lilt in her voice.

Nollen fought a smile at the question she always asked. "Like what? I want to marry your sister and have her move to the forest?"

Pricked by the teasing, Ida kicked her horse to leave.

"Ida!" He quickly caught up with her, as the mules slowed her progress. "I'm sorry. I was wrong to tease you."

Ida lashed out in frustration. "Why are we denied what others freely enjoy?"

"No one is denying you. Not me. Not Grandfather." He pulled his horse ahead to stop their trek. "Go back if you want. I can take care of the trading post."

"It's too dangerous alone, and you know it."

"*That* is what is stopping you. Same as Jarred even suggesting marriage," he pointedly said.

Ida snapped the reins to continue. Nollen quietly followed. Being the brethern's only link to the outside world came with difficult choices. He hated the fact that his sister felt such responsibility, as to forego happiness with the man she loved. True, the responsibility passed onto them by their parents, but surely, they could choose otherwise? He was now well in manhood, and a capable trader. Why should she continue in their covert role? Especially since their clandestine trips grew more hazardous.

Because lives depend upon us, that's why, his conscience answered the question.

It served no purpose to continue down a futile path of arguing. In his heart, he knew the truth. Despite the danger associated with the responsibility, it is one he would have chosen. His Oath and faith in Gott compelled him. Any dereliction of duty would only bring misery, both personally, and to those in the forest—the remnant of his people. Nollen shook the distracting thoughts from his mind to focus on the perilous journey home.

Once across a small river, Nollen and Ida armed their crossbows. This part of journey required alertness. The small clearing between woods brought them within a mile of the Ha'tar border.

Then it happened! The gushing thump-thud. Before they could react, a Ha'tar dragon rider landed in front of them. Ida dropped her crossbow when her startled pony reared. The mules also tried to bolt away from the dragon. Ida pulled hard on the lead-line to gain control of the mules. Nollen took up a defensive position with raised crossbow.

"That puny weapon won't help you," said the Ha'tar with a scoffing laugh. The rider's armor-like clothing consisted of dragon scales, fur, and leather. Upon his head, he wore a domed helmet with fur flaps to cover his ears from the harsh wind of flight. He carried a curved sword, and a long bow slung across his back.

The dragon stood four times the size or a war horse with pointed snout, powerful tail, and twisted horns. With an elaborated forged metal bridle around the dragon's snout, the rider controlled the beast. A saddle protected the rider from the dragon's scales, while also serving to carry extra weapons such as a lance and arrows.

"Gan!" Nollen sneered the name. "What do you want?" He kept steady aim at the rider.

"Finished trading? Too bad. You know the rules, Nollen of Far Point. If caught, you must pay a toll to pass."

"We're not in Ha'tar territory."

Gan haughtily laughed and spread his arms. "Anywhere a dragon can fly *is* Ha'tar territory!"

"Tell that to the harpys and Nefal."

"Nollen," Ida nervously hissed in warning.

"Listen to your *older* sister, *little* Nollen. The toll, and you may pass."

The dragon roared, as if adding its threat.

Thwarted, Nollen reached into his saddlebag to pull out a brown leather pouch. "Gold has become scarce due to Javan's demands. Two markats from the Halvor mountains. I took them in trade for badly needed supplies."

"Markats? Who would trade such rare green stones for supplies?" huffed Gan in disbelief.

"One desperate enough to want to live."

Gan slyly smiled. "You mean flee Javan's justice."

Nollen shrugged. "Think what you will but take the stones and let us pass." He threw the pouch at the Gan.

Gan caught it. He moved the dragon to block their path of departure. "I must examine them." He opened the pouch to withdraw the stones. He fought a smile at the sight of cut and shiny markats not raw stones. "Whoever traded *these* was indeed desperate." He then frowned upon further inspection. "Where is the setting?"

"I don't know. I only received the stones in trade."

Gan sneered. "You wouldn't try to cheat me by keeping the gold setting?"

"My brother doesn't cheat people like some others!" Ida bravely chided.

The dragon's roar frightened Ida.

"Oh, Ryu didn't like your implication," said Gan.

"I—I didn't mean you," Ida stammered.

Nollen moved his horse between Ida and Gan. He held his crossbow ready, though not aimed. "You know what she meant. The stones are of high quality, so let us pass." When Gan remained silent, Nollen spoke over his shoulder to Ida. "Take the lead."

Gan didn't move in response to their departure. Neither Nollen or Ida looked back, for to do so, could cause trouble.

"Should I retrieve my crossbow?" Ida carefully asked over her shoulder.

"No. Gan probably took it as a trophy," Nollen groused.

"What about Gilroy? We can't be seen returning by a different direction."

"We'll change course once we are safely away."

A sudden gust of wind with a thump-thud, told them that the dragon had taken off. Still, they travelled another mile before Nollen veered off into a patch of woods. The forest grew thicker. Thirty minutes later, the sound of rushing water could be heard.

Nollen turned in the saddle to shout back at Ida. "Through the passage under the falls, so we can approach Gilroy like usual."

She waved in acknowledgement.

When they reached the narrow passage, they couldn't hear anything due to the crashing sound of the waterfall. This fall rose to a height of sixty feet, a dwarf compared to the massive Great Falls, yet powerful enough to prevent crossing the river without a ferry.

On the other side of the falls, Nollen pushed his horse up a steep incline. From the crest, the forest descended into a glen on the north side of the small fortress town of Gilroy. Fading sunlight cast long shadows at the tree line.

"We need to hurry to make it before the gates close!" Nollen urged Ida. Distance widened between them, as Nollen pushed his pony in hopes of getting the gatekeeper's attention. "Hey! Hey!" he shouted and waved his arms.

The gatekeeper spotted him and waved in return. "Hurry!"

Nollen reached the gate a few moments before Ida. She struggled with pulling on the lead rope of the protesting mules.

"You made it just in time," said the gatekeeper.

"Thanks for waiting, friend," said Nollen.

"Be glad that I saw you. Mistress," he greeted Ida.

Nollen led the way to the Gilroy inn. Located in the western quarter of the town, the inn backed up to the wall. The bottom floor consisted of the tavern, dining room, and kitchen. Above the main floor were six guest rooms. A hallway from the tavern served as a connection to the eight-stall barn. Beside the barn was a corral, with access from the street. This served for mounted travelers. Those with a wagon or carriage, went to the livery down the street.

A large rear courtyard housed a private well, chicken coop, hog pen, hay shed, and area for two milking cows. The courtyard could be reached via a back door from the kitchen and alleyway gate.

Nollen and Ida drew rein before the barn. Twin fourteen-year-old boys, Abe and Bart, ran to greet them.

"Nollen! We wondered if something happened!" Abe took hold of the bridle.

Nollen dismounted and ruffled Abe's red hair. "Almost. The Ha'tar are getting bolder in crossing the border. You and Bart take care of our horses and mules. There will be an extra treat when finished." He removed his saddlebags and crossbow. He waited for Ida to retrieve her bags. They entered the inn.

"Hello, Friend Jonas!" Nollen hailed the innkeeper.

"Ah, speak of the dead or rather we thought you were when you didn't arrive yesterday," Jonas happily replied.

Nollen and Ida placed their bags and his bow on a table where they sat. "What can I say? Trading and the Ha'tar don't always keep to a time schedule."

"Gan?" asked Jonas with annoyance.

"Aye. When I offered him markats instead of gold, I thought that was the end for us." Nollen indicated a weary Ida.

Jonas smile kindly at Ida. "A good meal, hot bath, and soft bed will help you feel better, my dear." He shouted over his shoulder, "Sharla! Our friends are back. Bring the best."

Sharla called a happy response from the kitchen.

Jonas fetched two tankards of ale. He then sat beside Nollen, leaned close, and spoke in a private tone. "Tell me, is all well?"

Nollen drank before he replied. "As well as can be." He cautiously glanced around the room. Only four other patrons occupied the inn. He reached into his saddlebag to carefully remove a small carved wooden box. "For your sons."

Jonas slowly opened the lid enough to see the content. He quickly shut it. He blinked back the water rising in his eyes.

"He sends his best," Ida quietly to Jonas.

Jonas discreetly wiped his eyes. Sharla arrived with two heaping plates of food. She happily greeted Nollen and Ida.

"Come, woman, let them eat while we prepare the room and bath."

Chapter 4

In the still of the night, Nollen quietly left the room where he and Ida slept. He didn't need a candle or lantern, as Jonas kept hall oil lamps lit so guests could find the latrine. Downstairs, he saw Jonas seated at a corner table. A single candle provided light. The small wooden box he gave Jonas earlier sat on the table. Nollen took a seat opposite him.

"You haven't given them to the boys yet?" Nollen asked.

"No. How can I tell them where these came from?"

Nollen looked incredulous at Jonas. "What? They don't know their heritage?"

Ashamed, Jonas lowered his head. "I'm afraid of what may happen if they learn. I don't have your courage."

"Courage comes from our Faith. At least that's what Papi and Grandfather always told me. I'm still learning it for myself."

Conflicted between defense and frustration, Jonas leaned across the table. "You live isolated at the outpost. Here, in town, the pressure is mounting." His hand grasped the box.

"You said they took the Oath. Have they recanted?"

"No."

At Jonas' discomposure, Nollen sat back, guarded yet concerned. Such behavior was unusual for Jonas. There could be only one reason. "Something happened after I left."

Jonas slowly nodded. "The Magistrate came to Gilroy, *not* to visit his cousin." His expression turned fearful. "Javan issued another edict. This one deadlier than before." He tapped the box. "Prison has been replaced by *execution*."

Nollen took a moment to digest the disturbing news.

Jonas pushed the box toward Nollen. "Take them back."

"No, Jonas ..."

"Take them!" Jonas quickly left the table. The box remained.

Nollen's jowls flexed in painful anger. He snatched up the box and hurried back to the guest room. He thrust open the door, which disturbed Ida. Realizing his mistake, he slowly shut it so as not to completely wake her. Too late.

"Nollen?" Ida sleepily said.

"We leave at first light," he spoke in a tight voice.

"Why?"

"We need to be going." He shoved the box into his saddlebag then climbed back into his bed. A small table separated the two beds. He turned away from her.

"Nollen," she spoke in a motherly, scolding voice.

He sighed and turned to face her. "Jonas gave me back the box." Surprise made her prop herself on her elbow, which prompted him to explain. "He's afraid because a new edict means *death*."

"Dear Gott," she whispered in distress.

Nollen stared at the ceiling. "Our numbers are dwindling."

"No!" Ida tossed back the covers to sit on the edge of the bed. "Fear is a weapon of the enemy. Do not let it take hold."

He looked directly at her to say, "Jonas has."

"Then we will pray for Gott to strengthen him."

Nollen nodded agreement, yet said, "We still leave at first light."

After a whispered heartful prayer for Jonas and his family, Ida slipped back under the covers. She quickly fell back asleep.

Nollen lay awake staring at the ceiling. To hear the normally sure-minded Jonas admit fear deeply disturbed him. True, they lived in a remote location. However, that didn't mean they were impervious to trouble; actually, more so with their secret activities. Yet, Jonas knew all this, so why succumb to fear?

"Javan," Nollen bitterly breathed the name. He recalled his grandfather's question concerning anything unusual from Javan. Declaring death to those of the Oath surpassed *unusual* - it meant to terrorize.

"Gott, please, let this tyranny end soon," he earnestly prayed before he rolled over to try to sleep.

When the first light of dawn peeked through the shutters, Nollen rose from bed. He gently woke Ida. Together they packed to leave.

Downstairs, the aroma of breakfast reached their nostrils. Nollen detained Ida from entering the kitchen. Instead, he steered her to the front door.

"You're not leaving without something to eat," Sharla's voice came from behind.

"We've caused enough disturbance," said Nollen apologetically.

"I won't take no for an answer," Sharla kindly rebuffed. "You may not sit to eat, but you will take this." She held out a basket.

Ida accepted it. "Thank you."

"You'll find everything ready in the stable." Sharla smiled at Nollen. "The boys rose early to make preparations for you."

"Thank you," Nollen spoke with a touched smile. He and Ida headed for the stables.

Abe and Bart waited with the saddle ponies, and harnessed mules attached to the lead-line. "Mama said you had something for us," said Bart.

The statement caught Nollen off-guard. A nudge from Ida made him speak. "I did. Only your father thought it too generous."

Abe and Bart exchanged knowing glances at the dodge before Abe spoke. "Mama told us everything, and we are willing to accept the risk for our Oath."

Nollen's gaze shifted between the twins. "It would be wrong to go against your father's wishes."

"I will take the blame." Sharla arrived. She briefly held up a worn medallion before hiding it back in the pocket of her skirt.

"Are you certain?" Ida asked Sharla.

"Aye. We prayed about it last night." She indicated her sons. "Please, Nollen, the box." When he hesitated, she added, "I sent Jonas earlier to the market, so you need not fear he will intervene."

Nollen cocked a wry smile. "What excuse did you give? That Laren holds back on his goods to start them arguing?" He retrieved the box from his saddlebag.

Sharla chuckled and replied, "They don't need an excuse to argue."

Nollen held the box between both hands, his expression woeful. "This is not how I wanted it to be. Jonas—" He couldn't finish for being upset.

"He will come around in time." Sharla took the box. "Gott grant you safe journey." She waved for the twins to open the stable doors and gate.

Without looking back, Nollen and Ida rode from the inn. This time they headed to the west part of town. Through this gate, they took the path down to the river ferry.

Destry, the ferryman worked on the dock. He responded to Nollen's hail. "Well, well, you appear in one piece. Everyone in town began to wonder when you didn't arrive on schedule."

"Gan," was all Nollen said.

Destry shook his head and huffed. "The Ha'tar are growing too bold."

"The river appears swollen," Nollen observed.

"Heavy rains while you were gone."

Nollen dismounted to lead his pony onto the large ferry. "Then I suppose your fee is double." He helped Ida with the mules.

"No, only one and half times, *if* you remembered the gift for my wife." Destry made certain all the animals were safely onboard before he closed the gate.

Ida rummaged through her saddlebag. "One carved onyx brooch." She gave it to him.

"A very nice one," Destry said with admiration. "My regular fee." He pocketed the brooch then shoved off.

A pulley attached to a sturdy line stretched above and across the river. Destry guided the craft over the choppy water. Nollen and Ida worked to keep the ponies and mules calm for the crossing. The current ran swifter than normal due to the rain. Instead of ten minutes, it took double the time to complete the crossing. Workers on the opposite shore, helped secure the ferry, and lead the animals to shore.

After paying Destry, Nollen and Ida continued their journey northwest. Travelling the hilly and terrain would take the better part of the day.

By afternoon, they reached the woods west of the trading post. Once through these woods, they would travel the open meadow to the trading post. Anyone riding The Doane needed to be alert for signs of harpys. The malevolent birds always caused trouble for the human inhabitants.

The late afternoon sun sank low on the horizon when they reached the forest edge. Far Point appeared as a mere speck on the far side of the two-mile wide meadow.

"Gott keep us safe," Nollen prayed aloud. He armed his crossbow just before they left the safety of the trees.

"Perhaps they won't attack since the mules are empty." Ida tried to sound hopeful, as they began the open trek.

"We can only hope," groused Nollen. "Just to be safe, let's pick up the pace." He kicked his pony into a lope.

Sight of the outpost grew larger. Five buildings consisted of a main house, barn, store, storage shed, and chicken coop. The size and good condition told of a profitable business. Soldiers on horseback and one riderless horse came into view.

"Looks like we have visitors," Nollen warned over his shoulder. He slowed his horse. "No need to appear anxious."

Ida followed his lead in taking the animals down to a walk. "Who do you think?"

"Hertz. Who else?" he groused. "Take the ponies and mules to the barn while I deal with him."

"Don't anger him," she warned.

"Me?" he retorted with sarcasm. "I stared down Gan, didn't I?" He drew rein between the barn and store, dismounted, and gave the reins to Ida.

A short, barrel-chested man dressed in official attire of black and gold waited on the porch. Hertz flashed a caustic grin. He fingered the signet medallion around his neck.

"You're late, Nollen," he scolded.

"No. I made it before curfew."

Hertz sneered at the rebuffed. "Your note said you would be back yesterday. Why are you a day late?"

Nollen mounted the steps to the porch. "Rains swelled the river, and we had to wait for the ferry." He unlocked the door.

Hertz laid hold of Nollen. "A moment, *if* you please," he spoke in a tone not accepting opposition.

Nollen shook him off to enter the shop, which incited the official.

Hertz hurried to follow. "You are late with your taxes. I am here to collect. With interest, of course."

Nollen flashed a toothy grin of mockery. "Does it not say in the charter that interest can only be collected for deliberate avoidance of the tax? How can it be deliberate if our return was delayed by an act of nature?" When Hertz seethed at the retort, Nollen pressed his point. "You wouldn't want me to bring that to the Magistrate's attention, now would you?"

"Do you have witnesses to this *natural* delay?"

"The ferryman of Gilroy. A relative of the Magistrate Bernal, I believe."

With great indignation, Hertz reached into the pouch he carried. He slammed a small leather-bound ledger on the counter. He flipped open the pages. "Your tax is five gilders."

"Five? The normal amount is four. Are you adding illegal interest?" Nollen challenged.

"A ferry tax levied by the Magistrate last week. While you were out of town." Hertz grinned with triumph. He pulled out a piece of worn paper from the back of the ledger to give Nollen. "You just admitted to using the ferry at Gilroy."

Nollen tossed the paper back to Hertz before he turned to retrieve the money. Hertz noted the collected amount in the ledger then held out the roughhewed pencil for Nollen's signature.

Hertz gathered his things. "My compliment to your sister." His laughter lingered, as he exited the trading store.

Nollen waited until the sounds of hooves faded before he proceeded to the door. "May harpys hound your journey home!" he swore under his breath. He proceeded to the barn. The ponies and mules were stalled.

Ida put hay in the feed troughs. "What did Hertz want?"

"Money, what else?" In anger, he kicked over an empty bucket. "Every time he finds a loophole to collect more. I thought my ferry story would work to avoid the fine, but Bernal levied a ferry tax while we were gone."

Ida gripped his shoulder. "A few extra coins are a small price to pay for what we do."

Nollen released his anger with a long sigh. "Aye."

"Time to secure everything for the night."

"Why can't the jackals be afraid of the harpys like the rest of us?"

She locked the main barn door from inside then nudged him to a private side door.

Chapter 5

FOUR OF JAVAN'S SOLDIERS ENTERED THE INN OF GILROY SHORTLY after midday. Upon sight of them, Jonas felt a tightening of anxiety in his chest. He caught Sharla's apprehensive glance. Steeling his resolve, he forced a smile to greet the soldiers.

"Welcome to the Inn of Gilroy. I'm Jonas, the proprietor. If you need—"

"Food and drink. And be quick about it!" barked the squad leader. The soldier sat nearest the fire.

"Right away!" Jonas signaled Sharla to the kitchen while he fetched a pitcher of ale and four tankards. He set the pitcher down in the middle of the table. He no sooner handed out the tankards then the soldiers began to drink.

"Another pitcher!" ordered the leader.

Jonas scurried away to fulfill the command.

Abe rushed in from the stable hallway. He wore a long coat over his doublet since he worked in the cold. He spoke in hurried words to Jonas. "Papa, soldiers—"

Jonas punched Abe's arm, and jerked his thumb toward the hearth table. "Where's Bart?" he asked in near whisper.

"Pitching hay," Abe replied in a similar tone.

"Go back to the stables, and both of you keep out of sight."

When Jonas moved from the bar toward the table, Abe took the opportunity to dash back down the hall.

"Here you are. The second pitcher."

"Where's the food?"

"Food is coming!" Jonas spoke loud enough to be heard in the kitchen.

Seconds later, Sharla and another maid, carried trays with plates of steaming roast, vegetables, and fresh hot bread.

Once served, Jonas waved the women away to address the soldiers. "Enjoy."

The leader seized Jonas's arm. "I have a few questions for you."

He tried to maintain a calm, agreeable demeanor. "I'll answer if I can."

"Any strangers been in here recently?"

Jonas heaved a noncommittal shrug. "Strangers pass through Gilroy all the time. I see new faces every day."

"Would you recognize two foreigners?"

"Foreigners?" Jonas repeated, confused.

"Aye, *foreigners!*" the leader spoke with mocking emphasis. "Are you deaf? Or incapable of answering a simple question?"

"No," insisted Jonas. "I just can't recall any foreigners. Is that why you're in Gilroy?"

"Aye!" grumbled the leader, his mouth filled with food. "We seek to catch them before they make trouble."

"What kind of trouble?" asked Jonas. When the leader sneered at him, he quickly added, "So I can be on the lookout since an inn is a natural place to come when new in town."

"It is believed they want to make contact with those of the *forbidden* Oath," chided a soldier.

"As if those people don't cause enough trouble," groused another.

"You believe they are in The Doane? The foreigners, I mean," Jonas immediately corrected his near blunder. He made an impulsive glance to the bar where Sharla listened while she pretended to work. A jerk on the arm, brought his attention back to the table.

"Does the woman know?" asked the leader.

Sharla hurried over when Jonas beckoned her. "He wants to know if you've seen any foreigners—"

"And traitors!"

Sharla timidly replied. "No, sir. We're just surprised by the news, that's all."

The leader's narrow gaze shifted between them. He gave a warning. "Lying would be unwise."

"No. I swear! There have been no foreigners here," Jonas insisted.

The leader shoved Jonas away. "Leave us to eat."

Jonas and Sharla crossed to the bar. "We'll give them whatever they want. Hopefully, by doing so we can avoid any more confrontation," he said.

"I'll tell the cook." Sharla disappeared into the kitchen.

She didn't speak to the cook, instead, she hastened out the back door. Bart worked under the hay shed. She grabbed his hand to head for the stables. Once there, she waved for Abe to join them in a dark corner.

"Saddle two horses and ride to Far Point. Leave by the rear yard and take the waterfall path. Warn them that Javan's men are looking for two foreigners, who want to contact the *brethren.*"

"Why?" asked Abe.

Sharla glanced around for signs of anyone nearby. "Remember what Arctander said last time we saw him?"

The boys stared expectantly at her. "You mean …? Bart barely spoke when she covered his mouth.

"What about Papa when he finds us gone?" asked Abe.

"I'll tell him you went to fetch the furs Nollen promised." She pulled some coins from her apron pocket. "Take this, your extra cloaks, and lanterns." She pointed to the tack room. "Go, quickly. I must return." She kissed each on the cheek before she exited the back-barn door.

Inside the kitchen, Sharla found a scrap of paper and wrote a quick note. She folded and crinkled the note before she placed it in her pocket. She returned to the main dining room where she met Jonas at the bar. He carried an empty pitcher.

"The fourth round," he groused.

"Well, you said give them what they wanted."

"At this rate they'll drink a whole cask," he murmured, as he filled the pitcher.

"Never mind, innkeeper! You're too slow, and we're finished," the leader partly slurred his words.

Jonas waved acknowledgement and placed the pitcher on the counter. "I'll have the boys fetch your horses."

Sharla grabbed Jonas' arm to detain him. "They're not in barn."

"What? Why?"

"I thought the soldiers would be here longer, so I sent them to fetch the furs."

"What furs?"

She partially took the note from her apron pocket. She opened it far enough to display writing, but not clear enough to read. "The ones Nollen promised in trade for the Gorlander ale."

Noise of the soldier's departure drew Jonas' attention. Frustrated, he pushed passed her to head down the hallway to the stables.

Sharla ran through the kitchen, and out to the rear courtyard. Abe and Bart led two saddle horses through the alley gate. "Hurry!" she anxiously waved them to leave.

Abe and Bart quickly mounted and galloped out of sight.

"Gott protect them," she prayed. A cold gust of wind sent her indoors.

Armed only with work daggers, Abe and Bart dutifully obeyed their mother. Instead of taking the inn alleyway to the main street, Abe turned into an adjoining alley. He and Bart weaved their way through alleys to the north gate. At the intersection of the main road, they paused to look for soldiers. None.

"Act natural," Abe said.

"May Gott help us pass unnoticed," Bart said in quick prayer before he and Abe moved their horses into the flow of traffic.

With the day's commerce passing in and out of the gates, they left town unhindered.

"Don't look back," Abe harshly whispered when Bart stirred. "We'll take it easy until around the bend."

A bend in the road took them out of sight of the town watch. They kicked the horses into a gallop up the incline and toward the forest. Safely under cover of the trees, Bart drew rein to observe Gilroy.

"Looks like we made it. I don't see the soldiers," he said.

"Now it's just jackals and harpys," Abe dryly commented.

They would follow the same route Nollen and Ida did by going under the waterfall.

Jonas opened the corral gate for the soldiers. He stood safely out of the way to let them pass.

Destry came along side Jonas to watch the departure. "Those are the same ones I ferried over. Did they also ask you questions about some foreigners?"

"Aye, but I haven't seen any. What about you? Ferry any foreigners lately?"

"No." Destry's gaze observed the corral. "Where are the boys?"

Jonas made a sour frown. "Sharla sent them to Far Point. Apparently, the furs I ordered for winter have arrived. I just wish she had waited until after the soldiers left."

"I just came from the ferry, and the boys didn't ask for passage."

Jonas scowled in further annoyance. "Well, maybe they reached it after you left," he made excuse.

"No. The last people I ferried were Nollen and his sister."

"I thought you brought the soldiers?"

"I mean before them," Destry quickly corrected himself. "Come to think of it," he began in an afterthought, "they wanted the names of every passenger for the past month."

"Why would they want that?"

Destry shrugged. "Maybe to help identify the foreigners. Did they ask about Nollen?"

Jonas was taken aback by the question. "Why would they be interested in him?"

"Well, he is a trader, and travels frequently."

Jonas pressed his lips together in consideration. Seeing Destry's interest, he brusquely said, "I need to get back to work. Shut the gate as you leave."

Destry waited until Jonas returned inside before he went to close the gate. As he did so, he stepped on something. He moved his foot to pick it up. He brushed off the dirt and muck to discover a medallion. Stunned, he glanced at the inn then back to the medallion. The brief surprise became replaced by sneering anger. He pocketed the medallion, shut the corral gate, and hurried down the street.

Chapter 6

"I HATE NIGHT TRAVEL," GUNNAR COMPLAINED. HE AND AXEL rode through a dense patch of woods. He trimmed the light from the lantern attached to his saddle by way of a short pole. This helped illuminate a radius around them.

"So, you have said for the past nine days," teased Axel.

"And I'll keep saying it until you see reason."

Axel lowly chuckled. "You said harpys don't fly at night."

"I also said jackals hunt at night!"

"Hence the light. To scare them away. Another of your suggestions."

Gunnar again tended the lantern. "Lady Blythe may have been generous, but if you insist on traveling The Doane at night, we're going to need more oil. I'm not sure if what's left will last until morning. I keep dimming it, but *if* jackals do appear, there won't be enough to create a flash to blind them."

When they emerged from the trees, Axel noticed a dim glow in the northern part of a meadow. He reined his horse and drew Gunnar's attention to the horizon.

"Perhaps it's a house or campfire. Whoever is there may have some extra oil or know where we can purchase some."

"We better hurry, the flame is flickering."

Gunnar kicked his horse into a lope. At hearing a high-pitched squealing howl, he hit the base of the lantern to coax more light. The flame flickered with brightness then died. Another high-pitched howling bark was immediately followed by two responding calls.

"Jackals!" Gunnar shouted in warning. He snapped the reins to urge the horse into a gallop.

Axel also pushed his horse for more speed.

The sound of multiple jackals joined the noise of attack, as the pack raced from the trees in pursuit. Dog-like in appearance, the variant color fur ranged from golden brown to dark gray. The large pointed ears lay back during pursuit.

Gunnar reached behind him into his rolled blanket. It took a moment, but he withdrew a single-handled wooden clapper with metal filings. A jackal drew alongside his horse. With a violent jerking motion, he snapped the clapper at the jackal. It created a sharp metallic shot-like sound, that startled it. At a second crack, it backed away.

Gunnar heard the approach of another jackal on his left side. He had to reach over with the clapper. He made the snapping motion just as the jackal leapt at him. The clapper slammed down on the jackal's head. It made a short surprised whimpered when it fell stunned.

"Gunnar!" Axel called with concern.

"Keep going!" Gunnar continued to use the clapper, while he urged his horse for every ounce of energy the animal had.

Up ahead, came loud shouts and the bang of metal. Two torches appeared to be running towards them, then revealed people carrying the torches. Both shouted, one sounded male, and the other female.

The man tossed a projectile that hit the ground with a *pop* followed by a flash of light. Three more projectiles sent the jackals in retreat.

Axel and Gunnar reached the man.

"Get to the barn!" he told them.

The woman already headed that way, so Axel and Gunnar changed course. They slowed their weary and frightened horses to allow her time to open the barn. A secret panel outside clicked, and a crack appeared between the two barn doors!

Once inside, they saw the man running back, yet pausing to throw a couple of projectiles. When he reached the barn, a massive bird loudly screeched and swooped down from the roof. He dashed inside to avoid the bird. He shut the door using an interior lever.

"Was that an owl?" she asked.

"Aye," he replied breathlessly.

"An owl in The Doane is not good," Gunnar commented to Axel, but Axel's response became interrupted.

"What are you doing traveling The Doane at night?" he questioned, through still recovering his breath.

Axel gauged him to be young, perhaps around age twenty. He observed the woman when she lit an interior lantern. There appeared a family resemblance, though she was slightly older.

She spoke to the young man. "I don't think they're from around here. I've not seen such clothing."

"She's right," said Axel. "We offer our thanks, Master …?"

"Nollen. This is my sister Ida. We own this trading post."

"Far Point?" asked Axel.

"Aye," Nollen said, cautious at the curious reaction.

Ida intervened. "You can put your horses in the last stall. It's big enough for two. You'll find a water barrel inside by the back door. Hay is in the opposite stall." She hung the lantern for light to work by. "If you're hungry, there is leftover stew from supper."

"Thank you. That would be nice," said Gunnar.

"I'll have it warm and ready." Ida left by a side door.

"You still haven't answered my question. Why are you traveling The Doane at night?" insisted Nollen.

For a moment, Axel regarded Nollen. Despite the young man's understandable wariness, a sense of familiarity struck Axel, joined by a feeling of confidence. Doubtful Nollen sensed it. When his stare made Nollen uncomfortable, Axel diffused the tension with a smile. "We'll answer your question after we tend our horses."

"And a hot meal," added Gunnar in a light tone.

Nollen did his own sizing up of the foreign men. "I'll wait." He sat on a nearby tack chest. "Those are magnificent animals. I've never seen such large black horses with powerful, graceful necks, long manes and fetlocks," he commented. "They must be nearly seventeen hands high."

"You have an eye for horseflesh," said Axel.

"I'm a trader. I've seen all kinds of animals. But not this breed. Not in Eldar"

"These are special." Gunnar stroked his horse's neck.

Silence ensued, as Axel and Gunnar tended to their mounts. After fifteen minutes, the horses were relieved of their saddles, bridles, rubbed down, fed, and watered.

"This way." Nollen led them through the side door, which served as a walled corridor between the barn and house.

Gunnar admired the structure. "Wisely done. The jackals and harpys won't see you."

Nollen stopped to challenge Gunnar. "I thought you weren't from here?"

"He's not," Gunnar said of Axel. "I was born here, though returning after a long absence."

"His guide?" Nollen jerked a thumb at Axel.

"In a manner of speaking."

"Then *you* should have known better than to travel at night."

Nollen's rebuke prompted Gunnar to flash a toothy grin of triumph at Axel.

"His lantern ran out of oil," Axel dryly replied. "Perhaps we can purchase some from you?"

Ida appeared in the threshold of the house door. "The stew is ready." She stepped aside for them to enter. "There is hot water in the basin, and towels to clean up before eating. You can hang your cloaks near the front door."

While Gunnar and Axel followed her instructions, Ida placed bowls of stew and a platter of bread on the table. Nollen poured drinks into two tankards.

"It's an herbal cider brewed especially for a night drink. Helps to calm the nerves. Thought you could use some after that ride," Nollen explain when Gunnar and Axel sat to eat.

Gunnar sniffed the cider. "Ginger and lemon balm?"

"Aye. Along with apples and late season berries."

"Please, sit with us." Axel motioned to the table. "Mistress. Master Nollen."

"We've already eaten." Ida sat beside Axel.

"Then a cup of cider to calm your nerves after coming to our rescue." Axel smiled, easy, and compelling. He raised a tankard in salute.

Ida returned Axel's smile. "Nollen."

He fetched two more tankards, filled them, and handed one to his sister. He placed the pitcher on the table before he sat opposite her.

"We would like to offer thanks," began Axel.

"You already thanked us. That is enough," said Ida kindly.

"No. I mean *thanks*." Axel drew a symbol on the table with his finger.

Gunnar cautiously watched the siblings' stunned reactions.

Axel calmly continued. "You recognize it," he spoke confidently.

Nollen balked. "It would unwise to say so. And ill-advised to make such a sign among strangers.

Axel gazed directly at Nollen. His earlier sense of familiarity grew stronger. "I'm not among strangers, am I?"

"I ... I don't know what you mean."

Axel grinned at the feeble denial. "Of course, you do, Nollen, son of Alfred. Ida, daughter of Erica."

Dumbfounded, it took a moment for Ida to speak. Even then, her voice barely rose above an astonished whisper. "How do you know us?"

Axel reached into a pocket of his jacket and pulled out an old medallion. "By way of this." He laid it on the table. Despite the age, it showed a lion wearing a crown over a knotted cross.

The siblings stared at it until Ida bolted from the table. She crossed to a sideboard. From a hidden compartment, she withdrew something and brought it back to the table. She placed an identical medallion next to the one Axel produced.

"What are you doing?" Nollen demanded of Ida.

"Look at them," she urged, and indicated the medallions. "This isn't a coincidence."

"How can you be sure?"

With tender compassion, she regarded her brother. "Because of what happened to Marmie and Papi."

Nollen sat back with arms folded, his anger seething.

"What happened to them?" Axel inquired.

"Three years ago, Javan's men arrived at dawn, banging and shouting at the door. Our parents were accused of being spies, which was all they said before dragging them outside. When they seized us, Papi invoked the family sanctuary law. They took our parents but left us." Ida's voice slightly cracked.

"Sanctuary law?" Axel asked Ida, only Gunnar answered.

"An ancient law that states the children are innocent of any actions committed by the parents, unless proven complicit." He turned to Ida. "I assume they did not include you both due to lack of evidence."

Ida simply nodded, unable to speak due to emotions.

Nollen painfully sneered. "They were executed!"

"They weren't spies," Axel spoke with conviction.

"We know," began Ida with forced words. "Grandfather—"

"Ida! No!" Nollen scolded.

She ignored his outburst to continue in a stronger voice. "Grandfather told us everything, of how it is Javan's method for exterminating *our* people. From that day, we assumed our parents' responsibility."

Anger made Nollen hiss at her. "Ida!"

"They are of us!" She picked up the medallion.

"Or a trick to betray us!"

Axel seized Ida's hand to stop further anger between the siblings. "This is no trick. I came here because your parents sent me this."

"They couldn't have sent it. I just told you they were executed three years ago!"

Axel fought to remain calm in the face of Nollen's vehement objections. "I don't know how or when they sent it, but I know it came from them because of the note included." When Nollen sneered in dispute, Axel withdrew a crumbled piece of paper from the same pocket as the medallion. "Read it."

Nollen snatched the paper. *"The horn has been found!"* His brows drew level in annoyed confusion. "I don't understand. What horn?"

Axel ignored the question to ask, "Do you recognize the handwriting?"

Nollen stubbornly pressed his lips together.

His patience exhausted, Axel took the medallion from Ida and held it in front of Nollen's face. "You know this seal! And recognize your father's handwriting," he said emphatically.

"Nollen? Is it from Papi?"

"Aye," he grumbled an admission. He gave her the note.

Axel continued. "According to Ida, you have sworn to the same responsibilities as your parents. So, I say again, you *know* this seal."

Nollen nodded. "According to the ancient scrolls it is the seal of Eldar's king."

"And?" Axel pressed, his eyes prompting to the point that Nollen shifted uncomfortably in his seat.

"A sign between us, the Shining Ones, followers of the True King." Nollen look at Axel from under shrouded brows. "We haven't had a king in two centuries."

Thoughtful, Axel traced the cravings on the medallion. "Fulfilling their sworn duty, *your* parents sent this to *their king,* as the long-awaited signal that the time has come."

"Time for what?" asked Ida, cautious.

"To gather the remnant and pave the way for the True King's return."

Nollen huffed. "First you say they sent it to you, now you say to their king."

Axel sat up in the chair and spoke with a clear voice of declaration. "I am Axel, in the royal line of Oleg, leader of the Shining Ones." He held up his medallion with the crown facing Nollen.

Ida impulsively gasped and covered her mouth.

"What's wrong?" asked Gunnar, alert and ready for action.

Ida ignored Gunnar to stare wide-eyed at Axel. She slowly lowered her hands. "You are the prophesied Son of Eldar. The one who would *come from a far to reclaim the throne.*"

"I am."

Ida wept. "How long we've waited for this day, yet never thought to see." She seized his hand to kiss it. "My liege!"

Axel gently smiled at Ida. "There is much to do before then." He said to Nollen, "In answer to your earlier question; we rode through The Doane at night to find *you* and your sister."

Nollen's earlier combativeness turned to consideration. "What does this have to do with the horn Papi mentioned?"

"The Horn of Kolyn is the horn of triumph. One of the Six Treasures of the King. It's been missing for the past two hundred years. Since that horrible day ...," Axel's somber voice trailed off.

Sensing Axel's discomposure, Gunnar intervened. "Let me ask you something, Nollen. What is an owl doing in The Doane? Harpys would never tolerate a rival predator in their domain."

Nollen shrugged. "A few times an owl has ventured here from the Ha'tar territory. It usually flies away after a day or two."

"Here? Meaning Far Point?"

"Aye. Does that trouble you?"

"It should trouble you! Owls can be nocturnal spies for the enemy," Gunnar declared.

"We never thought of that," Nollen droned. "It's only happened two or three times ..." he stopped when Ida grew pale, almost to the point of swooning. "Ida?"

"Dear Gott," she murmured in distress. "An owl was here that day! I watched it fly off when they left with Marmie and Papi."

"Maybe it led them here," suggested Gunnar.

Baffled, Nollen shook his head. "Nothing happened the other times. Could just be coincidence."

"It attacked you earlier."

When Gunnar's statement upset Ida further, Axel comforted her. "Though we can't ignore its presence, we won't know for certain if it was sent to spy or an innocent hunt for food—"

"Oh!" she suddenly interrupted him. "The stew is cold. Let me warm it up." She grabbed the bowls.

Mindful of Ida's departure to gather her emotions, Nollen leaned on the table, his voice lowered to speak privately. "You don't believe it is a coincidence, do you?"

Axel again stared directly at Nollen. He replied in a grave tone. "The enemy will do anything to prevent me from completing my task. To maintain the power of the evil one."

The sobriety made Nollen visibly shiver. He swallowed back his momentary discomposure to ask, "What is your task?"

Axel's earlier reticence returned. Gunnar again intervened with a loud, exaggerated stretch and yawn. "I think I'll be ready for sleep after eating."

Axel took Gunnar's cue, and flashed a smile of encouragement at Nollen. "Gunnar's right. Everything else can wait until morning."

When Ida returned with warm stew for Axel and Gunnar, Nollen left the table. He moved to the front window to stare at the darkness. After serving them, Axel watched Ida join Nollen at the window. They exchanged a few quiet words. Gunnar nudged Axel to continue eating. He did so yet cast several cautious glances at the siblings. At one point, he caught Nollen's intense stare. Small wonder after their dramatic arrival and revelation. In abrupt manner, Nollen said something to Ida then went upstairs.

She returned to the table. "Please, my lord, be patient with Nollen. He tends to be quick-tempered but has a good heart."

"I'm not angry. He's young. He still has much to learn."

"He has already learned much since assuming our father's role—in accordance with the Oath."

Axel grinned "If I didn't believe you both trustworthy, I would never have spoken so freely." He stood. "Now, it is time we retire."

"But you haven't—" she began to object but stopped at seeing empty bowls.

"It was delicious," said Gunnar.

Ida simply nodded and pointed. "The room to the right at the top of the stairs."

Axel picked up his medallion before he and Gunnar went upstairs. Upon entering the guest room, they found Nollen stoking a small fire in the brazier.

"It's not much, but it should provide ample warmth for the remainder of the night," said Nollen. "Also, there is a privy at the end of the hall with ample supplies for bathing and shaving. A pump draws up cold water. I can bring up a bucket hot water, if you want."

Gunnar scratched his scruffy face. "A shave would be welcomed. He might prefer a beard, but for me, whiskers are irritating."

"Your hospitality is much appreciated," began Axel. "Forgive my earlier outburst. You have every right to be suspicious of me, and protective of your parents' memory."

"No, my lord, it is I who should apologize for my coarse behavior."

"Accepted, as I hope you accept my apology."

"Of course. Our Faith instructs us to forgive." Nollen made a sardonic self-debasing grunt. "Only I seem to need it more since I have difficulty with my temper."

Axel clapped Nollen on the shoulder. "Patience will come as you get older."

"I'll fetch the hot water."

Gunnar closed the door upon Nollen's exit. "You took a great risk telling them," he said in mild rebuke.

Axel sat on the end of the bed to stare at the door. "Nollen will have a part in our venture. How, and why exactly, I don't know yet. I must pray and meditate more upon his involvement."

Gunnar fought a real yawn. "Can it wait until morning? It took nine *nights* to get here. Not the mention eluding harpys and fighting jackals. Getting clean, and a good night's sleep, is necessary."

Chapter 7

NOLLEN SAT IN THE DARKNESS OF THE FAMILY AREA OFF TO ONE side of the kitchen. He stared at the low, dying fire. Ida retired, but he couldn't sleep. Too many questions whirled in his head along with painful memories of his parents' death. Memories, he thought long buried. All stirred up by the arrival of Axel and Gunnar.

Contemplation made him realize that other incidents also brought back the pain and anger. Each time the commitment to his covert activities grew stronger and more urgent. Revenge? Perhaps, but those at the forest compound depended heavily upon him and Ida. In fact, many he secretly encountered on his trading routes, trusted him with their lives.

He let out a heartfelt sigh when Jonas came to mind. This relationship went beyond the Oath to a beloved friend and cousin. When word spread about their parents, Jonas immediately came to comfort and console them. He remained for several weeks to help with the legalities that came with Nollen assuming the responsibility of running Far Point. Being seventeen-years-old at the time, he looked up to Jonas, his elder by fifteen years. Back then, Jonas seemed so sure-minded and strong. Alas, a few days ago, Jonas acted so different. He even admitted to fear.

Nollen briefly glanced at the medallion he held. His fist clenched it in confusion. What could have changed Jonas? Were there hints of it the past three years that he missed? Jonas' words echoed in his mind:

"Javan issued another edict. This one deadlier than before. Prison has been replaced by execution. … I don't have your courage."

"Oh, Gott, what is happening?" Nollen lowly lamented.

He again gazed at the medallion. This changed his focus to Axel. In their brief time together, Axel stood in marked contrast to Jonas. A man of fortitude, courage, and faith. A man who offered immediate trust to strangers. Yet there was something more, something deeper. True, he claimed to be the Son of Eldar, but what Nollen began to sense was more personal than the possible fulfillment of prophecy. Axel knew his parents—or at least knew of them.

Nollen intensely studied the medallion. It had been passed down from father to son for six generations. A sign of their sworn duty, and enduring Faith. A sudden thought struck him. *This is the family's medallion, so what did Papi send with the note? Did he have a second one?* He glanced at the stairs, perplexed by the unanswered questions.

Hearing footsteps, he stood to face whoever was coming. Ida. She held a lantern as she arrived in the kitchen from a bottom room. "You couldn't sleep, either?" he asked.

The question startled her. "Nollen. Have you been up all night?" She placed the lantern on a hook that hung from the ceiling. She used a match to take a flame from the lantern to light the stove.

Nollen crossed to the kitchen. "What do you mean *all night?* You just went to bed."

"It's five o'clock in the morning." She observed his perplexity. "What troubles you? The Prince?"

"Among other things." He held up the medallion. "Like how did Papi send a medallion when this is still here?"

"Because the one he sent has a special encryption engraved on it," said Axel. He arrived unnoticed. He was partially dressed, his surcoat open. His beard now nicely trimmed, and he appeared refreshed after a night's rest.

"Did you sleep well, Highness?" Ida asked.

Axel smiled an affirmative, though more interested in answering Nollen. "On the back, you'll find words inscribed. You probably didn't notice the difference last night."

"Aye. *Faith, loyalty, hope, and courage*," Nollen read the inscription on the family's medallion.

"Now read mine." Axel handed it to Nollen

"*Kynge Ece*? I don't know these words. Is it your language?"

"It is ancient Eldarian and means *king forever.* When the coup happened, six of these medallions were secretly made and distributed to faithful men, along with instructions to send it *only* when the horn had been found."

"So, you have the others also."

Axel took back his medallion. "No, one is all that is needed. And, to answer to your next question," he preempted Nollen, "I knew it came from your father because each family had a pre-arranged sign."

"Ah!" began Nollen in confident refute, "he didn't mention his name or Far Point."

Axel grinned at the attempted contradiction. "Do you think Oleg's descendants lost interest in those trusted men? Or their faithful families? Centuries are meaningless when The Oath and prophecy are involved."

"How? Spying?" Nollen practically demanded.

"No!" Axel emphatically said. "It isn't *spying* when serving the cause of righteousness and justice. The information is used for good, *never* evil. I knew this," he held up the singal medallion, "came from the trusted family, who lived somewhere in The Doane. After our arrival, we discovered the location of Far Point. Your names confirmed that information."

Gunnar arrived. His face clean-shaven. He stretched and yawned.

"Did you not sleep well, my lord?" asked Ida, concerned.

"He snores." Gunnar jerked his thumb at Axel.

"I do not!" Axel refuted with a laugh.

"Well, someone does. I heard it throughout the night."

Perplexed, Nollen said, "Ida doesn't snore."

"And Nollen has been up all night," she added.

Baffled, Axel glanced at Gunnar, who insisted, "I heard it."

"Maybe from outside?" Ida innocently asked.

Her question prompted swift action, as Axel, Gunnar, and Nollen headed for the front door. As soon as the men emerged onto the porch, an owl took flight from the rooftop over the window of the guest room.

"Answers my question about the owl," groused Gunnar.

"I don't understand. Owls snore?" asked Ida.

Gunnar ushered her back inside. Axel and Nollen followed. Nollen locked the door behind them.

"Owls snore when hungry. Meaning, it didn't come here to hunt. Otherwise, it would have been satisfied and left," Gunnar explained.

Ida fought against fear. "Then it will lead them here."

Nollen placed a comforting arm about her shoulders.

"How close is the nearest town?" asked Axel.

"Vanora is a two-day ride southeast," replied Nollen. "We have time," he tried to reassure Ida.

"I don't fear for me, but the Prince. He can't be found." When Nollen hesitated with indecision, Ida continued with urgency. "We must take him to the forest compound for safety—"

A sharp rap at the door, and the call of Nollen's name, interrupted Ida. Gunnar placed himself between Axel and the door.

"Nollen! Ida," came another call.

"Sounds like Abe," Nollen said to Ida.

"Who is Abe?" asked Gunnar.

"My cousin's son." Nollen peeked out the window. The rising sun revealed the twins. He opened the door to admit Abe and Bart. "What are you two doing here?"

"Mama sent us," Abe began in hurried explanation.

"Aye, soldiers came looking for foreigners. Something about wanting to contact *traitors.* Us, the brethren," Bart briskly added.

"She sent us to warn you," Abe concluded.

"Did they identify these foreigners?" Axel's voice made the twins notice he and Gunnar. Sight of them startled the boys.

"It's all right!" Ida hastened to calm Abe and Bart. Her focus shifted to Axel to explain. "They are of us."

"I gathered that from what was said." Axel smiled at the twins.

"Are you the ones the soldiers are looking for?" Bart bravely asked.

"It would appear so." Axel observed the twins' dusty and wrinkled appearance. "You made haste to obey your mother and bring warning. The sign of faithful and courageous youths."

Abe remained guarded. "If you are of us then you understand her concern."

Axel showed them his medallion. The twins marveled, with Bart speaking. "Foreigners take the Oath?"

Axel chuckled. "Gunnar was born in the Freelands. Me. Well, my family dates back hundreds of years to Eldar." He made direct eye-contact with Bart. "It is time for my return from afar."

It took a moment for Bart to comprehend, but when he did, his eyes grew wide with astonishment. "You, are *he?*"

"I am."

Bart seized Abe and began to laugh with glee. "Arctander was right!" he said to his brother.

"But they can't find him here," Abe objected.

"We know," said Ida. She sent a prompting glance to Nollen.

"You realize if we leave before our scheduled time, Hertz will suspect our involvement," Nollen offered as reasoned argument.

"We are already involved! Now so are they." Ida indicated the twins.

Nollen took a deep breath then curtly nodded. "Fetch what is needed while we saddle the horses," he instructed her.

"And the boys? Should they come with us?"

"No," replied Axel. He took hold of each boy's shoulder. "Your bravery will be remembered. For now, return to your mother. Say you delivered the message, but do not speak of me—at least not yet," he added to Bart's beginning objection. "Time will come for all to be revealed. Do I have your word?"

"Aye, my lord," Bart staunchly declared.

"Aye," agreed Abe.

"Help Ida and take whatever you need. You'll ride with us to the forest trail," Nollen told the twins.

"We'll meet you in the barn." Gunnar said of he and Axel.

Nollen made his way through the covered passage. His pony, and Ida's, were stalled opposite the largest one. He finished saddling his pony when Gunnar and Axel arrived. Both now fully dressed.

Axel noticed the full quiver and crossbow attached to Nollen's saddle. "You always travel armed?"

"Trading is a risky business in The Doane."

"How long will it take to reach where we're going?" asked Gunnar.

"At least three days. If nothing, happens, Gott willing." Nollen spoke the last statement more to himself then in reply.

"Gott will help us," Axel assured him, though his response surprised Nollen. "He knows your heart, and Oath." He observed the animals Nollen saddled. They stood almost two hands shorter than the ones he and Gunnar rode. Thick-necked and sturdy looking bays. "What breed of horse is this?"

"Highland ponies. Great stamina for the long-distance travel required for trading," replied Nollen.

"Only good for short bursts of speed, if I remember correctly," Gunnar comment.

"Aye, though they have better temperaments than mules." Nollen tightened the girth on Ida's horse. He placed another crossbow and full quiver on its saddle.

By the time the men were ready, Ida arrived, also dressed for travel. She wore a dagger on her belt. She carried a heavy saddlebag along with Nollen's cloak and dagger belt. He took possession of his items while she placed the saddlebag on the back of her horse.

"There's another saddlebag just outside the door. I couldn't carry everything," she told her brother.

Nollen retrieved it to place on his horse. He donned his cloak.

"Rather heavy saddlebags for two-days travel," said Gunnar.

"One contains everything pertaining to our Oath and secret duty. If they come here, it is best these things are not found." Ida indicated the one on her horse. "The other holds provisions for our journey." She motioned to the one on Nollen's horse.

"Trading ledgers and papers?" Nollen urgently asked.

"Burning in the stove," she dolefully replied. She looked up at feeling Axel's hand on her shoulder.

"Do not think of this as an ending, rather a beginning."

She blinked back the tears to smile. "I know."

"The sun is up. At least we won't face jackals," said Gunnar.

"We must ride almost two miles in the open," warned Nollen.

"Then let's hope the harpys aren't early risers."

Nollen moved to the main door and unlocked the mechanism. He took a hold of the rope before he vaulted into the saddle. "It's best to be ready for the gallop when I open the door." He waited a moment for the others to mount. "Gott protect us," he prayed, and pulled the rope.

The mechanism drew the door open to one side. As soon as there was room enough, Nollen led the way outside. Axel followed, then Ida, with Gunnar in the rear. Abe and Bart waited, both mounted. Each had a bag stuffed with new provisions. They fell in among the group.

Nollen headed west and urged his pony into a steady lope. Axel and Gunnar held their horses back to match the ponies' speed. They just reached the half-way point in the meadow when the screeching cry of a harpy sounded.

"To the trees!" Nollen urged his mount, yet even at top speed, the pony was easily passed by Axel's horse.

When Axel realized the widening distance between him and Nollen, he drew rein to slow his horse.

"Keep going!" Nollen shouted and waved at Axel.

Nollen armed his crossbow. He turned in the saddle to aim at the diving harpy. He ducked since the bird came too close to shoot. The harpy did a sharp bank directly at Ida. Before Nollen could get a clear shot, the harpy's talons snared her on the right shoulder. She tried to avoid the attack and jerked back on the reins. The pony reared, and she fell off backwards.

"Ida!" Nollen cried out. Her pony crossed his line of sight. Once again, he couldn't shoot.

Axel rushed his horse toward Ida. As the harpy made for a second attack, he shouted, *"Bi Gott's gebod egle!"*

Almost immediately, the loud deep cry of an eagle echoed in the meadow. The arrival of the massive bird caused the harpy to break off its attack of Ida. It rose to meet the eagle for an airborne battle. Despite being half the size, the harpy would not yield. The short, decisive encounter ended when the eagle knocked the harpy from the sky. Badly wounded, the harpy tried to rise. The eagle landed on top and killed it.

Nollen leapt from the saddle beside an unconscious Ida. Gunnar was already there and examined her wounds. Abe and Bart anxiously watched for their horses.

"Is she …?" Nollen couldn't finished the dreaded question.

"No, just injured and stunned," replied Gunnar.

"Ida?" Nollen tenderly touched her face. She moaned, blinked, and opened her eyes. "Thank Gott," he sighed in relief.

"We need to get under the cover of trees to tend her wounds," began Axel. "You take her," he told Gunnar. "I'll fetch the pony."

Gunnar lifted Ida onto his horse. She was woozy, but awake. She seized the saddle bow to remain astride. Gunnar mounted behind her. His arm encircled her waist in support. She jolted when he urged the horse to move.

"You won't fall. I've got you," he reassured her. She relaxed.

At a gallop, they crossed the remainder of the meadow. In the woods, Nollen guided them to a hollow near the edge of a small river.

"We should be safe here for a time. Harpys don't like water," Nollen said to Axel. He moved to Gunnar's horse to help Ida dismount. He escorted her to a portion of the bank where she could rest against the slope. "Abe, Bart, take care of the horses."

Axel opened his saddlebag and withdrew what appeared to be herbs and a pestle. All the while, he mumbled unintelligible words.

"What are you saying?" Abe asked.

"A prayer for Gott's mercy and healing." Axel set about making a paste for salving the wound.

"We've never heard that language before," said Bart.

"It's ancient Eldarian," Axel spoke while he tended Ida. She groaned in pain. "Gunnar, mix some willow bark in the wine." He then said to Ida, "The salve contains neem, which should help with healing and swelling. The wine mixture will ease pain, and help you relax."

Nollen leapt to his feet at hearing a soft call of a large bird. He made ready to draw his dagger when an eagle landed on a nearby pine branch.

"Be at ease. She won't hurt you," Axel said.

Nollen knelt beside Axel. "Is it the same one from the meadow?"

Axel just nodded, as he finished bandaging Ida's shoulder wound.

Nollen looked cautiously at the eagle. "Where did it come from?"

"I summoned her," came Axel's nonchalant reply.

The eagle screeched, as if in acknowledgement.

"Softly, Ottlia. This is Nollen, his sister Ida. And brave youths, Abe and Bart."

The eagle squawked again, as if speaking to Axel.

"Aye. Of my people."

"You understand it?" Nollen asked, amazed.

"Her, not *it*. Ottlia is the mate of Artair, the eagle king." He then spoke to Ottlia. "Keep watch. Ida needs rest before we continue."

With an affirmative cry, Ottlia took off.

"Fetch some provision. We'll eat breakfast while she rests," Axel instructed Nollen.

Nollen returned with a loaf of honey bread and a small dry sausage. He gave some of each to Axel, Gunnar, Abe, and Bart. When he offered some to Ida, she refused.

"I think I'd rather sleep than eat right now," she said.

Axel leaned close to Nollen. "The willow bark can make one drowsy. She'll be fine. You eat."

"It's not wise to stay here too long," said Nollen.

"We'll be safe with Ottlia keeping watch."

"This bread is excellent," said Gunnar with a mouthful.

"Ida is a good cook," said Nollen.

"Aye, her stew was also delicious." Gunnar shoved more bread in his mouth.

Nollen sat beside Ida while she slept. In watching her, his thoughts drifted back to his earlier contemplation. *Things are happening so fast,* his mind complained. He closed his eyes to contain his frustration. He never liked sudden changes. Even in their clandestine trips, they planned everything down to the last detail in hopes of being prepared for the unexpected. He felt a nearby jostling of his arm and woke with a start. He had unexpectedly fallen asleep. In surprise, he found Axel sat beside him.

"I realize our sudden presence is troubling, and you have many questions."

Axel's statement confounded Nollen. *Can he read minds?*

"Despite all that, I ask for your trust."

Surprise turned to unintended sarcasm. "We're leaving Far Point, aren't we?"

"Not by choice."

Nollen didn't reply, rather looked at his sleeping sister.

"She will recover."

"How can you be certain? Harpy wounds can be deadly."

"Because I trust Gott to answer my prayer."

"You make it sound so easy," Nollen complained under his breath.

"Faith isn't easy. If it was, it wouldn't be faith, now would it?"

"Or trust," Nollen countered.

"No, trust isn't easy either. Except, it should be among *our* people," Axel pointedly said. "I have given enough answers and proof to earn your trust. Why do you still doubt? They don't." He nodded toward the twins.

Nollen noticed Abe and Bart watched their conversation with rapt attention. *What must they be thinking?* His internal question prompted a verbal reply. "Not … doubt."

"Then what?"

Nollen's search for words ended in a shrug. "I don't know exactly." He rubbed the sudden fatigue from his eyes.

"Fear?" asked Gunnar.

Nollen's head snapped up and he declared, "No!"

"Doubt often accompanies fear," said Axel.

Frustrated, Nollen lashed out. "The situation is happening so fast, I'm just trying to comprehend!"

Ida stirred at the shouting. Axel laid a hand on Nollen's arm. He made a slight motion to Ida. Nollen acknowledged the need for calm with a nod.

In a lower voice, Axel asked, "That is understandable. However, let me ask you this: Did you need complete understanding when you took the Oath, or was faith and trust involved without all the answers?"

Stymied, Nollen slumped back against the bank. His expression thoughtful, as he glanced to Abe and Bart. Axel's question recalled his own disquietude earlier about Jonas.

"Well?" Axel gently insisted.

Though unable to fully look at Axel, Nollen replied with certainty. "No. Papi always said the answers will come in time."

Axel cupped a hand around Nollen's neck in a supportive brotherly manner. "Faith and trust also compel me in this undertaking. Some of my questions were answered before leaving for Eldar. Others will come when I need them. And right now, Nollen, brother of the Shining Ones, I need *you* and Ida to help me. Like they did," he said of the twins. "They hadn't met me nor heard what I told you; yet obeyed their mother to help warn me of the enemy's plan."

Determined, Nollen sat up to fully meet Axel's gaze. "You have my help."

Ida woke, which drew everyone's attention.

"How are you feeling?" asked Nollen.

"Better. How long have I been asleep?"

Nollen couldn't answer since he unintentionally slept.

"Not long. Maybe an hour," Axel replied. "Let me check your shoulder." He examined her wound. He grinned. "It's already starting to knit. Should be healed by tomorrow."

"What?" she said in surprise.

"Impossible. Harpy wounds take days, sometimes weeks to heal," added Nollen.

"See for yourself." Axel motioned Nollen to view under the bandage. Stunned, the young man looked twice.

"Something wrong?" asked Ida to Nollen's reaction.

"No. It's healing. Like the Prince said."

"Prince," Bart murmured, and began to smile.

"Axel," Gunnar sternly warned. "Mustn't let straying ears hear."

Bart colored with embarrassment. "Aye, sir."

"Eat before we continue." Axel handed Ida the remaining portion of breakfast.

Once finished, Nollen helped Ida to mount her pony. "If you become fatigued, don't hesitate to tell us."

"Truly, I'm better. I felt no pain with activity."

"All the same. I'll be keeping an eye on you."

"We should avoid our regular routes," she pointedly suggested when he mounted.

"Altwald will be safer," he emphasized.

Ida visibly shivered, and screwed her eyes shut at the mention of *Altwald*.

Keen to her disturbance, Axel inquired, "What is Altwald?"

"An ancient forest some believe haunted," Nollen replied, as he led them south along the river bank

Gunnar's face became rigid. "I remember hearing the legends of Altwald as a child. It's said not even the Ha'tar dragon-warriors or Nefal will enter it because of the Cursians."

"Do not speak their name!" Ida chided.

Axel's features went from recognition at Gunnar's mention of *Cursians* to sympathetic at Ida's warning. "Why do you believe it is forbidden to say their name?"

"It is *unwise,*" she answered with discrete insistence. "So is traveling through Altwald."

"If you have a better suggestion, please tell me," said Nollen.

Her face filled with dejection at his reply.

"Fear not. Gott is directing our journey," Axel encouraged her.

"Will it add time?" Gunnar asked Nollen.

"Not if we succeed. It will take the remainder of the day to reach the outskirts of Altwald. We'll make camp and proceed in the morning. Daylight is needed to navigate it safely." Nollen drew his pony to a halt. "This is where we part ways," he told the twins. "Tell Sharla, thank you."

"We shall," Abe assured her.

Bart spoke to Axel. "We will remember our word, and all that we witnessed today. Gott watch over you, my lord."

"And may He guide you safely home."

They waited until the twins rode out of sight to continue the journey north by northwest.

Chapter 8

In a rushed gallop, Hertz and Magistrate Bernal led a group to Far Point. The group consisted of ten soldiers and Bernal's cousin Destry. Heavy smoke rose from the house chimney. The store appeared to be closed with no customers or activity outside. Good! Maybe they arrived in time.

Hertz violently drew the reins to bring his horse to a skidding stop in front of the house. The soldiers did likewise while Bernal acted gentler in stopping his mount. Destry brought his horse alongside Bernal.

Despite his sixty years, Bernal appeared spry and agile when dismounting. "The barn and store!" he ordered the soldiers, who immediately dispersed to follow orders.

After he climbed the steps to the house porch, Hertz banged his fist on the door. "Open up!" No response, so he shouted, "Nollen! Open this door. Now!"

Met with more silence, Bernal added his pounding on the door and yelling command. "Nollen of Far Point, this is Magistrate Bernal. Open this door immediately!" Furious at the persistent silence, he ordered the captain, "Break it open!"

Together, the captain and two men, used a bench from the porch to break open the door. It yielded with a mighty crash that splintered timber. The soldiers moved aside to let Bernal, Destry, and Hertz enter. Heavy smoke from the fire also filled the room.

Coughing and backing out the door, Bernal barked at the captain, "Search for them!"

Hertz and Destry also coughed and wiped their eyes in recovery from the dense smoke.

"I fear they may not be here," said Hertz between coughs.

"They couldn't have known we were coming," rebuffed Bernal.

"Unless he received warning," suggested Destry. He turned to Hertz. "I told you that might happen because of those boys!"

Hertz's eye narrowed in warning at Destry.

"That you did," Bernal groused in agreement.

A soldier ran from the barn. "Magistrate!" He saluted and gave his report. "The mules remain, but the ponies are gone."

Bernal swore.

"There is more, Magistrate," continued the solider. "They weren't alone. By the looks of it, two more horses were stabled here."

Bernal swore again.

"My suspicions proved correct." Destry's eyes darted to Hertz.

"The *miller* proved correct," rebuffed Hertz. "He sent word that foreigners inquired about Far Point. You merely capitalized on his report."

When Destry opened his mouth to dispute, Bernal interrupted him. "It doesn't matter *who* was right, the facts are now confirmed."

"Magistrate!" The captain emerged from the house. He held a badly charred book cover. "The fire was meant to destroy ledgers."

Fury made Bernal knock it from the captain's hands. "We should have included them in the charges three years ago!"

"There was no evidence then," said Hertz, much to Bernal's chagrin.

"There is now! So, take your so-called legal expertise and put them to good use." Bernal angrily strode to his horse with Destry at his heels.

The sting of insult rose on Hertz' face. He lingered on the porch to collect his emotions. The constant barrage of abuse from Bernal, and his infuriating cousin, wore on his nerves.

"Hertz!" called Bernal.

Squaring his shoulders to hide wounded pride, Hertz responded to the summons. He approached Bernal. "Aye, Magistrate."

"Confiscate everything! And draw up a warrant for their arrest on the charge of treason for aiding the enemy! Anyone harboring Nollen and Ida of Far Point will face the same punishment—death!"

"Jonas may know their whereabouts. Not only do Nollen and Ida frequent the inn when traveling for trade, I've recently learned, they are cousins," said Destry.

Bernal slyly grunted with satisfaction, but it was short-lived when Hertz questioned Destry.

"What evidence do you have of their family connections?"

"I won't betray my sources, but this was found at the inn stable." Destry pulled a medallion from his coat pocket.

Bernal seized it. His triumphant pleasure returned. "Using this, we can invoke the Elector's edict, and persuade Jonas to tell us what he knows." Biting sarcasm crept into his voice when questioning Hertz, "Unless, you have any objections?"

"No, Magistrate. The finding of an outlawed medallion warrants investigation."

"Investigation?" spat Destry with indignation. "These followers of the True King are a blight upon Eldar."

Hertz fought his temper at the outburst. "You misunderstand. I meant an *investigation* by way of interrogating Jonas. With all the legalities in order."

When Destry rolled his eyes in frustration, Hertz continued. "Due to the rising unrest, it is a necessary delay to quiet the likes of the Ganels and Freelanders."

"I hope someday the Elector stops all this legal double-talk and takes direct action."

"He has—by issuing this edict of death for these traitors," Hertz rebuffed.

Bernal intervened to stop any further argument. "Destry, return to Gilroy. Act as if you know none of this. Hertz will be along in a few days, once all the legalities in order."

"I don't dispute you, but a delay may give Jonas time to flee or provide an alibi," said Destry.

"Enough!" exclaimed Bernal. He took a deep breath to calm down. He waved Hertz away to speak privately to Destry. "Cousin, hear me. I share your impatience, and desire to rid Eldar of these *followers*. However, you must understand, in my position, I must proceed with caution." He snatched a glance to be certain Hertz wasn't listening. He lowered his voice. "There are those who believe the foreigners present a greater threat to Eldar then a few secret followers."

"How so?"

Bernal shook his head. "I cannot say. You must trust me in this. For the good of our family, and in service to the Elector."

The refusal didn't set well with Destry. "While you listen to that *lawyer*, those like Jonas multiply, and threaten our livelihoods. It's polluting our town."

"I can only act within the bounds of my office. At least for now." Bernal sent his own withering glance toward Hertz.

"What if someone acted without your knowledge? Something that would not implicate you?" When Bernal hesitated with uncertainty, Destry quoted Bernal, "*For the good of our family, and in service to the Elector.*"

Bernal closely scrutinized Destry. "Well, what I don't know, I can't forbid or approve."

A small sly smile formed on Destry's lips. With a last, sniggering glance at Hertz, Destry rode from Far Point.

Hertz returned. "You didn't tell him everything, did you?"

"No! Though I fail to see how two men can do what you say. There aren't enough of these outlaws to raise an army."

Hertz glared along his shoulder at Bernal. "You still don't grasp the enormity of their arrival, do you?"

"You expect me to believe a two-hundred-year old myth is suddenly reality?"

"I *expect* you to do as told regardless of what you believe!"

Irate, Bernal sneered a warning. "Don't press me."

Hertz rose in the saddle. This time, he did not hide his anger at the threat. "If you want me to continue acting the fool to your lead, keep your temper, and a civil tongue. Or my next report to Dolus may not be so favorable!" He jerked the horse's head around to leave.

Screeching and hooting, drew Hertz's attention skyward. A harpy and owl circled overhead. He drew his horse to a halt and held up his left arm. The owl landed on his arm while the harpy alighted on the ground. This gave Bernal time to come alongside Hertz.

"Were there others with Nollen and Ida?" Hertz asked the owl. The bird bobbed its head in affirmation.

"How would it know?" asked Bernal, a bit wary.

Hertz ignored Bernal to once again speak to the owl. "Gather the black-jackals for pursuit." The owl took off. He spoke to the harpy. "Inform Lord Dolus that they are on the move."

"What can Lord Dolus do that we haven't?" chided Bernal.

Hertz didn't reply. Instead, he kicked his horse into a gallop. Playing lackey to such an incompetent, arrogant individual as Bernal grew tiresome. Despite his commoner heritage, Bernal prided himself on being astute and shrewd. To maintain his cover, Hertz fed Bernal's warped pride. Yet the longer he spent in The Doane, the more he chafed.

Unmasking the traitorous couple at Far Point prompted Dolus to send him to keep an eye out for anything suspicious. Back then, he had no idea the extent to which his patience would be challenged by Bernal. He only knew the Magistrate by name, no personal dealings until he arrived in The Doane three years ago.

With each correspondence, Dolus reminded him of his assignment, and how Bernal served only as a dupe. His primary target of surveillance were the children of Alfred and Erica. On that fateful day, Alfred cleverly used the law to his advantage. This infuriated Hertz, who believed he accounted for every legal possibility. Ida and Nollen might have been innocent then, but Hertz knew it would only be a matter of time before they revealed their true allegiance. Now, by their own treasonous actions, he could close the net. The time of his role-play would soon come to an end.

Chapter 9

BY LATE MORNING OF THE FOLLOWING DAY, NOLLEN LED THEM across a glen to a narrow band of trees. All the time they followed the small river, Ottlia circled above. The river narrowed and began a descent to a lower spot where it appeared as a creek that ran under a natural bridge.

Ottlia's loud cry caught Axel's attention. He briefly reined his horse to listen before Ottlia flew off. The others stopped across the bridge where Nollen and Ida dismounted. Axel hurried his horse to join them.

"Ottlia won't go any further. Why?" he asked Nollen.

The young man didn't immediately answer, rather gave instruction. "It is best to cover the horses' eyes and lead them through Altwald."

"How far is it?" asked Gunnar.

"Altwald is less than a quarter mile ahead, but it's five miles across." Nollen gently placed the cloth over his pony's eyes then slipped it under the bridle for security before he tied it underneath.

"Why are we doing this?" Axel asked.

"To save their lives," Nollen soberly replied. Since the answer appeared unsatisfactory, he elaborated. "The inhabitants are said to have powers that blind animals for hunting. Their prey includes harpys, owls and jackals. That is more than likely why Ottlia left."

As they neared Altwald, the surrounding area grew colder and darker. An almost black, dense forest lay before them. Nollen paused before entering the darkness. He placed a finger to his lips for silence. He flashed a plaintive smile of encouragement at Ida before moving into Altwald.

An ominous sense of evil enveloped everything. The uneasiness made them wary and alert. Massive gnarled trees with clinging vines created an almost impenetrable canopy. Many of the trees appeared dead. However, by the height and girth, they were very, very, old.

When the sun rose to its apex, nothing but a gray dullness reached the forest floor. Once in a while, a shaft of light broke though the canopy to illumine the path before them. Yet not even sunlight revealed any color among the bleakness. The grimness of Altwald almost forbade speech. When any dared to voice words, they did so in hushed uneven tones.

"We're at the half-way point," said Nollen.

"You navigate like an expert," observed Axel. He walked behind Nollen, and just slightly ahead of Ida. Gunnar followed in the rear, yet close to Ida.

Nollen pushed aside a dead vine. "Papi and Grandfather brought me here for a fortnight of training. They taught me the secret ways in and out." He just finished speaking when an eerie cry came. "Hide your eyes!" he shouted in warning. He placed his head to rest against his pony's neck with eyes screwed shut.

A loud blast of light filled the area. Ida screamed in surprise when the force knocked her sideways into Gunnar. He let go of his horse, and partially opened one eye in time stop her from falling to the ground.

When the horses and ponies neighed in fright, Axel shouted, "*Bi gestedige!*" The animals immediately calmed down, though still nervous.

Grunts and hisses sounded close-by. Opening their eyes, revealed that they were surrounded by creatures resembling a cross between man and troll. The creatures wore primitive clothes of animal skins and reeked of decay. Upon the heads were helmets made from hides with slits over the eyes. Each held a sharp, slate-tipped spear.

"Trespassers!" hissed a creature. He wore the most outlandish trimmings on his helmet and clothes. "Give us your animals, and we'll let you pass."

Nollen began to speak when Axel grabbed his shoulder. Axel took a few steps towards the creature, which prompted the group to thrust out their spears in a threatening gesture. Axel stopped yet kept his focus on the leader.

"You will take nothing from us, nor stop our journey through your forest. *Hyrst Cursians of mi fader!"*

The leader drew back in terror. Even behind the slits, his eyes grew wide and his whole body trembled. He lips quaked, as he exclaimed, "Son of Eldar!"

"I am!" Axel declared.

Screams and shrieks of horror came from the creatures. Immediately, they dropped their weapons. All fell to the ground, some prostrate, while others cowered in the protected fetal position.

Nollen and Ida watched in amazed befuddlement at the sudden turn of events.

"Mercy, Son of Eldar! Do us no further harm. Your forefather's curse has bound us for centuries," the leader urgently pleaded.

"Mercy is what placed you in this state rather than being sent to eternal torment for your evil treachery."

"You think this is better?" the leader dared to ask.

"Silence!" commanded Axel.

The leader cringed and covered his head. "What do you want of us?"

"Escort us safely through Altwald. After that, I will tell you more."

"As you command."

At the leader's agreement, a few began to grumble.

"It's been two weeks since we've eaten meat."

"Aye, horse flesh—"

"Quiet, fools!" the leader snapped. "Pay them no mind, Son of Eldar. Hunger makes them impertinent," he spoke in quick apology.

Axel didn't reply rather made a curt wave to move.

Between awkward bows of acknowledgement, the leader picked up his spear to take the lead.

Nollen, Ida, and Gunnar uneasily eyed the others, especially the two objectors. A half-mile further, the leader changed course.

Nollen leaned close to Axel to speak confidentially. "This isn't a way I learned. Do you trust him?"

"It's not a matter of trust, but self-preservation."

"Aye, if we survive," Nollen huffed in reply.

"I mean *their* self-preservation, not ours."

Confusion at the answer silenced Nollen. In fact, the whole encounter unsettled him.

Ida grew nervous when the two objectors inched closer to her and her pony. Gunnar moved to walk beside her. His actions caused the two objectors to back away. Rough hushed chatter came from the creatures.

"They don't like us," Gunnar whispered in attempted humor.

"I don't care for them, either," Ida replied.

A rocky, root-tangled descent forced them to walk single file. This time Axel took the lead with Nollen behind him, then Ida, with Gunnar again in the rear-guard position. Slow and careful, the humans guided their blinded mounts down the rough terrain.

Near the bottom, Ida briefly looked up to get her bearings. Taking her eyes off the descent, made her trip. She released the pony's bridle so as not to injure it in her fall. That was when the two objectors moved in. Already frightened by Ida's fall, the pony bolted at a sharp poke. Fortunately, being on an uneven slope, the spear only grazed its shoulder.

"Binny!" Ida exclaimed the pony's name. She scrambled to her feet to go after the frighten animal.

Already at the bottom, Nollen loosed his pony to catch Binny. The blindfolded pony breathed heavy with fright. "Easy, girl." The pony snorted and chomped at the bit.

"Binny." Ida's soothing voice and hand on the pony's neck turned to concern at seeing blood. "She wounded!"

"Bring them here!" Axel commanded

The leader repeated the order. However, the objectors fought those sent to fetch them, and fled.

For the remaining Cursians, the sight of blood made self-control difficult. Even the leader fiendishly eyed Binny.

"We must leave, and fast!" Gunnar harshly advised Axel.

"How far to the border? Axel asked Nollen.

"I'm not sure. But I see daylight up ahead."

When the Cursians rallied to attack, Axel drew his sword. He brought the cross-guard before his face. "*Leoht!*"

Bright, blinding light instantly radiated from the blade. Gunnar, Nollen and Ida shielded their eyes. The Cursians shrieked in pain. Soon the shrieks turned to pitiful whimpers then silence.

When Axel lowered the blade, the light vanished. He breathed hard, his face pale. Concerned, Gunnar grabbed Axel's arm in support.

"I'll be fine," Axel quietly spoke.

The Cursians lay fallen. Some dead, others moaned in agony. The leader among those still barely alive.

Axel sheathed his sword to kneel beside the creature. His voice filled with rancor. "The treachery of the Cursians never ends, does it?"

Too weak, the leader offered no reply. However, the look of defiance clearly visible even in defeat.

Such obstinacy infuriated Axel. He seized it by the collar to jerk it up into a sitting position. "Hear me, creature of darkness. If any Cursian leaves Altwald to aid the enemy, the curse Gott instructed my forefather to pronounce will immediately become eternal torment! Do you understand?"

Defiance turned to begrudging words of spiteful acknowledgement. "Aye, Son of Eldar!" He fell back when released.

Axel stood. "Let's move quickly." He motioned Nollen to lead on. Despite the stunned expression, Nollen did as bade.

Ida spoke soothingly to Binny as they went. Axel walked beside her with Gunnar in his normal rear position. After two hundred yards, they emerged from Altwald. The sun sat low in the late afternoon sky. After another hundred yards, Nollen stopped to remove the blindfold from his pony. The others did the same.

"We'll still lead them, as their eyesight needs to adjust." Nollen took stock of the surroundings. "We should find shelter before dark."

"How much further to our destination?" Axel inquired.

"I'll let you know when I plot a new course. We came out farther from where I intended."

"We seem to be near Emory Pass," reckoned Ida.

"Aye," agreed Nollen. "There is a hollow a mile away."

The sheltered hollow proved large enough for people and animals. Fifty yards in front of the hollow ran a creek. Ida tethered Binny. She immediately unsaddled the mare to examine the wound.

"It's not too deep, just jagged edges," she told the others.

Axel brought the same satchel he used when treating Ida. Binny snorted and stomped when he touched her wound. "Easy, Binny girl. We'll have you better by morning." He stroked the pony's neck.

"It might be a graze, but still take a week to heal."

Axel straightened from his attention on Binny to look at Ida. "What about your wounds? Does it hurt?"

Momentarily stymied by the question, Ida touched her right shoulder. "I feel no pain."

"Even when you fell down the slope?" asked Nollen, puzzled.

Ida shook her head in wonderment.

Axel grinned, and told Nollen, "Remove Ida's bandage."

To the siblings' surprise, the wound was completely knitted with only a red scar visible, but no blood or scab.

"How?" asked Ida.

"I told you, I prayed for Gott to heal you. Why are you surprised?"

"I've never received an answer so fast."

Axel simply smiled and returned to Binny.

"I'll start a fire," said Gunnar. "Ida, food."

She made an absentminded nod and fetched her saddlebag.

Chapter 10

AXEL INSISTED ON TAKING THE FIRST WATCH. THIS WOULD GIVE him time to reflect and pray. Throughout his youth and adulthood, he focused every waking moment on preparation for this undertaking. Each phase of training drove to heart the significance of what he must do. To succeed, reliance upon Gott became paramount.

By the day of his departure, he believed he understood the scope of his task. However, since arriving in Eldar, reality showed that his abstract grasp only scratched the surface. The people he heard and read so much about became flesh and blood.

He glanced to where the others slept. Nollen and Ida, children of faithful parents, who sacrificed their lives to send the long-awaited signal. His gaze lingered on Nollen. The sense of his critical involvement deepened with each passing day.

"So, young," he sighed under his breath.

His gaze passed to Gunnar; the loyal friend and soldier assigned to aid him fifteen years ago. Many a time his mere presence bolstered Axel during the hardest challenges of preparation. Axel wryly grinned. Gunnar probably just pretended to sleep. His smile faded when he turned back to the fire. Not even Gunnar knew the full extent of the task. He alone bore the burden.

The last image of his father sprang into his mind's eye. A man of strong faith, vision, and mettle. Yet, on the eve of his death, tears freely flowed. Tears of separation, of encouragement, and of faith when imparting the truth to his son. Axel tried to comfort his father with the confession that he already knew what must be done, and why. Gott showed him years earlier, but he chose to keep it secret.

When the flames became blurry with remembrance, Axel wiped his eyes. "Gott, do not let me falter now that I am here." He stared at the flames to silently pray for peace of mind, and strength of spirit.

"Highness … I mean, Axel."

He went so deep in prayer that Nollen's voice startled him. "Why aren't you sleeping?"

"I came to relieve you. It's been three hours."

"That long?" Axel murmured in surprise.

"Pardon?" Nollen asked, not understanding.

"Never mind." Axel flashed a plaintive smile. "Did you sleep?"

Nollen shrugged. "Some." He tossed another log on the fire and stoked it to produce more heat.

"Questions?"

Nollen glanced along his shoulder at Axel. "Wouldn't you have questions after what happened with Ida and the Cursians?"

"Faith and trust, remember."

"You say that as if what you did were commonplace, and not miraculous. What manner of powers do you possess?"

Axel stirred with annoyance. "I have no power in myself. I only do what Gott allows." He placed a firm hand on Nollen's shoulder to get the younger man's undivided attention. "Being true to our Oath and Faith is what gives us strength beyond this mortal frame."

"I still call what you did—miracles."

"I call them fatiguing." Axel fought a yawn.

"Sleep. Unless this strength you speak of helps you stay up all night," Nollen lightly teased.

Axel chuckled, and patted Nollen's shoulder. He made his way to his saddle blanket. Upon laying down, he immediately fell asleep.

After another three hours, Nollen woke the others. Gunnar immediately sat up to the touch. Ida took some effort, while Axel acknowledged Nollen with a grunt.

"It's still dark. Why did you wake us?" Axel fought back a yawn.

"To eat breakfast before we leave."

Axel realized he smelled food. "Sausage?"

"With onions. I also warmed the honey bread." Nollen returned to the fire where breakfast waited.

Ida stretched and flinched in pain.

"Does your wound hurt?" asked Gunnar.

"No," she groaned. "Sleeping on the ground isn't comfortable."

Nollen set the skillet on a rock so everyone could eat. He tore off pieces of honey bread to distribute. Each used their knife to skew pieces of sausage and onions to place on the bread.

"How far will we travel today?" Axel asked between bites.

"About twenty miles. Which is why we need to start before dawn, otherwise, we may not make it until after sundown," replied Nollen.

Axel popped the last part of his breakfast in his mouth. He wiped the dagger blade on the skirt of his surcoat then sheathed it. He took a drink from his flask. "Then let us be going."

Nollen smothered the fire with dirt. His pony stood ready with the bedroll secured to back of the saddle. He helped Ida with her bedroll and saddle. Shortly, they left camp to head northwest by west.

As they rode, Axel observed the forest. The massive trees rose tall and straight. Although the oaks and other deciduous trees stood bare of leaves, they appeared healthy. The robust pines maintained their green needles. Light freely filtered through the branches. Unlike Altwald, this forest displayed an abundance of life.

Axel rode beside Nollen. "By the size of the trees, I reckon this is also an old forest."

"Aye. The same age as Altwald, only not cursed," said Nollen.

"Does it have a name?"

Nollen hesitated to respond. "One that is not spoken often."

"Forbidden?"

"Secrecy."

Axel grinned at Nollen's discretion. "Do you fear being overheard?"

Before Nollen could reply, the cry of an eagle came from overhead. "Ottlia?"

"She rejoined us last night. The name?" Axel motioned to the trees.

"Heddwyn. The forest is called Heddwyn."

Axel chuckled. "You said you didn't speak ancient Eldarian."

Nollen flushed with embarrassment. "I don't. I just know the name of the forest."

"It means *place of the blessed.*"

"That makes sense," Nollen grumbled, still red-faced at Axel's amusement.

With Ottlia as sky-guard, they safely continued through Heddwyn. By midday, they paused at a stream to refresh the animals, and eat a quick meal of stale honey bread with slices of cheese and apple.

By late afternoon, Nollen drew the group to a halt near a clearing. He placed a finger to his lips then waved the others closer. He spoke a whispered warning to Axel and Gunnar.

"Less than a mile is the Ha'tar border. We must proceed with caution, and quietly. The Ha'tar have grown bold in crossing the border to harass and loot."

"Ottlia will warn us," said Axel.

"What match is an eagle against a dragon?" chided Nollen, fighting to keep passion from making his voice too loud.

"Did you learn nothing from the Cursians?" Gunnar challenged Nollen in unguarded rising tone.

"Light from a sword won't blind a dragon."

"Nollen," Ida scolded.

The deep distance cry echoed in the valley.

"Oh no, we attracted attention!" Nollen kicked his pony for a hasty departure.

Axel gave Gunnar a withering glare before he sent his horse after the siblings

"What? I didn't realize my voice would carry," Gunnar replied, as he urged his horse for speed.

Without looking back, Nollen weaved his pony through the trees and up a gentle rise to a clearing. A sudden swooping forced him to violently draw rein. The pony protested the rough stop.

A juvenile dragon looped around for another pass at Nollen. By this time, Ida, Axel and Gunnar arrived. They too checked their mounts to dodge the dragon. Although a juvenile, it was three times the size of Ottlia, yet nowhere near full-grown.

Nollen's pony reared when the dragon spewed a weak steam of fire in its direction. He fell hard to the ground, the wind knocked from his lungs. He lay stunned. The dragon changed direction to head for Nollen. Ida maneuvered Binny to avoid trampling her brother.

Gunnar drew his sword and moved his horse to shield Nollen. He swung the blade at the dragon. It altered course to avoid the attack. In doing so, the talon on the end of its wing, slashed a cut along Gunnar's right cheek. He rocked in the saddle and grimaced in pain.

Axel drew his sword to charge the dragon. It dove at him, and tried to spew a steady, narrow stream of fire. The third attempt proved greater than other two, and capable of injury. Axel used his sword to deflect the fire without being singed. He swung the sword. The impact slashed off part the juvenile's wing.

Unable to fly, the dragon crash-landed. Axel maneuvered his horse to come at the dragon from behind. The juvenile turned its head to throw more fire. Axel's sword met its neck and severed the head.

He jerked his horse to a stop. He rose in the saddle when he heard a nearby whistle. "Gunnar! More trouble."

"No. All is well!" Ida quickly said. She dismounted to help Nollen sit up. She responded with a similar whistle.

Jarred, and a half- dozen men, arrived in a rush. "Ida!" Fearful, he fell to his knees beside her and Nollen.

"We are well," she assured him.

"Speak for yourself," Nollen gasped a reply. He gingerly touched his chest. "It hurts to breathe," he complained.

"The fall knocked the wind from him," she explained to Jarred.

"Too bad it didn't knock some sense into him," Jarred teased.

Nollen flashed a toothy sarcastic smile. "Help me stand." He grabbed Jarred.

Axel moved beside Gunnar. "That's a nasty cut. I'll tend it when we reach safety."

Gunnar grunted in painful reply.

"Jarred!" called one of the men. He stood by the dead juvenile. He held up the damaged wing. "The Ha'tar may be here soon."

"Can it be buried?"

The man shook his head. "I don't think there is time."

"Do what you can to conceal it." Jarred turned his attention to Axel and Gunnar. "I take it there is a reason Nollen and Ida brought you here, but explanation can wait. We must leave." He again spoke to the man, who worked to conceal the dragon. "Howie, you and Conary do what you can quickly, then follow."

Nollen and Ida mounted, while Jarred and his men moved on foot. By the time, they reached the forest on other side of the clearing, Howie and Conary raced to join them.

"From the air, it should look like a mound," Howie reported.

Thump, thump of air movement reached their ears.

"Quickly! Take cover!" Jarred sprinted in the direction of safety.

Nollen, Ida, Axel, Gunnar, and the others reached a hollow just as the Ha'tar dragon-rider came over the far tree line. Those mounted, got down to keep the animals quiet. Everyone shrunk back into the hollow as far as possible. For several moments, they anxiously waited, as the Ha'tar dragon-rider circled overhead. Finally, he left in the same direction he came. They remained in the hollow to make certain he wouldn't return.

"Is he gone?" Gunnar whispered to Jarred.

"I believe so." Cautiously Jarred stepped out of the hollow. The glow of twilight came from the west. "The sun is setting. Ha'tar don't fly at night."

"Will we make the compound before nightfall?" asked Axel.

"We're within a mile of our destination," Nollen said.

"Best walk the horses. The entrance is low and narrow," Jarred advised Axel and Gunnar.

After a quarter mile, they began a winding descent that forced them to walk single file. Though being dusk at the top, the light grew much darker on the way down. Fortunately, their eyes adjusted during the journey.

Jarred waited for everyone to reach the bottom. He confronted Axel and Gunnar. "You must swear never to reveal what you are about to see in terms of location and number of people."

Axel looked directly at Jarred. "My word of honor before Gott."

Jarred's brow wrinkled at hearing *Gott*.

Ida's hand on his arm drew Jarred's marked attention from Axel. "They can be trusted."

Jarred's glance shifted to Nollen, who nodded in confirmation. Jarred cupped his hands around his mouth and made a warbling sound of a evening bird. He received a reply warble. The ponies and horses became startled by a metallic snap and creak. They held the reins to steady the frightened animals.

A section between two large pines began to rise with the sounds of pulleys. The camouflage rose only high enough to permit passage. Once inside, two men closed the section. The group arrived at the hidden from another direction. People warily watched, as Jarred led the strangers from the south entrance further into the compound.

From the longhouse, Arctander emerged, eager in manner. His eyes shifted between the newcomers before resting on Axel. He fought a hopeful smile, as he hurried his approach.

"You are he, the one we have awaited, aren't you?" It was more a statement than a question.

"I am Axel—"

Arctander seized Axel's left hand to remove the glove. He saw the engraved band. "Of Oleg's royal line! The Son of Eldar!" he announced. "My liege!" He kissed Axel's ring.

Jarred, and all the people, gasped or murmured in wonder.

"You know about the sacred ring?" Axel questioned.

Arctander reached beneath the collar of his shirt to show the amulet he wore. The engraving matched the band. "I am the sole surviving priest of Gott sworn to the secrets of the True King."

Axel examined the amulet. "How are you the last?"

"Influenced by Dolus, Lel, Javan's father, ordered the massacre of our order a decade ago. Though seriously wounded, I managed to escape, and find my way here."

"He is our Grandfather. The one we spoke about," Ida told Axel regarding Arctander.

"No need to stand out in the cold night air. Come inside, rest, while we prepare to celebrate your arrival! Jarred."

"Prepare food and bring the best ale!" Jarred ordered the people.

At either end of the longhouse were separate rooms. Arctander lead Axel and Gunnar to the west room.

"How did you receive the wound?" he asked Gunnar.

"Dragon's wing thumb scratched me."

Arctander suddenly became concerned. "Adult or juvenile?"

Gunnar and Axel appeared uncertain, so Ida answered, "Juvenile."

"Merciful heaven!" Arctander murmured with dread. "Nollen, fetch Peni, quick!" then to Gunnar, "Sit on the bed, my lord. Peni will be here shortly."

Confused, Gunnar asked, "What's the problem?"

"How do you feel?"

"I've felt better, why?"

Arctander attempted to be diplomatic. "I don't wish to alarm you, however, wounds from a juvenile dragon are poisonous."

"Poisonous?" repeated Gunnar in surprise. "I don't recall that." He grew thoughtful. "Then again, I hadn't encountered a dragon before today. Only heard about them."

"How poisonous?" Axel asked.

Arctander examined Gunnar's wound. A greenish ooze came from the cut. "Peni can tell us more. She is our physician."

Nollen arrived with a very old woman. She wore a satchel on her shoulder that slung across her seemingly fragile frame. Axel and Gunnar appeared leery upon sight of her.

"Don't be fooled by her age," Arctander told them. He said to Peni, "The wound is from a juvenile dragon."

Peni examined it, and asked, "How old was it?" When Gunnar shrugged ignorance, she asked a clarifying question. "Did it have fire or not?"

"Fire. Weak attempts though," replied Ida

"Enough to cause injury," insisted Axel.

"That's the most dangerous time," said Peni. By Axel's harsh expression, he required further explanation. "Poison is their only defense until mature enough to produce powerful fire. However, during the time of transition, the poison is most potent."

"Lethal?" Axel demanded when Peni crossed to a side table. He went after her. "I asked if it's lethal," he firmly repeated.

"Possibly." She withdrew various vials, plants, small box and pestle from her satchel.

Axel fought to contain his disturbance at her answer. "What mixture are you using?"

"Do you know herbs?"

"Aye, only I don't recognize these plants."

Peni glanced up and down at Axel. "You are a stranger to Eldar."

"The *Son of Eldar*," Arctander emphasized to Peni.

"Indeed," she sounded only mildly impressed. "I'm using jewelweed and yarrow mixed with clay as a poultice to draw out the poison. Followed by a tea of elder flower and willow bark to help with pain and prevent fever." She heard Gunnar moan in pain. "Make him comfortable so he can sleep when I'm finished," she instructed Axel.

Nollen and Ida helped Axel to strip Gunnar down to his shirt and pants. He didn't fuss, since the poison made him lethargic. Once they had Gunnar under the covers, Peni sat on the bed to begin treatment. When finished, she stood.

"Now it's up to Gott," she said soberly.

"How can he die from this scratch?" Axel challenged.

"My lord, I told you, during transition, the juvenile's poison is most potent and dangerous. I will tend him throughout the night, but only Gott can heal him."

Fighting worry and aggravation, Axel brusquely said to Arctander, "No feast tonight! Not until Gunnar is healed."

"Aye, my lord. We shall keep vigil for him tonight." Arctander bowed. He began to draw Nollen and Ida from the room.

"I want to stay and help," said Ida with compassion.

To her offer, Axel softened his attitude. "You have done much for us already. Go with your grandfather and rest." He looked to Nollen. "Both of you. Peni and I will be enough."

Chapter 11

BY MIDNIGHT OF THE PRAYER VIGIL FOR GUNNAR'S HEALING, neither Nollen nor Ida could stay awake. Nollen willingly listened to Arctander's instruction to sleep, but Ida hesitated due to concern for Gunnar. Not until Jarred's insistence did she submit and retire with Nollen to Arctander's personal chamber.

To Nollen's annoyance, sleep didn't last long. He estimated three hours at most. Despite bodily fatigue, his mind wouldn't allow him to rest. So as not to disturb Ida, he carefully donned his cloak and carried his boots to leave quietly.

In the main room, the vigil continued, only with less people. Jarred remained with the group while Arctander slept on a cot near the far hearth. Nollen carefully pulled on his boots and managed to sneak out without being noticed.

He braved the cold to find a spot by the compound fire. This area of warmth helped the night watch ward-off a chill when needed. The men must have been on patrol since no one sat around the fire.

His earlier contemplation about Axel became confounded by incidents since leaving Far Point. The harpy attack, Ida's wound healed, the Cursian encounter, and the dragon battle that left Gunnar fighting for his life. All these things confirmed Axel as the Son of Eldar. So why was he still so unsettled in spirit?

Nollen stared at the fire trying to comprehend. The flames turned mesmerizing and drew his mind back to the horrible day of his parents' capture, then receiving word of their execution. The fire grew misty through tears of anger, pain, and confusion. Without realizing it, his thoughts turned into dreams of sleep.

"Nollen," he heard a voice speak his name. Gentle at first then insistent, and finally accompanied by a rough shake. Startled, his eyes snapped open. He sat at the compound fire with a hand on his shoulder. Jarred.

"Oh! I must have fallen asleep." Nollen blinked his eyes to focus.

"What are you doing out here? Last I saw, you were in Arctander's room," said Jarred.

Nollen rubbed the back of his neck. "I couldn't sleep."

"So naturally you ended up out here sleeping," Jarred teased.

Nollen huffed a chuckle.

"Breakfast will be ready soon. However, Arctander wants to speak with you in his study."

Nollen stood and stretched before he returned inside. Upon entering the private room, he saw Arctander sat at the desk conversing with Ida.

"Did you sleep better outside?" Arctander asked, battling a smile.

"Hard to tell," grumbled Nollen.

Ida poured a drink. "Warm cider."

Nollen mumbled thanks and drank. "What did you want to speak to me about?"

Arctander motioned for Nollen to sit. "With Sir Gunnar falling ill, we didn't get the chance to discuss how the Son of Eldar came to Far Point. Ida just told me about the jackal attack you thwarted when they arrived."

Nollen considered what to say. "Well, after that, Ida fed them. He told us who he is and showed us a medallion. He claimed Marmie and Papi sent it. Ida immediately believed him."

"But you didn't? Why?" asked Arctander.

Nollen shrugged since he drank. "It seemed incredible at the time."

"Answers to prayers usually do."

Nollen drank to cover a frown.

"All his actions since have proven his claim," Ida said.

"Oh, I no longer doubt his claim." With knitted brows of consideration, Nollen stared at the cider in the cup.

"Then what do you doubt?" asked Arctander.

"I don't know if I'd use that word. Troubled, perhaps." Yielding to anger, Nollen pushed himself off the chair to confront Arctander. "Why wasn't I told about this medallion that Marmie and Papi sent?"

Taken back by the outburst, Arctander stared at his grandson. "Alfred never told you?"

"No! According to *him*," Nollen waved at the door, "it was a prearranged signal. Something I should have known about since I took over for Papi." His voice cracked when he mentioned his father.

Arctander's expression softened from confusion to compassion. "You were young at the time, and still unsure of your future responsibility, so we agreed to wait."

"*We?*"

"Alfred sought my advice before sending the medallion. He wanted to tell you but didn't believe you were ready yet."

Incredulity made Nollen momentary mute. "Did you know?" he challenged Ida.

She shook her head. "No. They didn't tell me either."

"For your protection, in case anything went wrong. Which it did," Arctander said, pain crept into his voice. Nollen's indignation prompted him to ask, "Don't you understand? Alfred *wanted* to tell you, but our decision helped to keep you from sharing their fate! By being able to claim true innocence, and invoking sanctuary law, you are alive today to help the Son of Eldar!"

Arctander moved from behind his desk to further entreat Nollen. "The task entrusted to our family centuries ago, now falls to you. It is your destiny to finish what Alfred started, and do what I cannot. If I leave the compound, and Dolus learns I am alive, our people will be slaughtered."

Overwhelmed, Nollen couldn't speak.

Arctander's eyes grew misty, and voice tender. "I realize it is a heavy burden for one so young, but there is no one else."

Nollen cast a side-glance to Ida.

"You know it is passed down from father to son. It is why you inherited Far Point rather than Ida," said Arctander.

Nollen abruptly moved to stand in front of the hearth. Overcome by conflicting emotions, he seized the mantle. First, he assumed the responsibility to maintain Far Point, continued the covert missions of mercy, and now supposed to help fulfill prophecy? Changes were happening too fast!

"Nollen. You're not in this alone."

He heard sympathy in Ida's voice, but couldn't look at her. When she touched his arm, he whirled about. Despite the visible battle to contain his emotions, irritation slipped out. "That's easy for you to say."

At her recoil, Arctander scolded him. "If you lack the courage to do what you must, don't take it out on your sister! Find the resolve in here." He pulled a large book off his desk and thrust it into Nollen's hands. "The Ancient Book."

Nollen grew hesitant, as he held the sacred writings. "I wouldn't know where to start."

Arctander briefly took the book back to open it. "Read from here on about the Son of Eldar. And don't stop until Gott shows you what needs to be done." Using a stiff arm, he pointed Nollen to the desk.

"I'll send in breakfast," Ida offered.

"No! He won't eat until he is finished," chided Arctander.

Nollen knew better than to argue with his grandfather. Thus, he spoke no dispute when Arctander drew Ida from the room.

With open book in hand, he sat to read. Since very few copies of the Ancient Book remained, he hadn't read anything from the revered pages. Mostly he listened to either his father or grandfather when they read and expounded on passages. Soon, he became lost in the pages, digesting every word and phrase. He paid particular attention to those regarding Axel.

The remnant suffers under the staff of the enemy.
Woe to them who divide the spoils of the Chosen!
The people who live in darkness shall see a great light
when the yoke of oppression is lifted off their shoulders.

That is the day each generation longed to see since Oleg's overthrow. Could they really be witnessing it now?

There shall come one from the offspring of Oleg, a son
to gather that which were lost of the children of Eldar.
Wisdom, strength, and justice will rest upon him.
From him, the sacrifice will be satisfied.

The word *sacrifice* gave Nollen great pause. It was a word all too familiar to those of the Faith. Thoughts of his parents brought immediate tears. He slammed the book closed. He needed to get a hold of his emotions before he continued. He wiped his eyes then crossed to the bookshelf. Whereas the Ancient Book contained words of prophecy, it didn't provide a timeline to events. Unfortunately, only six other books sat on the shelf.

Nollen quickly thumbed through each. By the fourth one, he grew frustrated at not finding the answer he needed. Finally, in the fifth book, he discovered a timeline. A scant recounting since the time of Oleg, vague and unspecific. He turned when the door opened. Ida entered with a tray of food.

"I know what Grandfather said, but that was about breakfast." She placed the tray on the desk.

"What time is it?" asked Nollen, baffled.

"One o'clock."

"I hadn't realized so much time passed," he muttered, more to himself.

"Have you found what you needed?" she asked, hopeful.

"I'm not sure yet." He thoughtfully traced the etching on the front cover the book he held. "There seems to be no record of our family's *activities,*" he said with discretion.

"There aren't any," Arctander said. He stood in the threshold.

"Why? I kept notes."

"You did what?" Arctander exclaimed. Anger propelled him further into the room. "You didn't leave them at Far Point to be discovered?"

"No!" chided Nollen in rebuff. "I'm not that foolish. We burned all ledgers and papers before departure. Ida brought those connected to our Oath and Faith." He held up the book. "But why is there no history of our family to help me understand what I must do?"

"Because it is a duty of Faith rather than lineage. Did you learn nothing from the Ancient Book?"

"Of course," Nollen huffed in refute. "Only it contains no history. Nothing tangible."

"The Prince is tangible," said Ida in her soft-spoken confidence.

Nollen plopped in the chair beside the shelf. He fought a yawn and rubbed his eyes.

"You're tired. Fatigued minds are slow to grasp information, and comprehend implications," began Arctander. "Rest. Understanding will come when you are refreshed."

Nollen didn't argue, rather collapsed onto the cot he occupied earlier. Within moments, he fell asleep. He wouldn't wake until the following morning. His first thoughts dealt with Axel.

Axel didn't notice the flame flicker, as the lamp ran low on oil. Nor did he see the gray light of day peeking through the shutters. He sat beside the bed, elbows on his knees, hands clenched, and eyes focused on Gunnar. Peni slept in a chair near the window.

Gunnar lay still, slowly breathing, but not moving or making a sound. Axel knew the journey required sacrifice, only it surprised him how unprepared he felt at Gunnar's condition. Treating Ida did not cause him personal distress. However, Gunnar hit close to his heart. Fifteen years his constant companion, and not so much as a sniffle. With all that lay ahead, it couldn't end like this so soon.

Axel became aware of a presence next to him. He sat up, a bit surprised to discover— "Nollen."

"I didn't mean to disturb you. I simply came to see how Sir Gunnar is doing this morning."

"Morning?" At that moment, Axel noticed the lamp had extinguished, and daylight filtered into the room. "I guess my prayers and contemplation went deeper than anticipated."

"Grandfather, and others, also spent the past two days in prayer."

"Thank you." Axel heartily gripped Nollen's arm.

Nollen's focus changed to Gunnar. "He doesn't look any better."

"At least he slept peacefully. No deterioration in his condition."

Nollen didn't appear satisfied by Axel's attempt of encouragement. "Why could you heal Ida and not Gunnar?"

"I didn't heal anyone. Gott did," Axel replied in emphatic dispute. "I merely applied medicine while praying for her healing."

Nollen's attention again shifted to Gunnar. "Will Gott answer and heal Gunnar?"

Axel also watched Gunnar sleep. "I don't know. However, I trust Gott to do what is best for all concerned."

"How can death be best?" Nollen demanded. Instead of waiting for an answer, he withdrew.

Ida entered just as Nollen left. She carried a tray. "Nollen?" He didn't reply. Dejected by his silence, she forced a smile and indicated the tray for Axel. "I brought you breakfast."

Axel's gaze continued passed Ida to the door. "Has he always been so angry, or just since your parents' death?"

Ida paused in placing the tray on the small table beside the bed. "Since their death," she murmured. "But he has a good heart."

"A good heart can grow bitter if anger is left unchecked." Axel watched emotions make her momentarily mute.

"I know. It is my greatest fear for him. We, Grandfather, Jarred, and I, have tried to help him. Sometimes he listens. Other times, he regresses. Just like you saw now."

"Because each time something made the anger resurface. This time, it was our arrival."

She nodded, yet again quick to insist, "He knows your coming is for our good. He spent the better part of yesterday reading the Ancient Book."

"Knowing it and accepting it are two different things."

Ida deflected the disturbing conversation. "Please, eat."

He politely declined. "Not until Gunnar is recovered."

"It's been two days, you must eat," she gently insisted.

"I feel no hunger, only great concern."

Arctander entered. Jarred accompanied him, and Nollen returned. "We came to inquire about his condition," said Arctander.

Axel's gaze briefly shifted from Arctander to Nollen. The young man still appeared stoic. "Unchanged, which is good, since he is no worse."

Peni woke. She opened the shutters to allow in the full morning light. She moved to examine Gunnar. "The fever is gone." She took off the bandage. The green ooze had diminished. "No further infection. Another good sign," she spoke the last sentence to Axel.

Suddenly, Gunnar inhaled in a deep gasp, and his eyes snapped opened. He became befuddled. "Where am I?"

Axel sat on the bed. "Easy, old friend, you're safe."

"Axel? You're not hurt?"

"No. I am whole. So are Nollen and Ida."

Gunnar followed Axel's indication of the siblings. He balked upon sight of Peni. "Where am I?" he asked again.

"The hidden compound," said Nollen. "Don't you remember our journey here?"

Gunnar's brows furrowed with confusion at Nollen's response. "Nothing has happened since?"

"No."

Axel touched Gunnar's shoulder to get his attention. "You've been recovering from the dragon wound the past two days."

Gunnar stared at Axel trying to comprehend. "Just two days?"

"Aye. Why?"

Gunnar closed his eyes, swallowed, and tried to breath normally. "It couldn't have been a dream. Too vivid."

"What was?"

Gunnar shook his head, utterly perplexed. "I'm not certain I can describe it. A vision, a dream, I'm not sure which."

"You mustn't become upset. Remaining calm is crucial to recovery," advised Peni.

"Listen to her, my friend. Rest and recover. In due time, we will discern what troubles you," Axel added his counsel.

Gunnar weakly smiled. "Seeing you alive and whole is already helping."

"Would some broth be good for him?" Ida asked Peni, to which the old physician nodded.

"I may need more than broth," said Gunnar, which caused Axel to chuckle.

"Speaking of eating," Ida said to Axel.

"Breakfast sounds good now. Only I will take it with everyone else. Unless you've already eaten?" he asked Nollen.

"No, it's being placed on the table now. Ida brought you the first plate."

Axel smiled. He held Nollen's shoulder to steer him from the room. "Do you see the good now?"

"He's healed, or at least on his way to recovery. Although it took longer than expected."

"Time means nothing to Gott, only to us." Axel fought a yawn when they reached the table in the main room. "The same with sleep. Though the eternal never rests, as soon as breakfast is done, I will sleep."

Chapter 12

ELDAR'S MAGNIFICENT FORTIFIED CITY OF SENER STOOD AT THE base of the majestic Halvor Mountains. The Plain of Sener separated the grand city from the sheer-faced mountains that served as the northern border. Crossing down from the north to approach Sener proved hazardous any time of year, but deadly during the colder months. The Plain provided good visibility for the city watch.

Lake Helivan guarded Sener's main entrance. Helivan narrowed near the center over which a massive bridge allowed access to the city. Two enormous gate towers guarded the southern portion of the bridge. These also housed guards, and the great mechanisms needed to close the huge thick iron gate. At the north end, two more gate towers flanked the bridge. Access could be cut-off at both ends to trap any would-be attackers on the bridge.

On the east side of the city, the River Stille flowed into Lake Helivan. Beyond the Stille lay the Freelands, though only a portion of what once was a vast domain. The River Endelos served as the western barrier to Sener. It also emptied into Helivan. Across the west bank, lay the Forest of Ganel.

With the flowing force from the upland rivers feeding it, the waters of Lake Helivan proceed south to form the mighty River Leven. Two miles across, the swift, powerful current traveled one hundred miles before dramatically ending at the Great Falls. Over the one-thousand-foot drop, waters rushed down the precipice with a deafening roar.

As for Sener itself, the walls, buildings, castle, tower houses, and bridges were all built with beautiful crystalized quartz quarried in the Halvor Mountains. When polished, the nearly impregnable city shone in a sun-splashed array of blue and purple hues. Lesser gray marble paved the streets. Blown glass of various colors dominated the taller keeps, and towers of the castle. Throughout the day, sunlight caught different glass reflections with a dazzling sparkle. At least, that is how Sener once looked. Over the past two hundred years, the city's brilliance faded to muted colors. The dampened splendor matched the subdued mood of the kingdom.

The castle dominated the center of Sener on the highest point in the city. From the marbled columns of the great hall hung black and gold velvet banners depicting jackals and harpys. The dozen beings representing the territories were dwarfed by the sheer size of the hall.

On the raised throne sat Javan, a portly man of fifty with a thick salt-and-pepper beard. Arrayed in rich apparel of gold trim with black and fur he sat impatiently listening to a man from the Freelands. The humble man with balding yellow hair, knelt before the platform. His clothes, once of good quality wool and cloth, appeared faded and worn.

"Enough, Gorman! I grow tired of excuses from the Freelands," Javan interrupted.

"Most noble Elector, I brought what I could for Tribute. Even Minister Beltran can vouch for my diligence in this matter." Gorman indicated a frowning bald man in the end of the platform.

"Well?" Javan demanded of Beltran.

With stiff, reluctance, Beltran nodded. "It is so, Elector."

Javan's glance shifted from his Second Minister to his First Minister, Dolus. He stood on the opposite side of the lower platform from Beltran. Despite the stooped back always making him look awkward, Dolus made an affirming nod.

Javan snarled and waved Gorman away. He scurried backwards and bowed to Javan while he muttered gratitude.

Javan glared at beings gathered to one side. The group included various representative from five of the Six Territories. The three Ha'tar were Fod, Gan, and Kyn. Gan replaced his dragon-rider apparel with a rich robe and cloak to match his companions for an official visit to Sener. Standing nearly eight feet, three male Nefal representatives flanked the Ha'tar. Two muscular Nefal warriors wore the barest of clothing consisting of leather and metal. The plumed helmets were complete with a nose guard. They carried massive spears. Lord Argus of the Nefal augmented his appearance by wearing a robe and jeweled headdress.

Two representatives from The Doane kept to themselves a few steps from the group. The most out-of-place were three male representatives from the Forest of Ganel. Elegant in feature, form and dress, they stood out from the rest. Their official clothes made of white linen trimmed in various shades of blue, red, and violet. Long, rich, thick hair of black, brown, and blond reached past their shoulders. Each wore a jeweled dagger.

Javan's raised voice demanded attention. "Do all of you offer the same excuse as the Freelands?" When no one spoke, he scolded the Freeland representative. "Well, Master Gorman? See what obstinacy you have inspired!"

"If I pleases you, Elector, I will give answer," said the black-haired representative from Ganel.

Javan cocked a sardonic smile. "Lord Ronan. I'm surprised you haven't spoken before now."

Ronan ignored the slight to continue. "There is only so much gold in Eldar. If you take all of it, how can we continue to pay the tribute you require?"

"He's right!" agreed Governor Ebert of The Doane. "We can barely sell or trade, much less make Tribute."

"There is gold in the Halvor Mountains," said Dolus.

"The Eagles jealously guard the mines," said Argus of Nefal.

"Are you afraid of the eagles, Lord Argus?" asked Dolus.

Argus snarled with insult. "I fear nothing. However," he admitted. "The dangers outweigh the benefits of attempting such an undertaking."

"Benefits?" Javan's loud, angry outburst echoed in the hall. "Do the Nefal not *benefit* from my protection? Do not all of the Territories *benefit* from the stability I bring to Eldar?"

"He can't control the harpys," Jabid grumbled to Ebert. He also represented The Doane.

"What did you say?"

The question startled Jabid. "I … I," he stammered fearful at being overheard. He let out a cry when Beltran seized him. In terror, he blurted out, "You can't control the harpys!"

Ebert hurried to add, "We can't conduct trade with harpys menacing the province. Without trade, we can't feed our families, or pay Tribute."

"The harpys protect our southern border," refuted Dolus. He continued his argument to Javan. "They too must eat and provide for their young. As birds of prey, they take what is needed to survive, and *that* benefits Eldar."

"Killing innocent people does not benefit Eldar!"

Beltran clouted Jabid for his impertinence.

"Harpys don't kill people," Dolus harshly rebuked.

"For that baseless accusation, The Doane's next Tribute will be double!" Javan told them. "Throw them out!"

Beltran ordered guards to take charge of Ebert and Jabid.

Once the commotion of the departure had faded, Javan addressed those remaining. "Are there any more objections?"

No one dared speak.

With a haughty laugh, Javan left the hall.

"Will you trespass into the Halvor to fetch gold?" Fod of Ha'tar asked Argus.

The Nefal lord sneered. "If I do, it will be only for our *benefit.* Let your dragons contend with the eagles." Argus turned on his heel to leave.

The sting of insult still flush on his cheeks, Fod confronted Ronan. "What of Ganel? You seem amply supplied for Tribute."

"We have our ways," Ronan spoke in tempered reply. He gave a courtesy nod before turning to depart.

"Maybe the Ha'tar will discover your supply and help ourselves!" Gan shouted.

To this threat, Ronan whirled about. His dark eyes ablaze with anger. His voice deep and foreboding. "Hear this! If any Ha'tar set one foot in our forest, or use your dragons in any way against us, you risk the *full* wrath of Ganel!"

A resonant power in Ronan's speech forced Gan to retreat a step. At the reaction, Ronan took a deep breath to calm down. This time, he didn't make a formal acknowledgement. Instead, he abruptly withdrew.

With his companions in tow, Ronan headed to the main courtyard. There, he found The Doane men mounted for departure. "Ebert! A moment," he called.

Ebert now wore a hat and cloak for travel. He checked his horse at Ronan's call. "What do you want?"

"Only to ask a civil question. You mentioned the harpys killing. When did it start?"

Ebert shrugged, a bit annoyed. "I don't know, a few years. Why?"

"It's important. Please, try to be specific."

Ebert glanced with consideration to Jabid. "Two?"

"Closer to three years, I'd say," replied Jabid. "It began with old man Drayper."

"Aye, three," said Ebert with growing conviction.

Ronan said to Jabid, "Tell me about Drayper."

Ebert's hard hand on Jabid's arm, stopped his reply. Ebert glanced to see the guards and other milling about the courtyard.

"Ebert, this is important," Ronan again stressed, yet mindful of his tone and volume.

Ebert leaned down to speak privately. "Wyck's Inn tonight." He kicked his horse to leave.

Ronan stepped back to allow the departure. In turning, he spied Dolus watching from a balcony. He boldly returned Dolus' stare until he felt a hand upon his shoulder. He heeded the silent warning of his companion. They proceeded out the main gate on foot.

"What shall we do in the meantime?" one asked Ronan.

"Irwin, I want you to double-back, and try to learn what Dolus has planned," he instructed the blonde Ganel. To the brown-haired man, "Cormac, shadow the Nefal, and determine *if* Argus intends to disturb the Eagles. I will speak with the Freelanders. We'll rendezvous at the inn before meeting The Doanes."

"He gets the friendlier task," Irwin snickered to Cormac.

Ronan didn't accept the humor. "There is nothing friendly about what is happening!"

"What about the Ha'tar?" asked Cormac. "They pose more of a problem than the Freelanders."

Ronan's brows knitted together in consideration. "They have been threatening our borders for years. However, I feel our friends need more encouragement." He motioned to them. "Go. We'll rendezvous at the inn before the meeting."

Dolus returned inside. The large, lavish study was filled with hunting trophies; eagles, wolves, jackals, and various other game animals. The dominant prize was a massive and magnificent white lion with a glorious mane. It stood on a platform between two oversized windows that lead to the balcony.

Javan sat at the desk. "Well? What do you make of their excuses?"

"They spoke the truth. Gold is becoming scarce. It is all part of the plan. When the gold is gone, they will be forced to give up their most sacred treasures."

Javan sneered a snicker. "Revealing the Horn of Kolyn." He then blustered with anger. "It is taking longer than you said it would!"

"It may not be much longer, Elector." Dolus made his way to a harpy—a real harpy, not a stuffed trophy. He stroked the bird's head. "Aras and his flock have confirmed that *he* is here—in Eldar. Just like I reported earlier."

Javan's eyes narrowed in guarded concern. His voice betrayed a hint of anxiety. "Oleg's heir."

"Indeed, Elector." Dolus leaned on the table to bring his face eye-to-eye with Javan. "He is here for one reason, and one reason only—to fulfill the Blood Oath. Once this is done, you will have the throne and title of *king forever.*"

Javan lightly bit his lip at the response. "Are you certain?" He made a dismissive wave at Aras. "It is just a bird."

Aras squawked in anger, his double-crest rising.

"Easy," Dolus soothed Aras. "He didn't mean to insult you."

Javan recoiled at the intimidating display. "How can you understand it?" he asked.

Dolus heaved a nonchalant shrug. "Part of my training before entering your father's service. The same, which made this possible." He motioned to the lion.

Javan's expression flexed between annoyance and uneasiness. "Your ways are unsettling, and confusing. Why capture it rather than kill it?"

Dolus sighed to quell his rising frustration. "Allow me to explain *again.* Capturing Gott's spirit guardian will help to prevent any interference—"

"Killing it would make certain of no interference."

This time anger filled Dolus' voice. "Capturing it allows *us* to control the situation until the Blood Oath is fulfilled. Any prior action, and you risk forfeiting the *crown.*"

For a moment, Dolus held Javan's gaze. The cool cunningness of the First Minister made Javan shy. He quickly recovered his momentary discomposure, and with hard-set features exclaimed, "Find the horn!"

The slamming of the door at Javan's exit made Aras flap his wings.

"He will be dealt with in time," said Dolus. "For now, return to The Doane. The Son of Eldar's whereabouts is more important than Javan's vain threats."

Aras made an acknowledging cry before he flew out the open balcony.

Dolus moved to stand before the lion, to look at it face-to-face. He cocked a fiendish grin. "You will be destroyed along with Oleg's descendent. Othniel, great spirit lion of Eldar obliterated for eternity! Gott will not save you. He has abandoned you for a carelessly spoken bargain."

For the briefest moment, the eyes of the lion seemed to display anger. Dolus didn't see the reaction, as he returned to the desk.

He picked up a bell, and continuously rang it before slamming it down, annoyed by the sluggish response.

The door opened, and Sylvan, a middle-aged man, entered. Although his wore his hair shorter, his facial features resembled those from Ganel. "You rang, my lord?"

"Have you made a full accounting of today's Tribute?"

Sylvan appeared pained to answer. "I fear it is far short of what was required, my lord."

Dolus took note of Sylvan's discomfort. "That troubles you?"

"My lord," Sylvan began, discrete, yet hedging, "my displeasure is of little concern."

"Will that *concern* affect your duties?" Dolus pressed.

Sylvan straightened, his pride wounded. "I have faithfully discharged all the responsibilities you have given me."

Dolus flashed a sly smile. "Indeed. However, very soon there maybe tasks which will require more than faithful discharge. Tasks that force a choice between Territorial loyalty, and service to the Elector. Do you understand?"

Sylvan visibly swallowed. "I do." He boldly continued, "And if you recall, my lord, I willingly entered your service."

Satisfied by the gutsy reply, Dolus patted Sylvan's shoulder. "Bring me any information the archives contain regarding Oleg's relics."

Sylvan bowed and left.

After leaving Dolus, Javan hastened his steps to his private chamber. He slammed another door. This time in the face of his valet when the poor man sought to aid him.

Every argument with Dolus caused him the same angst and reconsideration. The only thing that helped reassure him, was standing before the portrait of his father that hung near the desk in his chamber.

Javan revered his father, the powerful Elector Lel, who strengthened the hereditary office like none before. Of course, with Dolus' help, a thought which made Javan sneer.

Dolus arrived in Sener just as Lel was diagnosed with a terminal illness. Charismatic and cunning, Dolus quickly gained Lel's favor. Playing upon the dying Elector's work to solidify the family's hold on Eldar, Dolus suggested a bold plan: execute the remaining priests of the Shining Ones, followers of the True King. Fresh from that success, Lel appointed Dolus First Minister, and set in motion the events to secure the crown for Javan. Lel died shortly thereafter.

Little did Lel know the dire agreement required of Javan in exchange for the throne. Yet even that didn't matter. His own desire for the crown and the title of *king* drove his decision to abide by his father's wishes, and Dolus' plan.

His agitation from this argument was short-lived, and he slyly grinned. "You'll be happy to hear, the Great Lion has been captured, and the Son of Eldar is alive and here. What you started, will soon come to fruition. I shall become *king forever*."

Chapter 13

LOCATED ACROSS THE LAKE JUST PAST THE TOWER HOUSES, Wyck's Inn became a popular gathering spot for those coming and going from Sener. The sprawling complex consisted of a store, tavern, main inn, a personal home for the owner, and two barns capable of stabling up to twenty horses. Out in the back were a chicken coup, carriage house, two wells, and a gristmill along the lake. Several other houses and farms were located nearby to serve as support for the Inn.

Being large and noisy made it easy for people to come and go without much notice. This helped informants earn a living by spying for whomever paid them. Despite the covert side that frequented his inn, Wyck proved to be nobody's fool. Those who provided support for his establishment, included former soldiers hired to provide security. If any unscrupulous individual disturbed his customers and caused trouble, he had his men quickly put an end to it. After all, the local livelihood of all involved depended more upon honest commerce than dishonest skullduggery.

Ronan and his companions arrived an hour after dark. Being the height of the dinner time, finding Ebert and his friend could be difficult. Fortunately, The Doane men were creatures of habit. Thus, Ronan knew where to look. The Ganels weaved their way through the crowd to join them. Ebert waved to a man across the room. He grinned and nodded.

A moment later, he arrived at the table with three tankards. "Our best cider," he said to Ronan.

"I'd expect nothing less from you, Wyck," said Ronan with a chuckle.

Wyck's face widened into a broad, friendly smile. Clean-shaven, short and bald, nothing about this mild-mannered man suggested an innkeeper of formidable mettle. "So, what will it be this time?"

"The usual."

"Why am I not surprised? Can't you at least order something different than onion soup with bread?"

"And rob you of the enjoyment of having our same argument?" Ronan lightly bantered.

"At least Ebert and Jabid order meat," fussed Wyck in a good-natured retort.

"We of the Ganel—"

"*Don't eat meat,*" Wyck mimicked. "There, I finished our argument. Can I at least convince you to try some cheese and pine nut fritters? Maybe mushroom and leek pie?"

The offer intrigued the Ganels. "Very well. Bring both, along with the soup and bread."

"You don't eat meat yet accept cheese?" questioned Ebert.

"You don't need to kill a beast to get milk," said Ronan.

"And eggs in the pie?" challenged Jabid.

Irwin replied, "A domestic chicken lays one egg a day. Can you see a mother hen guarding thirty offspring in a single month? Hundreds in a year? No. Chicken eggs are produced regularly, so they are not in danger of going extinct. Wild birds only lay eggs once a year. We don't eat those, since it would reduce the population to dangerous levels."

Jabid shook his head. "You have strange ways of reasoning."

"Not so. Everything we do is to protect our forest and cultivate its growth. Do you not protect and nourish that which you love?"

For a moment, Jabid considered the question. "I guess I haven't thought of it that way."

Ebert grew frustrated. "They know trading commodities is our way of life. He's just luring you into a philosophical debate."

Ronan and his friends smiled at the characterization.

"Now what is it you wanted to know?" Ebert continued in his terse manner.

Ronan waited to answer since two women, and a man, brought the food. Once they left, he replied in a discrete tone. "Tell me about Drayper."

Ebert shrugged since his mouth was full. "We did already."

Ronan frowned at response. "Don't play coy. This is *not* a philosophical discussion, rather one of the utmost importance," he leaned across the table to add, "to *all* Eldarians."

Ebert paused in eating to regard Ronan.

"You raised objection when Dolus said harpys don't kill humans."

At the reminder, Ebert's eyes shifted between the Ganels before he glanced about the inn. He lowered his head to continue eating, yet spoke, "He died the day before The Doane *traitors* were captured."

Ronan stared at Ebert, stunned by the implication. Ebert continued to eat in his attempt to ignore Ronan's reaction.

Ronan's voice barely rose above a whisper. "You think—"

"I think nothing!" Ebert quickly rebuffed. "I just told you *when* it happened. Nothing more."

"Terrorizing for information," Cormac said in a side comment to Ronan.

Ebert and Jabid heard. When he caught Cormac's glance, Ebert nodded confirmation.

Satisfied, Ronan said, "Let's enjoy the meal. And perhaps more philosophical discussion." He ribbed Ebert.

"Only if you trade for it. I've given enough away already," Ebert huffed a reply.

"Uh, oh," warned Cormac. He indicated the entrance.

Two Nefal warriors accosted Wyck. The low ceiling height of seven and half feet forced the Nefals to hunch their shoulders. One held the innkeeper by the front of his shirt.

"Where is the Ganel?" The Nefal's loud, deep, menacing voice rose above the noise to capture attention.

"What have you been doing? Stirring up trouble?" Ebert challenged Ronan.

The Ganel leader ignored Ebert. Instead, he shouted, "Here!" to stop the Nefal from harming Wyck.

The Nefal tossed Wyck aside, along with anyone one, or anything, that impeded their path to Ronan. They left a wake of downed security men, overturned chairs, plates, and tables.

The lead Nefal warrior sneered with contempt at Cormac but spoke to Ronan. "Lord Argus wants you!"

"What seems to be the problem?" Ronan calmly asked.

"He asks too many questions about us." He pointed to Cormac.

"A friendly inquiry," said Cormac, also unphased.

"There, no harm done." Ronan turned back to eating.

"Come. Now!" The Nefal pulled Ronan to his feet.

In response to the violent seizure, Ronan snatched his dagger and slashed the Nefal's arm. The painful action made the warrior release him and retreat. With the ceiling being too low, the Nefal struck the back of his head on a thick support beam. This pain made him step sideways and off-balance. He crash-landed on a table filled with food and patrons.

Ebert and Jabid hid under their table, while Cormac and Irwin rose to join Ronan.

When the second Nefal attempted to grab him, Ronan ducked to one side. This gave Cormac a clear chance to slash his dagger across the Nefal's thigh. The warrior stumbled and fell into their table. On hands and knees, Ebert and Jabid scrambled out from under the smashed table.

"Quick! Out the back!" Wyck waved to Ronan.

The Ganels hurried from the scene, as Wyck's security tried to deal with the Nefal.

"We'll keep them occupied while you leave," Wyck hurried to explain. He herded them out the side door to the stable yard.

"No need to ask how things went with you and the Nefal," Irwin dryly quipped to Cormac.

Their horses stood ready for departure.

"We'll talk later!" Ronan vaulted into the saddle.

They rode hard from the inn and headed west.

By midnight, the Ganels reached a remote inn along the route home. The road straddled the border of Ha'tar territory and the banks of Lake Helivan. Any inn or settlement along this road was heavily fortified, with the gates shut at night. A traveler risked reprisal for disturbing a host after curfew.

However, for this inn, Ronan didn't need to disturb anyone. He withdrew a key from his saddlebag to unlock a side door at the gate. They dismounted to guide the horse through the narrow opening. He locked the door before they proceeded to the stables. Sight of a lamp in an open doorway stopped their progress.

"Who goes there?" demanded a male voice. The lamp flame flashed upon a blade of steel.

"Be easy, Friend Brock," said Ronan with assurance.

The lamp rose higher when Brock stepped out from the threshold. "Ronan? I didn't expect you until tomorrow."

"The Nefal didn't agree with our time schedule," said Irwin. The Ganel continued to the stables with Brock.

"What did you do this time to provoke them?"

Irwin chuckled in refute. "Not me. Cormac."

Ronan shoved the reins of his horse, and Cormac's mount, at Irwin. "Tend to them then join us."

Cormac flashed a wry smile at Irwin before he left with Ronan and Brock.

"Food?" asked Brock once inside the inn.

"No. Just something to drink—and a private room," said Ronan in a tone suggesting no interference.

Brock pulled a key out from a hidden drawer behind the counter and tossed it to the Ganel leader. Ronan took a candle from the counter and placed it in a holder. He used flame from the lamp to light the candle. He accepted a tankard of ale from Brock while Cormac carried two tankards. He held the candle to light the way to the secret room.

Once in the cellar, Ronan set the candle on a barrel to unlock the door. The dim light revealed a room just large enough to hold two beds, a table and four chairs. Cormac set the tankards on the table, sat, and took a long drink. They waited in silence for Irwin to arrive. When he did, Ronan locked the door.

Irwin let out a grateful sigh after drinking some ale. "For being so remote, Brock manages to stock some of the finest ale. Any food?" At their contrary glares, he shook his head. "I suppose it's too late."

Ronan began the discussion by chiding Cormac. "From the Nefal encounter, I gather you weren't successful in *unobserved* surveillance."

"No, I was," insisted Cormac. "How they found out it was me, I don't know."

Irwin spoke in Cormac's defense. "It shouldn't surprise you. Sener is full of prying eyes and listening ears. For even a fleck of gold, every man becomes a spy. It's a wonder we leave alive whenever we visit."

Ronan took a drink before he asked Cormac, "What did you learn?"

"It seems Argus may accept Javan's challenge and venture into the Halvor mines. Probably best to warn Artair."

Ronan nodded in agreement. "Aye. Once we are safely home." He then spoke to Irwin. "Were you able to get any information about Dolus' plans or too many eyes and ears to trouble you?"

Irwin finished drinking before he replied with sly satisfaction. "Any fleck of gold is as good another."

The response intrigued Ronan and Cormac.

"You discovered his plans?" asked Cormac with astonishment.

"Not exactly. Rather confirmed what we already suspected."

"When the gold is gone, Javan will ask for our sacred treasures as Tribute," said Ronan with grim conclusion.

"Aye, but there is more," said Irwin in a tone suggesting new information. "I didn't understand it until Ebert spoke about Drayper's death in relation to the capture of Alfred and Erica."

"That he was one who betrayed them," chided Cormac.

"Aye, but more to the *reason* for their capture and execution."

"How so?" asked Ronan, growing impatient.

"There is a possibility, though I couldn't find confirmation," Irwin's demeanor grew grave and serious as he said, "that *Oleg's heir* is in Eldar."

Stunned mute, neither Ronan nor Cormac blinked or reacted. Both let the news sink in. With suddenness, Ronan seized Irwin's arm.

"Are you certain of this?"

"I told you, I found no confirmation, but that is what Dolus believes. It guides his action. That's why he's increased the demand for Tribute in hopes to quicken—"

"Discovery of the horn," Ronan dreadfully said. He sat back in his chair to contemplate the latest development. "Alfgar must be told. Artair also." He closed his eyes with a painful sigh. "If only we hadn't lost Othniel."

"Gott won't abandon us. Not with the Son of Eldar's arrival," Cormac tried to encourage Ronan.

"We return home with all speed."

Cormac restrained Ronan from rising. "The horses need to rest at least three hours. And so, do we."

"We can be back in the saddle before dawn," added Irwin.

"Aye," Ronan reluctantly agreed. "For now, let us pray to Gott that what you learned is true, and the salvation of Eldar is at hand."

Chapter 14

DURING THE NEXT FOUR DAYS OF GUNNAR'S RECOVERY, AXEL mingled among the people of the compound. These faithful followers of the Faith had been hunted to the point of near extermination. Despite the hardship, they generously welcomed him and Gunnar. Many inquired about his journey, but more often he listened to their stories. Each tale brought new insight about the people he came to find. Tales of hardship, tears, and desperation, yet all balanced by hope. His arrival turned abstract impressions into reality. Now, reality brought a clarity of purpose to his task.

Retreating from the crowd to contemplate what he heard, Axel made his way to Arctander's room. The priest worked at the desk and greeted him with a smile. Axel freely wandered about the room and handled relics of the past.

"It's amazing how all these have been preserved," he said.

"Why amazing? Gott promised to keep knowledge of *you,* the True King, alive," said Arctander. He grew somber in reflection. "Why *I* survived is a mystery. Other men were worthier than I to carry on this task."

Axel grunted a chuckle. "Oleg thought differently when he entrusted your family with such an important mission." He placed down the small box he examined to face Arctander. "Tell me, how many more Shining Ones live outside this compound?"

"Some are scattered throughout The Doane. Most live in the city of Milagro."

"Lady Blythe," said Axel with a grin of remembrance.

"You met Blythe?" Arctander asked, curious.

"The other way around," Axel light chuckled. "She met *me* at the last watering hole before Milagro. She knew of my coming and waited for me. We stayed with her, and she generously provided supplies for our journey to Far Point."

Arctander affectionately smiled. "My niece is considered a prophetess among our people. The daughter of my younger sister."

Axel's smiled widened. "Now that you mention it, there is a family resemblance between her and Ida." His smile faded to ask, "Are there others outside The Doane?"

"Aye. The majority reside at the Fortress of Mathena in Ganel. Lord Ronan is governor of the territory. A devout follower. His father, Edwin, was a very dear friend and fellow priest." Arctander's earlier solemnity returned. "Ronan helped me escape to Heddwyn after he witnessed Edwin's death." He shook off the dreary melancholy to continue. "You must make yourself known to him. His great-great-grandfather was Melvern."

Axel perked up at hearing the name. "One of the original six Oleg trusted."

"Aye. Like my family, Ronan may know the whereabouts of *certain* items."

"You mean the Six Treasures?" said Axel, cautious. "They have been reported missing since the coup."

"Not *missing*, hidden. Although, some exact locations have been lost over time. Thus, a backup plan is in place." Arctander moved past Axel to approach the rough-hewed bookshelf. He removed two books before pressing a knot in the back wood. A portion of the wall swung open. He reached inside and pulled out a large wrapped object. He placed it on his desk to reveal the cover. "The Book of Kings."

Axel gazed in awe at the gilded cover embossed with the royal signet. "My family's heritage."

"This is the Treasure entrusted to my family. Take it when you leave, along with a letter from me to Ronan." He wrapped the book to give to Axel, who refused.

"Give it to me when Gunnar is fully recovered. What about the Freelands? Gunnar fled his home in Stellan."

Arctander put the book back in its hiding place. "Hard to tell. There may be some followers left after the massacre of priests. However, it took years before survivors found the courage to venture forth into Eldarian society again. Every time we feel on the brink of freedom, the enemy clamps down with a vengeance. The latest act of evil led to the loss of Othniel. Some quit the Faith when news reached us and left the compound." Pain made Arctander wince.

"Othniel, the Lion of Gott's spirit," Axel thoughtfully said.

"Aye. His presence gave us hope that Gott had not abandoned us." Arctander gripped Axel's shoulder and spoke with enthusiasm. "But now, you are here! The Son of Eldar will lead us to the promised victory!"

Axel fought to keep a pricked frown from his face. However, Arctander was keen to his reaction.

"You fear we do not fully understand your presence." Arctander picked up the Ancient Book. "As the last priest, I know very well why you are here. In accordance with my duty, I have instructed others. Many are willing to support you in anyway necessary."

"What I must do, none of you can support," Axel spoke with resolute bleakness.

Arctander quoted, "*The weakness of men resides in hasty words.*" He stoutly regarded Axel. "Do not underestimate us."

"The cost is high."

"I've already lost my wife, son, and daughter-in-law."

"Are you willing to lose Nollen, Ida, and your own life?"

"I believe you already know the answer."

"I'm not Gott. I can't read your mind. I can only go by your actions. Your faithfulness is a witness of *your* devotion. Ida," Axel softly smiled. "For such a kind-hearted individual, she is surprisingly committed. Nollen …" He paused with due consideration. "He has yet to know his own mind due to the anger he holds."

Arctander let out a heavy sigh. "It is true, anger clouds his faith."

Outside the door, Nollen carried a load of firewood. He began to pass when he overheard Axel mention him by name. He paused to listen to Axel's assessment and his grandfather's lament concerning his faith.

"Nollen, the firewood." Ida's voice interrupted his eavesdropping. She motioned to the interior hearth.

Instead of taking the firewood to the hearth, Nollen hurried outside. He dropped the wood and he ran up one of the stairways to the rampart. Piqued by the exchange, he slammed his fists on the rail. How could his grandfather question his faith? Did not his dedication to the Oath prove anything? What about abandoning Far Point to bring Axel and Gunnar to the compound?

"Nollen?"

Hearing a male voice, made Nollen turn further aside.

"Nollen," Jarred repeated, firmer when ignored.

"What?" he demanded.

"Ida said something upset you."

"How would she know?"

"Leaving in a rush with the firewood gave her a clue. Now, I find you up here instead of helping with feast preparation."

"I brought them here, isn't that good enough? Maybe it was a mistake," Nollen answered before Jarred replied.

"Why would it be a mistake? He is the Son of Eldar."

"Is he?" challenged Nollen, his face flushed with rage.

Jarred became confused by the outburst. "From what you and Ida told us, who else could he be? Arctander confirmed it from the Ancient Book."

Nollen again turned aside. Yes, the book confirmed what he witnessed, so why did he continue to struggle so hard against reality?

Jarred placed a hand on Nollen's shoulder in effort to gain his attention. Nollen struck aside Jarred's arm and marched further down the rampart.

"What has made you so angry?" Jarred questioned.

Nollen whirled about, ready to speak, but a lump in his throat prevented any words from being uttered. It was the answer he fought to discover, but so far incapable.

"Whatever is it, give it to Gott. For if you allow it to take hold, bitterness will follow. And *that* is Ida's greatest fear for you. Please, don't break you sister's heart. Or Arctander's. Or mine. You mean too much to all of us." Having said that, Jarred left the rampart.

For the next hour, Nollen's mind bounced between the conversation he overheard to Jarred's warning. He sat at the furthest observation point where he stared into the forest. He knew that his temper tended to get the better of him from time to time, but bitterness? *No, I don't think I've acted bitter toward anyone,* his mind argued.

What about faith? Were faith and loyalty to the Oath separate? He always considered them one in the same. Apparently, others did not. His vacillation only produced more questions than answers.

Frustrated, he murmured under his breath. "Oh, Gott, what is happening? Why am I suddenly so conflicted? Even reading the book has only served to confuse me. What manner of man is Axel?"

"Nollen."

He didn't have to look back, as he recognized Ida's voice.

"Will you join us for the feast? Or continue to brood?"

Nollen turned to face his sister. Ever since their parents' capture, Ida took on the role of mother. Although back then, he didn't think a seventeen-year-old needed a mother. Time showed him otherwise. Her wisdom and patience often balanced his tempestuous impulsiveness. At her gaze of worry, Jarred's words flashed through his mind; *bitterness. That is Ida's greatest fear for you.*

He flashed a small humorless smile. "I'm no longer angry, if that's your concern."

"Then join us." She held out her hand, hopeful.

He simply took her hand to escort her from the rampart.

The interior of the longhouse transformed from its everyday appearance into a festive atmosphere. Decorations of fall garlands and ancient banners hung from the rafters and support poles. Tables were filled, and ready for feasting. Laughter came from those assembled. Nollen and Ida took their places near the high table. Three seats were vacant, those to be occupied by Arctander, Axel, and Gunnar. The Ancient Book sat on the table in front of Axel's seat.

Arctander accompanied the honored guests from the sick room. After six days, Gunnar looked better. With the infection treated, he worked on regaining his strength from the near-death experience. A visible scar remained on his cheek. Once at high table, Axel and Gunnar sat while Arctander remained standing.

Arctander held up his hands for silence. "Brothers and sisters, this is an auspicious occasion. One long awaited, and we are blessed to be among those alive to see it."

Axel watched everyone bang on the table. Everyone except Nollen. When he caught Nollen's eye, Axel smiled, hopeful. At what appeared to be sudden awkwardness, Nollen averted his glance when Arctander again spoke.

"Today, we welcome Prince Axel, rightful heir of Oleg. The promised Son of Eldar."

At the declaration, Jarred stood, tankard in hand to offer a salute. "The Son of Eldar!"

Everyone, including Nollen, stood with raised tankard and repeated Jarred's salute.

"Thank you." Axel took hold of Arctander's arm in a signal to sit. "Your generous welcome is much appreciated."

"It is the least we can do, as we are blessed by your presence," insisted Arctander.

"The blessing comes from Gott, whom I also serve in undertaking this venture. But," he added with a smile at seeing Arctander's disappointment. "We gladly accept your warm hospitality, and gratefully partake in celebration." He spoke concerning himself and Gunnar.

Arctander's face brightened. "Then let us begin by reading a passage from the Ancient Book. Highness."

Axel rose with open book in hand. "Hear Gott's account concerning my ancestor." He read,

"The weakness of men resides in hasty words.
Faithlessness results in actions that cannot save.
Treachery and deceit lie behind the dealings of false men.
Yet my covenant with Oleg will remain.
I do not deal foolishly like men.
My word is forever.
From my far hidden place one shall come
to remove the stain of oppression."

He closed the book. All eyes focused upon him in expectation. Again, he caught Nollen's gaze. This time the young man appeared guardedly curious. Axel began to speak, and first directed his words to Nollen.

"I do not know what outcome awaits, yet by these words, I place my trust in Gott to guide my path." His eyes swept over those gathered. "Gott has proven faithful by the fact that I am here. By the fact, *all* of you are here." His eyes darted back to Nollen. "Alive in faith, sustained by trust, encouraged by hope." He nodded in conclusion to Arctander before he sat. For a third time, he met Nollen's gaze. He noticed a struggle raged in the eyes of the young man. *Gott, help me learn what it is he fights against,* he silently prayed.

With a smile of delight, and unaware of any issues, Arctander stood. "My lord, your presence is a tremendous blessing to our souls, for you embody the substance of our hope these past two hundred years."

Axel smiled an acknowledgement. His mind still on Nollen.

"Now let us pray and enjoy sweet fellowship!" Arctander offered a prayer of praise and thanksgiving.

They spent the remainder of the night laughing, singing, dancing, and making merry. There were challenges in feats of strength, juggling, and entertainment. Axel willingly participated, while Gunnar declined, though he took great pleasure in watching Axel. For a few hours, the danger and weightiness of their journey gave way to fun and gaiety.

Several times Nollen and Axel took part in the same event. Sometimes they joined together on a team, like tossing bags at a target. The team scoring the most points won. Other times they stood in direct competition as single participants. Such was the case during the quarterstaff competition.

"For someone who claims not to handle a sword, you do well with the staff." Gunnar spoke the jovial compliment to Nollen between rounds.

"It comes from years of fending off jackals," Nollen joked in reply.

Jarred announced the next pairing. "The first semi-final match will be between Nollen and Prince Axel!"

Ooos and *ahhhs* arose from the crowd, but the announcement caught Nollen off-guard. Gunnar's pat on his shoulder made him recover from the initial surprise.

"Don't fear going too hard with him," Gunnar said.

"I won't," Nollen replied with determination.

The tone made Gunnar curious, but before he voiced a question, Nollen moved to take up position for the match.

Axel stepped to the center of the circle, only his expression showed one of pleasure. However, upon meeting Nollen's intense glare, his enjoyment faded.

The word *"begin"* was barely uttered when Nollen launched at Axel. The quarterstaffs came together with a loud clap of wood. They exchanged a series of fierce blows—well, fierce on Nollen's part. Axel expertly parried.

When they came together in locked staffs of pushing force, Axel spoke so only Nollen heard. "Fighting when angry is never good."

Nollen grunted and left off, which made Axel briefly lose his footing at the release. Nollen struck the back of Axel's left leg. Axel's knee buckled, but he caught his balance in time to make a backward parry of Nollen's next attack. He swiped at Nollen's feet and caught him in the ankle. Nollen whirled about at impact, and barely managed to block another swipe from Axel. When both righted their position, they exchanged another series of blows.

Nollen breathed heavy, both from exertion and passion. He grew sloppy in his effort to get at Axel. Taking advantage of the carelessness, Axel's swipe impacted Nollen's right side. This move intensified Nollen's rage. He recklessly launched an attack. This exchange ended when Axel knocked Nollen to the floor. The butt of the quarterstaff pointed at Nollen's face. Axel stared at him with intense inquiry.

Cheers erupted from the crowd. This prompted Axel to change his demeanor. He backed off, lowered the quarterstaff, and extended a hand to help Nollen stand. There was only a brief hesitation before the gesture was accepted. Once on his feet, Nollen fought to contain embarrassed irritation.

"The winner!" Jarred held Axel's hand up.

At this brief distraction, Nollen left the longhouse.

Axel gave the quarterstaff to Jarred and hurried in pursuit. "Nollen!" he called, only to be ignored. He caught Nollen at the stairs to the rampart.

"Leave off!"

"Not until you explain your anger." Axel held fast.

"How can I when I don't know my own mind?"

"So, that's it. You overheard me speaking with Arctander."

"What of it?" Again, Nollen shrugged to be free.

"Rather than become angry, why not ask for an explanation?" Axel rebuffed.

"What is there to explain? You think I don't know my own mind, while my grandfather questions my faith."

Axel noticed Ida and Jarred watched them from the threshold. He drew Nollen to a private corner of the compound. He kept his firm tone low. "We spoke out of concern not accusation. You need to learn the difference."

Nollen's lips pressed together to contain his emotions. Still, his eyes grew misty.

The reaction made Axel inquire; "Does the concern of others for your welfare disturb you?" At further distress, he took Nollen's face between his hands. "Look at me," he said with unction.

Nollen's inward battle was clearly evident.

"There is great fear behind the anger," said Axel.

Nollen closed his eyes to swallow back the emotions.

"Though some is directed at me, I know the source comes from what happened to your parents."

Nollen heavily sighed, his eyes lowered.

"But the fear. Expectations? Fear of failure, perhaps?"

Nollen screwed his eyes shut at the question. An unintended gasp escaped.

Moved by compassion, Axel said, "Now, I understand. It is because of what happened to them that anger drives you to prove yourself. Yet always with the fear of failing to live up to expectations."

A sob escaped, as Nollen fought to contain his emotions. His words came halting and pained. "Grandfather said it falls to me to finish what Papi started." Through tears of vulnerability, he dared a glance at Axel. "I don't know if I can."

Axel held Nollen at arm's length to look him directly in the eyes. "You must stop battling anger of the past and imagined expectations to freely act as your heart and Oath dictate. When you do that, Gott will give you strength to succeed."

"Is that what you're doing? Acting without fear when everyone expects you to fulfill prophecy?"

"I do not deny that I feel the weight of my heritage. But," he stressed. "I have fully embraced my task and trust the outcome to Gott. You, my young friend, must do the same."

"Expectations?" Nollen huffed.

Axel wry grinned at the challenge. "No, encouragement. Same as Gunnar and others have done for me. As Ida, Jarred, and Arctander have tried to do with you."

"I often scoff at their counsel."

"Admitting that is a good place to start healing. The complete way is committing to memory passages from the Ancient Book. Think on them whenever fear and anger rises. And pray. That is what I do. Otherwise, I might have left Eldar at the first hint of opposition. Overwhelmed by what awaits me."

A great cheer rose from the longhouse. Axel grinned at the sound of celebration. "What say you we return, and let our hearts and souls be revived in the enjoyment of simple pleasures?"

"Aye."

Chapter 15

IN THE WEE HOURS OF THE MORNING, JONAS AND HIS FAMILY ROSE to prepare for the day. Guests of the inn were not yet awake but would be soon. Breakfast needed to be ready. Suddenly, the front door burst open, startling Jonas and Sharla.

Hertz lead a group of soldiers inside. "Jonas of Gilroy, you are hereby under arrest for aiding and abetting the enemy."

Immediately, soldiers surrounded them. Jonas gaped in fearful astonishment. Sharla covered her mouth when she cried out in terror.

"Wha—what? I've done nothing of the kind!" Jonas protested.

"You know Nollen of Far Point, do you not?" asked Hertz.

Jonas balked at the question.

"Oh, come. We have at on good authority that he stays here frequently when traveling for trade."

Jonas swallowed back his discomposure. "I know *of* him." He shrugged with a nervous laugh. "So many people come and go from here. It's impossible to personally know them all."

"He was seen here two weeks ago speaking with you!"

Jonas again tried to pass it off with a quaking smile. "I speak to all my customers."

"Apparently, news hasn't reach Gilroy," Hertz scoffed. "Nollen, and his sister, are accused of high treason by conspiring with foreigners against the Elector." He glared at Jonas. "*You* were last person to see them before they fled."

"Papa!" Abe and Bart were roughly escorted by soldiers.

"Maybe your sons can tell us." Hertz nodded.

A soldier grabbed Abe, and mercilessly twisted the boy's arm behind his back. Abe screamed in pain that forced him to his knees. Bart went to help his brother when a soldier jerked him back.

"No!" Sharla tried to intervene. A soldier struck her so hard that she fell to the floor.

"We didn't help them!" Jonas shouted. "For pity sake, leave the boy alone."

Hertz waved for the soldier to stop. He released Abe. Despite a whimper of pain, Abe crawled to his mother to check if she were injured. They helped each other to stand. Bart glowered with angry tears at the soldier who held him.

Hertz renewed his interrogation of Jonas. "What help did you give Nollen of Far Point and those foreigners?"

"Foreigners?" repeated Jonas, puzzled. "I helped no foreigners."

"Really? Then how do you explain this?" Hertz pulled out a medallion.

Instinctively, Sharla felt the pockets of the apron she wore over her dress. When she realized Hertz noticed, she stopped.

Unaware of Sharla's reaction, Jonas blurted out, "It's not mine! A guest must have dropped it. It could belong to anyone."

"Search her!" Hertz commanded.

Abe shielded Sharla. "It's mine! I must have dropped it."

"Where?"

"The barn."

"Don't tell him anymore!" Bart urged Abe.

Hertz seized Bart's face to look at him. "Tell me what?" The boy remained stubbornly silent. "That you belong to an outlawed Faith?" He roughly released Bart to command, "Search them all!"

Struggling proved useless when the soldiers obeyed. One discovered a medallion hidden in the fold of Sharla's skirt. Bart had a medallion in the sole of his shoe. None were found on Abe or Jonas.

"So, this could be yours," Hertz said to Abe.

"It is," the boy bravely admitted.

"You?" Hertz questioned Jonas.

Mortified, Jonas shook his head.

"Interesting that your family admits it, but you do not."

"Jonas?" Sharla urgently pleaded.

"It's no use, woman!" he rebuffed before he confessed to Hertz. "Nollen brought two for my sons. He showed them to me first, but I refused to have them in my house—because of the edict," he hastily added. "They must have accepted it without my knowledge."

"Papa! How can you betray Nollen? Betray us?" Bart chided.

Passionate fear overtook Jonas. "She's responsible!" He pointed at Sharla. "I warned her about the Oath of Faith, but she wouldn't listen. Now look at us, woman!"

Despite tears, Sharla glared at Jonas. "What I see, is a cowardly husband who sacrifices his family to save himself!"

Hertz stepped in front of Sharla. "You know the penalty for admitting to being a follower of the forbidden Faith."

"Better that than betraying Gott's appointed True King."

"Take them!" Hertz ordered the soldiers concerning Sharla, Abe, and Bart. He marched outside.

Jonas stood dumbfounded, as he watched his family dragged from the inn. He hurried to the window where he saw a crowd had gathered. Soldiers bound the boys and Sharla with iron shackles.

Hertz mounted. He addressed the crowd. "Members of the outlawed Faith." He motioned to prisoners. "See that you don't allow your town to become further polluted by their heresy!"

Jonas drew back when Hertz pointed at him. He stepped from the window when a soldier returned. Jonas felt a fist meet his jaw then his midsection before another blow to the head rendered him unconscious.

Feeling something wet on his forehead caused Jonas to awake with a start. It took a moment to realize he laid in a bed where Destry hovered over him.

"Where am I?" Jonas asked in a hoarse voice.

"My house," answered Destry.

"How did I get here?"

"Galt and I brought you." Destry motioned to his brother.

"You should be glad we did," added Galt. "The mob tore apart the inn and made off with everything."

"What?" Jonas tried to rise, but pain in his head and ribs made him collapse back onto the bed. "Why would they do that?" he hissed between clenched teeth of pain.

"To protect the town so no one else will suffer because of those *followers*!" Galt spat on the floor after speaking the word *followers.*

Jonas moaned in disbelief. "How could they turn against me?"

Galt and Destry appeared unsympathetic.

"Because you endangered the town," said Galt.

"We convinced the mob to spare you since Hertz found no medallion to tie you to the outlawed Faith," said Destry.

Jonas spoke in desperation. "I meant how could my family turn against me?"

Destry heaved shrug of indifference. "Does it matter? It's too late now. The damage is done."

"Thanks to Nollen of Far point!" Galt again spat on the floor with disdain.

Jonas blinked back tears of anger. "I curse the day I let him into my house!"

Destry sat on a chair next to the bed. He placed a hand on Jonas' shoulder. "Maybe if you tell Hertz where Nollen could be hiding, he will spare your family."

Jonas wiped his eyes. "I would gladly tell, if I knew. I was ignorant of any problem until Hertz arrived. Wait," he said with sudden disturbance. "He mentioned I was under arrest. Why didn't he take me also?"

Destry and Galt exchanged curious glances before Destry replied. "Perhaps, he hopes to gain your cooperation."

In urgency, Jonas seized Destry. "Your cousin is Magistrate Bernal. Write and implore him to drop the charges. Tell him, I swear to learn where Nollen is hiding."

Destry removed Jonas' grip. "It is best I stay out of this. *You* need to discover the truth to save yourself."

"The inn is how I learn information. Tongues becomes unguarded when the mind is too inebriated to think clearly."

"Then as innkeeper you've heard many secrets," said Galt pointedly.

Jonas nodded because he swallowed back pain. "I've heard nothing about foreigners. Nor of any connection to Nollen."

After a brief knock on the door, Destry's wife entered. She carried a tray of food. "Is he strong enough for luncheon?"

"What time is it?" asked Jonas with surprise.

"Noon," replied Destry. "You've been unconscious since it happened—" His reply became interrupted at hearing the alarm bell.

"The Ha'tar!" the wife cried out with fear.

"Quick! Get the children to the cellar," Destry told her.

"Wait!" Jonas called with a painful grunt. He managed to sit up.

"You're in no condition," chided Destry.

"I will defend my town!" Jonas stubbornly said.

Destry helped Jonas from the room and outside. Even as men scrambled to pre-assigned positions for defense, they heard the loud echoing *thud, thud, thump* of approaching dragons.

Nearing Gilroy, the dragon-riders split. Two headed for the north side of town, two went south, while Gan, the leader maintained a straight flight path.

Men at the armed ballistas prepared to fire the massive hollowed tipped arrows. Each tip contained a lethal dose of poison that released upon contact. Even a deep graze from the arrow could cripple a dragon. These men earned their station by demonstrating superior marksmanship.

Others manned catapults containing balls of water. The balls were carefully crafted using the same light, breakable material as the arrow tips. Each weapon was individually loaded onto the ballista or catapult before being filled with either the poison or water.

Another group consisted of longbow archers tasked with targeting the Ha'tar riders. Teenage boys served as messengers between groups, or to fetch any necessary supplies. Older men formed the fire brigade. They used horse-drawn carriages bearing barrels of water to quickly douse fires caused by dragon's breath.

When the dragon-riders came within range, the dragons spewed fire. Simultaneously, the catapults launched water balls. One ball disintegrated when it met a stream of fire. Another ball struck a dragon in the face, which caused it to bank away from Gilroy. One hit a dragon square in the mouth, as it made for a second spewing of fire.

A ballista fired at the dragon hit in the mouth by the water ball. The rider tried to avoid the arrow, but unsuccessful. The hollow penetrated the underside of the dragon. Blue liquid showed the release of poison. Angry at being wounded, the dragon's roar filled the air. It began to wobble in flight. The rider fought to turn the dragon and retreat. The beast didn't respond, as it grew weaker. Soon, it could barely flap its wings. Without the ability to safely jump from the dragon, the rider tried to steer for a landing. Too late. A dying gasp of breath, and the dragon fell from the sky. The rider was thrown when the dragon turned over in a free-fall. The dead dragon landed on the road to Gilroy. The rider crashed into the town's main gate before he tumbled to the ground where he lay unconscious.

Gan sounded a horn to gather the remaining dragon-riders and begin a second run. Another ballista fired just ahead of a dragon's arc. The arrow ripped through its right wing. A trail of blue poison following the trajectory. The rider jerked back to stop the turn and headed for the safety of the trees.

Two water balls hit another dragon in the face. Startled, it balked and refused to obey any commands. The rider struggled to regain control. The more he tried, the more the dragon refused, till it turned to retreat.

His companions forced to withdraw, Gan blew a horn then turned his beast to follow the out-of-control dragon. His dragon was the last to disappear over the far tree line.

Smoke rose from several fires. The brigade did its job to contain the flames to a few buildings.

Three men rushed outside the main gate. One held a longbow ready, while the others fetched the downed, unconscious Ha'tar. Placing an arm over each shoulder, they drug him inside Gilroy. The gatekeeper locked the gate-door when they were returned.

Hearing a moan, they lowered him to the ground. A group of men, including Destry, Galt, Jonas, and Gilroy's three aldermen arrived.

The eldest alderman told the sentry, "Make sure he's fully awake."

He slapped the Ha'tar's face to encourage him. The eyes opened, though slowly blinked to focus. The Ha'tar sneered at the crowd gathered around him.

"Why did you attack us?" the alderman demanded.

The Ha'tar coughed. A stream of blood trickled from his mouth.

"Answer him!" the sentry commanded.

By the sight of blood, and dimmed gaze, the Ha'tar was dying. "We kill you for what you did!"

"We haven't done anything to the Ha'tar," rebuffed the alderman.

The Ha'tar spoke in halting, painful words. "Men of Doane kill young dragon …"

"No! I tell you," insisted the alderman.

"Liar!" The Ha'tar coughed up more blood. "Find body near …" His eyes became droopy near death.

The sentry slapped his face again. "Where?"

"Hedd … wyn …" The Ha'tar died.

Pronouncement of the place brought murmurs from the crowd.

"Get rid of him," the alderman instructed the sentry. His gaze swept over those gathered. "Who here has been near or in Heddwyn?"

"No one goes near there," said one man.

"Aye. It's enchanted. Haunted even," said another.

"I know someone who does," said Jonas, almost under his breath.

Destry heard, and asked, "Who?"

"Nollen of Far Point. He called it his secret trading route."

The first man who spoke, accosted Jonas. "Your friend killed the dragon and brought the wrath of Ha'tar upon us!"

"He's not my friend!" Passion stirred Jonas to continue. "He's responsible for what happened to my family!"

"You expect us to believe that?"

"Aye! It wasn't until Hertz showed up that I learned he deceived me and bewitched my family!" Fervor brought Jonas to the brink of tears. "All of you have known me since my youth. When have I ever lied or hurt anyone in Gilroy? Destry? Galt? Alderman Flynn," he pleaded.

"Hertz didn't arrest him," said Destry to Flynn.

"The more important matter is dealing with the Ha'tar," chided Flynn.

"The only way to do that is to capture Nollen of Far Point, so he can face Ha'tar justice," said another alderman.

"Aye!" agreed the crowd, wholeheartedly.

"Hertz said Nollen is a wanted fugitive. Something about aiding foreigners. Since Heddwyn is his secret route, he could be hiding there," said Jonas.

"Do you know this route?" demanded Flynn.

Jonas nodded. "I know where it leads."

"Destry, take Jonas to Magistrate Bernal. Tell him what happened. And find Nollen of Far Point!" ordered Flynn. "In the meantime, keep a sharp eye out for the Ha'tar," he told the sentries before he dismissed the crowd.

Chapter 16

ALMOST TWO WEEKS AFTER ARRIVING AT THE COMPOUND, Gunnar was completely healed from the dragon wound. The red scar faded to a thin pink line. Jarred gave orders for extra hunts to provide meat to aid Gunnar's recovery and honor Axel. The vigil Arctander held for his benefit transitioned to daily prayers for the task that lay ahead of them. Everyone willingly participated. A fact not lost on him and Axel. Though a necessity, leaving would prove difficult, as in such a short time, these unselfish people had grown dear to them.

Gunnar stood with Axel at the table in the sick room to pack their saddlebags. He paused to gaze about the room. A tender smile appeared. "This is the longest we've stayed in one place since we left."

Axel joined Gunnar in observation. "Aye. And these beloved people are the reason we came." He returned to packing.

Gunnar did the same. "I take it you discovered what lies behind Nollen's anger."

Axel kept working as he replied. "The same fear that grips all when an unexpected responsibility is thrust upon them."

Gunnar paused in reaching for supplies. "Failing to live up to expectations."

"Aye."

"I assume you told him otherwise."

Axel ceased packing, his expression uncertain. "I'm not sure if it did any good. Only time will tell."

"Maybe if it comes from one with whom he is less combative."

Axel cocked a wry grin. "You always could get through to me when my father could not. Hand me the medical kit."

"Do you think he'll accompany us to Mathena?"

"I don't know. Whether he does or not, it is our next destination."

Both turned when the door opened. Nollen entered followed by Arctander and Jarred. Arctander carried a wrapped oblong shaped object. Gunnar nudged Axel and made a discreet motion to Nollen. The young man wore a cloak and gloves in preparation for travel.

"Don't forget this." Arctander handed the object to Axel.

In turn, Axel gave it to Gunnar. "Keep it safe."

Gunnar carefully tucked it in his saddlebag.

"Everyone is gathered in the compound to send you off with a prayer of blessing." Arctander reached into his pocket to produce a sealed letter. "This is for Ronan. I explain our meeting and confirm your identity."

Axel placed the letter inside a breast pocket of his surcoat. "So, you will be our guide again." He grinned at Nollen.

"It's only fitting since I brought you here," Nollen replied with a voice devoid of emotion. "We best be going." He left.

"Is he still angry about what he thought he heard pass between us?" Axel asked.

The old priest sighed with lament.

"I'm sorry. I thought I convinced him."

"It's not your fault, my lord," began Jarred. "Nollen tends to be stubborn, but he didn't hesitate to serve as your guide again."

"Let us not dwell on it, as we have arranged a proper send off," Arctander told Axel.

Axel and Gunnar donned their cloaks and gloves. They placed the saddlebags over a shoulder. When they arrived in the compound, everyone began to sing the ancient tune celebrating the True King. It took Nollen a few stanzas before he joined in. Jarred moved alongside Ida to raise his voice in song. Arctander also joined the chorus. To Axel's amused delight, Gunnar sang. Gunnar nudged Axel. Though he knew the words, he kept his voice low.

"You need more singing lessons," Gunnar teased Axel when the song concluded. He took the bag from Axel to attach them to their individual saddles.

Axel observed Ida was not dressed for travel, and her pony not among those ready for departure. "I believe it is good for you to remain here."

"It took much convincing," said Jarred.

Axel grinned. "I'm sure it did. Faith makes her brave in the face of great danger."

Ida blushed. "In truth, I'm not as good at pathfinding as Nollen. Nor possess his keen sense of direction."

Axel took Ida's hand to kiss it. "Thank you for all you've done."

Ida gaped in astonishment at his action. "My liege, it is I who am honored to have helped you in what little ways I could."

"Let us send him off a prayer of blessing," Arctander said. He raised his hands to address the crowd. "This is a day you will tell your grandchildren. The day we praise Gott that our redemption is near." He motioned for Axel and Gunnar to kneel. "Accept Gott's blessing." He placed his hands upon Axel's bowed head. "Gott, we commit to your purposes, Axel, heir of Oleg, the True King according to your promise. Guide him on his journey. Fill him with your courage to face the task you have set before him." He moved one hand to Gunnar's head. "We also ask you to strengthen Sir Gunnar, loyal friend and servant to the Son of Eldar. Make him fearless in the face of danger, and mighty in what battles they may encounter." His gaze shifted to Nollen. "Help my grandson, Nollen, to understand the challenges placed before him. Grant him strength and determination to faithfully fulfill the duty he has accepted this day."

Struck by the prayer, Nollen humbly bowed his head.

Arctander removed his hands and stepped back. "Rise, Son of Eldar. Go with Gott's blessings, and our prayers for success."

Axel saw faces filled with hopeful expectation. "With Gott's help, I will see you again." He vaulted into the saddle.

Ida grabbed the bridle of Nollen's pony after he mounted. "Stay safe." Her voice cracked. He forced a smile of attempted reassurance.

Jarred drew Ida back from Nollen. "Frick!" He signaled a man to open the secret passage.

Without looking back, Nollen led Axel and Gunnar from the compound. Men closed all the hidden passages behind them.

After traveling north for two hours, Nollen turned due west. Shortly, the forest trail allowed for all three to ride together rather than single file. Nollen explained his change in course.

"We'll head west for two days before turning north to enter Ha'tar territory. The closer to the border with Gorland the better. The Ha'tar fear the Gorlanders, who are experts in killing dragons."

"Could we travel through Gorland and avoid Ha'tar?" asked Gunnar.

Nollen shook his head. "That would require a lot of negotiations with the border guards. I don't have enough with me to trade for safe passage. By keeping the border stations in sight, we may be able to use the Ha'tar fear to our advantage."

"I take it you've done this before," said Axel.

Nollen nodded. "Part of my training."

"Trading, aye. But I meant this route."

Nollen looked squarely at Axel. "So, did I. Secrets of knowing safe passages in and around Eldar is necessary for survival."

"Then you have contact with more than just those in the compound?" began Gunnar, eagerly. "Are there any of the faithful left in the Freelands?"

"A few in Stellan, but most live in a small settlement not easily accessible. Even using secret passages, the arduous journey takes two weeks. I've only been there twice. Once with my father, and another time with Jonas."

"Who is Jonas?"

"The innkeeper at Gilroy, and my cousin. Our relationship is a closely guarded secret." A pained expression crossed Nollen's face.

"Is there something about Jonas that troubles you?" asked Axel, keen to Nollen's discomfort.

"Nothing of importance." Nollen waved it off.

"I think it is," insisted Axel. "Is Jonas among the remnant?"

Visible discouragement made Nollen hesitate. "I'm not sure. I thought …" He couldn't finish and heaved a shrug.

Sensitive to Nollen's despondency, Axel changed the subject, "In your travels, have you been to Sener?"

"Once, with my father when I was fifteen. After that, he wouldn't take me again."

"Why? Did you get into some teenage mischief?" Gunnar teased.

Nollen cocked a impish grin. "Nothing that caused undue trouble. Just exploring." His smile slowly faded. "Still, it is a very dangerous trek from The Doane since there are no secret trails. If one evades the harpys and jackals, then they must navigate safely around the Great Falls. From there, it's either pay exorbitant ferry fees to journey one hundred miles up the Leven or travel the free roads on either side of the river."

"I mentioned the dangers to him when we first arrived." Gunnar motioned to Axel. "His task will take him to Sener."

Nollen curiously followed Gunnar's indication.

Axel deflected the topic. "I think bringing Tribute would be the most hazardous time for travel."

"It would be, except Javan wants all the gold. The penalty for robbery of a representative is death." Suddenly, Nollen rose up in the stirrups to peer ahead. "The trek narrows before we descend into a gorge. With the Ha'tar border two hundred yards north, it's a good place for an ambush." He sat back in the saddle to arm his crossbow. "Swords are no good." His statement stopped them from drawing their blades.

Nollen's pony expertly picked its way down the rocky descent. Rather than guide their mounts, Axel and Gunnar let the horses follow the pony.

The exposed descent made for anxious moments, as they occasionally glanced skyward. A small river ran through the gorge bottom. Gnarled trees with exposed roots lined the river bed. Bare branches extended over the banks and provided some cover.

Nollen drew his pony to a halt at the edge of the water. He allowed it to drink from the river. He put up his crossbow. When Axel and Gunnar arrived, he said, "Let them drink. Two miles after we cross the river, there is a steep climb out."

Racked by an involuntary shiver, Axel's brows knitted in regard of the gorge. "There is coldness to this place. A foreboding sense of evil."

Nollen spoke in a near solemn whisper. "This is where many priests and others fell when they fled the onslaught. It's called—"

"Weastow!" breathed Axel in dreaded awe. "The Place of Sorrow."

"Aye," droned Nollen. "The trees have not bloomed since. Those responsible pronounced a curse upon this place in hopes of preventing the passage from being used again. That's what Grandfather said when he showed me this place after my parents …"

Sympathetic to Nollen's discomfort, Gunnar kindly said, "I'm sure that wasn't easy for him—or you."

Nollen jowls tensed trying to fight back emotions. "He felt it necessary. I didn't know why until last night."

At the statement, Axel spoke with understanding. "He told you to bring us this way."

Nollen didn't reply. Instead, he pulled up the pony's head to guide it into the river. Cold water reached his knees. The gentle current proved safe enough to cross without issues.

In silence, they travelled the remainder of the gorge then made the difficult climb out. At a covered hollow, Nollen dismounted.

"We should rest them before we continue."

Nollen tethered his pony in such a way as to graze on forest scrub. He checked the pony's legs and hooves for sign of injury or loose shoe. Satisfied at finding everything well, he pulled out some provisions from his saddlebag. He sat on a stump beside the pony to eat.

Axel and Gunnar followed the example. Axel sat beside Nollen. After a few moments of eating, Axel asked Nollen, "You didn't agree with Arctander's suggested route?"

Nollen shrugged since his mouth was full.

"What route would you have chosen?"

"Doesn't matter now," Nollen mumbled as he chewed.

"Do you resent being forced into doing things you would rather not?" asked Gunnar.

The question surprised Nollen. "What made you ask that?"

"Ever since we arrived, you act with resentment at everything." Gunnar ticked off a list. "Ida revealing the medallion, leaving Far Point, arriving at the compound, misunderstanding what was said, and now this route."

"I don't mean to," Nollen offered in feeble defense.

"You're afraid you can't live up to expectations."

At Gunnar's statement, Nollen bolted to his feet. Rather than reply, he tore the reins from the tether and mounted. Axel and Gunnar took it as a sign to leave.

A short time later, heavy rain fell. A steady downpour followed them the rest of the day. By nightfall, they reached a set of ruins. Part of a roof remained intact, but the walls crumbled and broken.

"It's not much, though with a fire, we can get warm." Nollen removed his bedroll and saddlebag. He left his pony saddled, and again tethered in such a way, as to graze. The pony drank from water gathered inside a rock depression.

"If we can find any dry wood under here," complained Gunnar.

Nollen proceeded to the rear of the shelter. He reached down and flung aside a leaf-covered ratty piece of canvas. It revealed a partially constructed fire pit. "Hasn't been used in a while but should work."

"Another of your secrets?" teased Gunnar.

Nollen flash a confident smile. While he started a fire, Axel and Gunnar prepared places for sleeping. The ground under the shelter felt cool and damp.

"We can make tea and heat up the food," said Nollen.

"Won't the smell attract the Ha'tar?" asked Axel.

"They don't fly in the rain or at night, unless forced to." At Axel's skepticism, Nollen motioned to his mouth. "Water and fire don't mix. And dragons have poor eyesight at night."

Axel chuckled. "I'll fetch the food and skillet."

Gunnar knelt beside Nollen to speak in a private tone. "You're not the only one who fears living up to expectations." He nodded toward Axel, whose back was turned to fetch the items.

Nollen's quizzical gaze shifted from Gunnar to Axel. When Axel returned, Gunnar helped stoke the fire. Nollen looked up and met Axel's gaze. For the briefest of moments, he hesitated to accept the skillet. Axel's silent curiosity made Nollen shy away to heat the skillet.

Gunnar intervened. "I'll slice the onion. You do the sausage," he said to Axel.

Nollen silently accepted the ingredients to cook the meal. The smell of crispy sausage with caramelized onions filled the shelter.

With reminiscence, Gunnar closed his eyes and popped a piece of sausage in his mouth. "Reminds me of when I was a boy in the Freelands. My mother made the best sausage. I never thought I'd taste its like again."

Nollen paused in eating to say, "The meat we use is from the Freelands."

"I thought you've only been there twice."

"Aye, but the Nefal need salt from our southern marshes. They also fancy turquoise for ornamental reasons. Being as Far Point is nearest to the turquoise quarries, we have a long-standing trade agreement for Freeland hogs."

Alarmed, Gunnar swallowed hard. "Nefal travel The Doane?"

"No!" Nollen hastened to reply. "They ship the hogs and goods to Vanora via a caravan. Salt and turquoise are returned in the same manner."

Though reassured about the Nefal, the answer still made Gunnar curious. "How do the Nefal get Freeland hogs?"

"They breed them. Supposedly from some hogs they captured decades ago after a dispute with the Freelanders."

"I'm surprised the Nefal don't invade The Doane and take what they want," said Axel. He ate his portion of sausage.

"For all their size and strength, Nefal fear jackals," Nollen said with a chuckled.

"Why would giants fear any animal?"

Nollen took a drink of tea before he answered. "The same reason dragons don't fly at night – poor nocturnal eyesight."

Once again, Axel comprehended Nollen's cryptic answer. "So, when we reach Ha'tar territory we'll travel at night, yet stay near the Gorland border for extra security during the day."

Nollen smiled before he ate a final piece of sausage.

Axel grinned in admiration. "With your cleverness, you shouldn't fear expectations. You do yourself a disservice." Nollen shied at the compliment, so he asked, "What can you tell me about Lord Ronan?"

"Well," began Nollen, thoughtful. "I've only met him a handful of times. When I go Mathena, I usually meet with Baron Irwin to discuss supplies along with the latest news."

"Is Ronan a frequent visitor to Heddwyn?"

Nollen shrugged. "He was there on a few occasions when we brought supplies. He may have visited other times. Grandfather knows him better than me. So, did Papi," he droned slightly then concluded, "Yet, from those times, I found him to be an honorable man, dedicated to the Faith.

Since the discussion made Nollen uncomfortable, Axel cleaned off his knife from eating. "I'll take the first watch." He drew his sword. He took up position beside the fire to face the forest.

Moments after Gunnar and Nollen fell asleep, the night grew still with only the sound of a crackling fire breaking the silence. No nocturnal bird, crickets or even a breeze stirred the trees. Axel looked at his sleeping companions. Nothing disturbed them, yet he sensed something unusual about the stillness.

Movement caught his attention a second before it appeared. A large white wolf. Firelight revealed bright icy blue eyes that stared directly at him. No menace in the steady gaze, rather a beckoning compulsion. Axel approached the wolf. It opened its mouth and spoke audible words.

"Put up your sword, Son of Eldar."

"You know who I am?"

The wolf nodded.

Axel sheathed his sword. "How?"

Again, the wolf spoke. "Animals once lived in peace with humans. Wolves served as sentries for your ancestor. The forest, and all in it, became cursed when Oleg fell. I am Bardolf, alpha of the White Wolves of Heddwyn. We guard the few humans, who have taken sanctuary here. Those faithful to the True King."

"Then you know Arctander."

"Aye. The last priest."

"He is sending me to Ronan of Ganel. I travel with his grandson, Nollen." Axel motioned back to the shelter.

"I remember seeing him with Arctander."

"What do you want?"

"To see you safely to Sener. The fate of all creatures lies in your hands now. Sleep. Nothing will disturb you." Bardolf disappeared into the shadows.

Gunnar stirred. He sat up when he didn't see Axel by the fire. "Something wrong?" he asked upon Axel's return.

"No. I just learned we are being watched over, and I can sleep undisturbed." He went to his bedroll beside Nollen.

"Watched by who? Owls?" Gunnar sarcastically quipped.

Nollen woke at hearing voices then Axel's reply.

"No. A large white wolf."

Nollen propped up on his elbow. "You've seen Bardolf?"

"You know what he's talking about?" asked Gunnar, confused.

"Bardolf is the leader of the White Wolves of Heddwyn," Nollen explained. "I saw him when Grandfather showed me Weastow."

"He remembers you," said Axel.

"I heard tale that the White Wolves disappeared," said Gunnar.

"No," said Axel and Nollen in unison.

At Gunnar's intrigued reaction, Nollen clarified. "The White Wolves of Heddwyn, that is. I don't know if any other pack exists." He grew somber. "Othniel's death deeply disturbed Grandfather. He wondered how we would survive without Gott's spirit roaming Eldar."

Gunnar gaped in astonishment. "The Great White Lion is dead? He was our hope as we fled."

"'*The fate of all creatures lies in your hands now,*'" Axel muttered the quote.

"What?" asked Gunnar, not having heard clearly.

"Just repeating what Bardolf said to me before he left. The fate of Othniel brings a more profound meaning to it." Axel laid down and stared at the shelter ceiling.

"Are you going to tell us?" inquired Gunnar.

Axel slowly shook his head and closed his eyes.

Chapter 17

NOLLEN WOKE WHEN SOMETHING WET TOUCHED HIS CHEEK. HE became startled by the sight of a white wolf near his face. He scrambled back in momentary fright.

Axel chuckled at the reaction. "Bardolf brought his pack. Ula has been trying to wake you for several moments."

Nollen took a deep breath to calm down. The gray light of pre-dawn filtered into the shelter. "I guess I slept deeper than I expected." Ula pulled the blanket totally off him. "All right! I'm getting up." Upon standing to gather his bedroll, he noticed the pack. "How many are there?"

"Ten." Axel fastened his bedroll to the saddle.

The fire had been doused. Nollen took his prepared bedroll to his pony. "What about breakfast?"

"We'll eat as we ride. Bardolf senses a disturbance and wants to leave immediately." Axel mounted.

Once Nollen was ready, they followed Bardolf from the ruins. Immediately, Nollen noticed a course deviation.

"This is not the way," he objected.

Bardolf made several yelps to his pack then spoke to Nollen. "There is a smell I can't identify. This way will circumvent the unknown."

Nollen gasped in astonishment. "It speaks!"

"Not *it,* Bardolf," Axel said as a reminder.

Nollen's amazement was slow to fade. "I've never heard an animal speak before."

"Because we were made mute to humans until the Son of Eldar's arrival," Bardolf explained. He walked in front of them.

"Would have been nice if such speech happened when we encountered the juvenile dragon," Gunnar wryly quipped.

Although typical dry humor from Gunnar, Axel flinched with guilt. Gunnar didn't notice, since he rode in the rear. Still, Bardolf replied to the surly comment.

"Until Eldar is fully restored, we will only speak to a few humans, as necessary. Now be quiet, something may be following us."

The gray of morning gave way to sunrise. Rain clouds moved off to reveal blue sky. Two hours later, they made an arching turn to reverse course.

Bardolf stopped before a narrow ravine. He made several yelps to the pack. While the wolves dispersed, he spoke to the humans. "You must walk the horses. The ravine is narrow and grows short where some natural stone cross it."

Stone arches, tree roots, and branches formed a canopy to shade the cramped ravine. The serpentine path stretched for over two miles. At several bends, light briefly vanished beneath large, lengthy stone ledges.

After the fourth bend and overhang, the ravine widened to reveal forest. Before they reached the end of the ravine, Bardolf stopped, hackles up, and growled. Axel quietly drew his sword. Nollen grabbed his crossbow, while Gunnar carefully unsheathed his blade.

With a loud growling bark, Bardolf launched forward. The pack immediately responded to join him.

Axel, Nollen, and Gunnar moved to the ravine opening to discover the wolves fought twelve—

"Jackals?" Nollen said in surprised confusion. "What are they doing in Heddwyn? And during the day?"

Two jackals broke from fighting the wolves to charge the men. Nollen fired his crossbow. The dart struck one jackal in the shoulder. It yowled in retreat.

Gunnar stepped in front of Axel to intercept the second jackal. He batted it aside with the flat of his blade. The jackal leapt at him. It bit down and grabbed part of his surcoat. He clouted the jackal's head with the pommel. It made an angry yelp. At the second clout, the jackal released him.

It snapped at Gunnar, which made him retreat in avoidance. Before he could swipe at the jackal, a wolf took it down by the neck. The vicious attack ended with a loud pitiful yelp from the jackal.

"My thanks," said Gunnar. The wolf returned to the fight.

After ten minutes, two jackals fled. Any wounded jackal that moved, was killed by a wolf.

Nollen approached one of the dead animals. "Something's not right. This looks like a jackal, but not one I've ever seen."

Gunnar and Axel joined Nollen in observing the dead animal. Nollen continued, "It's larger. More like a wolf than a dog, and with black fur. The muzzle bigger with yellow teeth and longer fangs. Also, green foam at the mouth, but everything else appears similar."

"You're right," agreed Gunnar. "It doesn't look like the jackals we encountered since arriving."

Bardolf approached them. The wolf leader was cover in blood, but not from any wounds. "The enemy has penetrated Heddwyn using Black Jackals as advanced scouts." He yelped at the pack. Three wolves responded in yips and ran off.

"I've not heard of Black Jackals before," said Nollen.

Bardolf explained. "They are only used by the enemy for special assignments. The last time they were sent to track the priests, and flush them out of hiding. When your grandfather reached the safety of Heddwyn, they stopped at the border, frustrated at being unable enter." He snarled at the dead jackal. "Now they are dispatched to hunt the Son of Eldar. I sent three of pack to stop the jackals from leaving Heddwyn and betraying the Son of Eldar's whereabouts."

"What about the compound? Could they be in danger?"

Bardolf barked again at the pack. A lone male hurried off in a different direction. "Raff will stand watch."

"Thank you," said Nollen, grateful.

Ula limped over. Axel sheathed his sword. He knelt and beckoned to her. "Lie down and let me see." When she obeyed, he examined her right front leg. "A bad bite. Gunnar, my saddlebag."

He and Nollen led their mounts from the ravine. Gunnar removed the saddlebag per instruction.

After removing the needed items, Axel warned Ula. "This might sting a little." He applied some salve. Ula yelped, but his hold kept her from withdrawing her leg. He wrapped a cloth around the wound. "Now, the bandage needs to stay on for a few days. No chewing it off."

Ula lowly growled. She tried to lick it.

"No. This is needed to help the salve work." At her stubbornness, Axel spoke to Bardolf. "Tell her to behave."

Bardolf simply showed his teeth. Ula submitted by laying back her ears and lowered her head.

"Where to now?" asked Gunnar.

"The trail is up ahead, so we can ride rather than walk," began Nollen. "Unless you still smell something unknown," he said to Bardolf.

Bardolf sniffed the air before he turned his attention to the ground. He moved up the trail and sniffed the ground as he went. Once there, he called back, "It is safe to continue."

Axel motioned Nollen to take the point behind Bardolf. Six wolves continued with them. Ula limped along near Gunnar in the rear of the line. He kept an eye on her, but as the hours passed, she fell further behind. When they paused to eat, and refresh the horses, Ula had disappeared.

"Did you see where she went?" Axel asked Gunnar.

"No. I lost sight of her over that last climb."

Axel noticed Bardolf stare back in the direction they came. "Bardolf, do you see Ula?" he called.

Instead of answering, Bardolf vanished behind the rise. A moment later, he reappeared with a badly limping Ula. Axel placed aside his food to approach. This time, Ula growled and bared her teeth. At Bardolf's reproving snap, she moved off with her tail between her legs. Yet, she growled at Axel as she went. He watched her lay down and gnaw at the bandage. She even snapped when Bardolf or another wolf approached. Before Axel could take a step towards her, Gunnar grabbed his arm.

"She's obviously in great pain. Best to leave her alone."

Nollen aided Gunnar's effort by handing Axel back his food. Reluctant, Axel returned to eating.

After thirty minutes of rest, they continued toward the Gorland border. By twilight, they reached a tree line that led to an open river plain. In the near distance, stood a brightly lit blockhouse.

Nollen stopped just inside the shadow of the trees. He pointed out the blockhouse to Axel and Gunnar.

"That is a Gorland border station on the raised platform. The lesser light below it, is the actual border."

"Looks like a dam of some kind," said Gunnar.

"It is," began Nollen. "A strategic one, actually. Depending upon our relations with Gorland, the dam can be opened or closed. This time of year, the Leven tributary is low, and easy to cross without a ferry. Which also means the dam is partial close for control, yet still allows Gorland access to water."

"Do you ever use water as a trading commodity?"

"Oh, no! That's the quickest way to start a war—or end up dead!" Nollen then thought out loud, "But I do trade purification herbs. Gorlanders fear we could poison the water."

"Do you have any of those herbs?" Axel asked.

Nollen shook his head. "I didn't think we'd need them." He judged the fading twilight. "Should be totally dark within half an hour. We'll cross the river and make camp just on the other side."

"I thought we travel Ha'tar at night?" said Axel.

"Aye, but after days to get here, we'll rest before starting night travel."

They waited until the light faded and stars appeared. Once at the river's edge, Nollen dismounted to test the depth of the water. He waded in waist deep. He shivered from the cold but could withstand the current. He returned to shore.

"The current is crossable. Cold, but safe."

"Bardolf, you don't need to come any further," Axel said.

"No, we will escort you. Black Jackals won't stop us."

Axel smiled. "Very well. Swim on."

Men, horses, and wolves crossed the hundred-yard-wide river, as quickly and quietly as possible. On the other side, the wolves shook off the water. They followed the men to an abandoned shack a quarter mile inland.

"All can come inside. No need to tip our hand to any wandering patrols." Nollen lead his pony into the shack.

"Don't tell me, you have some hidden secrets here also," quipped Gunnar. He tethered his horse beside Nollen's pony.

"Well, I do travel between The Doane and Ganel more frequently," Nollen spoke in witty reply.

"Matches to a start fire, perhaps?" Gunnar moved to the hearth.

"No fire. This close to the border station, they'll see the smoke. Between all of us there should be enough heat for the night. You can light the lantern though."

Gunnar did so and trimmed the flame.

"What about water for the horses?" asked Axel.

"There is small, supposedly abandoned, well out back." Nollen removed the saddle from his pony.

"Cleverly disguised under debris, I assume." Axel smiled. Being closest to the door, he grabbed a bucket. "Take care of my horse. I'll find the well," he instructed Nollen.

Axel no sooner stepped out of the shack when it happened. A menacing growl accompanied by an attack from behind that knocked him to the ground. He used the bucket to bat aside the animal. He turned on his back and caught a glimpse of Ula foaming at the mouth. She attacked again. His raised the bucket to shield his face.

Gunnar raced outside. He held the lantern in one hand, and his sword in the other. The pack became agitated. Bardolf nipped at Ula in an effort stop the attack.

Nollen ran outside with his crossbow. He watched Axel use the bucket to fend off Ula. "Raise the light!" he urged Gunnar. He took aim. "Axel, roll left! Now!"

Axel heeded. Nollen fired. Ula let out a loud short yelp when the crossbow dart pierced her neck. The impact knocked her to the ground. Axel scrambled to his knees. He breathed heavy from the excretion of battle. Ula's limbs twitched then became still.

After a wary moment, Bardolf sniffed and nudged Ula. She didn't move. He howled. The rest of the pack joined the song of lament.

Axel dropped the bucket to approach Ula. He knelt. "I'm so sorry, Bardolf."

Bardolf whimpered, and nudged Ula again.

Distressed by the wolves' grief, Nollen spoke with painful regret. "I had to shoot!"

Sympathetic, Axel glanced at Nollen. "He knows that. He mourns his mate."

Gunnar grew uneasy. His gaze scanned the surroundings. "If they keep howling, it could draw attention."

Axel touched Bardolf's head. The alpha made a short huffing bark. The pack grew silent. Axel noticed Ula chewed off the bandage.

"Gunnar, bring the light closer." When able to see clearly, Axel reached to examine the now badly infected jackal bite.

Quickly, Nollen knelt and seized Axel's arm. "Don't touch it!" Poison! Like the dragon's wound."

Startled by the abrupt action, Axel asked, "Jackal bites are poisonous?"

"Since they weren't normal jackals, it has to be poison. How else can you explain the sudden onset of green infection, and foaming at the mouth, as if rabid?"

"Bardolf," began Axel with concern. "Did any of the others suffer bites during the fight?"

Bardolf first exchanged barks, yelps, and low growls with the pack before replying to Axel. "One." He then turned to Nollen to identify the second. "Raff."

"The compound!" Nollen bolted up.

Gunnar prevented Nollen from leaving. "You can't go back. Not now."

Nollen's violent jerk to be free made the older soldier stumbled off balance. Axel hurried to catch Nollen.

"Leave it be! Bardolf and his pack will deal with Raff," Axel sternly said. His grip tightened when Nollen tried to move away.

Bardolf came beside them. The large wolf rose on his hind legs to place his front paws on their arms. He spoke with urgency to Nollen. "It is our duty to defend the compound. You must stay with the Son of Eldar to guide him safely through Ha'tar territory!"

Conflicted, Nollen glanced in the direction they came.

"If necessary, we will stop Raff like you did Ula," Bardolf spoke in sober assurance. He rubbed his head against Nollen with a whimper.

Nollen's shoulders sagged at the declaration. He swallowed back regret to pet Bardolf. "Thank you."

Bardolf jumped down to speak to the pack. They left.

Chapter 18

THE DAY WENT ALONG JUST LIKE ANY OTHER AT THE COMPOUND; foraging, hunting, teaching children, meal preparation, and other activities. As became her habit each day since Nollen, Axel, and Gunnar left, Ida stood on the rampart staring in the direction they traveled. Of course, she never expected to see anything. Simply gazing into the forest helped to focus her prayers.

When Axel and Nollen returned to the festivities, she knew something passed between them. Axel gave her a quick smile and wink, while Nollen seemed a bit more relaxed. Yet when Nollen volunteered to act as guide, she sensed a renewed tension. What exactly that meant, she didn't know. It could just have been anticipation of the arduous journey to Mathena. Thus, she determined to keep a daily prayer vigil on their behalf.

Naturally, she and Jarred joined Arctander and the brethren in nightly prayers. Yet, this was her time to be alone with her thoughts and meditation.

Ida heard the footsteps and knew without turning that it was Jarred. He came to fetch her when lunch was ready.

"Any new impression or revelation?" he asked.

"No. But I believe Gott hears everything and is with them."

He tenderly kissed her forehead. "Come, time to eat."

Upon reaching the main compound, a man called, "Jarred!"

"What is it, Kaden?"

"Jonas is here."

"Jonas?" asked Ida, alarmed. "Is he alone?"

"Aye."

"Has he come alone before?" she asked Jarred.

He shook his head. "No, he hasn't."

"He says the news is urgent, and insists upon speaking with you and Arctander," said Kaden to Jarred.

When Ida frowned, Jarred said, "It must be very important for him to risk coming alone."

"Still seems strange," said Ida, wary

"You and Nollen fled Far Point. The news may be the repercussions from that."

"I suppose," she said in tentative agreement.

"I'm not going to just let him in," Jarred assured her. "I'll check with the other scouts. Speak with Arctander and see what he thinks." He waited a moment for Ida to enter the longhouse. "Come," he said to Kaden.

Once again, Jarred mounted the stairs to the ramparts. He made a warbling call. His brows knitted with caution, as he waited. When it took longer than normal to receive a reply, he asked Kaden, "Are you certain Jonas is alone? No signs of anyone else?"

"Not at my station. He approached by himself."

There! Two all clear responses. Jarred relaxed. He patted Kaden's shoulder. "Bring Jonas to the compound." He then descended to where Ida and Arctander waited. "The scouts gave the all clear. I sent Kaden to fetch him."

Unconvinced, Ida wrapped her arms around herself, as if warding off a chill. "I can't shake this uneasy feeling," she said to Jarred then to Arctander, "He refused the medallions you sent for the boys."

"Granted, that is disappointing," agreed Arctander. "However, Jonas has always been supportive of our family in times of crisis."

"Aye," she droned, still uneasy. "I pray Nollen and the Prince are well."

Arctander offered an encouraging smile and placed a comforting arm about her shoulder. "We'll know soon enough. No need to worry needlessly."

At a warbling call, Jarred motioned to the men at the main gate to allow entrance. Kaden escorted Jonas into the compound with Jonas on horseback.

An immediate look of surprise registered on Jonas' face at seeing … "Ida!" His head turned side-to-side in scanning the compound. "Is Nollen here?"

Alert to Jonas' reaction, Jarred spoke. "I take it you didn't expect to see her."

"No!" Jonas fought to regain his composure. "I mean, not after what I heard about Far Point." He forced a smile at Ida. "I'm glad to see you whole, cousin."

At the familiar address, Arctander confronted Jonas. "What have you heard?"

Recovered from his brief shock, Jonas grimly replied. "After the authorities ransacked Far Point in search of Ida and Nollen, they came to Gilroy looking for me! I tried to withstand them, but," his tone turned bitter, "they took my family!"

"Sharla and the boys?" exclaimed Ida in horror.

Arctander ignored her outburst to press Jonas. "Why did they come after you and your family?"

"Because of this!" Jonas removed the box from his saddlebag and flung it on the ground. It broke upon impact.

Ida immediately recognized it. Sudden realization made her glare at Jonas. "You—"

Simultaneously a sentry shouted, "Attack-" his warning cut short when struck down by an arrow.

"Traitor!" Ida finished her angry declaration.

A hail of arrows flew over the walls. Several people fell when hit.

"Men to the ramparts!" Jarred ordered.

"I must get you to safety!" Ida seized Arctander.

They dodged arrows, as Ida hurried Arctander to the southeast corner of the compound. The secret south entrance opened, and soldiers rushed in. Ida grabbed a nearby piece of wood for defense.

"Go!" she told Arctander.

"Not without—"

A soldier seized Arctander. Ida swung the wood and hit the soldier's face with a loud smack. He fell to one side. A second soldier arrived. Ready for her attack, he ducked, and seized the wood. They wrestled for control. He sent a punch to her stomach. Winded, she let go, and fell to her knees. He tossed the wood aside. When he reached down to grab her, she slashed his hand with her dagger. Wounded, he backed away to assess the injury.

Ida wobbled when trying to stand, so Arctander helped her. They continued to move southeast. She cried out when seized. She fought, but a blow across the face stunned her. It was the same soldier she wounded. Two more soldiers grabbed Arctander.

The surprise attack ended quickly. Ten dead, or badly wounded lay around the ground. One soldier drug a wounded Jarred to where the rest gathered in front of the longhouse. Jarred fell to his knees when the soldier released him. He sat back on his heels to observe the outcome. He grimaced with discomfort and held his side wound. It wasn't lethal or debilitating, more a painful inconvenience.

Hertz and Magistrate Bernal rode through the main entrance. Four soldiers followed with bound and gagged scouts in tow.

"Well done, Jonas." Pleased, Bernal's gaze swept the crowd. He huffed with mockery at sight of Arctander. "Do my eyes deceive me? Arctander? Jonas didn't mention you would be here."

"I didn't know if he was still alive," said Jonas.

"Liar!" Ida sneered.

"I advise you to keep your tongue. You and your brother are already in enough trouble," Hertz warned. He spoke to Captain Udell, "Have you found Nollen of Far Point?"

"No, sir. This is everyone."

"The foreigners?" Bernal asked Hertz.

Hertz dismounted to accost Ida. "Where are the men who came to Far Point?" When she didn't reply, he seized her by the throat. She gasped for breath at the sudden stricture. "You realize, I could kill you right now since you've been declared a traitor. Just like your parents."

"Let her be!" Jarred managed to stand. Soldiers immediately grabbed him.

Hertz ignored Jarred to concentrate on Ida. "Well?"

"I don't know," she hissed through clenched teeth.

Hertz whipped out his dagger to hold in front of her. A whimper of fear escaped her pressed lips.

With a snarl of disapproval, Bernal snapped, "Put it away! Killing her won't get what we want. Word of her capture will."

Hertz shoved Ida back. She stumbled before she regained her balance. Hertz sheathed the dagger to mount his horse.

"Bind them and bring them to Vanora!" Bernal ordered Udell.

On the edge of an overhang, Raff laid and watched the attack. His muzzle twitched in a snarl. Some foam dripped from his mouth. He licked a long scratch on his left rear leg. Although not a puncture wound, green puss showed that some poison had entered his system.

Upon sight of Arctander being led away with the others, Raff stood. He whimpered at pain in his back leg. He sat in such a way as to take weight off the injury. Unable to track any further, Raff howled. He ignored the fact that howling drew attention from the soldiers. However, when two came within sight, Raff stood, hackles up, and growled.

A soldier aimed a bow. Raff snapped in their direction. The arrow loosed just as wolves leapt upon the soldiers. The pack arrived. The men never stood a chance against five wolves.

Bardolf approached the downed Raff. An arrow protruded from Raff's side. Still alive, he whimpered at Bardolf. "Strangers at the compound."

"Arctander?" asked Bardolf.

"They took him. They took everyone."

"Which way?"

Raff couldn't response anymore and breathed his last.

Bardolf ran to the compound. The rest of the pack joined him inside the protected circle. They investigated each human. None moved when nudged, licked or otherwise encouraged.

"Dead," a female mournfully said to Bardolf.

The alpha sniffed the air then the ground. "Strangers attacked from all sides."

"What should we do?" asked another male.

"Follow, and to stop them from leaving Heddwyn!" With a curt bark and howl, Bardolf led them in pursuit.

As the pack reached a bend in the trail, one stopped. His attention drawn back into the woods. "Bardolf!" He waited until the others doubled back to him.

"What is it, Dag?"

"I caught Orlie and Lido's scent."

Bardolf sniffed the air. At a familiar yelping cry, they broke off pursuit of the humans to race up the incline. After three-hundred-yards, they came upon a distressing scene. Orlie and Lido lay dead, along with one of the Black Jackals.

"We're too late!" Dag loudly said in distress.

Numerous snarls and growls alerted the wolves. Slowly, Black Jackals appeared. Their fangs dripped with foaming saliva, as they surrounded the pack. The wolves formed a circle with their hind ends to each other, to stare down the jackals. A very large she-jackal moved toward the pack.

"We meet again, Bardolf," she taunted.

"Fia!" Bardolf growling in angry reply. "I should have guessed it was you from the foul scent."

"Two hundred years is a long time. Scents, and appearances, can change."

"But not your evil blight on the forest."

Fia lowered her head, ears laid back, her fangs totally bared. "Tell me where the Son of Eldar is, and I might let you live."

Bardolf's loud bark sent the wolves on the attack. Being larger and heavier, they easily took down a jackal. This would be a fight to the death.

Bardolf lunged at Fia, the she-jackal not afraid to take the full-force of his attack. Bardolf landed a bite on the scruff of her neck. He managed to avoid her retaliatory snap. Again, he lunged. This time, he grabbed Fia by the throat. Feeling the sharpness of her fangs near his ear, he gave her a violent shake. Unfortunately, this allowed Fia to break free. She leapt at him. Bardolf jumped back to avoid her bite. He came at her from the side and knocked her to the ground. His powerful jaws clamped down on her throat. Fia couldn't escape. Blood oozed from her wounds, but Bardolf wouldn't let go. Fia's struggle grew weaker. Her breathing became labored. Not until she became still, did Bardolf release her.

Sadly, other wolves were not so fortunate. In the end, all Black Jackals lay dead with only Dag and Bardolf remaining from the pack.

Bardolf slowly approached a weary Dag. "Any wounds?"

"I don't think so."

Bardolf sniffed to inspect Dag. The subordinate male submitted to the alpha's examination. "The blood on your fur is jackal."

"What now?"

"Warn the Son of Eldar."

Bardolf headed back into the forest. Suddenly, Fia sprang to her feet intent on attacking Bardolf. Dag intercepted her. The younger wolf might have matched Fia in strength, but not in speed. He tumbled backward when Fia pounced on top of him. His yelping whimper cut short by her lethal bite.

The force of Bardolf's attack knocked Fia off Dag. With ferocious anger, he made an end to Fia. This time not releasing her until certain she was dead. Finally, he backed away. He howled, long, hard, and mournful. He alone survived.

Chapter 19

AFTER THE WOLVES LEFT, GUNNAR AND AXEL AGREED TO Nollen's request to wait an extra day before continuing. He found it difficult to concentrate on anything else than the fate of those at the compound. When not occupied with tasks of survival, he spent the time brooding. Gunnar and Axel didn't press him, though they offered words of encouragement from time to time.

Nollen's thoughts bounced between events since their arrival, to recollections of childhood, and fateful events of life. His family faced danger for as long as he could remember. Only recently, the peril increased. Not that he faulted Axel. No, life grew more harrowing the past decade when Dolus became Javan's First Minster. Learning from Jonas that Javan issued a new edict calling for death happened before meeting Axel. Yet since fleeing Far Point, his heart, mind, and faith became shaken, challenged, and tested. Ida's wounding scared him, Arctander's doubt disturbed him, while Axel perplexed him.

A recent conversation echoed in his mind. It started with Gunnar's question: *Do you resent being forced into doing things you would rather not?* Followed by Gunnar listing off actions that made him pose the question: *Ida revealing the medallion, leaving Far Point, arriving at the compounding, misunderstanding what was said, and now this route.* The most disturbing part came with Axel's summation: *You're afraid you can't live up to expectations.*

Nollen never considered his actions as being *resentful.* Nor did he consider *fear.* Still, those words struck a nerve deep within him. True, duty was thrust upon him at the death of his parents. Yet a duty he spent his whole life preparing to assume. It just came in a most unexpected, and horrific manner.

Nollen sat outside the shack near the threshold. He glanced back inside to see Axel sitting at the table. His elbows rested on the rickety wooden top, hands folded with his forehead touching his knuckles in a posture of prayer. Despite the danger, Nollen sensed a serenity in Axel. With that serenity, came an unusual strength that seemed to defy circumstances. It gave Axel an unwavering confidence.

Confidence, Nollen's mind echoed in realization. "Not fear or resentment but confidence to act."

"Did you say something?"

Nollen balked in surprise to see Gunnar standing in the doorway beside him. "Just thinking out loud."

Gunnar glanced skyward. "Twilight. We should eat before we leave. We can't wait any longer."

Nollen swallowed back his disappointment at the thought of leaving without knowing the fate of his family. However, he knew they must continue. Inside, he noticed the horses and his pony were saddled. Gunnar replied to his unspoken curiosity.

"I did it while you kept watch and Axel prayed." Gunnar gave each a slice of bread with a thin piece of sausage, cheese, and apple on it.

Nollen sat opposite Axel to eat. "What were you praying about? If you don't mind me asking."

"Wisdom, guidance, and protection for us, as well as those at the compound."

"Let's hope Gott answers you," droned Nollen.

"I'm confident he will."

Nollen paused in eating at hearing the word *confident.* "It's still hard not to worry about them."

"I never said I didn't worry," began Axel. "I just know when and how to release my worries. Praying is one way."

Nollen grew thoughtful at the statement. "Ida and Marmie always said the same about prayer."

"I thought you prayed," Gunnar commented to Nollen.

"Aye. Just differently, I suppose." Nollen noticed the fading light outside the door. "Time to leave." He popped the last bite of food in his mouth then fetched his pony.

"Should we light a lantern?" asked Gunnar. They led the animals from the shack to mount.

"No need. Gilen knows the way. Don't you, boy?" Nollen stroked his pony's neck. Gilen snorted and tossed his head. "Also, we'll keep the light from the Gorland border stations to our west to help stay on course."

"How far apart are the stations?" asked Axel.

"Every ten miles. This portion of the Ha'tar territory stretches for sixty miles, so we'll pass six stations."

"We should be able to travel it in two or three nights at most," said Gunnar.

"No, the terrain is too difficult. We'll be lucky to make ten or twelve miles in a night," groused Nollen. He then proceeded to explain why. "Dragons prefer steep, rocky places. If they can't find it, they'll create it by destroying everything. That's why the further we travel from the river, the less trees. They decimated the forest to suit their liking."

"Hence night travel," surmised Axel.

"Aye. We'll be out from under cover soon." Nollen motioned to the thin trees. "Any light can be seen for miles."

"Which means no fire again," complained Gunnar. He drew his cloak about his shoulders against the night chill.

"How desolate is this place? Any other creatures we should be worried about?" asked Axel.

"An owl maybe, but the rest are harmless rodents, insects, and bats. Dragons won't allow any other large predator to live."

As the hours passed, the moon rose higher. Abundant stars shone brightly in the clear night sky. The nocturnal heavenly lights did little to improve the bleak gray landscape.

Several times, they needed to dismount and carefully lead the horses down, up, around, and through crags, tunnels, and rocky peaks. After each grueling trek, they stopped to partake of water, catch their breath, and allow the horses to rest.

During one descent, Gunnar slipped, and slid down a rocky patch of ground. Fortunately, they were near the bottom.

"Are you hurt?" Axel helped Gunnar to stand.

"Twisted my ankle, but I'll manage."

"We're nearly done for the night," said Nollen. "Beyond the bend is a cave where we can rest for the day."

Nollen suddenly stopped when he moved around the bend. He held up an arm to wave a warning. Axel and Gunnar immediately halted. Nollen beckoned them closer. He spoke in a whisper.

"Looks like a juvenile has found the cave." He pointed to the young dragon nestled down in the opening. "We need to double-back."

When he turned his pony, Gilen slipped and whinnied in surprise. Nollen immediately grabbed Gilen's muzzle. Too late! He peeked out to see the juvenile rise, and stare in their direction.

"I thought you said dragons have bad eyesight at night?" chided Gunnar close to Nollen's ear.

"They can still hear and smell." Nollen grabbed his crossbow. "Back into the crag!" He pulled the reins and ran.

Gunnar half-hopped, half-ran on his injured ankle. He reached the crag last, just as the juvenile flew overhead. Nollen held his crossbow ready.

"Can you see well enough to shoot?" Axel harshly whispered.

"I don't want to shoot if I don't have to. A dead juvenile will alert the Ha'tar to the presence of trespassers," Nollen replied in hoarse voice.

They ducked when the juvenile roared, and once again, passed overhead. An answering dragon call caused great concern.

"Two dragons?" hissed Gunnar.

"Stay here." Nollen slung the crossbow over his shoulder.

Axel seized him. "Where are you going?"

"To climb up and see what's going on. Stay out of sight." Nollen carefully climbed the lowest part of the crag for a better view. He sank back at the sight of the juvenile with an adult dragon. The beasts seem to exchange verbal calls. The adult roared while the juvenile whimpered. When the adult banked away, the juvenile followed. He watched the dragons disappeared beyond the rocky horizon. He climbed back down.

"Well? What did you see?" asked Axel.

"Mama dragon showed up, and both flew east. Away from us, and the cave." Nollen took Gilen's reins to leave the crag.

"Will it be safe? It won't come back, will it?" Gunnar grunted as he followed.

"I don't know. This is the first time I encountered one here. So, close to Gorland is dangerous for any dragon. If I were to guess, I'd say the juvenile got lost, and the mother came to find it." Nollen lead them deep enough into the cave to avoid being seen.

"Sit, and let me bind your ankle," Axel said to Gunnar.

Gunnar sat on a large rock with a huff of painful effort. "It feels swollen, so I don't think the boot will come off."

"Then I'll bind it from the outside for extra support." Axel knelt in front of Gunnar.

"I'll do it!" Gunnar snatched the bandage cloth from Axel.

"It will be hard at that angle." Axel reached for the bandage, but Gunnar refused to yield. Axel frowned, which prompted Gunnar to speak in a troubled tone.

"This isn't right. I'm supposed to protect and tend to you, not the other way around. First the dragon, now this." He waved Axel away with the intent to bandage his own ankle.

"You couldn't help—" Nollen began to refute, when Axel drew him to the other side of the cave.

They stopped beside the horses where Axel quietly spoke. "Gunnar feels he failed me. Don't argue with him."

"Being wounded and injured is not failure."

"Not to you and me. However, in his mind, it is." Axel glanced to Gunnar, before he spoke again. "Sometimes what is in our minds, is not the reality others see, or *expect.*" At Nollen's pensive expression, he said, "Gunnar does not have to prove his loyalty or courage to me."

"Does he know that?"

"Of course. Pain, hurt, fear, or any negative emotion can overshadow knowledge." Axel grew sober in self-reflection. "That is something I prayed about earlier."

"For him or me?" Nollen asked, though he tried to keep accusation from his voice.

Axel lifted his gaze to meet Nollen's. "For myself. The battle between self-doubt and faith rages in all of us."

The confession pricked Nollen. "I'm sorry," he offered in apology.

The conversation became interrupted by Gunnar's grunting. He rose and began to cross toward them.

Nollen intercepted him. "Sit. I'll fetch the food and drink." He tried to steer Gunnar to where he sat when Gunnar jerked away. At Axel's negative shake of his head, Nollen let Gunnar hobble back to the rock. Yet thinking better of it, he moved to kneel in front of Gunnar. "I *will* wrap this better." He snatched Gunnar's hand when the older soldier went to shoo him away. He boldly, yet privately quoted, "'*You're not the only one who fears living up to expectations.*'"

Gunnar fought annoyance and amusement at the clever retort. He relaxed against the cave wall to allow Nollen access to his ankle.

Chapter 20

THE LARGEST FORTIFIED MANOR HOUSE IN VANORA SERVED AS residence, and headquarters for Magistrate Bernal. It consisted of four wings; one for the family, one for administration, soldiers' barracks, and the smallest building for servants. The dungeon was located beneath the barracks. It had three small cells for individuals, and a large single area for multiple prisoners.

The last rays of daylight filtered in through small, high, barred windows of the large room. Soldiers herded those from the compound inside. Being late fall, the trek from Heddwyn to Vanora proved hard on the young children and elderly. The cold nights caused some to develop fever, while hunger gnawed at all of them. Those stronger helped the sick and weak during the arduous journey.

Despite great fatigue, Ida aided an elderly man to sit on the uneven cobblestone floor beside his wife. Her own strength nearly spent, she awkwardly knelt beside the couple. "At least we are done traveling," she tried to encourage him.

The wretched plight of his people pricked Arctander. "For pity's sake, at least bring us food and drink!" he entreated. A soldier shoved him aside. He groaned in pain when he hit the wall and sank to his knees.

"Grandfather!" Ida moved to help him. "No need to mistreat an old man," she bitterly shouted at the soldiers. Their answer was the loud slamming of the door and clicking of the lock.

Jarred managed to have his wound wrapped during the journey, but no further treatment. He endured the irritation. He gingerly knelt on the other side of Arctander. “Sadly, Bernal is not known for pity or mercy. Are you hurt?”

“No, just sore,” complained Arctander.

“Ida?” a female asked in disturbed surprise.

“Who calls?” She used the wall to help herself stand.

“It is you!” Sharla threw her arms around Ida and wept.

“Sharla?” Stunned, Ida held the woman at arm’s length. She gently brushed Sharla’s tears aside. “What are doing here?”

Arctander motioned for Jarred to help him rise. “We heard you had been taken captive.”

Abe and Bart approached. “*We* didn’t betray him. We kept our word. Papa did,” Bart told Ida. The youth’s features fought sneering rage.

“We know about Jonas.” Jarred tried unsuccessfully to keep the bitterness from his voice.

“What?” asked Sharla with some confusion. “You know of his betrayal? How?”

“Because he led them to the compound!” spat Jarred.

“Oh, Gott,” she lamented, and shed more tears.

Abe comforted his mother when Jarred continued.

“A number were killed before they brought us here.”

Arctander’s hand on his shoulder and stern look, stopped Jarred. With compassion, Arctander spoke to Sharla. “Jonas told us of your capture. He blames Nollen … and me. I’m sorry.”

Sharla shook her head and wiped away the tears. “You need not apologize for my cowardly husband. We,” she motioned to the boys, “knew the risks of our Faith, and willingly accepted it. We just didn’t expect betrayal to come from … *him.*” She scowled in painful anger.

Arctander gave Sharla a fatherly hug about the shoulders.

“Was Nollen among those killed?” asked Abe with worry.

“No! Thank Gott, he was not there when it happened,” Ida quickly replied

"Then Nollen is safe?" asked Sharla, to which Ida shrugged ignorance. "Is he with the foreigners?"

"How do you know about them?" asked Jarred, guarded.

Ida intervened to stem Jarred's ire. "Remember I told you *they*," she nodded to Abe and Bart, "came to warn us, and *he* was there."

"Aye, but did they tell Jonas?"

"No! I said we kept our word," Bart insisted.

"The boys only told me since we've been here," Sharla informed Jarred. "Hertz came with a warrant and accused Jonas of helping Nollen and the foreigners."

For a moment, Jarred contemplated the various answers before inquiring, "Did Jonas leave Gilroy at any time recently?"

"No," replied Sharla with certainty. She took note of their consideration and concern. "Why?"

Frustrated, Jarred shrugged. "I'm not sure. It's growing more complicated."

Ida cuddled up to Jarred's arm. "You're tired. We all are. And I can see your wound troubles you. Emotions are raw, and none of us are thinking clearing right now."

Jarred kissed her forehead.

"Despite all that," began Arctander with a growing smile. "We are alive to see prophecy fulfilled. We must be strong. Our redemption is near."

Bernal, Destry, Hertz, Captain Udell, and Jonas entered the magistrate's office. Two servants followed, and immediately lit four lanterns and stoked the fire to life.

Only a desk, three chairs, and two file cabinets, occupied the cold damp room. Little furnishings combined with unadorned gray walls made for a dreary atmosphere. The décor showed a place for conducting harsh business, and not comfort.

Bernal warmed his hand over the flames. "Fiske, fetch mulled cider," he barked at a servant.

"Will you keep them here, or take them to Sener?" Destry asked. He rubbed his hands to get them warm.

Bernal looked to Hertz. "What says our legal counselor?"

"There is an edict that calls for anyone accused of being a follower of the forbidden Faith to be taken to Sener for public execution. The fact we captured a long-thought-dead high priest, will be of great interest to Lord Dolus."

Bernal cocked a satisfied smile. "It will also prove our loyalty to Javan and strike a blow at the other Territories."

Hertz nodded, as he blew on his hands to warm them. The fire slowly began to raise the room temperature.

"How soon can arrangements be made for transport?" Bernal asked Udell.

"With forty individuals, I estimate two days."

"Why send them all when just a few would do?" said Destry. At Hertz's annoyed glare, he explained, "The objective is to draw out Nollen of Far Point, and these foreigners. Only key people need to be sent. The rest, kept here as incentive."

Pleased, Bernal chuckled. He clapped Destry on the shoulder. "I think you should be my counselor."

Hertz grew rigid at the insult. "Magistrate, there are *other* matters he is unaware of, besides his ignorance of the law."

For a long, uncomfortable moment, Bernal and Hertz glared at each other. Finally, Bernal broke off the tense stare-down with a huff and impatient wave.

"Do as you think best!" He snatched a tankard off the tray when Fiske returned with refreshments.

"Master Destry's suggestion has merit. Those chosen should be Arctander, Ida, Jarred, and," he flashed a glance at Jonas, "your family."

Jonas paled, disconcerted. "Why? I've done as you asked."

"We did not find Nollen or the foreigners at the compound," Hertz coolly said. "Until they are captured, your family will be treated like the traitors there are."

Desperate, Jonas appealed to Bernal. "Magistrate, please, I beg you to spare them! Keep them here if you must, but don't send them to Sener."

Bernal ignored the plea by taking a drink.

Hertz stepped between Jonas and Bernal. "Do you wish to join your family, as a branded traitor? Because if you don't do as pledged, and bring us Nollen and the foreigners, *that* is what will happen."

"Will they be spared if I do?"

Hertz heaved a non-committal shrug. "Who can say? But they face certain death if you fail again." He summoned the servant. "Fiske, see Master Jonas is made comfortable."

"Aye, my lord. Sir."

Destry aided Fiske by taking hold of Jonas' arm. "I'll stay with you."

Hertz spoke after the door closed on their departure. "Udell. Place a guard at the door to be sure Jonas doesn't act foolishly."

Bernal waited until Udell left to ask, "Why *did* you include his family? They served the purpose of getting him to talk. And he led us to the compound."

"Oh, you of little brains!" complained Hertz with exasperation. "The more bait, the better the trap to draw out Nollen, and the foreigners."

Bernal abruptly turned his back to again warm himself by the fire.

With a smug grin, Hertz withdrew. In the hall, another servant handed him a letter. Recognizing Dolus' seal, he hurried down the corridor then up a flight of stairs to his quarters.

Once inside the dark room, he struck a match to light a lantern. He ignored the night chill to read. His eyes grew wide, and he impulsively spoke with alarm, "The Son of Eldar!" He took a breath to calm down, as what they suspected had been confirmed.

He swiftly crossed to a bell rope and pulled it multiple times. He re-read the letter while he awaited the servant's return. He looked up when the door opened. "Light the fire and send for Captain Udell. Be quick!"

Dim moonlight shone through the dungeon window. Ida sat against a wooden pillar as she tried to comfort a sick child. Arctander and Jarred moved about the chamber to offer encouragement and reassurance. The past few days had been difficult for those who lost loved ones at the compound.

Hearing the jingle of keys in the lock, Jarred stood from kneeling beside a grieving widow. He braced in anticipation, and briefly shielding his eyes from the bright light of torches. Behind the soldiers with torches, came Udell. Several more soldiers followed the captain.

"Him, him, her, her, and those two boys." Udell pointed to Jarred, Arctander, Ida, Sharla, and her sons.

The soldiers grabbed each person indicated.

"What's going on?" demanded Arctander.

"You'll find out soon enough, old man." Udell waved for them to be taken from the chamber.

Torches and lanterns helped little to navigate the winding steps leading up from the dungeon. Ida stumbled and was jerked to her feet by the soldier who escorted her. Once out of the barracks, Udell lead the group across the courtyard to the administration building. The night felt even colder outside, as a north wind blew in clouds that threatened rain.

Up a flight of stairs, and down a long corridor, they finally arrived in an anteroom. It felt a bit warmer than the cold damp dungeon. Glowing embers filled a brazier while several candles provided light. Udell exited by way of another door.

"What do you suppose they want with us?" Sharla anxiously asked Ida.

Ida held Sharla's hand in support. "Whatever it is, we'll face it together."

Udell returned with Hertz. The counselor's gaze swept over the group, then came to rest on Arctander.

"Dolus will be very pleased to learn about you," said Hertz.

"What pleases Dolus, is of no concern to me."

Hertz chuckled with mockery. "Oh, you'll think differently when you all arrive in Sener."

Sharla pressed her lips together in terror and tightened her grip on Ida. Ida paled when Hertz mentioned Sener.

Arctander straightened with defensive fury. "Send me alone and leave them here."

"I can't do that. I *won't* do that," rebuffed Hertz. He boldly approached Arctander. "And you *know* why." He looked at the others. "All of you know why." No one spoke. "Heroic silence," he jeered.

"Silence of Faith, not heroics," corrected Arctander.

"Your Faith is a curious oddity, as it serves no purpose but to bring death." Again, Hertz gazed at each of them. Despite rising tears of fear, the women withstood him; the boys appeared anxious, but uttered not a word. Jarred and Arctander displayed the most defiance.

"We leave at first light." Hertz turned on his heels.

"You expect us to be fit for travel when we haven't eaten in nearly three days?" Jarred brazenly challenged.

Hertz's gaze shifted from Jarred to Udell. He nodded to the captain. "See to food and drink." He left.

Chapter 21

THE GRAYISH-PURPLE LIGHT OF POST-TWILIGHT SHONE AT THE opening of another cave. No incidents or rain impeded night two of their travel through Ha'tar. Nollen checked Gilen's legs and hooves in readiness for the third night's journey. Axel squirmed on his bedroll. Gunnar sat up to rub his injured ankle. Axel rose to a sitting position at Gunnar's low, throaty growl.

"What's wrong?" he asked.

"Nothing," chided Gunnar. He placed his hand against the cave wall to stand. He slowly placed weight on his right foot. "Feels a bit better." He took two steps with full weight before he grunted in pain and quickly came off his right foot.

"You won't need to walk. We'll ride most of the way," Nollen said. "I already divided the provisions for breakfast." He pointed to a large flat rock close to where they slept.

"Don't you mean supper?" Gunnar dryly commented.

"Call it what you will, only eat as we ride," Nollen retorted.

"There are only two portions here. What about you?" Axel asked before he took a bite.

"I already ate. I also inspected your horses. They look fit. No hoof nicks or fetlock cuts."

They led the animals from the cave. Axel held the bread in his mouth to mount. Since he used his left leg, Gunnar easily mounted, but careful to settle his right leg down once astride.

Nollen headed northwest from the cave to travel a short gorge. Emerging onto a flat plateau, light shone a short distance to the north. Nollen indicated the lights.

"That is the third border station. Between here and the fourth, is mostly open terrain." Nollen glanced up at the partly cloudy night sky. "Hopefully those are just passing clouds and no rain. The plateau may be flat, but still rocky. Water will only add to the difficulty."

"Are your eyes adjusted enough to see through rain?" asked Axel.

"Not as well as Gilen." Nollen patted his pony's neck.

An hour later, a totally dark sky released a downpour. They descended into another gorge filled with streams of running rainwater. Occasional overhanging rocks and ledges provided some shelter. The floor of the gorge was fed by small waterfalls along the rock face. For another hour, they travelled the gorge.

Around a bend, a group of bats emerged from a hollow cave. Startled, Gilen reared. Nollen fought to bring the frightened pony under control. One bat flew directly into Nollen's head and shoulders. The impact knocked him to the ground, while the bat's wing became tangled in his cloak. The bat squealed when he fought to toss it aside. The bat tried to bite him. A close growl was immediately followed by a wolf that snatched the bat away from Nollen's face. The bat's squeal became silenced when the wolf shook it and slammed it on the ground.

Nollen scrambled to his feet to better view the wolf that kill the bat. "Bardolf?"

Axel drew rein beside Nollen. "Are you hurt?"

Nollen didn't reply, still focused on Bardolf. The wolf left the dead bat to approach Nollen. He nudged and licked Nollen's hand.

"Thank you. I'm well. But what are you doing here?"

Sorrowful, Bardolf began to explain, "The enemy raided the compound. Some were killed, but the rest taken."

"Ida? Grandfather? Jarred?" Nollen murmured with alarm.

"Among those taken."

"Why are you alone? Are the others following them?"

Bardolf's head lowered. "We battled the Black Jackals. I alone survived."

Nollen's knees gave way, and he sat hard on the ground. He fought against weeping, but it proved useless. Bardolf whimpered, as he laid down beside Nollen and rested his head on Nollen's lap.

Axel dismounted to kneel in front of Nollen. "I grieve with you. But take heart, your family is alive."

"For how long?"

"Gott willing, long enough for us to complete our task."

"We're not going to free them?" Nollen spoke in desperation.

Axel seized Nollen by the shoulders. With intense urgency, he spoke. "What I have come to do will free all those faithful, and ultimately, save Eldar. Do you believe me?" His eyes searched Nollen's beleaguered face.

"I want to—"

"Aye or no! Indecision will not help them, or me."

"Did I hear wrong when you said, '*Not fear or resentment but confidence to act!'?*", Gunnar quoted in a tone that suggested he knew the answer.

Nollen took a deep, steady breath. He slowly shook his head. "No, you heard right." He looked steadfastly at Axel. "What exactly are you doing? Tell me straight, no cryptic statements."

"Preparing to do what I must. The first step was meeting you. Now, I need to take possession of the Horn of Kolyn. Then, I will confront Javan in Sener, and fulfill prophecy. Once that is complete, the horn will call the faithful to battle."

"Where is the horn?"

"Arctander said Ronan would know."

Nollen stroked Bardolf's head. "Will you come with us?"

Bardolf stood. "To the end." He licked Nollen's face, which made Nollen chuckle.

Axel pulled Nollen to his feet.

"How much further to the border?" asked Gunnar.

Nollen wiped the tears from his face and eyes. He fetched Gilen before he took stock of the surroundings. "I'll estimate that after we climb out of the gorge. We should see the fourth station from there."

Fortunately, the rain stopped when they reached the place to climb out.

"The trail is too steep to ride. Normally, I let Gilen go first, and I follow. If I lead and slipped, I could pull him down on top of me. It's best if we tie the horses together and let Gilen lead them while we follow. Will your ankle hold?" he asked Gunnar.

"I'll make it hold," came the determined reply.

"Line your horses behind Gilen." Nollen took the rope that hung on his saddle and threw it to stretch out the length. He tied one end to the back of Gilen's saddle. Next, came Axel's horse. Nollen threaded the rope through the dee ring on the saddle where the chest strap attached. He ran it out the rear dee ring for the rump strap then did the same on Gunnar's horse. He also wound up the excess rope and tied it to the saddle. He left enough slack between each horse for ease of movement.

"Is it safe at the top? We're taking a great risk sending them unprotected," said Axel.

"I hope so, because this is the safest way for them, and us."

"Bardolf. Go before the horses, and make certain all is well," Axel instructed.

Nollen waited until Bardolf was out of sight before he took the bridle to stand in front of his pony. "Gilen, we're counting on you to get these inexperienced fellows up safely." Gilen snorted and rubbed his head against Nollen's chest. With a confident smile, he stepped aside and slapped Gilen's rump. "Up, boy!"

Shortly, they heard the snorting of effort and sounds of loose gravel falling.

"Is something wrong already?" asked Gunnar.

"No. It's just steep and rocky." Nollen prevented Axel from starting the climb. "Wait a few moments more, otherwise loose gravel will be hitting you in the face." He listened closely. He didn't release Axel until the sounds of falling gravel ceased. "Gunnar, you go first. We'll keep pace."

"I'm not an invalid, boy!"

"I only—" Nollen began to protest when Axel waved him to take the point.

Nollen wasn't completely out of earshot when Axel emphatically said to Gunnar, "I *will* take the rear."

Despite a mumbled protest, Gunnar followed Nollen.

It wasn't long before Axel and Gunnar realized the slippery hazard of the trail. Though wide enough to ride, the unsure footing made for many slips, trips, and near falls. A few times, Axel had to brace Gunnar when his right ankle gave way. A few painful grunts and grumbles escaped Gunnar's gritted teeth of effort.

Near the top of the arduous climb, Gunnar slowed his pace. He labored to breathe due to pain. Axel tried to climb up and help, but the gravel moved beneath his feet. He fell to his knees.

"Gunnar! Take hold of the rope so I can pull you up," Nollen called. He threw the rope.

Gunnar fumbled to catch it. He groped along the rocks. "I got it but wait!" He looked down the trail. "Axel?"

"I'm right behind you."

"Can you get a hold of the rope?"

"I'll try." It took a moment of sliding and grabbing before Axel successfully held the rope. "Got it!"

"Hold on!" Nollen shouted.

To Axel and Gunnar's surprise, the rope moved faster than expected. They hurried to keep hold and walk upright. They reached the top in a rush. Gunnar fell face first to the ground. Axel stumbled over Gunnar's legs, but managed to remain on his feet.

"How did you …?" Axel stopped his question when he saw the rope still attached to Gilen's saddle. Nollen held the pony's bridle.

"I don't think I've been pulled by a pony before," huffed Gunnar. He sat up to brush off the dust and gravel.

"We should rest a while before continuing." Nollen took a drink from his flask then handed it to Gunnar. Axel drank from his own flask.

"I hope we ride from now on, because I don't think I can walk after that," Gunnar groused an admission.

"We ride." Nollen sat.

Axel inspected his horse. The animal breathed hard and lathered in sweat. "What about the horses? They haven't eaten anything but a few weeds between rocks."

"There's a creek less than two miles. I usually let Gilen drink, and freely eat of the scrub by the bank."

After a short break of ten minutes, Axel helped Gunnar mount. Twenty minutes later, they reached the creek. Staying in the saddle, they let their horses drink and eat whatever they could find.

Riding an hour further from the creek, ragged pine trees dotted the landscape. The clouds cleared to reveal the moon and stars through the cover of spindling evergreens.

Axel observed the bright night sky. "We made it under cover just in time." He then peered forward to view the change in landscape. "Nollen, are there markers to tell us when we enter Ganel?"

"Aye. Large stone runes carved with unicorns, lions, and ancient writing."

The terrain under the pines proved less hazardous, as scrubby vegetation and pine needles softened the ground. After three miles, they reached the edge of the spindly forest plateau.

Nollen drew to a halt. He pointed to the western horizon. "See those lights? The closest is the fifth Gorland station, with the furthest being near the Ganel border."

"We passed the fourth station? When?" Gunnar glanced back.

"I wasn't sure if the shortcut was accessible. Last time it was blocked by a rock slide." Nollen pursed his lips in annoyance. "There had never been bats in that cave before."

"How much time did we save?"

"At least half-a-day's ride."

"About five or six miles," said Gunnar, impressed.

"Well, the next station can't be more than ten miles," said Axel. He waved toward the far border station.

"About seven," said Nollen. "We'll stop for the night in the valley."

"But we haven't traveled all night," argued Gunnar.

"Can you make it up another climb out of the valley? Because it's the same with horses going first," said Nollen.

At Gunnar's huff of annoyance, Axel said, "We'll rest."

Nollen sent a wry grin in Gunnar's direction. "Don't worry, Once in Ganel, we'll be able to continue without hinderance."

Fortunately, the ride down from the plateau was not too steep or rocky. The horses easily made the trek into the valley. They entered a ruined stone structure.

"What is this place, another of your hideaways?" Gunnar wryly questioned. He gingerly dismounted.

"I have made use of it, but I'm not sure of its history. The Ha'tar aren't as skillful as whoever built this." Nollen led Gilen to what appeared to have been a stable at one time.

Axel made Gunnar sit before he followed Nollen with the horses. The partial overgrown roof provided shelter. There were small wooden troughs, rough and worm eaten, but useable. Nollen left enough slack in the tether for Gilen to graze. He poured some water from his large flask into the trough.

"They can nibble on the scrub," he told Axel. He placed the saddlebag over his shoulder and removed his bedroll.

Upon returning to the main structure, they found Gunnar had started a small fire with what debris he found.

"Being under cover, the Ha'tar or Gorlanders shouldn't see small flames," Gunnar explained to a frowning Nollen. Bardolf laid beside the fire, which prompted Gunnar to say, "Even he agrees."

Axel grinned, as he put down two saddlebags and bedrolls.

"Well, if you insist, why not make it so we can toast the bread," Nollen chided with sarcasm.

"Wonderful idea." Gunnar proceeded to stoke the fire.

"I didn't mean ..." Nollen huffed with frustration. "No, hot sausage. That *can* be smelled."

Axel couldn't stifle his amusement while he fixed the bedrolls for himself and Gunnar.

Nollen threw up his hands and left the building. He made search of the perimeter. He met Axel outside when he returned.

"Is everything secure?" asked Axel.

"Aye."

Axel grinned. "Gunnar is a seasoned warrior. He taught me everything I know about survival. Traveling hostile territory isn't new to either of us."

Nollen sat on a fallen hewn stone. "I realize that. But I've been charged with *your* safety on *this* journey. I can't do that if you both ignore my advice about places and people you know little-to-nothing about."

Axel sat beside Nollen. "Gunnar was born in the Freelands."

"He fled as a boy," Nollen countered. "Much has changed in the decades since."

"Aye, Eldar is worse than I remember." Gunnar hobbled over. He brought two pieces of toast with melted cheese. "There is a thin slice of sausage under the cheese." He gave them each a piece.

"You warmed the sausage?" asked Nollen, incredulous.

"No. I melted the cheese over it to prevent any smell."

Nollen didn't reply.

"How about we work together to see *our charge* safety through this ordeal?" Gunnar pointedly spoke to Nollen.

Looking up into the face of the veteran warrior, Nollen felt as if he were seeing Gunnar for the first time. He couldn't deny Gunnar's age and experience were well beyond his own. With his mouth full, Nollen nodded, and raised the remaining bread in a salute of agreement.

"Good. I'll take the first watch," said Gunnar.

Chapter 22

JONAS RODE WITH DESTRY FOR THE RETURN TRIP TO GILROY. THE four-day journey from Vanora gave him time to brood. His mind argued and reasoned over recent events and his actions. With each argument, Hertz's threat against his family repeated. The compound was simply the first logical guess. He couldn't have known Nollen wasn't there. It did yield results in the capture of Arctander and Ida. He felt a tiny twinge of regret for Ida. She hadn't done him harm like Nollen. Her only fault was being among the faithful who corrupted his family. The regret soon turned to bitterness.

During the journey from the compound to Vanora, Jonas avoided any interaction with Ida, Arctander, or Jarred. His father, Oberon, was Arctander's brother. Arctander might seek to use that relationship against Jonas, since the brothers were very close before Oberon's death. When alive, Oberon kept the family connection secret since the activities at Far Point helped the Faithful and could endanger his brother. That, and certain perks gained due to the commerce of trade. Being a stop along the trade-routes earned the inn a reputation of hospitality and brought in more customers. Jonas carried on his father's wishes, until one day, everything changed.

Despite being his uncle, anger swelled against Arctander. What culminated at Hertz's arrival with a charge of treason, began when Arctander converted Sharla and the boys to the Faith regarding the True King. His father spoke privately about Faith, but not with such devotion as Arctander. Fury and revenge drove Jonas to lead Bernal and soldiers to the compound. He blamed Arctander more than Nollen for the calamity that befell his family.

Family! Thought of his wife and sons gnawed at him. Jonas screwed his eyes shut against visions of the group leaving for Sener. He hadn't planned to witness the departure, it just happened. Sharla's glare pierced his heart, for in that moment, he saw her bitter disappointment and pain. If not for his impulsive burst of angry denial, he would be going to Sener with them.

Jonas forced his mind back to his present task – finding Nollen. Since leaving Vanora to head home, he wracked his brain for possibilities. However, there were just too many options. Oh, he knew some secret trading passages, just not which one Nollen would take. Throw two foreigners into the problem, and the issue became complicated. Where exactly would Nollen take them? And why? If he knew their identity, he might be able to determine a destination. Alas, no one Jonas questioned before they left could provide clarification. All anyone knew is the foreigners posed a great danger to Eldar.

What concern is that to me if my family dies? his mind argued.

"We've reached the ferry." Destry's voice broke through Jonas' dreary consideration.

"What?" Jonas sounded like a man woken from a dream.

"I said, we're at the ferry. Where has your mind been?"

"Down too many roads," groused Jonas.

"Hopefully one of them will lead to Nollen. Wait while I get the pulley tackle." Destry unlocked the ferry house door and went inside.

When Destry emerged, Jonas asked, "Why didn't you let Galt run the ferry in your absence?"

Offended, Destry chided, "Are you implying I don't trust my brother?"

"No, just curious."

Before Destry led his horse onto the ferry, he asked, "If you were leaving on an important trip, would you give Sharla the keys to the stockroom? Would you *trust* her to keep a good record while away?"

Jonas stiffened at the question. "Why bring my wife into this?"

"Because people aren't always what they appear. Like *your wife.* Now, wait while I prepare for passage."

Although the question about Sharla pricked him, Jonas thought better than to pursue the conversation. The relationship between Destry and Galt had no bearing on his current situation. He dismounted just as Destry was about to place the pulley tackle on the line for the ferry to cross to Gilroy. With the ramp down, Jonas hurried to lead his horse onto the ferry.

"I said wait! I need to prepare—" Destry's objection was cut short when Jonas poked a dagger blade against his side.

"No pulley. We aren't going to Gilroy. Head for the Great Falls basin."

"What? Are you mad? If—" Another poke in the side stopped further protest.

Jonas' eyes narrowed. "I have nothing more to lose. You, on the other hand, have your life to lose."

Destry stared warily at Jonas. "You realize I can cry out for help?"

"You wouldn't utter two words." Jonas pressed the dagger uncomfortably close.

Destry gasped in terrified surprise. His words barely above a cautious whisper. "I must be free to go about the ferry to do as you instruct."

"One false step."

Destry grimaced at feeling the blade point prick his side. He became dumbfounded at Jonas' determined desperation. "You really will kill me."

"Slowly raise the ramp and launch the ferry," Jonas said.

With Jonas just a step away, Destry moved about the ferry for launch. Once safely from shore, Destry turned the ferry to head due east. He used the rudder to steer and propel the ferry like a fin tail.

"What do you hope to gain by this? Hertz said if you found Nollen your family would be spared," said Destry.

"No, he said, they *might* be. Yet everyone knows, prisoners taken to Sener are executed. There is no mercy, only death."

"They're traitors! Believers in this rumored True King!" spat Destry with contempt.

"They're my family!" Jonas's passion brought him dangerously close to Destry, dagger first.

"Stay your hand!" Destry exclaimed in a panic. "I'm taking you where you want to go." He breathed a bit easier when Jonas backed away. "What do you plan on doing? Rescue them?"

"I'll do what I must."

"You denounced them. I heard you."

Jonas' icy glare made Destry recoil. "Enough talk! Tend to the ferry."

"You've changed, Jonas," droned Destry.

"So, would you if this happened to your wife and children."

Destry didn't reply to the statement, rather said, "It will take until midnight to reach the mouth of the basin."

Hours passed with little conversation. Most comments came from Destry about the current and locations. Occasionally, Jonas paced the ferry, vexed and impatient. He always held the dagger ready.

Even as the night grew later, Jonas showed no sign of fatigue. Destry, on the other hand, fought to say awake. He woke to a poke in the side, totally unaware he had fallen asleep at the rudder.

"Can you tell where we are now?" Jonas demanded.

Destry shook the sleep from his head. "Give me a moment." He looked over the side at the water, as he pushed on the rudder to feel resistance. He cupped a hand over one ear to listen. "I think we're near the basin mouth. The current feels stronger, and I hear water churning."

Jonas moved to the bow. He peered out into the darkness. He quickly went back the stern. "Head for the north shore."

"There is no mooring for the ferry."

"Run aground!" Jonas held up the dagger.

Destry pushed hard against the rudder to turn the ferry toward shore. It proved difficult to see a good landing spot. Shortly, the ferry lurched and jerked when it struck something. It skidded a bit further before it abruptly stopped. The motion threw Jonas and Destry to the deck.

Hearing a blade clang, Destry assumed Jonas became unarmed. He scrambled to his feet to charge Jonas. The mistake proved reckless. Jonas snatched up the dagger, but unable to avoid the charge. They fell hard against the rail.

The sudden stop upset the horses, while the fight between the men, agitated the animals further. They tried to get away, off the ferry, if possible. A horse ran into Destry and caused him to fall onto the deck. Jonas hastened to lower the forward ramp. Before he could mount his horse, Destry came at him again. This time, Jonas slashed at Destry, and landed a serious cut to Destry's chest. Jonas used the hilt to cold-cock Destry unconscious. Both horses bolted from the ferry. The sloshing of water and mud halted total flight, as the horses just managed to reach dry land.

Jonas sheathed the dagger and jumped into the shallow water. With all his might, he tried to push the ferry out to deeper water. He slipped a few times, but with each attempt, the ferry drifted away from shore. Unable to push again, Jonas stopped in waist high water to catch his breath. He watched the ferry become caught in the current. He wearily made it back to land. The horses grazed upon some water grass. Jonas picked up the reins of his horse to lead it further inland before he mounted. Whatever happened now, there was no turning back.

Chapter 23

IN HIS OFFICE AT SENER CASTLE, DOLUS FEVERISHLY WORKED ON dispatches for each Territory. The Son of Eldar's arrival called for acceleration of the plan. Execution still needed to be precise, just more forceful on compliance. Fortunately, Sylvan provided Dolus with any information the minister required. Both became buried in papers, books, and old manuscripts.

"Dolus!" shouted Javan.

Being so deeply immersed in his task, Dolus didn't notice Javan until he pounded on the desk. "Elector," he said in surprise.

"You were scheduled to meet me in the council chamber over an hour ago."

Dolus glanced at the clock on the mantle. "Forgive me, Elector. I just now finished composing the notifications for the Territories. As *we* discussed," he emphasized the agreement.

Javan held out his hand for the dispatches. Instead of yielding them, Dolus read the opening statement.

"*By decree of Javan, Elector of Eldar, rightful ruler of the Six Territories, be it known to all that the following Tribute is required a fortnight from receiving this directive,*" began Dolus. "I listed the items: Sword of Emet, Horn of Kolyn; Sadok; The Book of Kings, Star of Conant, and Shevet."

"You believe those relics from Oleg's reign still exist? That they survived the past two-hundred-years?" Javan asked with skepticism.

"According to lore, Oleg distributed them to the six high priests for safe keeping. After all, a king needs his crown, scepter, and sword."

"And the book? Just a bunch of old names."

"It establishes the lineage." Dolus' eyes narrowed in regard of the directive. "The horn is key to all the rest. Its sole purpose is to summons his followers. Thus, exposing all traitors." His eyes lifted from the paper to the lion. "By gaining possession of the other Treasures, we undermine any efforts to challenge your right to rule."

Still not fully convinced, Javan asked, "And this Star of Conant? I don't recall you mentioning that."

"A large diamond gifted to Oleg by the Eagles as an adornment to Sadok, the crown. It is said to give the one who wears the crown wisdom and insight beyond mortal ability."

"All of them could have been melted down, cut up, and sold for a great price."

"I made certain these items will be brought to Sener." Dolus proceeded to read: "*Failure to secure these Tributes will result in the utter destruction of the Territory – or Territories – responsible.*"

Sylvan fought to display any emotion to the threat, while Javan became annoyed.

"I understand the need for such a threat. Yet, if fulfillment proves necessary, how will it secure my reign if there is no one left to rule?"

Dolus moved from behind the desk. "I don't believe you have anything to be concerned about. The Ha'tar and Nefal will surely bring them due to the ancient alliance. Men of The Doane are cowards. Past actions have shown they are unwilling to oppose you. The main objectors will be the usual, Ganel, Freelanders, and the Eagles."

"Even using mortal representatives, the Eagles haven't brought Tribute in years," scoffed Javan. "Anything we've done to force them ends in failure."

"If we find the other Treasures, I'm sure we can compel the Eagles to give up Conant."

Javan knitted his brow, thoughtful. "How will all this affect the Blood Oath?"

"Without these, the Blood Oath will fail, thus securing Eldar from any claim but yours."

Javan's sneer turned toward the lion. "And we will finally be rid of this cursed creature?"

"The lion's roar will never again be heard in Eldar," Dolus declared.

With smug satisfaction, Javan commanded, "Send the dispatches immediately! And summon the Cursians. We will leave nothing to chance." He marched from the room.

In heavy silence, Sylvan watched the exchange. When the door closed behind Javan's departure, he said, "My lord, he forgot to sign the decree."

Dolus huffed with impatience. "My signature will be enough." He scribbled his name on each dispatch, folded the paper, and applied the official seal in wax. He held them out to Sylvan. "Dispatch the messengers."

Sylvan took them. "My lord, they can't travel at night. The danger is too great."

"What?" thundered Dolus. He looked toward window when motioned by Sylvan. Night had fallen. He sneered in frustration. "At first light."

"Aye, my lord." Sylvan bowed.

Once he left Dolus' office, Sylvan hurried to his private room at the rear of Sener Castle. The old dodge about the dangers of night travel worked almost every time. Not that there wasn't some truth to the statement about nocturnal hazards. Personal exaggerations, and concocted stories of ambushes gave him time to carry out his covert assignment.

Sylvan locked the door to his room. This time he didn't need to carefully copy the dispatches since he already knew the contents. He quickly wrote six short cryptic messages and slipped them into the interior pocket of his doublet. After he secured the dispatches in his personal desk, he left.

Being as his quarters were located at the rear of the castle, reaching the storehouse unseen proved relatively easy. Besides, if any servant or soldier questioned him, he pulled rank as Minister Dolus' personal secretary.

Inside the storehouse, he climbed the stairs to the very top room. He reached the hidden coop through a concealed door. Moonlight filtered through a slated window. He carefully lit a single candle. Added light revealed the dozen shield owls that occupied individual cages. A cross between a common pigeon and barn owl, the large specialty birds were highly prized for their ability to fly great distances at night. Six different colors coded the twelve cages.

"I have an important assignment for you, my beauties," he spoke to the birds.

He removed one bird from a different colored cage and set them on a table. From a box, he withdrew six small pouches, into which, he placed a note. He tied one pouch to the leg of each shield owl. He gently blew out the candle.

"This is of vital importance. Fly swift and straight, in the name of the True King!" He opened the window for the shield owls to depart.

Sylvan secured the coop and made certain the concealed door was well covered. He stopped on a lower level of the storehouse to pick up a small cask of mead. After that, he proceeded to the barracks where he informed the messengers of their morning assignment. Upon returning to his room, he was surprised to find Dolus there waiting.

"My lord?"

"Sylvan." The minister casually moved about the small chamber to inspect everything.

Sylvan used the action of setting the cask on a table near the door to regain his composure. "Is there something I can help you with, my lord?"

"Rumors have been circulating about a spy in the castle." Dolus paused in his course about the room. "What do you know about it?"

Sylvan shrugged. Despite clenched fists, he replied in a calm voice. "Not much. I've been too busy to pay much attention to idle chatter."

"Where were you just now?"

"I went to the storehouse, to pick up your mead for breakfast." He indicated the cask. "Then I told the messengers to report to me before dawn."

Dolus' eyes narrowed. "The dispatches?"

Sylvan unlocked the center draw of his desk to show them to Dolus. "Safe until morning."

Dolus examined each dispatch for signs of tampering. Satisfied at finding none, he placed them back in the drawer. With a last side glance to Sylvan, he said, "Good night."

"My lord." Sylvan bowed. He waited a moment before he locked and bolted the door. Most rooms had only a single lock, but few also had a metal bolt for added security. Being Dolus' secretary afforded him extra protection due to his involvement with state documents.

Since the confirmation of the Son of Eldar's presence, his assignment became more urgent and hazardous. Dolus' deal with darkness made him very dangerous. With this bold move to gain possession of the Treasures, Sylvan knew a personal choice must soon be made. He just hoped he survived to make that choice.

Chapter 24

THE FINAL NIGHT OF THEIR TREK THROUGH HA'TAR TERRITORY pelted them with heavy icy rain. Soaked to the skin, the cool night air added to the misery. Even the horses snorted and grunted in occasional protest of the storm. Only Bardolf seemed oblivious to the elements.

The driving rain made it difficult for Nollen to see the trail. It became particularly hazardous when they attempted to navigate a deep gorge. More overhangs provided periodic shelter from the rain, but also created dark shadows.

Emerging from the gorge, Nollen lost sight of the lights from the last Gorland border station. He paused after two hundred yards to gauge direction. He swore under his breath. "The station is south of us!"

"Meaning what?" asked Gunnar.

"Due to this blasted rain, I took a wrong turn, and we crossed the border into Gorland!" Nollen turned his pony. "We need to double-back to find the right trail."

"Halt!" A squad of Gorland soldiers blocked their path of retreat.

Nollen dropped the reins to hold up his hands. Axel and Gunnar followed his example. Nollen spoke to the soldiers. "We mean no harm. We got lost in the rain. Let us go in peace and return the way we came."

"Your speech is Eldarian."

"Aye. I'm a trader of goods."

"I don't see any pack mules."

"We're on our way to negotiate a trade route in Ganel when we took a wrong turn."

Bardolf arrived to take up a defensive position. When the lead soldier moved closer to Nollen, Bardolf growled, his hackles raised.

"Quiet, Bardolf," Nollen warned.

"It's a wolf!" the leader exclaimed. "Shoot it!" he ordered an archer.

Axel moved his horse to shield Bardolf. "No!"

The archer barely stayed his shot, and only did so by lowering his bow.

"Why are you protecting it?" demanded the leader.

"Bardolf acted in defense of us. That should tell you he is traveling with us as a companion," Axel sternly replied.

"I never heard that about a wolf," scoffed the leader. "And *you* don't sound Eldarian."

"They are Bertrandians come to Eldar to establish peaceful trade relationship," Nollen offered a hurried explanation. "I was giving them a tour of my trade route in hopes they would agree." He then spoke with eager animation. "Ah! I have something that may interest you. Of Bertrandian origin." He reached for his saddlebag.

"Slowly!" the leader warned.

"No weapon, just a trinket." Carefully, Nollen opened the left saddlebag. It took some digging, but he found what he wanted. "A necklace. Made from rare stones, and sure to please any woman." He held it out for the leader to take.

"Bring the lantern," the leader called.

A soldier came forward to illuminate the necklace for examination. Several soldiers *oooed* and *awwed* at the highly polished white marble like stones with an iridescent quality.

"I've never seen anything like this. This is Bertrandian?" asked the leader.

"It is *yours* if you allow us to leave peacefully," offered Nollen.

"Have you any more trinkets like this one?"

"Alas, no. The stone is so rare, it was the only one they brought to help secure the route."

For a moment, the leader examined the stone. His brows drawn in consideration.

"It is worth enough, that should you sell it, money can be divided among the squad," Nollen shrewdly suggested.

The leader waved. "Let them pass!"

The soldiers moved aside to allow access to the gorge.

"What is going on?"

Nollen, Axel, Gunnar heard a voice behind them.

"Sir! They mistakenly crossed the border and gave us these rare stones to leave in peace."

"Those are worthless moonstones, you idiot!"

"Run!" Nollen shouted and kicked Gilen into a gallop. He, Axel, and Gunnar raced for the gorge.

Twang! Twang! Two arrows whizzed passed them. In the driving night rain, lethal aim proved difficult. A third *twang!* Nollen cried out when an arrow deeply grazed his right shoulder. At the gorge, he made a sharp left turn, followed immediately by Axel. Two more arrows bounced off the rock walls after Gunnar made the turn.

"I hope you know where you're going this time!" shouted Gunnar.

Nollen didn't reply, as he steered Gilen through the gorge at top speed. He briefly slowed the pony when Bardolf ran in front of him. He knocked the hood from his head to clear his vision. Gilen began to skid around a sharp curve. Nollen shifted to stay balanced in the saddle. Bardolf stopped just ahead. The wolf barked before he went left. Nollen didn't see the turn until he was almost on top of it. Gilen slipped and stumbled when he drew rein to stop.

"This way!" Nollen shouted back to Axel and Gunnar. Seeing them draw near, he snapped the reins for Gilen to change course. With a neigh of protest, the pony launched forward.

Nollen looked back to see Axel and Gunnar make the turn. The gorge path opened into a wide river plain near a decline to an embankment. He turned forward just in time to see the trail end. He violently pulled Gilen's head to the right. Unfortunately, when Gilen responded, the momentum threw Nollen off to the left. He tumbled down the embankment and into the water near shore. He lay unconscious.

Axel caught Gilen. He and Gunnar carefully guided the horses down the embankment. Bardolf whimpered in an attempt to rouse Nollen. His head and shoulder were out of the water, but the rest of his body submerged. Axel silenced Bardolf when they heard commotion from the overhead trail.

"Where did they go?"

"Doesn't matter. This is Eldar's border."

Axel and Gunnar waited until they only heard rain. Axel signaled Bardolf to go up. With stealth, the wolf climbed the bank. He sniffed the ground, and the air. He ran back.

"They're gone," Bardolf reported.

Axel quickly got down from the saddle. He placed his hands under Nollen's shoulders and dragged him out of the water onto the shore. His examination caused the young man to wake with a start. "Easy."

Nollen groaned and tried to sit. He hissed in pain and grabbed his right shoulder.

"We need to find a place where I can medicine the wound." Axel steadied Nollen in aiding him to his feet.

Nollen took a moment to scan the surroundings. "This should be Ganel. Lake Helivan's watershed serves as a border between Ha'tar and Ganel. Only the crossing is further down." He carefully motioned south with his left hand.

"Can we travel along the shoreline to reach it?" asked Gunnar. He held the reins of all the mounts.

"It depends upon how high the water is." Nollen reached for Gilen with the intent to mount. He did so with aid from Axel.

They slowly rode along the shoreline. The animals sloshed through mud caused by the rain. Near the crossing, Nollen urged Gilen up the bank. Pain made him rock forward in the saddle.

"Are you well enough to continue?" Axel asked.

"I'll be fine in a moment. We need to cross the bridge."

"What bridge?" asked Gunnar.

Nollen swallowed back pain to speak. "Axel, behind that vine, you'll find a stone rune. Hidden among the writing is a secret button that will reveal a lever."

Once on foot, Axel lowered his hood for better visibility. He moved the vine. His hands traced the etchings of the runes. It contained both words and animals. "It's ancient Eldarian."

"I don't know what it says, but halfway down you'll find a word with the letter 'o'. Push the center of the circle."

Axel again followed instructions. A lever dropped out from the side of the rune closest to the water.

"Pull it all the way down."

It took some effort to make the lever move. Axel and Gunnar became startled by the sound of gears and scratching stone. From the water, rose a wall on either side of a soon to appear stone bridge. The wall served as a barrier to hold the water back.

"There is a rune on the other side that will hide the bridge," Nollen explained. He coaxed Gilen across the bridge.

Axel walked his horse across the bridge to the visible rune. "I take it this is it." After an affirming nod from Nollen, he asked, "Does it act the same as the other one?"

"Aye."

When activated, the walls slid back under water, and the bridge disappeared beneath the current.

"Press the 'o' again, and the lever with retract," said Nollen.

Axel hoisted himself back into the saddle. "Is there a place nearby where we can rest and tend your wound?"

Nollen groaned with great discomfort. He just nodded. He led them a half-mile from the watershed to an old lean-to shed. He fell to ground when he attempted to dismount.

Once again, Axel hurried to aid Nollen. He carried the young man inside. "Gunnar, fetch his bedroll."

Nollen shivered and moaned. Gunnar placed the bedroll down for Axel to lay Nollen on. He wrapped the blanket around Nollen from the waist down, leaving Axel access to Nollen's upper body.

Axel felt Nollen's forehead. "This is more than a simple wound. You've developed a fever. Do Gorlanders use poison on their arrows?"

Nollen shook his head. "C-c-o-old. Wet."

"This time I'm making a good fire to keep us warm. No argument," Gunner told Nollen. "If I can find dry wood."

"Hidden under a fake mound of moss. Back ..." Nollen spoke through shivers and made a feeble wave with his hand.

"You think of everything, don't you?" Gunnar hobbled off in a hurry.

"Covert family shelters," Nollen hissed through the pain of chattering teeth.

"Enough talk." Axel unfastened Nollen's cloak to reveal the angry wound for medicine. "I know the names of the six priests entrusted by Oleg. When Arctander gave me the Book of Kings, I suspected your family goes back to Eskil. Thus, secrets handed down for generations."

Nollen's face screwed in pain at Axel's administrations.

"The salve should help ease the pain."

Gunnar returned with an arm load of firewood. He cast a few anxious glances at Nollen while he prepared a robust fire to warm the lean-to. "Is he as bad as he looks?" he whispered his concern, so as not to disturb Nollen, who appeared to be sleeping.

"I fear so. He says Gorlanders don't use poison, but I've not seen a fever take hold so quickly," Axel replied in kind.

"We're traveling in cold, wet conditions."

"That's what he said. Only I'm not convinced. He showed no signs of illness or fever until I pulled him out of the water."

"You think there's a connection?"

Axel titled his head in consideration. "Something caused this to happen suddenly. Keep watch. I need to seek Gott for wisdom."

Gunnar drew his sword to stand at the opening of the lean-to with his back to the fire. He heard Axel softly begin to pray. Nollen reminded him of Axel in his youth. True, Axel's mind was determined on his course, even back then. However, he too fought against taking advice from his elders. There was also a time when Axel struggled with expectations. This prompted his suggestion of taking up the cause with well-placed comments to Nollen.

Still, mentoring another youth was not something Gunnar considered when they arrived. Nollen's likeability, and continued aid, it naturally seemed to shift in that direction. Mutually joining in the effort to protect Axel added another dimension to their association. Nollen also helped tend him during his recovery. Private thoughts soon turned to silent petition for the young trader's recovery.

For half-an-hour, Axel offered verbal petition until …

"Axel!" Gunnar hissed in warning. Axel joined him in the threshold where he carefully pointed to a growing light coming towards them. In guarded anticipation, they watched.

From behind the trees, came an animal-like figure obscured by an aura of light. It halted thirty feet from them. The light faded enough to reveal a magnificent male unicorn; its hide a light grey with a flowing white tail and mane, while the horn, silver. The horses and Gilen gently whinnied and lowered their heads, as if bowing. Bardolf laid down with a whimper of submission.

"My Gott, the legends are true," Gunnar murmured in awe.

The unicorn tossed its head and pawed the ground.

"Put up your sword," Axel hastily whispered. He nudged a mesmerized Gunnar to comply.

"What does it want?"

Axel placed a finger to his lips for silence, though his focus remained on the unicorn. He drew Gunnar aside to allow the unicorn access to the lean-to.

The unicorn approached Nollen and lowered its head to softly nudge his face. Then, it stepped back to bend its head, so the tip of the silver horn touched his forehead. Shimmering light radiated from the horn to envelope Nollen's body. He took in a sudden deep breath then relaxed. The light disappeared when the unicorn lifted its head. Nollen stirred and blinked before he finally opened his eyes. Startled at sight of the unicorn, he sat up.

Axel quickly entered to reassure Nollen. "Be easy!"

"It's a … unicorn!" Nollen stammered in amazement.

"My name is Alfgar, Nollen of Far Point."

"It speaks too!" Gunnar marveled. He moved inside.

Stunned, Nollen asked, "You know who I am?"

Alfgar tossed his head in affirmation. "I have watched you each time you came to Ganel in service of the Shining Ones. Just like I did your father and grandfather."

"Why haven't I ever seen you before?"

"The time had not yet come to make myself known. Now, you bring the Son of Eldar. All creation has longed for this day." He bowed his head to Axel.

Bardolf addressed Alfgar. "I brought them safely here though it cost the lives of my pack."

"Dear Bardolf." Alfgar lowered his head to comfort Bardolf as an act of consolation.

"Gott sent you in response to my prayer for Nollen, didn't he?" said Axel, in more a statement than question.

Alfgar again tossed his head in acknowledgement.

"Then you were right. The fever wasn't natural," said Gunnar to Axel.

"Helivan's watershed protects Ganel from intruders by causing sudden illness when anyone comes in contact with the water. The hidden bridge is the only safe access," Alfgar explained.

"He fell into the water when fleeing Gorland border guards. In the pouring rain, we accidently took a wrong turn," said Gunnar.

Alfgar asked Nollen, "Did you travel Ha'tar at night?"

"Aye."

"Then rest tonight. In the morning, I will escort you through Ganel to the Fortress of Mathena."

Chapter 25

FOR FIVE DAYS, NOLLEN, AXEL, AND GUNNAR FOLLOWED ALFGAR north through Ganel. Even in late fall, the dense and varied landscape wonderfully contrasted the bleakness of Ha'tar. Massive oaks, tall maples, and large spruce trees dominated the forest. Shrubs of various types created groves, while dormant grasslands provided abundant grazing in spring and summer. The noontime sunlight penetrated another patch of forest along their journey.

Constant riding helped Gunnar's ankle heal by staying off it for hours at a time. "Where is Mathena?" he asked.

"It lies just south of the River Endelos' origin at the foothills of the Halvor Mountains," replied Nollen. "We should reach it by nightfall."

They emerged from the woods into a large meadow. On a distant dominating plateau, stood the sprawling Fortress of Mathena. Awed by the sight, Axel drew rein. Gunnar came from the rear to stop beside Axel to stare at the fortress.

Enormous beige crystalline limestone walls stretched along the plateau. The city rose in height to a great cathedral and small castle at the apex. Even at this distance, ornate arches and decorated roofs told of different levels. To the east, a colossal aqueduct served as a bridge over the River Endelos. Water cascaded from the aqueduct to continue its course south.

Nollen, Bardolf, and Alfgar joined Axel and Gunnar.

"Magnificent," breathed Axel in wonderment.

"What you see, is a shadow of what Mathena once was," began Alfgar. "The same with Sener. Centuries of darkness have diminished their splendor. Now, come. We still have five miles to go." Alfgar again took the lead.

"Are we to cross the aqueduct?" asked Gunnar, a hint of nervousness in his voice.

"No, although that is the main entrance. We will use a lesser known gate," replied Alfgar.

"Is it the same gate I use?" asked Nollen.

Alfgar tossed his head and made a snort of affirmation.

A little over an hour later, they pushed through a grove of chokeberry bushes to arrive at the secluded gate. The enormity of the walls dwarfed them, soaring fifty feet above their heads.

Alfgar touched the gate with his horn. *Click! Slide! Creak!* The gate unlocked and opened inward. Alfgar entered first. Four soldiers immediately surrounded them, with swords drawn.

"Stand down!" came a shout from an officer. He bowed his head and placed a clenched fist to his left breast. "Greetings, Lord Alfgar. We weren't expecting you, but you are always welcome."

"Captain Cleary. Inform Lord Ronan I bring important guests. There can be no delay in meeting."

Cleary complied. "You two, do as Lord Alfgar says."

Nollen, Axel, Gunnar, and Bardolf entered behind Alfgar. A soldier quickly closed and locked the gate.

"For being a secluded gate, it is well guarded," said Gunnar.

"All entrances to Mathena are *well* guarded," Cleary rebuffed. He warily eyed Gunnar and Axel. "We know Nollen of Far Point. Who are you?"

"Ask no questions, Captain," Alfgar scolded. "The tunnel."

Cleary again bowed to Alfgar. "Leave the horses. My men will take of them," he told Nollen, Axel, and Gunnar.

With a nod from Axel, Gunnar withdrew the wrapped book from his saddlebag.

"What is that?" Cleary pointed at the book.

"No questions, Captain," Axel sternly said.

Cleary suspiciously regarded Axel. His inspection became interrupted by Alfgar's stomping hoof and furious snort. Taken aback by the unicorn lord's anger, Cleary made a quick salute before he led them down a narrow alley to an old wooden door. He took down a lantern that hung beside the door.

"Harvey, Coyle, lock and guard the door," he instructed the two remaining soldiers.

Cleary increased the flame before he entered the tunnel. It quickly became apparent why they had to leave the horses behind. A mounted man would not fit, as told by Alfgar, who carried his head low to avoid hitting the ceiling. The tunnel was part earthen, part stone, damp, and musty smelling. Shortly, they reached stone steps. Axel, Nollen, and Gunnar couldn't help but notice that Alfgar's hooves made no sound upon the stone. Forty steps led to the next level.

The second level turned right and continued in a gradual climb to another set of stone stairs. Forty steps brought them to a third level. They repeated the tunnel and forty steps to the sixth and final level. It ended at a door. Nollen, Axel, and Gunnar breathed heavy, and sweated profusely from climbing the stuffy passage.

They entered what appeared to be an antechamber. With no windows, Cleary used a match to take fire from a low lantern to light the room's other two lampstands. The soft glow revealed oak paneled walls and modest furnishings.

"You can refresh yourselves over there, while you wait. I will inform Lord Ronan," he said.

Two basins with pitchers beside them sat upon a richly carved oak sideboard. Towels hung over metal bars next to the sideboard. Nollen hung back to allow Axel and Gunnar first use of the basins.

Axel sat after his finished refreshing. "That climb was quite a workout. Is this how you come to Mathena?" he asked Nollen.

"Aye, the few times I needed to see Lord Ronan. Mostly, I meet Baron Irwin at an inn located on the southeast side of the city." Nollen took his turn at the basin.

"What room lies beyond this door?" Gunnar went to the door Clearly used to exit. Locked.

"The Great Hall," Alfgar replied since Nollen washed.

"Hardly good hosts to lock us in," chided Gunnar.

"Precaution." Alfgar tossed his head in Axel's direction.

"For me or them?" challenged Axel.

"Both."

"The Faithful will do anything to protect you, Son of Eldar," said Bardolf.

Axel sat forward to speak with sympathetic earnestness. "The sacrifice of your pack grieves me more than I can say."

Bardolf placed a paw on Axel's leg. "It is small a price compared to what awaits you in Sener."

A sober smile appeared, as Axel stroked Bardolf's head.

"You know about his task?" Gunnar asked.

"All The First Ones do. It is what we have longed for since the overthrow."

"Yet also dreaded," added Alfgar somberly. "Othniel tried to encourage us, but when he was captured, we feared the worst. That Gott had totally withdrawn his spirit from Eldar." He looked directly at Axel. "Your arrival has renewed our hope."

"Captured?" questioned Nollen. "We heard Othniel was killed. Grandfather mourned the news."

The unicorn lord snorted with anger. "I witnessed his capture, and unable to prevent it."

"Then the Great White Lion may still be alive?" asked Gunnar, hopeful.

"Difficult to say," chided Alfgar. "But the power used to trap him could only come from the enemy. Othniel is too wise and cunning to succumb to mere mortals."

"What happened?" asked Axel.

Alfgar eyes narrowed, and his voice filled with fury. "A trap was laid using information known only to The First Ones about your coming. As precaution, I accompanied Othniel since other signs had not yet appeared. However, the details were too specific to be ignored." He huffed another snort. "By the time we realized the deception, I became ensnared by a mesh of unbreakable vines. My horn caught so I couldn't use it to free myself. At the same moment, I heard the loud incantation summon a powerful bolt of light. It struck Othniel. He immediately became paralyzed. When mortals approached him, I grew still to avoid being seen." He sighed with great regret. "Not until they took him away in a cart, could I summon help."

"Why did you not call The First Ones to prevent his capture?" asked Nollen, confused and bit incredulous.

"Because such power would have be used to wipe us out! Leaving none to help when the Son of Eldar *truly* arrived."

Axel moved to Alfgar and stroked the unicorn's neck. "Such loyalty and sacrifice are beyond words capable of comfort. Nonetheless, accept my deepest gratitude, and pledge to fulfill my task."

Alfgar laid his head against Axel in such a way that his horn rested on the Axel's shoulder.

Cleary returned. He still carried the lantern. "Lord Ronan will receive you now. Please follow me." He held the door open for them to exit.

Cleary escorted them down an outer aisle of the Great Hall. Whereas the exterior of Mathena dimmed over the centuries, the splendor of the Great Hall remained intact. Arches of white veined marble reached to the curved mosaic painted ceiling. Color tiles formed patterns in the white marble floor. Four immense chandeliers hung from the ceiling. Ornate chains were used to lower them for lighting. Only two were fully lit, as the group made their way down the side aisle.

Once past the platform, Cleary turned right into the corridor that ran directly behind the platform. The hall consisted of no windows, and only two mounted wall lanterns for light. He paused before the only door.

After a quick knock of two raps, the captain opened the door and announced;

"Lord Alfgar, Bardolf, and guests."

By the furnishings and size of this room, it served as a study. More wood paneling, a large hearth, arched windows, and all trappings of comfort for the occupants. The magnificent view through the windows shown with the colors of a late afternoon sunset. Ronan stood before the fire chatting with Cormac and Irwin. They made the same bow to Alfgar as Cleary did earlier.

"My lord Alfgar. This is an unexpected pleasure," said Ronan. "Bardolf." He smiled a greeting. "Nollen, welcome," his tone turned sympathetic. "News has reached us about what happened at Far Point."

"The situation is more desperate than you realize, my lord. They raided the compound," Nollen dreadfully reported.

Alarmed, Ronan asked, "Arctander?"

"Taken. Along with Ida, Jarred, and those who survived." Nollen's words trailed off into hushed pain.

"Merciful heaven." Ronan swore.

"All is not lost," said Axel.

Ronan closely observed Axel. "By your speech and clothes, you are not Eldarian."

"No, I was not born here, but my lineage is very old."

"Ronan, Bardolf and I have taken great pains to bring you the Son of Eldar," announced Alfgar.

The shock of the Ganels was palpable. "You?" Ronan questioned Axel.

"I am Axel, from the royal line of Oleg." He withdrew the letter from the inside breast pocket to hand Ronan. "This is from Arctander. Written the day we left the compound - prior to the raid."

Ronan turned it over to view the waxy mark.

"Is it from Arctander?" asked Cormac.

"It bears his seal." Ronan broke the wax to read. He looked with expectant urgency to Axel. "The signet!"

Axel removed his glove to show the royal signet ring. He also nodded to Gunnar, who unwrapped the book. "The Book of Kings."

With gentle reverence, Ronan traced the markings on the gilded cover. The embossed signet matched Axel's ring.

"We are here because of this." Axel produced the medallion sent by Nollen's parents. He held it out to Ronan.

The Ganel lord's elation rose with each revelation. He passed the medallion to Cormac and Irwin.

"The rumor was true," breathed Cormac with excitement.

"And the enemy is reacting," stressed Axel.

"Indeed," said Ronan in agreement. "*My liege*, we are at your service." His voice filled with unction, as he knelt to pay homage.

Irwin and Cormac mimicked Ronan. "My liege."

"Rise, my lords." Axel tugged on Ronan's shoulder.

"We must send word to the Eagles and Freelanders that you are here!" Ronan enthusiastically said.

"Aye. The Shining Ones will rise up in your defense!" Cormac added his exuberance.

Axel tried to curb their eagerness. "All in good time, my lords. I must secure the Horn of Kolyn before I proceed to Sener."

Ronan widely smiled and leaned close to Axel. "The horn lies within these walls."

The statement surprised Axel. "Intact?"

"Aye, my liege. Whole and secure," Ronan assured him. A compassionate smile accompanied his words for Nollen. "Alfred was with me when we discovered it. That's how he knew to the send the signal."

Nollen swallowed back his emotions at news to ask, "Why didn't he tell me?"

Ronan gripped Nollen's shoulder to look at him directly. "You were young. He didn't want to expose you to danger before you were ready."

Nollen fought to restrain his anger. "That happened when he and Marmie were taken and executed."

Ronan soberly sighed. "Aye." He voiced the full anger Nollen obviously felt. "Since that day, I have diligently sought to learn who else knew of the horn's discovery! Only three of us were present that day; me, Alfred, and Kendryll. Kendryll mysteriously died shortly thereafter. Followed a month later by your parents."

Nollen's jowls flexed, his fists clenched. "Have you learned anything?"

"Alas, no, it remains a mystery." He took hold of Nollen by both shoulders. "What the enemy used for evil, Gott turned to good. The evidence stands beside you." His nodded to Axel. "Are you prepared to finish what your father started?"

Nollen stiffened at the challenge. "I have been his guide since he arrived at Far Point."

"Willingly or out of duty?"

Nollen's rigidity turned to perplexity. "What made you ask that?"

"For this endeavor, Faith, not simple loyalty to the Oath, is necessary for success." Ronan eyes darted to Axel.

Nollen followed the indication to momentarily regard Axel before he replied to Ronan. "I admit surprise and skepticism at first, as I didn't know about the horn or signal. However, after everything that has happened since, I'm confident of his identity, and *willingly* act, as my conscience dictates."

Ronan smiled with approval. "Alfred would have been pleased to hear you say that."

The statement brought visible tears to Nollen's eyes. He lowered his head to keep his emotions in check.

Ronan released Nollen to address Axel. "Rest for the remainder of the day, my liege. This evening will be the best time for more revelation."

"And celebration," added Cormac with enthusiasm.

"No feast!" Axel insisted. "The city is too large to maintain security of my presence."

Cormac became crestfallen, so Ronan suggested, "A private meal for those of us present."

"Agreed," said Axel, who tossed a smile to Cormac.

"For now, Captain Clearly will show you to the *private* quarters, my liege," said Ronan.

Clearly clapped the hilt of his sword in acknowledgement.

"This is where we part ways. At least for now," said Alfgar to Axel. "Gott be with you, Son of Eldar."

"My thanks, Lord Alfgar."

Cleary picked up the lantern. "This way, my liege."

Once in the corridor, Cleary led Axel, Gunnar, Nollen, and Bardolf to where the hallway ended. An unlit lamp hung on the wall. He pulled the lantern, which acted as lever. A panel slid open to reveal a small landing with a narrow stairway. When all were inside, Cleary pulled a level to close the hall panel. Again, they climbed stairs, only these were wooden and not stone.

"This must be directly over the study," said Gunnar.

"Aye," said Cleary. He lit four lamps.

The room appeared almost identical in size to the study yet for sleeping with four beds, wardrobe, hearth, table and chairs, desk, and two short gabled windows. A large paneled section walled off part of the room between the hearth and outer wall.

Cleary opened a panel door to explain the contents. "This partition contains a privy with a small tub for bathing. A pipe from the hearth provides heat. There are towels and soap inside. Water is drawn from a pump. The privy may not be of the finest quality but will serve. There are extra blankets in the wardrobe along with a change of clothes if anyone has need."

Gunnar inspected the paneled toilet while listening to Cleary. He looked circumspectly at the captain. "You speak as though you knew we were coming to have this ready."

"I don't think we are the first guests to occupy this room," said Axel. He made his own exploration of the trappings.

"You are correct, my liege," said Cleary. "For nearly fifty years this hidden room has housed secret guests or provide sanctuary for refugees.

Your father and grandfather were among those guests," he informed Nollen. "Take your leisure. I shall return when dinner is ready. However, if any need arises before then, pull this cord. It sends a signal to Lord Ronan's study."

"Thank you, Captain," said Axel.

Bardolf sniffed the perimeter while Gunnar checked the windows.

Nollen loaded wood into the hearth where Axel joined him. Nothing verbal passed between them. Everything became conveyed in glances: Axel sympathetic, yet pleased; Nollen sorrowful yet confident. It ended with Axel's smile of encouragement as Nollen continued to build the fire.

Chapter 26

A FEW HOURS LATER, RONAN RETURNED TO HIS STUDY. THE ROOM was arranged for dinner with platters of food and pitchers of ale on the extended table. He inspected everything while Cormac and Irwin held tankards of ale. With the room located directly above the study, it didn't take long for Cleary to escort Axel, Gunnar, and Nollen to join them. Fresh clothes told that they made use of the hidden room's accommodations. Nollen's hair was still damp. Bardolf lay down beside the hearth.

"I hope you find this simple meal satisfactory, Highness," Ronan politely spoke.

Axel graciously smiled. "It will serve very well."

Gunnar took a seat at the table. "I hope it tastes as good as it smells." He made quick observation of the food. "I see no meat."

"Ganels don't eat meat. That requires killing. As protectors of the wilderness, we only consume what is sustainable," said Cormac.

"I forgot that," murmured Gunnar.

"You will find our food most enjoyable in flavor and satisfaction," Ronan assured Gunnar. "Shall we pray." He offered a quick word of thanks and praise. "Please, help yourselves." He offered a platter to Gunnar.

"You said you forgot about Ganels. I take it you've been to Eldar before?" inquired Irwin.

Gunnar swallowed before he replied. "I was born in the Freelands yet fled as a boy. The last of Shining Ones to leave before Elector Gowan invaded the territory."

"That happened over thirty years ago. Where have you been since?"

Gunnar took a drink to wash down the food. "This is tasty, by the way," he said to Ronan then answered Irwin's follow-up question. "I was ten at the time of our escape." He grew reflective. "An arduous journey that took us through Bertand to Krynaston."

"Krynaston?" echoed Irwin in surprise. His stunned gazed passed to his companions. "We've only heard that name in lore and legend."

"I read about Krynaston in the Holy Book, but thought it lost to antiquity," said Cormac.

"It is real enough," said Axel, grinning. "I was born there. As were my father, grandfather, and all descendants of Leif, Oleg's only surviving son. It is a hidden place where Leif took refuge when he escaped the massacre. Few find it." He clapped Gunnar's shoulder. "Gunnar has been my mentor in arms and loyal companion since I was fifteen."

Ronan quoted the passage, *"From my far hidden place shall come one to remove the stain of oppression."*

"In ancient Eldarian, Krynaston means *royal hiding place*," explained Axel.

"I don't know anyone who speaks ancient Eldarian," said Irwin.

"When younger, I learned the meaning of some words when my grandfather translated the Holy Book," began Ronan. "But not pronunciation."

"Javan's ancestor forced Eldarians to speak another language so the people would forget their past, and Faith. So, in a sense, you were correct, with Krynaston being lost to antiquity. At least, as far as language is concerned. Real people do live there," Axel said to Cormac.

The conversation became interrupted by a tapping at one of the windows followed by a bird call. A shield owl! Ronan quickly opened the window to fetch the bird.

"Cormac, bring the cage!" he hastily said.

Cormac held it open for Ronan to place the bird inside. Ronan untied the small pouch before he secured the cage. He unrolled the scrap of paper to read.

"By all that's holy!" he loudly swore.

"What's wrong?" asked Irwin.

Ronan handed the paper to Axel. "This is from our agent in Sener. Your arrival has prompted Dolus and Javan to act. Although, we suspected their objective when the demand for gold increased with each Tribute."

"The Six Treasures," chided Cormac, perturbed.

Axel looked up from reading. "When I secure the horn this night, I will have two of them."

"The fate of the others is troubling," Cormac insisted, his worry slow to ebb.

"I'm certain this note was sent to all before the official directive dispatched. The Eagles and Freelanders won't yield any real Treasure they might have. Four should be safe," said Ronan.

"That still leaves two," groused Cormac, not convinced.

Axel tried to allay Cormac's expressed fear. "Whereas, I understand your concern, the horn and book are the most important to my task. The others are trappings of sovereignty. They will be revealed at the appropriate time."

"I wish I shared your optimism. However, it's difficult, as the Ha'tar and Nefal have been allies of Javan's family since the overthrow. If they know the whereabouts of the Treasures in their Territory, they will yield them up. *And* employ any means necessary to secure the rest."

"Our agent also reports, Javan sent for the Cursians," said Ronan in a tone of warning.

Axel shook his head and spoke with supreme confidence. "They won't respond. I made certain they understand that eternal torment awaits if even one leaves Altwald."

"You encountered them?" asked Irwin, surprised.

"Aye, on our route to Heddwyn."

"The shortest distance was through Altwald," said Nollen

Ronan's gaze showed mild disapproval to Nollen's comment. "Well, that maybe one less enemy to deal with."

"Perhaps, but the continuation of territorial power is dependent upon Javan and Dolus," Irwin reminded Ronan.

"The Doane has managed to resist them," boasted Nollen.

"Such resistance won't last if they unite forces against you," Irwin pointedly said.

Ronan added his voice to the argument. "Nollen, do you realize the Ha'tar and Nefal Territories were strategic in dividing Eldar – north from south?

"Of course." Nollen then offered a sly counterpoint. "Only a few hours ago, you asked me about *faith*. Does the thought of the Ha'tar and Nefal uniting shake your faith, my lord?"

Gunnar coughed to cover an impulsive laugh at Nollen's retort. Axel stroked his beard to conceal his pleasure. His eyes shifted between Ronan and Nollen.

Ronan's brief surprise at the retort turned into a chuckle. "Sounds like something Arctander would say."

Nollen cocked a proud smile. "Thank you."

Gunnar motioned to the cage. "I thought the harpys killed all shield owls."

"A few were saved and bred in secret. They serve as communication between the Faithful," explained Ronan.

"It's how I knew if there was trouble, and Ganel needed something urgently," began Nollen. "Otherwise, I followed scheduled visits."

"Hence the hidden trails," said Axel.

Nollen nodded since he took a drink.

"Were your normal routes more visible?"

"Aye, to keep up appearances, and gain intelligence."

"I take it there are secret passages from here to Sener," said Gunnar with a wry smile.

Nollen simply grinned, as he ate.

"The shield owls are how I plan to send word of you to *our* allies," said Ronan to Axel.

Gunnar became concerned. "They must respond to the directive. Knowing of Axel's presence may alter that."

"Rest assured, sir, we have planned for this eventuality. Almost two hundred years, in fact." Ronan grinned.

Gunnar leaned on the table, his face and voice firm in refute. "Javan hasn't been alive two hundred years. His demand for gold began when I was a boy."

"The desire to secure the Six Treasure has been around since Oleg's defeat. The method may have changed with each Elector, but there is always a counter plan to thwart them." Ronan's demeanor grew hostile. "Since Dolus' rise to power, the situation has grown harrowing."

"The man is evil!" Nollen bitterly sneered.

"And diabolically clever. So much so, none of us realized until too late." Ronan took a drink to stem his bitterness.

"Our agent can handle himself," Irwin tried to reassure Ronan.

"I take it the individual was chosen for that purpose," Axel said.

Ronan took a moment to calm down. "Aye." With thoughtful regret he regarded Axel. "Although it is now a tightly-held secret, Mathena was once the center of learning in the spiritual arena. People freely came to study, to gain knowledge, and wisdom." His angry disgust returned. "Dolus deceived my father with false piety. Once he learned what he wanted, he returned to Sener, and began his rise to power."

The news stunned Nollen. "Your father trained Dolus?"

The accusing question brought Bardolf quickly to the table.

"No! Using false devotion, he tricked my father into allowing him to study at our university. Father became his first victim when he convinced Lel to slaughter the priests. As a reward, Lel promoted Dolus to First Minister. He died shortly thereafter, and Javan came to power."

Axel leaned on the table to make inquiry. "Does such training include knowledge regarding The First Ones?"

Ronan's sheepish gaze shift to Bardolf. Unable to give a verbal answer, he soberly nodded.

"Dolus used it against Othniel," Bardolf growled in conclusion.

"I cannot adequately express the deep remorse of Ganel to have helped foster such evil," Ronan lamented. "Since then, we have used every means to combat Dolus, while hiding our shame."

"You too suffered loss due to Dolus' deception," said Axel.

"Personal, but not a danger to all Eldar. *That* is our greatest shame."

Bardolf sat and placed a paw on Ronan's lap. "The enemy's deceit was clever enough to fool Othniel and Alfgar. Place the blame where it belongs—on Dolus."

Ronan flashed a forced smile at the attempt of comfort.

Gunnar's brows knitted in consideration of the exchange. "So, what is the plan to defy the directive?"

"Not defy, circumvent by using duplicates. Fake glass for diamond, fool's gold, lesser wood."

Stunned, Nollen sat back. "Were those components hidden among the goods I brought and traded?"

Ronan cocked a sly grin. "You, no. Alfred completed the last delivery, which is how he came to be here when we unexpectedly discovered the horn."

Perplexed, Axel inquired, "You didn't know it was here?"

"We did. Just not the exact location." Ronan took a drink to wash down his food before he proceeded to explain. "My great-great-grandfather felt it too dangerous for one person to know, so he scattered clues about Mathena. We happened upon the last clue when putting up supplies for the deception." He cast a side-glance to Nollen. "Alfred provided the means to secure it until needed. Which would be after he sent the signal." He then asked Gunnar, "Does that satisfy your questions?"

"Aye." He took a drink, and muttered in the tankard, "For now."

Axel heard and scowled his disapproval. Gunnar simply shrugged and returned to eating.

After dinner, they prepared to leave the study. Cormac and Irwin each fetched a small lantern.

Axel regarded Nollen with some hesitation. He drew the young man aside. "Wait here."

"Why?"

Axel took a deep breath before he answered. "It is hard to explain, but I sense it is best for you to wait. Bardolf will stay with you." Nollen frowned, so he added, "Please, trust me."

"Of course," Nollen said, though disappointed.

Bardolf came to stand beside Nollen when the others left. Nollen crossed to a window. For a moment, Bardolf watched. The young human's angry grunt made him approach.

"Is it what Ronan said about your father that troubles you, or what transpired with Axel?"

Rather than respond, Nollen grunted with annoyance.

Bardolf wouldn't be put off. "I may be a wolf, but I am not insensitive to human feelings. You are troubled."

"Aye," Nollen soberly admitted. "Trust works both ways. Yet I don't seem to be given the same trust as my father or grandfather."

"That is not true. The Son of Eldar has trusted you with his life since leaving Far Point. There is no greater trust than that."

Nollen regarded Bardolf and considered the statement. "You're right." He turned back out the window. "Yet, it's hard to accept what Lord Ronan said about Papi not wanting to *trust* me back then."

"You were a youth." Bardolf raised up to place his paws on the window sill. "Having watched you secretly for years, I can tell you this. You share the same courage as Arctander and Alfred."

A touched smile appeared. "Thank you."

Ronan led them down a narrow metal stairway that made four spiral loops to reach the bottom. Centuries of damp earth and dripping water cracked the stone slabs used for flooring. This made for uneven footing. They moved a hundred yards from the staircase when Ronan stopped in front of an old wooden door. He opened the three top buttons of his surcoat to withdraw a key ring from an inside pocket. One large key, and one tiny pin-like key were on the ring.

"Irwin, Cormac, stand guard," he told his friends.

Axel and Gunnar accompanied Ronan inside.

"This is our secret storeroom. It has also served as a safehouse during time of great turmoil." Ronan's voice turned somber. "We just left, and made our way upstairs, when Javan's men attacked."

"We?" asked Axel.

"Me, my father, and Arctander." Ronan's eyes scanned the room. "It happened ten years ago. Yet each time I come down here, it feels like yesterday." He shook off the dreary recollection to continue with the task at hand. He set the lantern on a tall stack of wooden crates. "It's hidden in a place Javan's men would never suspect. A sealed crate marked *ladies unmentionables* and *toiletries*."

Axel chuckled. "Alfred's idea?"

"Aye. Not something a bachelor would have considered."

"You're not married?" asked Gunnar.

"No." A somber tone again crept into Ronan's' voice.

"Because of that fateful day?"

"Aye." Ronan grunted with effort in using a pry bar open the crate. Once the top came loose, he removed the lid. "Gunnar, the lantern."

Ronan waited for more light before he pulled out various items that ladies used for private toiletry. He removed the slats that formed a false bottom. He gently lifted a tightly wrapped oblong box. After laying it on the top of a nearby barrel, he carefully unwrapped it to reveal an ornately carved wooden box with a silver locked latch. He used the pin-like key open the latch to lift the lid.

Axel watched in anticipation. He gasped in awe when the light revealed a large mother of pearl horn with black veining. The mouth piece comprised of ornately carved gold. Using both hands, Axel carefully picked it up.

"This is not what I expected," his voice a near whisper of wonder. "Most are made from horned animals." He admired the variants of color at different angles. "What craftmanship formed this?"

"No one knows exactly," began Ronan. "Legend tells of a master jeweler commissioned by King Kolyn, Oleg's ancestor, to create it from the fragments of Teva's horn."

"Teva," Gunnar repeated. "Queen of the unicorns?"

"Aye. Unicorn horns are said to possess magical powers. According to the legend, she lost her magnificent horn in a battle to save Kolyn's life. Without it, she became a normal horse. His steed for the remainder of her natural life."

"We witnessed that power when Alfgar healed Nollen after he fell into the watershed during our flight from Gorland border guards," Gunnar told Ronan.

Eyes fixed on the horn, Axel lowly quoted, "*From the shattered pieces will come the call. A horn like none other shall summon them.*" He lifted his head to speak aloud to Ronan. "I always wondered what that meant. Even though my father told me Kolyn followed Gott's instruction to forge the horn, I didn't fully understand how, or why, until now."

"Since the overthrow, Gott's part has been omitted from the legend. Hard to believe it is three hundred years old."

Axel's fingers traced the gold carvings of a unicorn and lion. "So, her image used in the family crest."

"Along with Othniel, the Great White Lion," said Ronan.

"This must be kept safe for the journey to Sener, and the time of its sounding." Axel reverently wrapped the horn but didn't place it back in the box.

Ronan gripped Axel's arm to get his attention. "That comes after you fulfill the Blood Oath. How will you make certain of its security?"

"Blood Oath?" Gunnar repeated, stunned.

Axel heard Gunnar but couldn't look at him. Instead, he replied to Ronan. "You said there are duplicates. I will wear that one while this is protected."

"A bold move."

"A necessary one."

"The duplicate is in my study under lock and key." Ronan took the lantern and headed to the door.

Gunnar seized Axel. For a long moment, their eyes met. Gunnar's expression stern with inquiry; Axel somber yet resolute.

"Highness?" inquired Ronan, unaware of the reason for delay.

Axel clasped Gunnar's hand before he removed it to leave with Ronan. Cormac and Irwin joined them for the trip upstairs.

Once in the corridor, Axel instructed Ronan, "Give the duplicate to Nollen, and tell him to join us in the upper room."

"Aye, Highness."

Axel pulled the lamp level to take the stair to the secret room. The door barely shut, when Gunnar voiced his surprised annoyance.

"What is this Blood Oath?"

Axel let out a long, sigh of lament. "It is a burden I alone must bear. No one else can help me. Not even you, old friend."

"But what is it?" he persisted with harsh emphasis.

"A deadly pact Oleg hastily made before his execution."

Wary, Gunnar stared at Axel to ask, "How deadly?"

Axel placed the horn on a table to face Gunnar. "One that requires the ultimate sacrifice to satisfy it."

With horrific understanding, Gunnar gaped. "You can't mean—?"

"It is why I have come!" Axel poignantly declared. "And you must help me to see it through."

Mute by the imploring statement, Gunnar's expression turned pained. He slowly began to shake his head. "I have sworn my life to protect you. You cannot ask me—!"

Desperate, Axel seized Gunnar. "There is no one else!" He watched Gunnar continue to battle the difficult request. "Don't you understand? Everything depends upon it. That's why I prayed for Gott to prepare you." His voice cracked with fervent passion.

Dreaded realization made Gunnar murmur, "My feverish vision was not the nightmare I hoped."

"No. I knew Gott answered my plea when you expressed relief upon seeing me."

Gunnar's question came with strained painful anger. "Why did you not tell me before now?"

Axel lowered his head to gather his emotions. "Because the burden is greater than you can imagine." When he looked up, tears fell. "Oleg's recklessness may have bound me to this fate, but Gott promised not to abandon his covenant with Oleg. Although Nollen, and others, have parts to play, *you* are the only one who can help me complete my task."

Gunnar screwed his eyes shut to contain his agony.

At the door opening, Gunnar and Axel fought to stem their emotions. Bardolf entered first followed by Nollen, who, despite their effort, noticed both looked troubled.

"Is something wrong?" he asked.

"Nothing for you to be concerned about right now," Axel tried to sound encouraging.

"Axel!" Gunnar objected.

"Not now," Axel firmly rebuffed. He turned his attention to a confused Nollen. "Is that the duplicate?"

"Aye." Nollen held up the finely crafted horn.

Axel took it for inspection. "They did a good job thinning the ram's horn to make it appear opalescent. Nice metalwork as well."

"There is a difference?" Nollen innocently asked.

Axel smiled. "Let me show you." He motioned Nollen to the table where he unwrapped the real horn.

"Oh!" Nollen breathed in astonishment. He became confused. "Why the need for a duplicate if you have the original?"

"Because you will take possession of the real one while I wear the duplicate in hopes of fooling Javan and Dolus." He wrapped the horn and gave it to Nollen.

"You will trust me with this?" asked Nollen, astonished.

"Aye. Place it in your saddlebag for safekeeping."

"And, Nollen," began Gunnar in a grim, foreboding tone. "Guard it with your life. There will only be one chance to use it."

Nollen's deliberate gaze shifted between the horn, Gunnar, and finally fixed on Axel. "It will be kept safe, Highness."

Axel sighed, as if releasing all emotions. "Now, I must find a place of solitude for much-needed prayer." He pulled the cord Cleary indicated to signal need before he proceeded down the narrow steps.

Nollen's quizzical gaze found Gunnar, who raised a stern hand.

"Ask nothing, for I cannot answer."

"Can't or won't?"

"Both. Since he will not speak, I remain silent about what troubles him." He flashed a tender smile when he looked at the horn Nollen still held. "This I can say. He didn't understand why he felt a prompting in his spirit regarding your involvement in our venture. Now we know the reason." He tapped on the horn. His eyes lifted to stare directly at the young trader. "You've come a long way in a short time, Nollen of Far Point. Yet, a greater challenge lies ahead." He paused when a tremor of pain crept into his voice. "Only trust in Gott will see us through this."

Nollen soberly regarded the horn. "I won't fail him. I promise."

Gunnar nudged Nollen. "Hide it well."

Axel met Cleary at the threshold to Ronan's study.

"You require assistance, my liege?" asked Cleary.

"A private place for prayer and meditation."

"The room were you first arrived."

"It was locked, and we were unable to leave. I want free access to come and go," Axel objected.

Cleary flashed a modest smile. "I did that out of an abundance of caution. It will be left unlocked for your personal use." He escorted Axel to the room where he lit the small brazier and lamp. "Do you require a *certain* book perhaps?" he asked with discretion.

"Is one available?"

Using a small key hidden in the cupboard, Cleary open a concealed compartment to withdraw a holy book. "This is an original, and among the last in Mathena. Please replace it when you have finished." He bowed and withdrew.

Axel sat in such a way that the oil lamp illuminated the pages. With the book being so old, he gently turned the pages. Although he knew the passage by heart, he needed to read, to mediate.

The weakness of men resides in hasty words.
Faithlessness results in actions that cannot save.
Treachery and deceit lie behind the dealings of false men.
Yet my covenant with Oleg will remain.
I do not deal foolishly like men.
My word is forever.

Axel stared at the page for long time, as the words echoed in his mind. Overcome, he slammed the book closed. He nearly dropped it when his head fell, weeping and pleading. "Gott, help me! Take away this fear with the comfort of your words. Give me strength to do what I must to save my people … your people."

Chapter 27

THREE HA'TAR DRAGON-RIDERS GUIDED THE DRAGONS IN A descent to the ground. They flew deep into the northern part of Nefal Territory almost to the Freeland border.

On the ground, four Nefal bolt-throwers aimed at the Ha'tar. Those manning the bolt-throwers followed the path of descent. Behind them waited a squad of heavily armored Nefal warriors mounted on dire-buffalos. The enormous beasts weighed two-thousand pounds with massive shoulders, powerful necks, plated heads, and curved horns. The beasts' armor extended from the head plate, over the neck, to the saddle. Behind the saddle came the weapons' harness containing six spears; three on each side.

In front of the warriors, Argus sat upon his dire-buffalo. His beast was more elaborately armored; a sign of his position as Nefal chief. Two Nefal officials flanked him. Their dire-buffalos also fitted with augmented armor.

The dragons landed fifty yards away. The Ha'tar dismounted and moved in front of the dragons. Argus rode to meet them. The officials followed close behind while the warriors took up a defensive position.

Fod raised his hands in a peaceful gesture as Argus approached. "We come in peace, my lord."

Argus reined the dire-buffalo, and roughly retorted. "If I did not think so, you would not have landed, rather been shot down." He skeptically gazed at the other Ha'tar.

This prompted Fod to introduce them. "You remember my son, Gan. This is Kyn, my new *advisor* in all things political. He came with me to Sener, but not formally introduced."

"Dowid and Spoor." Argus indicated his officials. "State your purpose."

"The Six Treasures demanded by the directive."

Argus squirmed in the saddle. "What about them?"

"Do the Nefal have any of them?"

"Why should we tell you if we do?"

"Because it is in best interest of all."

"Need we remind you of the centuries-old alliance?" Kyn boldly spoke.

Spoor swore in Nefalese then spoke rapidly to Argus. He made angry gestures toward the Ha'tar. In a burst of rage, Argus raised a clenched fist and gave a short command. Spoor reluctantly became quiet.

Argus addressed Fod. "The alliance is a source of contention among the Nefal. It is unwise to mention."

"Being *unwise* doesn't change reality," Fod countered. He pressed his advantage. "Our ancestors' pledge binds us. Unless you would single-handedly break the alliance."

Spoor pulled a spear from the weapons harness. This prompted Gan to race back to his dragon to make defense. Fod's call stopped Gan from mounting. With a curt motion, Fod waved Gan to return.

Argus took a spear from the harness and used it to knock the weapon from Spoor's hand. In Nefalese, he loudly rebuked the advisor. He used the spear to motion Spoor to withdraw. Seething rage, made Spoor pull hard on the reins to turn the dire-buffalo around.

Argus moved his beast to again face Fod. "Be glad I kept the peace, or you would be dead!"

Fod struck a fist to his chest and made a slight nod of acknowledgement. "Tempers are raw on all sides. However, if we are to maintain our territories, compliance is necessary."

Argus scoffed. "The Freelanders and Ganels will never agree."

Fod heaved a calculated shrug. "Then let them suffer the consequences. Which could benefit both our territories."

Argus leaned on the saddle horn, his eyes keen on Fod. "Meaning when they suffer, we expand."

Fod slyly grinned. "Exactly."

Argus fought a satisfied smile. "Is the Ha'tar in possession of a Treasure?"

"Would I be here if we weren't?"

Argus sat back, and heartily laughed. "Which one?"

"You'll see at the presentation in Sener."

Argus' good humor faded. "You demanded to know ours while not telling the one you possess?" He gathered the reins. "Be off with you, before I order my men to shoot!"

In Ha'tarian, Kyn spoke words of hasty worry to Fod.

"My Lord Argus, wait!" Fod shouted. "I misspoke."

Argus paused in departure. He turned in the saddle to ask, "No more evasive answers, Ha'tar?"

Fod stiffened at Argus' insult but kept his reply neutral. "Direct answers. Both ways."

Argus put up his spear and returned. "The Treasure?"

"Shevet, the scepter. The Nefal?"

"Sadok. Although, I suspect the Eagles once again have the Star of Conant since it is missing from the crown."

"A logical assumption."

"How long have you known about Shevet?"

"A couple of years, why?"

Argus stroked his beard. "If each Territory has a Treasure, it can be used to strike a bargain with Javan."

Kyn moved close to Fod to speak privately.

Fod nodded to Kyn, then spoke to Argus. "A risky move."

"Why? Once Javan possesses them, he can proclaim himself *king forever* of Eldar."

"This move is to prevent Oleg's heir from regaining them," Kyn said.

The statement stunned Argus. He immediately summoned Dowid. He spoke a few terse words. Dowid's meek response included the clearly understood words *Son of Eldar.* Argus' snarl silenced Dowid. The chief resumed his discussion with Fod.

"What makes you believe Oleg's heir is in Eldar?"

"News of events in The Doane have not reached Nefal?" asked Gan, his annoyance roused.

"We heard reports of a disturbance at Far Point, and the warrants. How is that connected to the Son of Eldar?"

"No disturbance!" Gan spat. "That wretched Nollen is in league with the Son of Eldar. They killed a juvenile when fleeing into Heddwyn!" He motioned back to his dragon. "The offspring of my mount."

Kyn tried to soothe Gan. "They got what they deserved." He then explained to Argus. "Arctander, and forty followers of the forbidden Faith, were found in Heddwyn and taken captive by Bernal during a search for the Son of Eldar."

Argus swore. "The less of those Shining Ones the better."

"Agreed," said Fod. "How long have you been in possession of Sadok?"

"Very recently. Which makes me suspicious of how Javan knew so quickly."

"Lord Dolus is well-educated in the old ways. He manipulates Javan," chided Kyn.

Argus snorted with contempt. "He's a pox on us all."

"Dolus is powerful. It would be too dangerous to ignore the directive." warned Fod.

Kyn shook his head. The worry on his face came out in a shaky voice. "The directive is nothing but the loss of Territory. We risk eternal condemnation if we don't fulfill the alliance."

Fod reluctantly said to Argus, "I fear Kyn is correct. We must adhere to the alliance by obeying the directive and present the Treasures to Javan."

"Dowid said the same earlier," Argus begrudgingly admitted. He sat upright in the saddle. "Be assured, the Nefal will comply with both the alliance and directive. Return safely to Ha'tar." He withdrew with Dowid close behind.

Argus paused when he reached the Nefal troops to watch the Ha'tar depart. He sent a sneering glare to Spoor. "I hope you're correct, and this turncoat has Sadok! If not, I have committed each Nefal soul to eternal condemnation due to faulty information!"

"I am certain," said Spoor stoutly.

"Dispatch warriors to Brawly's farm immediately!" Argus ordered.

In the cellar of a remote farm on the northern outskirts of Nefal Territory, Henrick, a Freelander, worked feverishly to put the finishing touches on the fake crown. Sadok sat on a shelf at eye level for study while he worked.

Brawly, the Nefal farmer, anxiously waited. He appeared less muscular than a warrior, though still eight feet tall. "Hurry! They can come at any moment," he urged.

"I told you, this can't be rushed. If I miss the slightest detail, Dolus will suspect a fake," chided Henrick.

"If you don't finish soon, the entire plan will be discovered. Placing everyone's lives in jeopardy!"

Henrick didn't reply, as he delicately secured the last piece of colored glass to the crown made of fool's gold. He let out a satisfied sigh. "Finished!" When Brawly went to take it, Henrick bat his hand away. "The glue needs to set!"

"How long?"

"A few moments. Time enough to secure Sadok, and for me to leave safely."

Henrick put his tools in a satchel. He then carefully placed Sadok in a specially prepared box. Red velvet lined the box with a raised center to hold the crown in place. With a uniquely made key, he locked the box. Crossing to an iron stove, he tossed the key into the flames.

"Why did you do that? Now, you can't open it," chided Brawly

"That was also a duplicate. The real key is safely hidden with our Treasure." Henrick placed the box in a sack. He slung the satchel over his shoulder before he picked up the sack. "Make sure the way is clear."

Brawly climbed the steps to the cellar door. He slowly opened it enough to see the last rays of twilight fade. He stepped outside. No one. "All clear!" he cautiously called down to Henrick.

Henrick emerged just as Brawly brought a horse from around the back of the house. He secured the sack to the saddle, so it wouldn't move even at a gallop. He looked up at Brawly.

"I pray we meet again. Until then, Gott keep you safe, my friend." He heartily gripped Brawly's arm.

"May He give you safe journey." Brawly held the bridle for Henrick to mount. He stepped back to watch the Freelander head north and disappear into the forest.

Brawly returned to the cellar. He picked up the fake Sadok to admire Henrick's work. Suddenly, he heard a thunderous sound from upstairs followed by a female's scream. He set the crown down to hurry toward the house stairs. Nefal warriors arrived with swords wielded. Brawly never made it to the stairs.

A warrior spotted the crown. "It's still here."

Another warrior grabbed Brawly by the tunic and jerked him to a sitting position. Brawly's head fell lifeless to one side. Dead. The warrior searched him. From an inside pocket, he pulled out a medallion of True King. He held up the medallion for his companion to see.

"The information is right. A cursed traitor!"

"A lot of good it did him We got the crown."

Back upstairs, they stepped over the bodies of a woman and teenage boy to depart. The warrior with the crown stopped in the threshold.

"Burn it!" he ordered his companion.

While he continued to his dire-buffalo, the other Nefal used a lit log from the hearth to start a fire in the house. From outside, they waited a few moments to watch flames grow inside. Satisfied, they rode off.

Screams from behind made Henrick stop. He rode far enough not to be seen by the Nefal warriors, yet able to witness commotion at the house. He bit his lip, fearful of the outcome, yet unable to intervene. Even when the warriors left, the danger was too great to return. His eyes filled with tears when flames rose from the house. Snapping the reins, he continued his course toward home.

Chapter 28

LATE AFTERNOON OF THE SECOND DAY AFTER LEAVING NEFAL Territory, Fod, Gan, and Kyn approached Draca, the capital city of Ha'tar. It had been built beside a tributary forty miles from the great River Leven. Massive hewn stones formed the walls and the majority of buildings. Carved edifices of dragons, famous Ha'tar warriors, and battles adorned the gates, lintels, and most public places. Wood was used for stables, doors, windows, troughs or signs. Slate shingles topped the roofs. Narrow cobblestone streets wound through the city. Four large stone mills with enormous wooden wheels lined the tributary. Each mill also had a huge dock for barges used in commerce.

With Draca being too small for dragons, the beasts made their dens and nests around the outskirts of the city. Dragon breeders, and trainers lived among the rocky landscape.

Fod, Gan, and Kyn landed on a plateau overlooking Draca.

Fod instructed the dragon keeper to tend them well. He, Gan, and Kyn descended the steps to the road of Draca.

"You made a bold claim about Shevet," Kyn began to Fod. "When the other Nefal acted, I though all was lost."

Fod huffed a chuckle. "Despite his physical strength, Argus isn't too clever."

"Just be glad he didn't listen to his advisors more closely."

"What about Shevet? We may not have time to find the real one," Gan insisted.

"It depends if Hob talked," groused Fod. Near the city, he raised a hand to stop further discussion.

With the gates opened for daily business, they weaved through the crowd to the prison. A soldier greeted them.

"Lord Fod."

"Has Deputy Jen succeeded?"

"Not yet, sir."

Fod curtly pushed past the soldier to enter. The soldier hurried with a torch to escort them into the bowels of the dungeon. The echoes of lashing greeted them on the lower level. Weak cries of pain accompanied each lash. When they stepped inside the central chamber, the beating stopped.

Jen was a burly, dark, Ha'tar with a scarred face. He bowed. "Lord Fod."

Fod approached Hob. The middle-aged man slumped under the painful lashing. He hung by his wrists in the center of the chamber. Welts on Hob's face showed more abuse. Fod jerked up Hob's head by pulling his hair.

"This can end if you tell us the location of the real Shevet."

Hob didn't reply, too weak to speak.

"We could take you to Sener where Lord Dolus has more persuasive ways to get information."

"You risk exposing the fact you have a fake Treasure," Hob's feeble voice barely rose above a whisper.

Enraged, Fod spat in Hob's face. "Cursed traitor! Do you think the one you follow will save you?

"Even if Gott doesn't, I won't tell you where it is."

"You would die to keep this secret?"

"I would die to keep the Faith."

"So be it!" Fod removed his dagger and killed Hob.

Gan and Kyn flinched in surprise at the suddenness.

"Fader, why did you do that? Now, we'll never know where it is," said Gan.

Fod drew Gan out the chamber. "For years, we didn't know it was a duplicate until damaged. Hopefully, Master Abi can repair it so Dolus won't know either."

"You're taking a great risk," stressed Kyn.

Fod's temper exploded. "We don't have time to find the original! We either present what we have or admit failure. Which do you suggest?"

Stymied, Kyn reluctantly nodded.

Fod steered Gan to leave. "Time to pay Master Abi a visit to learn his progress."

When Kyn hesitated to accompany them, Fod curtly called his name.

From the prison, they again navigated the streets to the far side of Draca. Bells rang when the door to the silversmith's shop opened. Fod's grim expression told the workers why he had come. The eldest of Abi's craftsman hastened to meet them.

"This way, sir." He led them through the shop to a back room.

Abi, an older man of seventy, diligently worked at a raised table. He viewed the duplicate scepter under a well-used magnifying glass mounted on a wooden stand. Bright lamps surrounded the glass for ease of visibility.

The craftsman cleared his throat to get Abi's attention. "Lord Fod, Master."

Abi sat back and rubbed his eyes. He rotated his shoulders to loosen them from hours of work. "I suppose you're here to inspect my progress," he spoke, a bit terse.

"Hob is dead. He wouldn't betray the location of the real scepter," Fod scoffed.

"I'm not surprised. The followers of the Oath are fanatic in their Faith, unwilling to yield even in the face of death." Abi motioned to the scepter. "See for yourself. I have finished repairing the damage and was doing a last inspection."

Fod took hold of the intricately crafted silver scepter. He turned it over several times during his examination. "Excellent. I can't even tell it was damaged."

"Do you think it will fool Dolus?" asked Gan.

Offended by the question, Abi rebuffed Gan. "Boy, can you tell the difference between silver and nickel?"

Gan snarled with insult, which prompted Fod to scold him. "Be quiet! We didn't know it was only nickel plated until damaged."

"What about the box?" Gan impertinently asked.

To this, Fod didn't rebuke his son rather looked to Abi for the answer.

The silversmith moved from the table to a sideboard upon which sat an ornately decorated box. He gave it to Gan. His tone condescending. "I even found some red velvet at a dressmaker's shop. Unless you object to replicating this as well?"

Fod placed the scepter into the box. He closed the lid and secured it with the silver pin. "Stop by this evening for payment."

Abi smiled with great satisfaction.

As they made their way from the silversmith shop, Kyn delayed Gan in the pretense of being separated from Fod by citizens going about their daily business.

"Your father is playing a dangerous game. First provoking Argus, now with this replica scepter," Kyn privately said.

Gan seized Kyn, which slowed their pace even further. "Mind your tongue!"

Gan's anger didn't sway Kyn. "You know I'm right."

Gan roughly released Kyn to continue the trek. Kyn hurried to catch him.

"You must talk some sense into him."

Gan cautiously glanced ahead. Fod seemed unaware of the distance between them. He pulled Kyn into the shadow of a building. "I can't stop him from obeying the directive. Besides, which is better, bringing something or arriving empty-handed?"

Frustrated by the reluctance, Kyn pressed his argument. "One hint of falsehood, and nothing will save us."

Anger made Gan pin Kyn against the building. Unable to refute the statement, he hurried to leave. This time Kyn didn't pursue Gan. Instead, he headed in the opposite direction.

With daylight dwindling, most Ha'tar headed indoors for the evening. Clearing streets made for a swift journey to his apartment above a mercantile shop. Kyn climbed the exterior stairs like usual, so the landlord knew he returned home.

Inside, he locked the door and closed all the curtains. An oil lamp always remained lit during the fall and winter months. He slowly raised the flame enough to see. On a small piece of paper, he wrote a quick note, rolled it up, and stuffed it in a tiny pouch. He lowered the lamp light till almost extinguished then moved to the rear window. He slowly pulled back the curtain. Twilight faded. He needed to wait several hours to make certain most were in bed.

He pretended to make his usual preparations for the night, knowing the merchant could hear him by way of creaking floors. He packed a knapsack and placed it beside the rear window. He donned black clothes and a cloak. He removed his boots to soften his steps. These he placed by the knapsack. Once done with preparations, he listened to the noise from downstairs. Typical family having supper, even a few loud words. Finally, it grew quiet. By the time shown on the mantle clock, he suspected they had retired.

From a locked carved cupboard with decorative holes, he withdrew a cage draped in black cloth. Uncovering the cage, revealed a shield owl. The owl began a cooing hoot when taken from the cage.

"Easy," Kyn whispered, and stroked the bird's head. "We mustn't let the others know you're here."

He attached the message pouch to the owl's leg. He carried the bird to the rear window. Slowly, he opened the window to avoid making any sound. Outside on the wall, a large drainpipe ran from the roof to the alley behind the shop.

"Fly with Gott's speed," he quietly told the owl, and released it.

Satisfied that the owl safely left Draca, he slowly pulled on his boots. He put on the knapsack and secured it. He carefully climbed out the window and onto the drain pipe. He used the clamps as footholds to climb down. Fortunately, his window was the only one near the pipe, thus no chance of being seen. Such ease of escape was one reason he chose the apartment. Another reason was the proximity to Draca's rear gate.

Kyn didn't need to disturb the gatekeeper. He had managed to forge a key by striking a deal. It required leaving a certain amount of money in a prearranged location. Kyn planted a money pouch as agreed, and left Draca via the foot-gate.

Dark clouds obscured the moon and stars. Kyn dashed from the gate to the nearest boulder to hide and wait. Sentries walked the ramparts between lighted stations. Once they completed their course, a few moments past before another round of sentries. Kyn remained hidden until the pause between trips then ran north into the wilderness.

The path avoided dwellings of dragon breeders and trainers. Despite the cloudy darkness, he knew the path well. After an hour, he arrived at a ravine with a small cave. Before he made the descent, he looked to check if he had been followed. Satisfied, he slid down to the bottom then raced across to the cave.

Before he entered, he set down the knapsack to remove a candle and match. Holding the sack in one hand, and candle in the other, he walked to the rear of the cave. It was shallow and cramped, but room enough to move. He knelt and set down the candle. He felt along the rocks until he found it then began to dig. He smiled at hitting something with his fingers. Gently, he brushed aside dirt and pebbles to uncover a long sack. He unwound the binding to view what was inside. Shevet!

"Thank, Gott," he sighed with a smile.

He rewrapped Shevet, secured it in the knapsack, blew out the candle, and left.

Chapter 29

THE LATE AUTUMN WEATHER TURNED MISERABLY COLD, foretelling of a harsh winter. Bitter north winds and pelting rain did not deter Henrick, as he pushed himself to endure the unforgiving elements. His assignment would not be complete until he brought the True King's Crown safely back to the Freelands.

The events at Brawly's farm weighed heavy on him. Duty, grief, and urgency drove him to make the normal six-day journey in four days. He slept only when necessary and ate sparingly. With the danger of discovery hounding him, he dare not switch horses. Thus, by the time Stellan came into view, both he, and his horse were spent. The animal's head nearly touched the ground while blood oozed from its nostrils. Henrick fought to remain awake and not fall off.

The grandeur of Stellan dimmed over the centuries, but the Freelands' capital city still impressed newcomers to the Territory. The massive city of fifty thousand sprawled along the banks of the River Stille. Smaller suburbs and settlements encompassed the fortified main city. Soaring towers, battlements, cathedral, and castle dominated the cityscape. The river plain gently rose in elevation from the water's edge inland. Although it never went higher than a few hundred feet.

The latest rain included sleet and small hail. Within shouting distance of the watch, Henrick used his last ounce of strength to call out. "In the King's service!"

He slumped onto the horse's neck yet managed to stay in the saddle. Soon he felt hands and bolted upright in surprise.

"Easy, Henrick."

He tried to focus on the man beside him. "Mather?"

"Aye. We'll help you down before the horse falls over."

Mather and two soldiers guided Henrick from the saddle. His knees gave way when his feet touched the ground. Being held by soldiers kept him upright.

"The saddlebag … quick!" murmured Henrick.

A soldier retrieved it just before the horse collapsed—dead.

"Take me to Lord Gorman," he said to Mather.

"You need to rest."

"No! Gorman. Now!"

The soldiers practically carried Henrick through the gate. Despite his best efforts to walk, he collapsed. He clutched the saddlebag. He gasped for breath and fought against unconsciousness overtaking him.

"I must get to Lord Gorman," he muttered.

"Symeon, fetch that hay cart." Mather indicated an empty wagon with horse in harness near the gate.

Once the cart was positioned, they helped Henrick into the back. Mather climber onto the driver's seat.

"Return to duty. I'll take him to Lord Gorman," he ordered.

The sway of the wagon lulled Henrick to sleep. He didn't wake until Mather shook his shoulder. "What?" he exclaimed in surprise.

"We've arrived," said Mather.

Henrick slid off the cart. Still unsteady, he said to Mather, "Lend me your shoulder."

Inside the governor's house, Henrick kept focused on this task, and ignored the goings-on around him. He heard Mather speak a command to several soldiers, but the words garbled. Fatigue clouded his mind.

"Henrick!"

The loud, close voice startled him, until he recognized Gorman. "My lord." He indicated the saddlebag.

"Mather, lock the door!" Gorman took Henrick and led him to a chair. "Good Gott, man, what happened to you?"

Henrick smacked his parched lips. Keen to the need, Gorman poured cider into a tankard. Henrick greedily drank. Cider dribbled down his face. He fell back into the chair with a heavy sigh.

"Now, what happened?" repeated Gorman.

Henrick fought back tears. "Brawly, his family … killed just as I left."

"Sadok?" Gorman demanded, fearful.

Henrick patted the saddlebag. "Safe."

Gorman placed the bag on his desk to examine the contents. He lifted out the box. He searched the bag again. "The key?" He went back to Henrick, who had fallen asleep. "Henrick, the key?"

"Destroyed, as ordered, after I finished the replica and secured the real crown." Henrick fell unconscious.

Mather stopped Gorman from waking him again. "He must be tended to by a physician or end up dead like his horse. You know the real key is safe with Emet."

Gorman took a deep breath to calm down. He gazed with sympathy at Henrick. "Aye. See he is well-cared for."

Mather summoned two soldiers. "Take him to a guest room, and fetch Doctor Delling." Upon their departure, he again locked the door.

At a large window, they heard an eagle's call followed by tapping on the glass. Gorman instructed Mather to open the window. The great Eagle king moved inside to land on the back of a large cushioned chair.

"Artair?" Gorman breathed in awe.

Majestic in golden and white appearance, Artair was larger than the average eagle. He spread his wings and cried out.

Intimidated, Gorman and Mather recoiled. "I don't understand. Why are you here?" asked Gorman.

Artair bowed his regal head with a quiet squawk then looked up. "The time is near," he spoke in the common tongue.

Both men gaped, dumbfounded at hearing words.

"Do not be surprised by my speech. Gott is granting this for the sole purpose of uniting against the enemy."

"Forgive us, but conversing with an animal is a first for us," said Gorman.

Artair flew to the desk and landed beside the box. "Sadok?"

"Aye. My agent assures me he completed the task of replacing it with the replica. He destroyed the key—"

Artair spread his wings with an angry cry.

"According to plan!" insisted Gorman. "He used a duplicate key to secure Sadok, then destroyed it, insuring it couldn't be used again. The real one is safe with Emet."

Artair cocked his head to inspect Gorman. "You speak the truth."

Gorman withdrew a medallion from the inner pocket of his doublet. "My Oath and Faith compel me. I can do nothing else," he spoke with great sincerity.

Artair's head jerked toward Mather.

The captain showed his medallion. "In the King's service."

Artair nodded. "The Son of Eldar will soon begin his journey to Sener—"

Stunned, Gorman interrupted. "Then the rumors are true? Oleg's heir has come? We wondered when receiving the edict for the Treasure."

"It is true," confirmed Artair. "Alfgar and Bardolf are with him. My flock has taken to the air to scout our territorial borders for signs of enemy activity."

Gorman smiled with excitement at the news. "The First Ones are assembling. We feared that wouldn't happen after hearing about Othniel. You bring us hope."

"There has always been hope," said Artair.

"You misunderstand," began Gorman, resolute. "We would not have acted if we thought otherwise. However, the edict requiring the Treasure is most disturbing."

"The Nefal and Ha'tar will obey the directive," said Mather.

Artair spread his wings with another annoyed squawk. "The ancient alliance between the Electors, Ha'tar, and Nefal, require they also send warriors to defend Sener. The faithful of The True King must be ready to answer the call."

Gorman's delighted smile trembled slightly. "It is almost overwhelming to see prophecy fulfilled in our lifetime."

"Mortal years are fleeting, but duty calls," insisted Artair.

"And the Freelands will answer!" declared Mather. He slapped the hilt of his sword for emphasis.

Artair turned his head upwards and gave a loud, long cry that echoed from the room to outside. When he ceased, the echoes faded. "The Eagles are ready to join with mortals and welcome the return of The True King."

"The Star of Conant?" asked Gorman.

"Safe. You must prepare for *your* journey to Sener, with the Sadok replica, and troops.

"Of course. Since Javan expects me, Captain Mather will muster the troops."

"Gott protect you both until we meet at Sener."

"And may he guide you on your way, Lord Artair." Gorman bowed his head in polite salute. Mather did the same.

Artair made his way to the window where he took off in flight.

Chapter 30

IN THE GOVERNOR'S RESIDENCE AT MILAGRO, EBERT SAT BEHIND the study desk staring at the directive. Fire in the hearth faded due to lack of attention. Lamps flickered, the oil low. Darkness threatened to envelope the room, but Ebert remained motionless due to great consideration. Even when the door opened, he did not react.

"Ebert?" asked Jabid. No response. "Do you want to freeze or ruin your eyes?"

Jabid used the dying oil lamp flame to light three candles. He then stoked the fire and placed several logs on top of the refreshed coals. Finally, he approached the desk. Ebert's fixed expression and lack of reaction troubled him.

"What's wrong?"

When Ebert remained unmoved, Jabid snatched the paper from him. The action made Ebert bolt up to retrieve it.

"No!"

Jabid refused to yield. "Not until you explain why Blythe is so worried that she sent for me."

"She did what?"

Jabid crossly regarded at Ebert. "Do you know what time it is?" Seeing confusion, he said, "Ten o'clock at night. Blythe said you've been in here since noon. You won't talk, didn't come to supper."

"Read it!" Ebert snapped. He crossed to the reignited fire to warm himself.

Jabid leaned closer to a candle. "Dear Gott," he muttered. He then spoke aloud to Ebert. "The Six Treasures as Tribute."

"Dolus thinks *I* have the Book of Kings. I don't! Nor do I know where it is. If it still exists."

Guarded, though curious, Jabid probed. "You know why he wants the Treasures, don't you?"

Ebert huffed, "Aye. Although I thought it only rumor about Oleg's heir. Until the directive arrived."

Jabid held the paper up. "This means a decision must be made by *every* Eldarian."

Anxiousness propelled Ebert back to the desk. "If I defy Dolus and Javan, I'll lose everything! Home, position …"

"Blythe."

Ebert's jowls tensed against a flood of emotion. "She is the one I fear losing the most."

"The right choice can prevent that."

"You sound like Ronan," Ebert weakly refuted.

"There are similar sentiments among those who experience the peace of a settled soul."

Ebert looked to his feet, as he lost the battle of emotion. His voice trembled. "Blythe has mentioned the same over the years."

"She sensed a change in you due to the responsibility of being governor."

Ebert sniffled, and wiped a hand across his eyes. "She's right. So are you—about a choice. That is what I've wrestled with since receiving the directive. I just don't know what to tell Blythe."

Uncertain, yet sensing a glimmer of hope, Jabid asked, "Have you made a decision?"

Ebert took a deep breath to declare, "Aye. The Son of Eldar is the True King. Gott has shown me that." He pointed to the desk.

Being more concerned for Ebert when he arrived, Jabid didn't notice a book lying open. He slid the candle closer. Surprised, he picked it up to look at the cover. "Father's old holy book. How did you come by it?"

"I took it from Blythe's bureau. I needed answers."

Now confused, Jabid said, "I don't understand. If Gott provided you with answers why can't you tell Blythe? She would be overjoyed."

"Because I can't go to Sener empty-handed. The consequences are too deadly to even consider!" Agitation made Ebert pace.

For a thoughtful moment, Jabid watched Ebert. He vacillated between Ebert's confession, and the need for action. "When must you leave for Sener?"

"In the morning. That's why I've spent hours praying for wisdom." Ebert stopped in front of the hearth to once more regain his composure.

Jabid put the book down to join Ebert. "Do you trust me?"

The question briefly stymied Ebert. "What an odd question. Of course. We've known each other all our lives."

Jabid made Ebert face him, his eyes direct and earnest. "This goes beyond a lifelong friendship, even past our relationship by marriage. Your trust must be complete. No doubt or questions."

"I trust you with my life. Isn't that enough?"

Jabid grinned with a measure of relief. "Aye. Now, prepare for the journey, and leave the rest to me. I'll return shortly." He paused in leaving to say, "Oh, and tell Blythe."

"Where are you—"

Jabid raised a stiff hand. "I said no questions."

Jabid hurried from the residence to his home a few blocks away. He managed to avoid the night watch. Instead of entering by the front door, he travelled the alley to the rear. When a dog barked, he spoke a short command. "Quiet, Ziggy!"

Recognizing its master's voice, Ziggy wagged his tail. Jabid scratched the dog's head.

"Good, boy. Now lay down." He made a hand signal, which the dog obeyed.

Jabid made his way to a shed. For security, a portable lantern hung on a bracket by the door. After unlocking the door, he took down the lantern, entered, and bolted it from inside. Light illuminated the interior, which consisted of various tools and crockery for gardening and home repair.

He set the lantern down on a work bench. Using a hand, he felt underneath. He flinched at feeling something sharp. He withdrew his hand to view it in the light. A finger prick, but nothing serious. He tried again. This time he pulled a lever. Several floor boards slid apart to reveal steps.

Jabid held the lantern, as he descended to a damp earthen cellar. A rat squealed when he stepped on its tail. He ignored the rodent to retrieve a case and return upstairs. He placed both the case and lantern on the bench then shoved the level to close the floor boards. From the hollow bottom of crockery jar, he withdrew an old key. It fit the case lock. An ancient wood and leather book lay inside. Jabid smiled, and quickly relocked the case. Outside, he put the lantern back in place, locked the shed, and left.

Jabid just turned the corner from the alley, when confronted by a night patrol of two soldiers.

"Halt! What business to do you have this night, citizen?"

"I am Jabid, assistant to Governor Ebert." He reached into the breast pocket of this doublet to withdraw a piece of paper.

After reading, the watchman said, "If you are Master Jabid then you know this night's password."

"Peace and safety to you, friend," Jabid confidently replied.

A watchman returned the paper. "Why out so late?"

"No doubt you heard about the *new* directive. We leave at dawn."

"Is there any gold left in The Doane?" chided the second soldier.

"Hopefully what we bring will satisfy the Elector. Now, I bid you fair watch."

When Jabid returned to the governor's residence, Blythe and Ebert sat on a sofa in the study.

"I'm glad to see you took my advice," he said, pleased. He placed the case on the desk.

"What is that?" asked Ebert.

"The answer to your prayer." Jabid unlocked it and pulled out the old book. "The Book of Kings."

Astonished, Ebert examined it. "How? Where?"

"You know about our father but little regarding mother. This was entrusted to her family by King Oleg and handed down for generations."

Unseen by Ebert, Blythe nudged Jabid. Her expression scolding of her brother, though no words spoken. She quickly masked her displeasure when Ebert finished his examination of the book.

"It's locked," said Ebert.

"I have the key." Jabid patted the pocket of his doublet.

The answered satisfied Ebert. "This may well save us from Dolus and Javan, but what about the Son of Eldar?"

"By doing our part, we give him time to act," replied Jabid.

Ebert again admired the book. "Having this, I can get a few hours of sleep before we leave." He heartily gripped Jabid's arm. "Thank you."

Blythe took the book from Ebert and gave it to Jabid. "Off to bed with you." She tried to steer Ebert to the door.

"I should keep it with me."

"I will look after it since I intend to stay the night," said Jabid with a reassuring smile.

"All is well. Sleep in peace. I'll be along shortly." Blythe kissed Ebert's cheek. She barely closed the door on her husband's departure when she confronted her brother. "Why did you lie to him about the key?"

"For his own good. He may be a new convert but is untested. It is best some aspects of this remain secret." He tapped on the book cover.

"If he insisted on using the key to inspect the pages, he'll discover the deception."

"It can't be opened. The clasps are fake. No key will work."

"What if Javan or Dolus try to open it?"

"We claim ignorance of the sacred key's whereabouts."

In unconvinced anger, she continued to glare at him.

"Blythe," Jabid compassionately began. "You know I will do everything to protect Ebert. To protect you, and *our* people. It is a risk we must take. In the King's service," he added the phrase for emphasis.

Her anger waned at his argument. "Aye." She held his hand. "Promise me, that on the journey, you will instruct Ebert in the Faith. What he knows in his mind, must become settled in his heart."

"I promise." He embraced her and kissed her forehead. "Now, we both should rest." He picked up the case to retire for the evening.

Once in the guest room, Jabid rang to summon Deron, the steward.

Being near midnight, Deron arrived, sleepy. He tried to stifle a yawn. "You summoned me, sir?"

"The time of our salvation has come." Jabid showed Deron his medallion. "Send the signal. Only instruct them to follow a half-day behind us. We don't need word of mustering troops to jeopardize our plans."

Deron's fatigue immediately vanished at the news replaced by an excited smile. "Gott be praised. In the King's service, it is done!"

Chapter 31

JONAS GAVE LITTLE THOUGHT TO HIS ROUGH APPEARANCE. HE SKIRTED nearby homes on his way to Wyck's Inn. He grimaced and touched his chest. Without proper medicine, the wound inflicted by Destry still ached. He knew the authorities would be after him. Avoiding territorial patrols, dangerous animals, and other hazards lengthened the journey to Sener.

Being the wee hours of the morning, he hoped to reach the inn before anyone woke. As fellow innkeepers, he stood a good chance of convincing Wyck to help him. After all, the guild encouraged unquestioning cooperation against anything that impeded business.

Jonas reached the back of a stable before even the rooster crowed. He tethered the horse outside the rear gate. He would tend to the animal later. First, he had to contact Wyck.

Carefully, he opened the gate. Fortunately, the hinges were well oiled and didn't creak or squeak. He wasn't so fortunate upon meeting a dog, which began to bark.

"Shh! Quiet!" he tried to coax the dog. He pulled out a piece of sausage from the satchel and tossed it to the dog. Immediately, the animal quieted to eat the meat.

Too late! Light shown in a back window. Jonas flattened himself against the inn when the door opened. A person appeared holding a candle.

"What are you barking at, Mia, the neighbor's cat?" chided a male voice.

Jonas recognized him, and hissed the name, "Wyck!"

Wyck stepped out into the yard. "Who's there?"

"It's me. Jonas." He boldly stepped out for Wyck to see him.

Wyck raised the candle for better viewing. He remained skeptical at sight of the soiled man. "Jonas of Gilroy?"

"Aye." Jonas then added the guild motto, "For the good of patrons."

Wyck moved closer. He gaped in recognition. "By Gott, Jonas, what happened to you?"

"The same that can happen to you, and others, because of the edict," he grimly replied.

"Quickly, inside." Wyck ushered Jonas through the kitchen to a secluded storeroom. "Irin and others will be up soon, but you will be safe here for a while."

Wyck lit the storeroom lantern. Upon doing so, he noticed Jonas' unkempt and mired appearance. "When was the last time you ate? Or bathed for that matter?"

"Weeks since a bath. But, food, only what I could scrounge on the road." Weary, Jonas sat on barrel.

Wyck uncovered the remains of a meat pie and gave it to Jonas. He used his bare hands to eat. Wyck filled a tankard with cider. Jonas grabbed the tankard and washed down the pie.

"Easy, man. You'll make yourself sick," warned Wyck.

"An aching stomach from too much food is better than the pain of an empty belly," Jonas mumbled with a mouth full of pie.

Wyck pulled up an empty crate to sit. "What happened?"

Anger and distress made Jonas stop eating. "Somehow Hertz and Bernal discovered Sharla and the boys were of *the Faith.*" He sneered back a tremble in his voice to say, "They took my family! If they reach Sener ..."

Wyck sighed with great lament. "Dear Gott. We knew this day would come but … wait …" He then looked incredulous at Jonas. "Did you come all this way to rescue them?"

"Why else risk what I have?" Jonas rebuffed.

"It's suicide!"

Furious, Jonas stood.

Wyck also rose to continue his argument. "One man can't rescue anyone from the dungeons of Sener."

"Then you've seen them! With a large group."

"No group has passed here. And they must to get to Sener. Besides, I would have recognized your family."

Jonas grew hopeful. "I may still have a chance before they reach the city."

"By a *large group*, I take it you mean more than just Sharla and the boys."

"Aye!" Jonas waved with impatience to any prevent further inquiry.

"You may have arrived in time, but doubtful you can do anything to help them."

"Can you smuggle me into Sener?"

Wyck shrugged, baffled. "Why not just ride into the city?"

"Because I just told you, man! They took my family. We all tried to flee during the melee."

"Flee? You let your family be captured?"

"I didn't know that at the time. Only about the warrant."

"What warrant?" Wyck suddenly became suspicious. "What aren't you telling me?"

Jonas quickly covered his mistake. "I'm as confused as you. They arrived before dawn spouting words about a warrant and the edict. It became chaos. I suffered injury." He gingerly pulled back his doublet and shirt to reveal the chest wound. He then pointed to the fading contusion on his forehead. "When I came too, they were gone!"

"Why didn't they take you as well?"

Jonas flung up his hands in exasperation. "I don't know! Maybe they thought I was dead."

"Wyck?" a female voice called

Both men stopped to listen when the female spoke again.

"Wyck. Where are you? What's going on?"

"Irin," Wyck harshly whispered to Jonas. "Stay hidden. I'll talk to her—"

Jonas grabbed Wyck to stop his departure. "You can't tell her about me."

The door opened. Jonas released Wyck to seize Irin, pulled her inside and shut the door. He covered her mouth to stop any outcry.

"Jonas! Let her go!" Wyck accosted Jonas to free his wife.

"You did nothing more for Irin than I want to do for Sharla!" Jonas chided when he released her.

Irin clung to Wyck, startled, frightened, and confused. "What is he talking about?"

"The edict resulted in the capture of brethren. Sharla, and the boys included," Wyck somberly replied.

"Oh, dear Gott," Irin spoke in distress.

Jonas softened his attitude toward Irin. "I'm sorry for being so rough. I came here to save them before they reach Sener."

Irin looked to Wyck. "Is there any way we can help?"

Wyck shook his head with uncertainty. "I'm not sure. For now, take him to the secret room. He needs a bath and clothes."

"My horse is behind the stable gate."

"I'll take care of the beast. Go with Irin."

Wyck fetched Jonas' horse. It looked as miserable as its owner. The horse hobbled badly, so once inside the barn, Wyck lit a lamp to inspect the animal. He discovered multiple cuts on its legs. The deepest injury being to the right front knee, thus causing lameness.

Wyck patted the horse's neck. "Don't worry, girl. You'll get the rest and aid you need."

He proceeded to unsaddle the horse and rub her down with a liniment of calendula, echinacea, and wormwood. He paid careful attention to the knee injury by applying a simple solution of water and salt for disinfecting, followed by a healing mixture of oil and honey. He bandaged the wound then placed a blanket on her. He filled the trough with fresh hay and a bucket with water to drink.

A young groom arrived. He yawned and stretched. "Someone arrived already?" he asked Wyck. An older groom joined them.

"No, an abused animal that found its way to the back gate," Wyck made quick excuse.

"Tack and all?"

"Happened before when some poor soul ran afoul of harpys or the Ha'tar," said the older groom to his companion.

"Aye, and we always take care of them." Wyck patted the older groom on the shoulder. "If she wants more hay, give her oats instead. She can use the nourishment to help heal."

Wyck returned to the kitchen, which was now a hive of activity in preparation of food for the day. He noticed Irin emerge from the main pantry. He motioned her to a quiet corner.

"How is he?"

"Sleeping. He refused a full bath, just a quick wash. I went to fetch his old clothes to find him in bed fast asleep."

"I'm not surprised. He nearly rode his horse past its limits. If her wounds don't heal …"

"You have a way with horses."

He forced a smile at her encouragement.

"Have you thought about how to help?"

Wyck pressed his lips together in consideration. "I don't know what can be done without exposing *others*."

She whispered in his ear. "The Weasel may know something useful."

"My thoughts exactly. Prepare his favorite meal." He kissed her forehead and left the kitchen.

Even at this early hour, the main dining room began to fill with guests, both those staying at the inn, and locals. Wyck took note of the regulars, those who frequented the inn almost daily. Some came just for the food, others, for more nefarious opportunities.

A quick scan of the crowd told Wyck that The Weasel had not yet arrived. A little too early, perhaps. With his normal gregarious smile, Wyck strolled about the room greeting everyone. Of the guests who were leaving, he sent word to the grooms to prepare the horses.

He just moved behind the bar when The Weasel arrived. A scruffy middle-aged man in a well-worn uniform that harkened back to a former Elector, but none dare ask, as the Weasel didn't like intrusive questions. On the wall behind the bar, a panel could slide open to speak to people in the kitchen. Wyck used it to call Irin. When she appeared on the other side, he spoke.

"The meal for our special guest."

Wyck spoke a few private words to his teenage son, who helped to tend those in the tavern. The teenager nodded. Wyck proceeded to The Weasel's usual table.

"You're late." Wyck tried to keep a straight face as he scolded.

"You opened early," The Weasel countered.

Wyck heartily laughed.

Irin arrived. "We received an unexpected delivery of duck eggs. Fixed just the way you like, with roasted potatoes." She sweetly smiled and set the plate before The Weasel.

Their son arrived. "Apple ale." He placed an overflowing tankard beside the plate.

Wyck motioned for Irin and their son to leave when The Weasel cast a suspicious glance up at him.

"I take it you want something."

Wyck sat opposite. "Just answers to a few questions."

"A sample first before I agree." The Weasel ate some of the eggs then took a long drink of ale. He used his sleeve to wipe the ale from his stubby whiskers. "Ask."

"What happened in Gilroy?"

"You mean the Ha'tar attack?" he spoke with a mouthful.

Wyck's brows furrowed at the reply. "No, I mean," his voice lowered, "the edict."

The Weasel paused in eating. He then shoved a fork full of potatoes in his mouth. "You mean warrants for traitors."

Wyck made a careful glance at the other guests before he asked, "Who?"

The Weasel drank more ale. "The same one as before, those at Far Point." He ate the eggs. "Oh, and the innkeeper at Gilroy." He waved his fork at Wyck. "Wanted for murder that one is."

Wyck barely managed to keep the shock from his face and voice. "Are you certain?"

"Aye," he mumbled through food.

"The victim?"

"Magistrate Bernal's cousin. Now, you've asked your questions. Let me eat in peace." He used the fork to shoo Wyck away.

Understanding he couldn't press for any more answers, Wyck returned to the bar. It took a moment for him to regain his composure after the stunning news. What he knew of Jonas didn't fit with a charge of murder. Then again, considering Jonas' state upon arrival, a desperate man can act against nature if he feels threatened or trapped. But harboring a fugitive, even one of the Brethren . . . He needed answers.

"Delay anyone leaving for the stables," he ordered his son.

In long, deliberate strides, Wyck made his way to the rear courtyard. The grooms busily worked at the stables. He waited for them to turn their backs before he ran to the back gate. Once out of view, he circumvented the main building to a hidden door. This led to a room with no windows. It contained a bed and table with two chairs. Upon the table sat a lamp. Irin left it lit, only turned low, otherwise the room would be totally dark. Wyck increased the flame. He fought to keep his temper at seeing Jonas still asleep.

"Get up, man!" He slapped Jonas' feet.

The physical assault made Jonas wake with a start. "Wyck?"

"Don't play innocent with me. Answer me truly, or I will turn you over to the authorities!"

"What?" Jonas asked, confused in his groggy state.

Wyck seized Jonas by the collar. "Did you kill Bernal's cousin?"

Jonas blinked in befuddlement. "I—"

"The truth!"

"We fought. But he was still alive when I left."

Wyck's eyes narrowed in disbelief. "You swear by Gott that you did not kill him?"

Jonas fumbled over his reply. "The blow was meant to render him unconscious, so I could escape. If he died—"

"Then you are a murderer!" Wyck dreadfully pronounce.

"No! I didn't intend to kill. Just get away."

Wyck threw the clothes at Jonas. "Get dressed and leave!"

Jonas cast furrowed glance at Wyck, but the hostile expression muted any further argument. When finished dressing, he grabbed his satchel.

Wyck escorted Jonas outside. He stopped him from going to the stable. "Without a horse. I won't let you kill an innocent beast."

Jonas adjusted the satchel over his shoulder before he dashed into the woods.

From a nearby corner of an alley, a scruffy man peered out from under his hood to watch Jonas flee. Once Jonas was out of sight, he made his way to the front of the inn to wait. A few moments passed before The Weasel emerged. He nodded, and The Weasel approached.

Acting nonchalant, The Weasel said, "I did as you asked."

"And netted a good result." He discreetly handed him a pouch filled with coins.

Feeling the weight, The Weasel smile. "The Magistrate pays well—" His words cut short when seized him by the throat.

The man's hood partially fell back. "He doesn't know. And you'll say nothing that connects him to this."

The Weasel's brows rose in surprise recognition. "You're not—?" He coughed at being choked, and fought to say, "I won't."

He shoved The Weasel away. He replaced the hood before he headed for the bridge to cross into Sener.

Chapter 32

THE DOANE COMPRISED THE MOST SOUTHERN PART OF ELDAR. The vast territory stretched from border to border on the west and east. Being so large, multiple roads were needed to travel north to Sener. The two major roads began at the Great Falls and ended at Lake Helivan. They ran alongside the two-mile wide mighty River Leven. The east road travelled Nefal territory, while the west went through Ha'tar lands.

Since Tribute, trade, and military used the roads, an old law forbade any interference of those traveling these roads. Any person found guilty of thievery, harassment, or other crime faced imprisonment or death. This law defended travelers against people groups, but did nothing to protect against harpys, jackals, dragons, and other natural hazards.

When word of the directive reached Vanora, Bernal revised the plan and ordered all prisoners captured in Heddwyn brought to Sener. He knew Governor Ebert would bring the Tribute, yet such a gesture would elevate his standing in the eyes of Javan.

The distance between Vanora and the Great Falls' trailhead added fifty more miles to the journey. Herding a group of forty people including elderly, children, sick, and weak, made for a difficult time. Some days, cold rain impeded the already arduous trek, which resulted in only ten miles traveled. They needed to travel fifteen miles to make the one hundred and fifty miles to Sener in ten days.

Bernal's impatience to reach Sener increased with each delay. Learning of Destry's death while en route deepened his frustration. Although the evidence against Jonas was based solely on him being the last one seen with Destry, Bernal issued the arrest warrant. He taunted Sharla and the boys mercilessly, while he physically took out his frustration on weaker men of the group.

Arctander comforted Sharla after the latest encounter with Bernal. He walked with her and Ida in the middle of the group. Abe, Bart, and Jarred encircled them. Jarred bled from a fresh cut on his lower lip. Abe and Bart also showed signs of recent abuse. Ida tried to tend Jarred's wound while moving.

"I'm fine," he insisted.

"You're not," she compassionately rebuffed.

He flinched at her touch. He grabbed the cloth from her, and gingerly held it against his lip to stem the bleeding.

The group began a gentle climb to a bend in the road. Through the trees, they caught glimpses of the capital city.

"Sener is massive," said Abe with trepidation.

"The first time we see it, is before we die," droned Bart.

Their comments made Sharla whimper with grief.

"Courage," Jarred told the boys. He indicated Sharla.

Bart held his mother's shoulder. "I didn't mean to upset you. We," he nodded to Abe, "just hoped to see the City of The True King in splendor."

Sharla swallowed back her upset to flash a shaky smile.

Arctander spoke in a low, yet confident tone. "With the Son of Eldar here, we may yet live to see it."

Once on the last plateau, the city came into full view.

"The castle is at the apex," said Arctander to the wide-eyed boys.

"What stone is that? It's almost a purplish blue," said Abe.

"Never seen such coloring before," said Bart.

"It's the sunset's reflection in the clouds that you're seeing," droned Jarred.

"No," refuted Arctander. "Although the clouds make it harder to see, the crystalize quartz is the color Abe describes. It's called *royal stone* and quarried in the Halvor Mountains. Direct sunlight sparkles on the colored glass windows." He sighed with regret. "Sadly, it is less grand than when I first saw it as boy."

"Have you been inside the castle?" asked Abe.

"Aye. As first priest and representative of The Doane, my father was responsible for delivering the Tribute. When old enough, I became his assistant. After he died, the responsibility fell to me."

"Until Dolus ordered the priests slaughtered!" Jarred chided.

"Do not dampen our joy," Arctander scolded Jarred.

Rebuffed, Jarred offered a contrite apology.

Occupants of the homes furthest from Wyck's Inn, noticed the approaching group. Among those watching was Jonas. He hid in a nearby field behind a large hay stack. Despite his confrontation with Wyck, he had no intention of leaving the area. His determination paid off when he spotted his family. A sharp pain of distress made him screw his eyes shut. Since that horrible day, feelings of guilt for not protecting them warred with anger at their betrayal of embracing the outlawed Faith. Their haggard appearance enhanced pangs of guilt.

When his eyes opened, he spied Arctander and Ida. Sight of them made his anger flare. In his mind, Arctander bore the brunt of responsibility for the fate of his family. He may have failed at protection, but Arctander influenced Sharla and the boys. His eyes scanned the group. Still no sign of Nollen, the main culprit.

Jonas kept a discrete distance to follow the group. How to save his family remained a problem. He just needed to wait for an opportunity and be close enough to act.

Several young men from those first homes ran to the inn with news of the group. Patrons, staff, Wyck, Irin, and their son took up positions outside or at the windows to see Bernal and Hertz lead the procession. Captain Udell barked commands for soldiers to hurry the mass of haggard people. In turn, impatient soldiers shoved, yelled, and intimidated stragglers.

Bernal drew his horse to a halt before the inn to address the spectators. "Behold, the traitors! Cursed followers of the forbidden Oath!" he shouted with rancor.

"Look well, and heed what will happen to anyone else who defies the edict," Hertz added his harsh warning.

Wyck struggled to contain his astonishment at seeing Arctander among the captives.

Irin noticed, and quickly acted. "You're needed inside." She pulled on his arm.

Despite moving indoors, Wyck immediately took up position at the window. His jowls tensed. The elderly, children, weak and weary, were heartlessly herded past the inn, through the tower gate, and onto the bridge.

Slowly, patrons returned to their repast. Again, guests required his attention. With a heavy heart, Wyck returned to work.

Jonas managed to mingle among the crowd and avoid being seen by Wyck. Help from the fellow innkeeper to enter Sener would have been easier, but no longer possible. He edged his way to the bridge. A short distance from the tower gate, he spied a boatman's house. Two barges, and a dingy were moored at the dock. Goods too large or heavy for the bridge required a ferry. Everyone who visited Sener knew crossing Lake Helivan in daylight without a pass was unwise. He judged twilight to be about a half-hour away. He pulled up his hood to carefully make his way to the dock. Hearing someone approach, he hid around the corner of the boatman's house. He heard the door close and the bolt drawn for the night. A moment later, heavy rain began.

Dark clouds brought twilight sooner than expected. It also gave Jonas the chance to act. He dashed from the house and slid down the bank to the water's edge. This proved quieter than running on the dock. Fortunately, the dingy was the closest boat to shore. He carefully slipped into the dingy and untied the rope. Even with the hood up, he had to wipe the rain from his eyes to see clearly.

Gently he lifted an oar, and slowly pushed the dingy from the dock into open water. He kept his shoulders hunched to maintain a low profile. Near the bridge, he wrapped the cloak about him in an effort to appear as if the boat was adrift with no one aboard. He draped one arm over the side to hold the oar in the water when needed to steer. He ignored the cold making his hand numb. Unable to see due to driving rain, he accidently steered the dingy into a bridge pylon. He heard a voice overhead.

"What was that?"

Light reflected in the water from above. Jonas curled up toward the bow to avoid being seen.

"Looks like the stern of boat. Must have broken from its mooring."

Something moved under the boat, and brush against Jonas' hand. Startled, he jerked his hand out of the water, which caused the boat to rock and him to become visible.

"Hey! You there!"

Jonas placed both oars in the oarlocks and rowed toward Sener. At least, in the direction he thought was Sener.

For a second time, something struck the boat. The force sent the dingy spinning. The head of a serpentine creature broke the surface and grabbed an oar. Jonas nearly fell overboard when the oar was ripped from his hand. The creature submerged. A third knock from another direction, and the dingy went skidding along the water. Jonas fell to the bottom of the boat, stunned.

A thrashing tail broke part of the bow. Jonas scrambled to the stern to avoid a second swipe of the tail. He glanced over his shoulder. The creature's attack brought him close to shore. He used the remaining oar to strike the water and scare off the creature. He felt the oar impact something followed by an underwater screech.

This time, when the head surfaced, it rose up about five feet and bared sharp teeth. In fear, Jonas dove off the back of the dingy, intent on swimming to safety. The creature snapped and just missed him. Enraged, it destroyed the dingy.

Three soldiers appeared on the bank, with one mounted. The two on foot, threw Jonas a rope.

"Grab it!" a soldier shouted.

Once he had hold, the mounted soldier kicked his horse to hurry from the water's edge. Spray from the quick tow in nearly choked Jonas. He coughed and gagged when the soldiers drew him onto shore.

"What were you doing out there?" one chided.

"Don't you know about the lake serpent?" asked another.

Jonas shook his head, as he still recovered from the ordeal.

"Take him to the captain," began the soldier on horseback. "If he's not an idiot then likely a criminal. No one would be stupid enough to try that stunt."

Jonas didn't have the strength to fight the soldiers. He felt the coolness of evening through his wet clothes. Water sloshed in his boots with each step. They waited at the main city gate for the sentry to allow admittance. This wasn't the way he hoped enter Sener, and certainly not captured by soldiers. They went to the gatehouse in search of the captain.

A rotund older man sat at a table partaking of supper. "What is it?" he grumbled with a mouthful of food.

"We caught this man illegally crossing the river in a boat."

"And why would he do that?"

A soldier jerked Jonas' arm. "Answer the captain."

"Because I couldn't get across the bridge before the gate shut."

Displeased by the surly answer, the captain stopped eating. He stood to accost Jonas. For being large, he was also very tall, a trait not seen when sitting. "Flippant answers won't help. Perhaps a night in the dungeon will curb your insolence."

Jonas slightly flinched at the threat. He had to find a way to escape before they discovered his identity. He changed his tone to more contrite.

"I'm sorry, Captain. Being cold and wet made me forget myself. However, I meant what I said. I have important business in the city and was delayed by the prisoners brought in earlier."

The captain asked the soldiers, "He wasn't with Burris?"

"No, Captain. He was along in the dingy," said a soldier.

"Attacked by the lake serpent," added the other.

The Captain snickered, as he glanced up and down at Jonas. "What business could be so important as to risk your life?"

"Are you married, Captain?"

"What does that have to do with it?"

Jonas faked a hapless shrug. "Because if you were, you'd understand the consequences of missing a wife's birthday after a month-long absence. Her present was destroyed when the serpent attacked."

The captain heartily laughed. He composed himself enough to ask, "Do you think me a fool to accept such a lame excuse?"

"I take it you're not married."

Again, Jonas' flippancy irritated him. "Where do you live?"

"On the east side near the stock yards. I'm a tanner."

The captain roughly turned Jonas around to search him. He had no weapon other than the dagger he visibly wore.

Jonas protested when the captain took his dagger. "That's part of my trade."

"Being a tanner, I'm sure you have more. For now, I'll keep it." He motioned to the soldiers. "They will escort you home. *If* your story proves true, I'll return this," He held up the dagger. "*If* not … it's the dungeon, where we'll learn the truth." He used the dagger to wave them away.

Jonas didn't resist when the soldiers drew him from the gatehouse. He even walked confidently for several blocks. Then, when they turned a dark corner, he acted. He attacked one soldier by knocking him into a wall. When the other came at him, Jonas jabbed him with a hard elbow. He started to run away, when the first soldier leapt upon him. They fell to the street locked in struggle. Jonas managed to shove off the soldier and rise to his knees. That's as far as he got.

The Captain cold-cocked Jonas with the hilt of his sword. He and two others had followed unseen. "Is this him?" he asked one of his companions.

The man got down on his knees and rolled Jonas over. "Aye, it's him. He's the man wanted for murder." He stood and brushed off his hands.

"Take him to the dungeon," the Captain ordered.

Chapter 33

BERNAL DISMOUNTED IN THE COURTYARD OF SENER CASTLE. "Bring me Arctander. Take the rest to the dungeon," he ordered Udell.

Hertz waited with Bernal for Udell to comply. Despite the strenuous journey, the old priest fared well. His clothes were soiled, hair unkempt, and face besmudged. However, the serene gleam in his eye remained undiminished.

With contempt, Bernal spoke. "Your self-righteous confidence won't last long when Dolus gets a hold of you."

Arctander didn't reply.

Bernal roughly seized Arctander and pulled him to enter the castle. After a brief stumble at being man-handled, Arctander kept step with Bernal.

"Magistrate Bernal to see Minister Dolus. I bring a highly sought-after prisoner," he snapped at the servant who greeted them.

"This way, sir."

Arctander's step faltered a few times, but Bernal's hold kept him from tripping too severely. Hertz pushed Arctander from behind, though disguised it as an attempt to help right him. By the time they reached the hallway to Dolus' office, Arctander once again kept pace.

Bernal shoved Arctander into the room. He caught himself on a chair to stay on his feet. The last time he had been to Sener, Grimshaw served as first minister to Javan's father. The room changed much in fifteen years. More trophies accompanied by a deep unsettling shudder of coldness. *Evil reigns in this place,* his mind concluded.

His gaze about the room, abruptly stopped. Astonishment made Arctander's eyes grew, and murmur under this breath, "Othniel!"

"You recognize the Great White Lion," Dolus said.

Sylvan averted his eyes from Arctander, when the priest confronted Dolus.

"*You* killed him!" Arctander accused.

Dolus laughed in hearty mockery. He approached the lion. "A fitting prize that will soon be joined by the Six Treasures." He stroked the mane.

Arctander regained command of his faculties. "Be certain you aren't speaking prematurely since you don't possess the Treasures *yet.*"

Bernal cuffed Arctander on the head. "Mind your tongue!"

Dolus waved Bernal off. "He is of no consequence."

"He is the last priest of the Oath," chided Hertz.

"Exactly … the *last,*" Dolus emphasized.

"Not the last of the followers," began Bernal. "We brought forty. Most from Heddwyn, where we found him." He motioned to Arctander.

Dolus huffed a sarcastic chuckle. "It seems your Gott has turned against you. The Great Lion subdued, Heddwyn no longer a sanctuary, and the Six Treasures en route here." He crossed to the desk and picked up several pieces of paper. "These are pledges from the Territories stating which Treasure they are bringing. Shall I read them to you?" He waited a moment to spite Arctander's silence. "The Nefal possess Sadok; the Freelanders, Emet; The Doane, Book of Kings; the Eagles, Star of Conant; the Ha'tar, Shevet, and Ganel, the Horn of Kolyn."

Dolus left the papers to approach Arctander. "All this makes the Blood Oath moot and negates the Son of Eldar's arrival."

Arctander still didn't speak. His visible obstinacy was answer enough.

"Stubbornness only brings death!" Dolus declared, but even that threat didn't alter Arctander's tenacious silence. "Take him to the dungeon with the others!" he ordered Bernal. "You remain," he told Hertz.

As Bernal turned him to leave, Arctander caught a glimpse of Othniel. Only this time, the eyes of the lion moved, and appeared to show concern. Uncertain of what he saw, Arctander kept his gaze on Othniel even as Bernal drug him from the room. Othniel's eyes followed him, urgent and imploring.

In the hall, Arctander's mind raced to comprehend what just happened. The eye contact with Othniel stirred an awareness in his soul like never before. Yet how can an animal show signs of life when displayed as a trophy?

The dead can't move only the living, his mind reasoned. Despite all rational thought, his spirit sensed life in Othniel. So deep went Arctander's consideration that he was unaware of their arrival in the dungeon until Bernal spoke to him.

"Enjoy your short stay!" He pushed Arctander into the room and slammed the door.

Ida immediately greeted Arctander with a hug. "I didn't know if you would come back." Her voice cracked with fear.

Arctander only partially heard her, more intent on getting her undivided attention. "Be still," he quietly warned her. He led her to a corner where he motioned for Jarred to join them. "A most unusual, perhaps miraculous, thing just happened." A smile grew as he whispered with excitement, "Othniel is alive."

"Impossible!" Jarred's voice rose, which Arctander quickly silenced.

"It's true. I saw him in Dolus' study. Only mounted like a trophy." His hand on Jarred's shoulder stopped a protest. "I don't fully understand, yet, I know what I experienced. His eyes sought me. And when our gaze met, I sensed in my soul that the Great White Lion is alive! Somehow imprisoned by evil."

Jarred stared intently at Arctander. "You truly believe that."

"Aye. Think of what it means," he urged.

Ida struggled to comprehend. "It all seems incredible," she breathed.

"To us. But not to Gott." Arctander kindly smiled and stroked her cheek. "He brought the Son of Eldar to us. It is only fitting, Gott completes what is started."

She fought back tears. "Do you think we'll live to see it?"

He embraced her about the shoulders. "Whether we do or not, we have seen the beginning of the promise fulfilled."

Jarred took hold of Ida's hand. His brows wretched with contrition. "I have only one regret. That we are not married."

A whimpering sob escaped her pressed lips.

"Why regret? We are still alive," said Arctander to Jarred. He lifted Ida's head to meet his gaze. "And I am a priest."

Her sob turned to tearful laugh. "Aye."

The jingling of keys was followed by the door opening.

"Another one to join you!" announced a guard.

The man stumbled and caught himself on a post to keep from falling completely to the floor but landed hard on his knees.

"Jonas!" Jarred turned red-faced with rage.

Arctander stepped in front of Jarred. "Take no vengeance! His being here is an act of divine justice."

Jonas glared at Arctander. "Don't play your sanctimonious game with me, old man."

"Jonas!" Sharla firmly scolded.

He smiled in happy relief at seeing her. "Sharla. What of the boys?"

Abe and Bart moved to where Jonas could see them.

"You're all unharmed."

"No thanks to you," Bart chided.

Jonas' joy turned to annoyance. "Is that any way to speak to me?"

"He's right. You did nothing to defend us," chided Sharla.

Pricked, Jonas lashed out in defense. "I'm here because I came to find you and the boys. Rescue, if possible."

"Then how did you end up in the dungeon?" Jarred bitterly said.

Jonas fought his temper. "A story for my wife's ears only!"

"I have no secrets from them," Sharla rebuffed. "Why are you here?"

"I just told you." Jonas reached for Sharla. She avoided him. Her rejection reinvigorated his anger toward Arctander. "You poisoned my wife and sons!"

Jonas launched at Arctander and seized him about the throat to choke him. Jarred intervened, but unable to break Jonas' strong grip.

"No, Jonas!" Sharla screamed. Abe and Bart kept her from being caught in the melee.

Jarred landed a punch to the side of Jonas' head. The blow forced him to release Arctander. Ida tried to catch her grandfather when his knees gave way. He struggled to regain his breath. Guards rushed in to break-up the brawl. They roughly separated Jonas and Jarred.

"He attacked the old man!" Jarred protested.

"He deserved it!" Jonas spat.

"Oh! A trouble-maker." A guard sneered at Jonas. "Take them both to isolation."

"No!" Arctander spoke in a strained voice. He sat on the floor slow to recover. "Jarred defended me."

The guarded nodded for the others to release Jarred. He motioned for his companions to take Jonas from the cell. The lead guard warned Jarred, "Another outburst, and I'll have you flogged."

Sharla knelt beside Arctander. "I'm so sorry."

Abe fretfully said to Arctander, "We've never seen our father act so violent before."

"Aye. Why would he attack you like that?" asked Bart.

"I have become the visible target of his anger and bitterness toward Gott," Arctander soberly replied.

"Because of us?" asked Abe, disconcerted.

Arctander simply nodded. The boy struggled with the implications.

"We never disobeyed him or acted cross," Abe insisted.

Sharla cleared her throat to the contrary.

Abe grew sheepish to admit, "Aside from foolish mischief."

"It's true. We never sought to purposely hurt or provoke him," Bart came to Abe's defense. To this, she agreed.

With compassionate lament, Arctander watched the exchange between mother and sons. "It is a sad truth, that some people cannot accept change in others. Even when that change is for the best."

"What can we do to convince him?" asked Abe, desperate.

Ida supported Arctander when he swayed slightly upon standing. "Prayer," he began. "I know it sounds trite, but Gott has placed your father here for a reason. Trust Gott to work on Jonas' heart."

"We shall," said Sharla. She linked arms with her sons.

In Dolus' office, the first minister conversed with Hertz. Sylvan sat busily working at his corner desk.

"You seemed to have groomed Bernal well," said Dolus.

"There are times I had to pull rank, but he is quick to conform. However," Hertz' tone changed to guarded curiosity. "I'm unfamiliar with the report regarding the Book of Kings. Who sent it?"

Dolus gazed dubiously at Hertz. "Bernal, of course. You didn't know?"

"No. May I see it?"

Dolus returned to the desk and found the report for Hertz' inspection. "Well?" he impatiently demanded.

"This is impossible. The date is during the time we infiltrated Heddwyn and captured Arctander."

"What do you mean? Bernal doesn't have the Book of Kings?"

"He never did. I only recently discovered a rumor that it existed somewhere in the western half of the territory."

"Heddwyn?"

"We searched the compound and found nothing."

Dolus snatched back the report to wave it angrily in Hertz' face. "Someone has it and is pretending to be Bernal!"

Hertz sneered. "Nollen of Far Point!"

Surprised, Sylvan paused in his work to glance up to the discussion. Neither Hertz nor Dolus noticed.

"Who?" asked Dolus.

"Arctander's interfering grandson. He is believed to be with the Son of Eldar and serving as his guide to avoid capture."

Dolus became incredulous. "And you could not stop him? What is he? Another priest? A knight, perhaps?"

Hertz hesitated to reply but prompted by Dolus' angry sneer. He murmured the answer. "Far Point is a trading post."

"A merchant outwitted you?" The sarcasm in Dolus' voice raised to an outburst of incredulity. "I made a mistake in sending you to The Doane!"

"Master, if I may," began Sylvan, tentative. Once he had Dolus' attention, he spoke again. "I couldn't help but overhear. And the discussion makes me wonder. If this Nollen is with the Son of Eldar, why would he write and agree to bring the Book of Kings as Tribute?"

Dolus' narrow glare shifted to Hertz. "A very good question. Perhaps a lawyer can answer it?"

"To smuggle the Son of Eldar into Sener," said Hertz.

"I take it you would recognize this Nollen of Far Point?"

"Aye, Minister."

"Then keep watch at the gate! Sylvan, make sure Master Hertz find his way without delay." Dolus made a rough wave of dismissal.

After escorting Hertz to the front gate and relaying Dolus' instruction to the officer, Sylvan made a detour to the hidden coop. He scribbled a quick note and attached it to the leg pouch of a shield owl.

"Fly swiftly in the King's Service." He released the bird.

Chapter 34

GRAY LIGHT OF EARLY DAWN SHOWN THROUGH THE WINDOWS of Ronan's study. He, Cormac, Irwin, Axel, Gunnar, and Nollen gathered around the table to view a map of Eldar. All were dressed for travel. Nollen's usual clothes were replaced by a Ganel uniform of maroon and silver. A saddlebag hung over his shoulder. He held it steady.

Back in his own clothes, Axel wore the replica Horn of Kolyn. Gunnar too, donned his uniform. Both suits were cleaned and repaired from weeks of travel.

"We'll move in an arc that will bring us through a portion of the Halvor Mountains to approach Sener from the north." Ronan used a gloved finger to draw out the route on the map. "Once at Zorin, we separate."

"Ronan, are you certain you don't want to take this?" Axel patted the fake horn he worn. "Javan will grow suspicious when you arrive empty-handed."

"If we time our arrival as planned, there will be no chance for questions." He then spoke to Nollen. "Have you memorized the secret passageway into the Great Hall?"

"Aye. I've gone over it every day with Sir Irwin. What about the archers? Will they join us?"

Ronan shook his head. "They might reach the galleyway the same time, but by alternate means. Smuggling in the bows are key." He picked up a rather plain looking leather case. He undid the latch top to pull out the contents. On the table, he placed two ends of a bow with string attached at either end, and a center piece of silver. He demonstrated how to assemble the bow.

"Will it hold together when fired?" asked Gunnar, a bit skeptical.

Ronan handed him the weapon. "Try it. Pull as hard as you can."

Gunnar did a visual inspection of the silver center for secure fitting. He sighted a pretend target and pulled the string, as if shooting. He repeated the action several times. The center piece held. "Impressive." He returned the bow.

Ronan disassembled the bow and replaced it in the case. "Fifteen of my formal escort to the castle are expert archers, and armed with such bows—"

A scratching at the window interrupted Ronan.

"Another shield owl," said Cormac. Being nearest the window, he fetched the bird. He unhooked the message pouch to give to Ronan.

"Well," began Ronan with a muted chuckle. "It appears our precaution about using the secret entrance is warranted." He read aloud. "*Hertz in Sener. On lookout for Nollen of Far Point, b f k, and s f e.*"

"Come again with the letters?" asked Gunnar.

"Shorthand for Book of Kings and Son of Eldar."

Nollen swallowed back discomposure to say, "I shudder to think how Hertz came by that information."

Gunnar held the young man's shoulder. "Don't dwell on it. Such thoughts will distract you from what must be done."

"That easy for you. It's not your family."

"Nollen," Ronan compassionately scolded.

"No, he's right about that relationship," began Gunnar. He then said to Nollen, "However, I *do* have a deeply vested interest in the outcome. And not *solely* as a native Eldarian." He nodded toward Axel.

Nollen grew regretful. "I know. I'm sorry. Highness." He sheepishly glanced to Axel.

"No need to apologize," said Axel graciously. "Just remember, I depend upon you."

Determined, Nollen straightened and squared his shoulder. "Gott willing, I won't fail."

Axel heartily patted Nollen on the back.

"We should be leaving," said Ronan.

In the main courtyard, twenty mounted knights of Ganel waited in formation. Grooms held the reins of six horses. Three were formally saddled for the Ganel's official journey. Bardolf and Alfgar stood beside the horses.

"My lord Alfgar. I did not think to see you so soon," said Axel.

"There is uneasiness in the forest. Some of the enemy's creatures are causing havoc sooner than expected. Thus, my earlier return. My herd will also serve as escort. Five hundred strong." Alfgar tossed his head, stomped his right foreleg, and let out a loud neighing call.

An echo of unicorns came in reply, which caused the humans to look for the source.

"They wait on the isthmus with the rest of Ganel's forces," said Alfgar.

"How many men?" Axel asked Ronan.

"Ten thousand. Four thousand knights, fifteen hundred archers, and four thousand and five hundred foot-soldiers."

Bardolf approached Axel. "My pack may be gone, but we were not the last of White Wolves. Others live in the foothills of the Halvors."

"If only we knew how many from The Doane and Freelands will respond," Gunnar groused.

"More will rise when summoned," Axel said with certainty. He mounted and moved his horse beside Ronan to lead the troops from the castle.

Nollen and Gunnar rode behind Axel and Ronan. Cormac and Irwin followed, and directly in front of the troops. Through the winding city streets, they rode. Throngs of people on all levels bid them Gott's speed, and pronounced blessings on the Son of Eldar. This made Axel glance curiously at Ronan.

"Difficult to keep a secret when mustering troops." Ronan fought a smile in reply.

"You realize this means there is no turning back?"

Ronan lifted his chin with pride. "In the King's service, we ride to whatever fate awaits."

As they continued, Axel acknowledged the people. From upper floor windows, women threw flowers; yellow celosia and red chrysanthemums. Nollen caught a chrysanthemum. Axel caught a celosia. He smelled the fragrance then held it up for Ronan.

"What is this flower? I've not seen it before," he asked.

"We call it, the flower of hope. It grows from late summer to the beginning of winter. We hang the last blooms of the year to dry in our homes, as reminder of the *hope* that will come with spring." Ronan turned slightly in the saddle. "Nollen's red flower is a sign of trust and faithfulness."

"Then it is fitting he caught it for this venture." With steady regard, Axel held Nollen's gaze.

The young man tucked the flower stem through a clasp of the surcoat, so the blossom remained visible. Axel did the same with his flower.

Once they reached the halfway point of the city, they turned east toward the main gate and causeway aqueduct. Trumpets blew when the procession passed through the main gate. Gunnar grew nervous as they moved onto the causeway.

Nollen noticed the edginess. "Something wrong?"

Caught off-guard by the question, Gunnar roughly said, "No!"

Not convinced, Nollen continued. "What is it about the aqueduct that disturbs you?"

"Nothing," Gunnar gruffly dismissed the question.

Nollen leaned closer to ask, "Are you afraid of water?" Gunnar didn't react. "Of heights?" To this, question, he received a sideway glare of anger. Realizing his pushed too far, Nollen faced forward to continue over the causeway.

Gunnar spoke under his breath. "This is an unnatural height!"

"I won't argue with that," agreed Nollen.

Being the main water supply for Mathena, water on the aqueduct freely flowed in channels on either side of the causeway. Wrought iron metal work separated the causeway from the channels. The main thoroughfare was wide enough to accommodate large wagons and for riders to travel three abreast. It extended for half-a-mile over the narrowest part of Endelos in a gentle arch before descending to the isthmus.

Gunnar stared straight ahead. His fists clenched the reins. He didn't relax until they reached the other side.

"You realize we are now in the Halvor region? The Eagles' Territory," Nollen comment to Gunnar.

"Actually, we're on neutral ground," said Cormac. His remark made Nollen turn while Gunnar still faced forward. "This isthmus serves as the divider between the two sides of the river. We have another, *smaller* bridge to cross."

"As long as we're safely off the aqueduct I don't care where we are," said Gunnar.

Cormac winked at Nollen, who fought against amusement. Nollen felt Gunnar punch his shoulder in rebuke. Hearing an eagle drew attention to the sky.

"Ottlia?" said Axel.

"Aye. She and others patrol the isthmus to aid in our defense," explained Ronan.

A trumpet from the troops sounded. Mortal soldiers and unicorns came to attention. Ronan and the others moved to face the troops, while the castle escort joined the formation. When all grew quiet, Ronan's voice raised to be heard.

"This is the day our fathers and forefathers longed for, but to us, Gott has granted the privilege to witness. No, more than that, to be partakers by escorting the Son of Eldar to Sener. To join him in restoring the throne!" He drew his sword.

Axel stopped Ronan from raising his weapon.

"Highness?" asked Ronan, perplexed.

Axel briefly bowed his head. "Gott, help me," he whispered a plea. He sat straight up in the saddle to begin his address. "The journey we undertake will be one that shall test our mettle, our hearts, and our Faith. Before anything good can happen, there may come a time of darkness. A time more difficult than any have experienced before."

Cormac and Irwin put their heads together with murmuring between them. Similar reactions came from the troops. Ronan sat stoic. Nollen stirred with easiness. Gunnar's firm hand, grim expression, and stout shake of the head stopped any question or comment from the young man.

Axel raised both hands to regain attention. "I realize this is not what you expected me to say yet listen well. The enemy will do everything possible to cause doubt and fear. Regardless of what you think, see, or hear, place your trust in Gott. It is for his plans and purposes that I take up this challenge. That I ask you to join me in ridding Eldar of the darkness that has plagued our kingdom of far too long." He drew his sword to raise it high. "For Gott! For Eldar!"

With enthusiastic agreement, Ronan raised his sword. "For Gott! For Eldar!"

Humans and creatures repeated the shout several times. All became quiet when Axel sheathed his sword. Together, he and Ronan again took the lead.

Chapter 35

In his chamber, Javan yawned, as he sat up against the pillows. Dolus and Beltran stood beside the bed. Beltran held a glowing candelabra. Shafts of dawn's gray light appeared on the rims of the heavy window curtains.

"It is imperative, Elector," Beltran insisted.

Javan fought another yawn. "So, you keep saying! Still, you have not given me adequate reason."

"Arctander's arrival in Sener has caused unrest among the people. Soldiers report difficulty in keeping the peace. Several suffered injuries when breaking up fights about him."

"The people will become further agitated if he is executed," Dolus told Beltran.

Beltran ignored Dolus to press his argument. "Elector, your father ordered the execution of all priests. He feared that even one left alive would stir up the remaining followers of the True King, or even those sympathetic to their plight. Arctander's imprisonment is doing just that."

Angered by the brashness, Javan rose to confront Beltran. "Speak not to me of what my father did!"

Dolus physically intervened to keep Javan from assaulting Beltran. "We must proceed according to plan and take possession of the Six Treasures. That is the only way to thwart the Son of Eldar and subdue the people."

Beltran sneered in disagreement. "What about Arctander?"

"Because of your complaints, I ordered him placed in isolation," Dolus curtly replied.

"I doubt that will be helpful!"

"Make it so!"

Beltran sharply turned from Dolus to Javan. "Elector—"

Dolus hotly interrupted the protest. "Any further action against Arctander before we secure the Treasures would produce devastating consequences!"

Again, Beltran went to object, but stopped by Javan's harsh words.

"You heard *First* Minister Dolus! Be content with Arctander's move to isolation."

Beltran's lips tightly pressed together to contain his temper. He made a rigid bow to Javan before he turned on his heels to leave.

After the door slammed, Javan expressed his displeasure. "If the Son of Eldar doesn't arrive soon, I *will* order Arctander's execution! He can at least serve as a substitute."

"No!" began Dolus in adamant rebuff. "It would only make matters worse by jeopardizing your claim to the throne. The Blood Oath, and ancient alliance are very specific. One wrong step will doom everything we've worked for."

Javan's eyes narrowed in wrath. "Beware of exhausting my patience. Or I may add your name to the order when I finally deal with Arctander."

Rage instantly sprang into Dolus' glare. "Remember your own pact with me! Your soul for the crown."

Despite the ominous threat, Javan offered a rebuke. "And *your* continued position of power is also dependent upon *my* success."

The intense battle of wills became interrupted by a knock on the chamber door. A valet entered.

"What do you want?" demanded Javan.

Surprised by the vehement question, he meekly answered, "It's dawn, Elector. Time to prepare for your morning toilet."

Annoyed, Javan shoved Dolus away. "Off with you! We'll meet in the study after breakfast."

Sylvan carried a tray of food down to the dungeon. He approached the guard in front of a single cell door. "Breakfast for the prisoner."

"I didn't know he was allowed food," huffed the guard.

"Order of First Minister Dolus."

The guard unlocked the door to allow Sylvan entry. "Call me when you're ready to leave."

Arctander laid on the rickety bed and stared up at the tiny cell window. He didn't change focus when Sylvan entered and approached.

Sylvan bent over to place the tray on a chair beside the bed. He whispered in ancient Eldarian, "*In se kynge servir.*"

The signal phrase caught Arctander's attention. The old priest curbed a smile. "You take a great risk coming to see me."

"We both know the time is near.

"Aye." Arctander pushed himself to sit up. Stiffness and fatigue evident in his ginger movement.

Sylvan pretended to deal with the food while he spoke in a hushed, hurried tone. "I sent word you are here, and for the alternative plan to be put into action." He flashed a reassuring smile. "The food is safe. I prepared it myself."

"The others?" asked Arctander, fretful.

"Alive."

"Thank Gott," he breathed a sigh of relief.

"I must leave. Be of good cheer."

Sylvan moved to the door and called for the guard. Without looking back, he left to make his way to the largest prison cell. He frowned upon discovering two guards at a table playing dice.

"First Minister Dolus wants a count of the prisoners."

"Same number as when we moved the old man two days ago," came a guard's surly reply. He showed more interest in the game.

Angered by the disregard, Sylvan snatched up the dice. This brought the guards to their feet.

"Hey! Why did you do that?"

"Evidence to show First Minister Dolus. Gambling on duty is a serious charge that could mean death."

Rightly shamed, the guards came to attention. "Do you want to count them or should we?"

"I doubt either of you can count higher than the numbers on these dice." Sylvan pocketed the dice then waved at the door.

Once inside, Sylvan slowly made his way around the room with the pretense of counting. He paused before Ida and Sharla, who sat on the floor. He paid particular attention to Ida. His back was to the door.

"Are you the woman from Far Point?"

"Who wants to know?" Ida shot back. She looked past Sylvan to see Jarred approach.

Sylvan also noticed. He lowered his voice. "I mean no harm." He lowly repeated the signal phrase, *"In the king's service,"* and carefully revealed his medallion.

"What do you want?" demanded Jarred in a harsh whisper.

Sylvan kept his voice low, and discrete. "To assure you that *he* who was separated, is well. I just brought him food."

Ida sagged in relief and bit her lip to stifle any verbal expression.

Jarred's tone changed to agreeable when he asked, "Do you know what will happen to us?"

"It depends if the Treasures are successfully gathered or not. *And*, the arrival of a certain individual of prophecy."

The reference to Axel brought Ida to her feet. "*He* can't come."

Sylvan looked at her directly. "If he doesn't, everyone here *will* die." He used a small hand gesture to indicate the occupants of the cell.

Jarred sharply turned Sylvan to face him. "We would all rather die than see him submit to Javan and Dolus!"

"Hush!" Sylvan urged. He glanced at the door but saw no movement. "So, would I, but the fate of *all* Eldar rests with his coming." Again, he nervously looked at the door. "Now, I must go. I'll try to provide you with what information I can, *if* I can. Either way, keep the faith."

Sylvan called to the guards. "I've completed my count!" He nodded to them while he waited for the door to open. In the hall, Sylvan scolded the guards. "The count is accurate. However, some of the children appear worse than when they arrived."

"We have no orders for medical attention."

"Oh?" Sylvan huffed to contrary. "As I recall, the First Minister's orders were to see them kept *sound* until needed." He brought out the dice, and casually rolled them between his fingers. "Well, if you aren't following orders, along with gambling ..."

"I'll fetch a doctor immediately!" One guard saluted, but Sylvan detained him.

"Make certain this is the last time I discover any violation of orders. Do you understand?"

"Aye, sir!" they replied in unison.

Chapter 36

THE SMALL FORTIFIED TOWN OF ZORIN STOOD SITUATED IN THE foothills of the Halvor Mountains. These hardy people endured harsh winters, torrid springs, short summers, and unpredictable autumns. Yet for all their stalwartness in facing the elements, hospitality flourished. Traveling the wilds of the north took courage and stamina.

An early season snowfall began. Flurries mostly but accompanied by cold north winds. Mayor Lorne, a slender man in the middle sixties, waited outside the barbican for Ganel's approaching army. Three townsmen stood behind him. Watchmen remained vigil on the rampart.

Ottlia landed on the merlons. She spread her wings and made a loud, long cry. The reply of multiple eagles came from the flock overhead.

Mayor Lorne bowed when Ronan, Axel, Gunnar, Nollen, Irwin, and Cormac arrived. Bardolf accompanied the men while Alfgar remained with the troops.

"My lord Ronan, it is always an honor to receive you. Though it has been too long between visits," Lorne graciously spoke in friendly rebuke.

Ronan wryly smiled. "It is good to see you too, Lorne."

The mayor turned his attention to the newcomers. "Gentlemen, I bid you welcome to Zorin. All we have, we freely share to any who travel these parts."

"Lorne, these *gentlemen*, are more than mere travelers," said Ronan pointedly.

Lorne maintained his agreeable demeanor in reply. "That is obvious by the presence of eagles, a white wolf, and …" His tone changed to guarded, "if my eyes are correct at this distance—unicorns. The likes of which, I never thought to see."

"You are correct. Alfgar is among them," said Ronan.

"The fabled lord of the unicorns," Lorne spoke in awe.

Bardolf made his way to stand in front of Axel's horse, so Ronan introduced him. "This is Bardolf, an alpha among the White Wolves."

Bardolf sniffed the ground then the air in direction of Lorne.

"He's making certain there is no deception," explained Gunnar.

Lorne raise his hands. "He will find none." He glanced toward the army. "Yet other eyes may be watching."

Bardolf sniffed the area around the townsmen. To this action, Lorne said, "Allow me to make the introductions. This is Sheriff Haskel, and Aldermen Fane and Osborn."

The three men nodded when identified. Bardolf returned to his position beside Axel's horse.

"It appears all is well," said Gunnar.

Lorne stepped aside to motion to the gate. "Shall we." He led them into Zorin.

The compact town made the trip to the mayor's residence relatively short, perhaps two hundred yards.

"Master Fane will tend to the horses. He is our resident blacksmith and innkeeper," said Lorne.

Fane touched his forehead in salute. Once they dismounted, he barked orders to waiting youths. Nollen fetched his saddlebag before a youth took charge of Gilen. Gunnar and Axel also took possession of their saddlebags.

"You need not fear for your possessions," said Fane.

Nollen flashed an unconvinced smile. "Thanks for reassurance, but I will keep it with me."

"Have our horses back by dawn, as we are only staying the night," Ronan instructed Fane.

Inside the mayor's house, more people scrambled to meet them. A woman of near forty years old smiled and curtsied. "Lord Ronan. Sirs."

"Keena. Lorne still keeps you busy, I see," replied Ronan in good-natured banter.

"Some of his habits have improved," she lightly retorted. She snapped her fingers and motioned for servants to take hats, cloaks, and gloves.

"My daughter runs my household," Lorne enlightened the new guests. "Being a widower, I'm not very good with domestic issues."

"Supper will be ready in an hour. For the time being, I placed warm cider and scones in the parlor," said Keena.

"Our rooms first, please," said Axel.

"Of course. Follow me." She led them upstairs where she indicated rooms across the hall from the other. "I'm afraid we only have two guest rooms."

"We can share." Axel indicated Nollen and Gunnar.

"As will we," Ronan spoke of himself, Cormac, and Irwin.

Once inside the room, Gunnar made a safety inspection while Bardolf sniffed the perimeter.

"This wardrobe has a key. We can place our saddlebags inside." Gunnar took the bags from Axel and Nollen to put next to his then locked the wardrobe. "I'll keep it." He placed it in his pocket.

At the toilet stand, Nollen tested the water in the basin. "It's lukewarm."

"Better to warm our hands slowly from the cold," said Gunnar.

"Only mildly," groused Nollen. He dried his hands-on a towel. "Hopefully they'll light the fire to warm up this room."

Axel took Nollen by the shoulder to steer him to the door. "There is mulled cider in the parlor, and probably a good fire."

Lorne, Haskel, and Osborn had already helped themselves to the cider. They noticed the guests' arrival.

"Gentlemen. Is everything satisfactory?" asked Lorne.

"Once the room is warm," chided Nollen. He went to the hearth.

Axel soothed Lorne's pricked reaction to Nollen's snide comment. "I'm sure it will be fine later."

"Naturally. Please, help yourselves." Lorne indicated the refreshments.

Gunnar poured cups of cider for Axel and Nollen before he joined them. Ronan, Cormac, and Irwin arrived.

Lorne fetched refreshment for the others. He then raised his cup in salute to Axel. "Your health, *my lord*," he spoke with knowing emphasis. Osborn and Haskel echoed the title.

"The fire is warm, pray make yourself comfortable." Lorne offered a seat beside the hearth to Axel.

Nollen moved aside for Axel to sit. Gunnar refused when Lorne indicated a second chair by the fire. Instead, Gunnar, asked, "You mentioned *other eyes*, have there been reports of spies in the area?"

Lorne scowled, and heaved a shrug. "Since Zorin lies between Sener and the Halvor Mountains there are always spies lurking in the area."

"Some try to take advantage our of reputed hospitality, but easily spotted since they are unfamiliar with the area's wilderness," said Haskel.

"Anything unusual of late?" Gunnar continued his questioning.

"More frequent attempts. Nothing too suspicious," replied Haskel.

Axel tugged on Gunnar's arm to make his sit. "With such a large force leaving Mathena, Javan will know there is more to this journey than bringing a Treasure."

"Maybe not," began Irwin. "What territorial governor carrying such a precious Treasure would do so without proper escort and protection?"

"If only comprised of men it would not draw attention," countered Axel. "The inclusion of creatures, well, that's a different matter." He patted Bardolf's head when the wolf sat beside him.

"Aye," grumbled Irwin. He took a drink.

"I assure you, all precautions have been taken to safeguard what has already arrived." Haskel spoke the cryptic statement to Irwin and Axel.

Ronan gripped Haskel's arm in anxious warning. "Everything?"

"I have only received four," he said, a bit sheepish. "Yet all are safe."

"Fret not, we know where the other two are," said Axel. "When can we see them?"

"After supper, when the watch has secured the streets, and it is safe to venture out," said Lorne.

Throughout supper, Lorne's talkative nature provided amusing anecdotes of the town's people and Zorin's history. Not to be outdone, Osborn and Haskel joined in telling tales.

Gunnar heartily laughed yet shook his head in mild refute. "All this cannot be true. Surely some facts are exaggerated."

"Storytelling is a highly prized skill in Zorin," said Osborn.

"It is a means of entertainment to pass away the long dreary days of winter," said Lorne.

"For a widower or bachelor," Osborn snickered to Haskel about Lorne. He and Haskel showed signs of inebriation, though not totally devoid of faculties due to drinking.

"Why just them?" Nollen innocently asked.

Osborn and Haskel burst out laughing.

Cormac leaned close to say, "Because they aren't married."

Nollen's flush of embarrassment increased Osborn and Haskel's amusement.

"Go easy on the lad," said Gunnar with a wry smile. "Such innocent inexperience should not be ridiculed."

Osborn and Haskel battled to curb their merriment.

From outside, the watch called, "Eight o'clock, and all is well!"

Lorne rushed to finish his drink. "That is the signal. The streets are clear, my lord," he said to Axel.

When the men rose from the table, Bardolf left his place by the hearth to join them.

"Your cloaks and gloves are on that table. You'll need them." Lorne indicated the long flat hall-table near the front door. Cloaks hung on hooks just beside the table. Lorne took the lantern off a hook by the front door and lowered the flame. As he reached for the door, Bardolf cut in front of him, and barked. Startled, Lorne drew back a few steps.

"Let Bardolf go first. His nose can detect trouble before our eyes can see it," said Axel.

Lorne opened the door for Bardolf to exit. He waited in the threshold with the others at his back. They watched the wolf make a search of the area. Bardolf again barked at Lorne.

"He says all is clear," Axel translated.

"You can understand a wolf?" marveled Lorne.

"A gift from Gott to aid my task." At Bardolf's second bark, Axel asked, "Which way?"

"Left three blocks, then right for five more."

Gunnar looked up. "At least the snow has stopped."

Bardolf headed in the direction indicated.

As they left the house, Nollen spoke under his breath to Axel. "Why isn't Bardolf speaking words?"

Axel waved him silence, though he whispered a reply. "I don't know, but let's trust him."

They arrived at a warehouse. The double doors were barred and padlocked. Bardolf growled. There came responding growls and snarls from inside the warehouse.

Gunnar reached for his sword. "What creatures are inside?"

"Two dogs, trained to guard the warehouse," said Haskel, hurriedly. "Cass, Bebe, quiet!" he commanded through the door. The dogs obeyed and the noises ceased.

Haskel opened the padlock. Once he removed the chain, he lifted the bar and secured it in an upright position. He took the lantern from Lorne before he opened one of the doors.

Upon entering, two dogs were laying down. They immediately stood at seeing Bardolf. Despite the wolf being larger, they bared fangs and growled. Bardolf raised his head and made a low howl. Suddenly, the dogs backed away with submissive whimpers.

Haskel watched in annoyed surprise. "I trained them not to back down!"

"He didn't want to kill them for obeying you," said Axel.

Bardolf yipped at the dogs. Once more the demeanor changed, as the dogs greeted the wolf like lower pack members. When Bardolf made a low howl, the dogs joined in agreement.

"The watch is set," Axel said. "Your dogs will keep vigil with Bardolf while we proceed."

Haskel accepted the clarification with skepticism. "Osborn, shut the door when everyone is inside."

Weaving through crates, casks, and barrels, Haskel led them to the rear of the warehouse. He stopped by a small cart loaded with four crates. Harness showed that only a single horse was needed for the cart.

"Although marked with various supply identification, each one contains a real Treasure," he explained.

Gunnar circled the cart for inspection. He then checked the crates "These are sealed. How can we make certain they are the real ones?"

"Because of this." Haskel pulled out a medallion from the breast pocket of his doublet.

Axel examined it. Gunnar came to stand at his shoulder. "A high priest." He showed Gunnar the special marking.

"Our ancestor," said Haskel.

"*Our?*" repeated Gunnar, suspicious.

"We are brothers." Haskel motioned between himself and Lorne. "Osborn is our cousin. We are sworn to the Oath. By that pledge, I give you my word, four of the original Treasures are hidden in these crates."

"I wouldn't have brought you to Zorin if I were not certain of their loyalty," Ronan added his assurance.

For a long, heavy moment, an annoyed Axel held Ronan's gaze. "Your insistence on coming here was to secure these and place them among the supply train for transport them to Sener. *After* we separated. Why not tell us every aspect of the plan?"

"The same reason Lorne gave for his discretion in greeting you. Dolus has spies everywhere." Ronan grew uneasy under Axel's unwavering stare. "It is not a matter of trust. Everything has been done to aid you and protect the Treasures. Our lives depend upon your success!" The sincerity of his voice matched his expression.

Axel's jowls flexed in anger. He slapped the medallion into Haskel's palm to return it. He abruptly left. Bardolf quick to follow.

"My lord!" Ronan anxiously called.

Gunnar's hand on Ronan's chest stopped any pursuit. His glare clearly conveyed his meaning. Gunnar hurried after Axel.

Nollen sent Ronan a glance of sympathy before he too left. In a run, he caught up with Axel and Gunnar in the street. "Lord Ronan didn't mean any harm. I'm certain of that."

Axel's harsh expression made Nollen mute. The silence continued until they entered the guest room at the mayor's residence.

A nice fire glowed in the hearth, which had raised the temperature in the room. The two beds were turned down in preparation for the night. Axel leaned against the mantle to stare at the flames.

"I meant what I said about Lord Ronan," Nollen insisted.

Axel didn't respond.

"Let it be." Gunnar drew Nollen to the beds. "Take the smaller one."

"It's too early to turn in," chided Nollen.

Gunnar stood braced, his face stern against opposition. Understanding the futility of further argument, Nollen sat on the bed to remove his boots.

Chapter 37

THE DARKNESS OF THE ROOM, LOW EMBERS OF AN ALMOST extinguished fire, and rhythmic breathing from Gunnar and Nollen, told hours had passed since they returned. Axel sat in front of the hearth. His expression of deep contemplation showed no change from earlier. Hearing a rough moan, he watched Nollen stir restlessly on the bed before he settled down. A nightmare, perhaps? At least he slept.

Axel knew Nollen tried to encourage him earlier with his stated certainty about Ronan. Yet how could he explain that what troubled him had nothing to do with Ronan? Well, not directly, or in relation to the excluded parts of the plan.

When Gunnar made similar agitated moves in his sleep, Axel decided to leave. Bardolf stood, so Axel placed a finger to his lips for silence then motioned to the beds. With both hands he waved Bardolf to remain. The wolf laid down.

Despite the coolness in the hall, Axel carried his boots to quiet his trek downstairs. He entered the parlor. The clock on the mantle struck the hour of one in the morning. Since the room felt chillier, he replaced his boots.

At the hearth, he held his hand over the embers to feel for any remaining heat. He carefully placed kindling and a small piece of wood on the coals. A match holder hung on the wall. He lit the kindling, then gently used the bellows to encourage flames. The dry wood caught fast.

He moved the chair directly in front of the hearth and stretched his feet out to feel the warmth on the soles of his boots.

The activity only served as a minor diversion from his deep introspection. At each place along the journey, the weight of his task grew heavier. Yet in Mathena, the most difficult moment happened when Gunnar learned about the Blood Oath. Axel knew a time would come to inform Gunnar about the most unpleasant reality of his mission, just not that way. The hurt and disappointment in Gunnar's eyes pricked him. How could he keep such a secret from his most trusted friend?

To protect him, Axel's mind argued. The same reason Ronan gave for not disclosing an important detail regarding the Treasures hidden in Zorin. Axel heavily sighed, as he leaned forward in the chair, elbows on his knees. "Gott, help me not to falter," he prayed under his breath. "Give me the strength to fulfill your will and do what must be done."

"Highness?"

The voice sounded distant, more like words in his mind. He continued to stare at the flames, as he prayed.

"Axel?"

Startled by the sudden closeness of the voice, he bolted to his feet. "Nollen?" He took a deep breath to calm his fright. "What are you doing down here?"

Nollen donned his surcoat but didn't close it. His hair messed from sleeping, and he wore no shoes, just stockings on his feet. "I could ask you the same question. When I woke to use the chamber pot, I realized you weren't in the room. I became concerned." He glanced up and down. "You're fully dressed"

"I haven't gone to bed."

"Why? Are you still troubled about Lord Ronan?"

Axel didn't respond immediately due to consideration of what to say.

Nollen mistook the hesitation. "I meant what I said earlier. I don't believe he acted with any intent to harm or offend."

Axel forced a grin, and patted Nollen's shoulder. "I believe you."

"Then why did you leave the warehouse so angry?"

Axel took a deep breath. "I'm not sure that I can adequately explain. I'm still trying to comprehend *and* come to terms with what I must face in Sener." He motioned for Nollen to sit in another chair near the fire while he resumed his seat.

"You're going to take back the throne just like Gott promised."

With tender appreciation, Axel regarded Nollen. "Spoken with child-like simplicity."

The statement baffled, and briefly annoyed Nollen. "I'm not a child," he spoke in mild refute.

Axel softly chuckled. "No, I refer to the *faith* of a child, honest and trusting. Not fully comprehending the dangers that await." His voice trailed off.

"Well, I wouldn't go that far. I'm hardly inexperienced dealing with trouble."

"Nollen," Axel spoke in tone suggesting the need for attention. "What will happen in Sener will go beyond anything you can imagine."

Again, Nollen offered a bolstered answer. "Many things have already happened that I could never imagine."

Axel lightly bit his lower lip, at Nollen's attempt to lighten his burden. Firelight showed the rising of tears in his eyes. "I left the warehouse because *I am* keeping the darker side of my task secret—just like Ronan did by not telling me about the Treasures." He looked at his feet in an effort to regain his composure.

Although taken back by the confession, compassion stirred Nollen. He moved forward in the chair to grip Axel's arm. "Why? You can't take on Javan alone."

Axel's head rose. Tears freely ran down his cheeks. "There are aspects of my task which are so burdensome as to depress the soul. I would spare you from them."

Nollen's brows furrowed struggling to comprehend. Discouragement found its way into his voice. "How will this affect our winning back your throne?"

"Sometimes winning means you must be willing to lose."

Nollen's struggle visibly deepened. "I don't understand."

"In time, you will." Axel stood and pulled Nollen to his feet. He held the young man by the shoulders. "Promise me, that no matter what may happen, you will do the task entrusted to your charge. No one else can do what *you* must. Now, promise me," he urged.

"I promise."

Axel embraced Nollen. "Now, let's both go to bed. Dawn will be soon."

By morning, a few inches of snow blanketed Zorin and the surrounding area. Keena ordered a hearty breakfast prepared for the guests along with provisions for the journey. Conversation during the meal happened between Lorne, Cormac, Keena, and Irwin. They mostly spoke about the weather. Still, Axel perceived a tension among those gathered. He refrained from engaging in too much discussion to observe. Ronan appeared reticent, Nollen quiet, and Gunnar wary.

Gunnar's attitude didn't surprise Axel, as last night's incident in the warehouse heightened his soldier's intuition. Axel suspected Nollen's silence dealt with their conversation. Ronan. Well, that fell to him to deal with the Ganel lord.

When ready for departure, they found their horses in front of the residence. The cart with the hidden Treasures was pulled by one horse. Haskel sat in the driver's seat.

Ronan spoke to Lorne and Keena. "My thanks for your hospitality."

"Next time you must stay longer," Keena sweetly said.

A poignant smile appeared in reply. "If I can."

"My lord, it was an honor to meet you," Lorne said to Axel. "Blessings on your journey."

"Thank you. Mistress Keena." Axel nodded to her before he mounted.

Gunnar and Nollen also conveyed their thanks.

Ronan lead them from the mayor's residence. Although a short ride to the main gate, no citizens paid attention or wished them well as they had in Mathena. Axel noticed everything.

Soldiers broke down the Ganel camp in preparation for departure. Commanders greeted them when they dismounted.

"We should be ready to leave in twenty minutes, my lord," Cleary reported to Ronan.

"Very well. Have this cart placed in the baggage train under Sergeant Declan's personal care."

"Aye, my lord." Cleary signaled Haskel to climb down for him to take charge of the cart. He drove it to the baggage train.

With humble demeanor, Haskel addressed Axel. "My lord, please accept that everything we did was in your service, and not for personal gain, or with any ulterior motive."

"Duly noted."

Haskel cast an apologetic glance to Ronan before he returned to Zorin on foot.

Noticing curiosity from the others, Axel waved for Ronan to accompany him. They walked in search of a private place to speak.

"I owe you an explanation, and an apology," said Axel.

Surprised, Ronan vigorously insisted, "No apology, Highness. It is I who withheld information. Despite my good intentions, I couldn't sleep because of disappointing you."

"That makes two of us," droned Axel.

"Highness?"

"You are not the only one who withheld information, and for good reason. Protecting those in one's charge is a heavy responsibility."

"So is the burden you bear. I well understand the Blood Oath, and all the ramifications. Remember, my father was a priest," Ronan said with unction.

Axel saw the truth reflected Ronan's steady gaze. "Then let us part on good terms, no regrets to face what we must with a clear conscience."

Ronan smiled in agreement. "Willingly, Highness."

Axel guided Ronan back to the others with his arm around Ronan's shoulder. Upon return, he told Nollen, "You will again take the lead, since you boasted of memorizing the path."

Nollen cocked a confident grin. "As if I would forget any secret trail or hidden path?"

"Alfgar, I assume your herd will remain with Ronan," said Axel.

"Aye."

Axel glanced to Bardolf. "What of you, my friend?"

"I travel with you, while a pack will shadow us."

"What pack?" asked Gunnar. He glanced about the area.

Bardolf let out a loud, long howl. White wolves emerged from behind rocks and trees to join them. To the human's befuddlement, he explained, "They have followed us since we entered the territory."

"Why didn't you speak when we were in Zorin?" asked Nollen.

"Because I sensed uneasiness among them."

"Betrayal?" asked Gunnar, alarmed.

"No. Apprehension. Uncertainty. My speaking could have frightened them, so I chose to remain silent."

An eagle's cry alerted them a moment before Ottlia and another, larger eagle, landed on a nearby rock.

"Artair," said Axel in acknowledgement of the Eagle king.

"Son of Eldar. We will continue to patrol the skies above you for as long as possible. The nearer to Sener, the increased likelihood of encountering harpys."

"And Black Jackals," added Bardolf.

Axel shook his head, as he addressed Bardolf and Artair. "My path is set. It is important to protect the Treasures."

"We won't leave you unguarded," insisted Bardolf.

"Aye, the peace of all creatures depends upon you," agreed Artair.

"I deeply appreciate your concern. And I accept the wolves as sentries, but the Treasures must be closely guarded.

"Alfgar remains with Ronan," said Artair.

"Aye, and will fight on the ground, but keen eyes in air are needed to alert them to danger. To keep harpys away."

Artair awkwardly nodded his head. "Your reasoning is sound, Son of Eldar. Ottlia and the flock will remain with Lord Ronan, but *I* will watch over you."

Cleary returned. "My lord, we are ready to leave," he told Ronan.

"We'll be just a moment." Ronan gripped the hilt of his sword to address Axel. "Highness, the moment has arrived. Gott is with you, as are we all. By his will, we ride to Sener."

"Gott keep you safe, my lords," Axel said to the Ganels.

Ronan and his troops took the southern route from Zorin. Axel, Gunnar, and Nollen rode west.

"How long should it take to reach Sener?" Gunnar asked.

"Three days, according to Baron Irwin," replied Nollen. "That's without snow, harpys, jackals, or other hinderance."

"You don't sound very confident," said Axel.

"Oh, I'm confident about following directions," boasted Nollen. His voice changed to frustration. "What troubles me is finding alternatives in unfamiliar territory … should that be necessary."

Axel grinned and indicated the wolves. "It won't be a problem."

Nollen made a thwarted frown and mumbled, "I hate not knowing where I'm going."

Chapter 38

THE BRIGHT SUNSHINE BELIED THE BRISK NORTH WIND THAT marred the day. To escape the cold, servants rushed from one building to another at Sener Castle.

From the warmth of his study, Dolus watched the arrival of the Territorial representatives throughout the day. The Nefal came first, followed an hour later by the Ha'tar. By mid-afternoon, the Freeland delegation entered the main courtyard. Prior to sundown, The Doane men arrived. The Ganel delegation rode through the castle gate shortly after dark.

With a banquet scheduled for eight o'clock, Dolus knew the head chamberlain would assign billeting, and give instructions for the evening festivities. This would be an interesting meal, as he sought to gauge reactions among the representatives about the directive. So far everything was proceeding according to plan. Finally, after two-hundred years, the Treasures were again in Sener. He succeeded where others had failed. It was a mere formality to secure them.

Of course, the total culmination would happen when the Son of Eldar arrived, and the Blood Oath fulfilled. Until then, he satisfied himself with the knowledge that the Treasures served as a lure for Oleg's heir. He approached Othniel.

"Perhaps, I should have you moved to the Great Hall to witness the final act of my triumph." He cocked a malicious grin. "Then again, others don't understand your significance like I do."

Sylvan's return interrupted Dolus' regard of Othniel. Javan arrived with Sylvan, who held the door for the Elector.

Javan sneered as he asked Dolus, "Well, what news do they bring?"

"I take it you mean the representatives," said Dolus casually.

"Of course. Are the Treasures secure?"

"We'll find out this evening."

Irate, Javan chided, "You haven't taken possession of them yet?"

"Patience, Elector. The plan is proceeding smoothly."

"We are so close, nothing can go wrong!"

"It won't. The Treasures are within these walls. We must play our parts carefully while awaiting *his* arrival."

Javan's eyes narrowed. "You're certain he will come?"

"He must. The Blood Oath demands it."

Javan approached Othniel. After a moment of staring at the Great White Lion, he spoke over his shoulder to Dolus. "Have your men take possession of the Treasures during the banquet."

"That's not the plan," Dolus strenuously objected.

Javan wheeled about on his heels. "Hang the plan! I want this creature destroyed, and my crown secured!"

"At the proper time! A day at most." Seeing Javan's stubbornness, Dolus then spoke with unnatural authority. His face filled with a deadly aura. "Any hasty action, and you will forfeit the crown and title *king forever*. Is that understood?"

Javan flinched with fear, but quickly righted himself. "Are you threatening me?"

"No. I state reality." Dolus stood toe-to-toe with Javan. The power behind his transformation more intimidating up close. "You *willingly* made a devilish agreement in exchanging your soul for the crown. Break it now, and you won't live through the night."

Sweat formed on Javan's forehead, as he stared into Dolus' cold malicious eyes. He forced himself to speak. "We will proceed as planned."

Dolus' face changed back to its usual placid countenance. "Rest until the banquet. Sylvan will escort you to your chamber."

Sylvan fought to cover his discomposure at having witnessed the unsettling scene. "Elector," he quietly said.

No words passed between them, as Sylvan accompanied Javan to his apartment. Once there, Sylvan spoke.

"I will send in your valet."

"Sylvan," Javan's shaky voice began. "How do you tolerate him? How can you bear to work so closely?"

Sylvan cast a hasty glance at the door before he spoke, low and private. "It is not by my strength alone that I endure."

Javan's gaze turned suspicious yet guarded. "I think I understand."

"I hope so." Once again, Sylvan's cautious gaze shifted to the door. "To speak any further would be dangerous for us."

"It's already too late for me," droned Javan in a tone of resignation. "Leave Sener tonight and save yourself." He nudged Sylvan away.

Once in the hall, Sylvan altered his course to the guest wing of the castle. Since he helped with the billeting arrangements, he knew which rooms to approach, and those to avoid. Guards stood post at the door to each guest quarters. Being Dolus' personal secretary came with authority to wield as necessary.

When a servant answered his knock, he gave each a folded note for the representative with these written words, "*An invitation to a private meeting in the rear salon before the banquet.*"

Once he finished the task, Sylvan made his way to the lower level at the rear of the castle. He dimmed the hall lamp before entering a small room. Inside, he lit one candelabra, which proved enough light to see, but not shine under the door. The positioning of light also helped conceal his identity until absolutely necessary. Now to wait.

With the arrival of the Son of Eldar, his covert mission required more risk than originally anticipated. He prayed Javan would not betray him to Dolus but felt a prompting in his spirit to say what he did to the Elector. During the earlier confrontation between Dolus and Javan, he had difficulty maintaining a calm exterior when Dolus briefly pulled back his façade. Of course, he knew about Dolus' connection to the forces of darkness. His heritage and dealings with such evil before is why he was chosen for the assignment.

After twelve years undercover, the end grew near in anticipation of the long-awaited day that would fulfill prophecy. For whatever reason, if he didn't survive the night, he had a clear conscience before Gott that he faithfully discharged his duties.

A knock interrupted his pondering. Sylvan waited to hear it a second time. The knock-code, one used for decades between the Brethren. He peeked out only enough to see the Freelanders, Gorman and Mather. He used the door as a shield.

"Blessings, *froind*," he said.

"Blessings and more, *froind*," came the counter-sign.

Sylvan closed the door upon their arrival. He spoke in a partly disguised voice. "Be seated while we wait for the others."

Another knock-code. The Doane, only Jabid wasn't alone. Ebert accompanied him, which gave Sylvan pause when he spoke the password. "Blessings, *froind.*"

"Blessings and more, *froind.* From me and our new *bropor.*" Jabid's reply included an introduction of Ebert with the ancient Eldarian word for *brother.*

"Indeed?" said Sylvan, trying to mask skepticism.

"Indeed," insisted Jabid.

Sylvan opened the door wider to allow entrance. They moved further into the room.

Recognition brought Gorman to his feet. "Ebert?"

"A new convert," said Jabid, smiling.

Ebert raised his hands in greeting. "With the help of Jabid, and my dearest Blythe, I have been renewed in mind, heart, and spirit." He quoted the first line of the Oath using the names of those who helped him.

Gorman smiled in welcome. "Join us, *bropor.*" He indicated chairs at the table.

Sylvan listened to the exchange. Before he could ask further questions, a knock-code rapped upon the door. He opened to see Ronan. "Blessings, *froind.*"

"Blessings and more, *froind.*"

After closing the door, he asked Ronan, "You came alone?"

"Aye, to this meeting. To Sener, no."

"Where?"

"A few miles from here. Safe," he assured Sylvan. He moved further into the room. Like Gorman, he did a double-take at the newest member. "Ebert?"

Ebert heavily sighed. "I suppose I should expect suspicion because of my earlier behavior."

"No, I mean—"

Ebert waved off Ronan's attempted refute. "No apology. I acted shamefully."

"He quoted the Oath when I voiced surprise," said Gorman.

"I vouch for his genuine conversion," said Jabid. He held Ebert by the shoulder.

Ronan flashed a generous smile. "Then welcome, *bropor.*"

"Gentlemen," began Sylvan in tone suggesting attention. He moved close to the light to reveal his identity.

"You are Dolus' assistant!" Mather declared. The Freeland captain quickly overcame surprise to assume a braced posture.

"Be at ease, gentlemen." Sylvan lowered his voice to say, "I'm here *in the king's service.*" He produced his medallion.

Mather seized Sylvan's hand. His soldier's instincts demanded, "How can we be sure this not some deception? To get us to admit some treason?"

Sylvan remained calm against the accusation. "Your precaution is warranted, but misplaced, Captain." He nodded to the medallion. "You will find a signet on the back. Not of a high priest, rather a special crest."

Mather pulled it from Sylvan's grasp. He moved to the candelabra for inspection. His brows furrowed at spying the royal crest. "Are you using it to lay claim?"

"What?" demanded Gorman. He came alongside Mather's shoulder. "A royal seal?" He sent a narrow glare of suspicion to Sylvan.

"Cousin of the heritage," said Sylvan. "Arctander knew, which is why I was chosen. I lay no claim. I only seek to do what Gott has appointed."

"He speaks the truth," affirmed Ronan.

Mather's original skepticism returned. "Did you know about him?"

Ronan made an accenting nod. "My father took counsel with Arctander about whom to choose for the Sener assignment. Sylvan is Ganel, thus acquainted with certain traits Dolus possesses."

Sylvan offered further clarification. "My mother is Ganel. My father descends from Oleg's sister." He motioned to his appearance. "I took upon the dress and mannerism of Sener to facilitate my assignment."

"Those *traits* you mentioned?" Mather harshly inquired of Ronan.

"Whereas Sener served as the royal city, Mathena is the center of learning in the spiritual arena. In the past, many came to seek knowledge and wisdom, including Dolus." His voice turned bitter. "After learning what he needed, he returned to Sener and used that knowledge for evil."

Outraged, Mather asked, "Why was Dolus allowed access to such learning?"

"He deceived us!" Ronan rebuffed, though he struggled to contain his passion to a hushed voice. "He is so diabolically clever that we never suspected anything until we learned of his activities in Sener. His order to slaughter the priests, included my father!" He hit his chest in emphasis then motioned to Sylvan. "That is why we sent an agent, who possesses knowledge to withstand Dolus' evil."

Gorman spoke to Mather. "Since Ronan concurs, I accept."

Mather returned the medallion to Sylvan.

Jabid and Ebert watched, until Jabid finally spoke to Sylvan. "You risk exposure. The walls have ears."

"It is my duty, both to my kinsman, and the Oath."

"Why this meeting, to reveal yourself?" asked Mather. Although the others accepted Sylvan's profession, the captain remained alert.

"That is one reason. The other is more important." He moved closer to speak confidentially. "Don't drink the wine tonight."

"Poison?" hissed Ebert in alarm.

Sylvan curtly shook his head. "Drugged, not lethal, but enough to gain agreement to Javan's attempt to circumvent Dolus. I discovered about the wine because he wants to take possession of *them* tonight rather than at the fealty ceremony tomorrow."

"That would hinder our task," groused Ronan.

"Aye. Which is why I arranged this meeting. To forewarn and advise you to ask for *winter cider*. I set aside a cask for those allergic to wine."

"Won't Javan grow suspicious if we all do it?" inquired Mather.

Ronan answered, "He shouldn't since Ganels usually drink cider."

"That leaves we four," said Gorman.

Mather grew thoughtful with an idea. "We could prearrange it, say with a pretense of some malady."

"Good," Sylvan eagerly agreed. "Upon return to your chamber, send word to the butler in request of the cider."

Jabid shrugged. "I've never been a heavy wine drinker."

"True," agreed Ebert.

"Make whatever excuse you want to Jurren, he's the page assigned to your table," Sylvan instructed Jabid.

"Is there anything else we should know?" asked Ronan.

Sylvan straightened with pride. "If for some reason, I don't survive the night, tell my kinsman it was an honor to serve."

"What makes you think you won't?"

"An earlier situation that forced some unguarded words." He waved off further inquiry. "The details are unimportant. Now, leave at intervals. And Gott be with you all."

"And with you," Ronan replied.

Sener's great hall grew loud with the noise of festive revelry. Music competed with the din of laughter and loud voices. Javan sat at high table eagerly partaking of the food and wine. A demure woman near his age, sat beside him. She showed little expression despite the merriment going on around her. She nodded or offered a humorless smile to everything Javan said. Even the food on her plate received little attention.

Dolus sat to the right of Javan. He appeared to enjoy the banquet. Yet beneath his seemingly joyous exterior, his eyes shifted to the occupants at various tables.

Sylvan watched from his assigned seat nearest high table. His position allowed him the privilege of proximity in case Dolus required his services. With prearrangements made, Javan seemed unaware of any avoidance of wine. At least, at first.

"Grayden!" Javan shouted to the butler. "Fill every cup and tankard with wine. I will offer a toast!"

The butler repeated the order to the pages.

With calm discretion, Ronan, Cormac, and Irwin placed a hand over the tankard in refusal. The others took their cue from the Ganels to make similar gestures when approached.

After several moments, Grayden reported completion of the task. However, Dolus spoke before Javan picked up his tankard.

"I noticed the Ganels refused."

"What?" Javan's irate glare found Ronan. "Explain this effrontery!"

Unruffled, Ronan replied. "Elector, the Ganels do not drink wine. We never have. This is widely known. Our refusal should not come as a surprise. Nor is it an effrontery."

Javan snarled. "You are a bold one! What if I ordered it?"

"We would still refuse. Yet," Ronan hastily added to avoid more unpleasantness. "We will partake of your toast." He lifted his tankard.

"Let us hope your impertinence isn't spreading," Javan huffed.

Argus stood to declare, "The Nefal readily drink of your wine, Elector. Unlike the pitiful Ganels, who hide in their forest too afraid to come out and meet their betters."

Ronan's jowls flexed in anger at the insult.

Fod stood. "The Ha'tar join the Nefal! Further, we challenge everyone else to show their allegiance."

His patience thin, Ronan spoke in harsh reply, "You need not goad us into pretended show for favor."

Outraged, Fod slammed down the tankard, which caused some wine to spill. "You will answer for that insult, Ganel!"

Cormac restrained Ronan from rising. "Patience!" he warned.

"Enough!" Javan's shout caught attention. He made impatient waves for Argus and Fod to sit.

Ronan took a deep breath to regain his composure. He nodded for Cormac and Irwin to release him.

Javan waited for the tension to abate before he proceeded. "Pledges of fealty can wait until the morrow. For now, I have a special announcement." He smiled at the timid woman beside him. She shyly smiled in return yet avoided eye-contact.

He stood with tankard in hand. "Since the death of my first wife, I have led a lonely life. No more. Lady Johana has consented to become my wife." He waved a hand to signal all rise. He held up the tankard. "I toast myself, soon to be wed." He began to drink, but stopped to add, "And to you, my dear, for being the lucky woman." He gave her a side-acknowledgement. When he drank, so did everyone else.

With a sly eye on the crowd, Javan sat. He maintained a smile of cunning satisfaction. Since he didn't return to eating, those assembled waited, curiously attentive to Javan.

To this odd behavior, Dolus asked, "Elector, is there something else?"

Javan's smile never wavered. "Patience," he said to Dolus, then spoke loudly. "Master Ebert. Is the wine to your satisfaction? After all it came from The Doane."

Ebert struggled to mask his uncertainty. Jabid intervened.

"Please excuse him, Elector. He became ill en route and was advised by doctors to abstain from wine until the remedy is complete."

Javan's smile vanished. "What of you? Do you not drink?"

"I must keep a clear head to aid him. His wife would be cross if I did not," Jabid offered in hurried excuse.

"And if I ordered you to drink?"

"A difficult choice."

"Why difficult? Am I not the Elector?"

"Aye. Yet do I offend you or his wife, who is my sister? I must live with one while paying homage to the other."

Johana gently touched Javan's arm. "My lord, they already drank the toast. Please, do not let our happiness be the source of unrest for another relationship. I am honored by this evening." This time she smiled with genuine affection.

He kissed her hand. "As it pleases you, my dear." He turned back to Jabid. "What say you to such benevolence?"

Jabid raised his tankard. "My humble thanks, most gracious lady."

"Puny humans!" scoffed Argus.

Jabid shot a glare across the floor to the Nefal lord. "Graciousness is a trait barbicans lack."

Ebert seized Jabid when Argus bolted up ready to respond.

Javan shouted, "Away with you all!" He comforted an upset Johana. "You distress my bride! Grayden, clear the hall!"

Those assembled did not need to be told twice. Some left willingly, others grumbled at the disturbance which caused the early dismissal. No words passed between the representatives, as each retired to their chambers.

Chapter 39

DURING THE DAY, NOLLEN CONFIDENTLY KEPT TO THE prearranged course told him by Baron Irwin. However, drawing near to Sener, Artair reported a sighting of harpys. With Artair as the lone eagle, they decided to travel at night. A pack of twelve White Wolves stood a better chance against Black Jackals than a single eagle versus a flock of harpys.

Each man carried a lantern. The flames barely gave off enough light to see. The flames could quickly be increased should they encounter jackals. For now, they relied on the wolves as sentries.

A short snarling howl of a wolf somewhere in the darkness, caused Nollen, Axel, and Gunnar to stop. Bardolf made a short clipping yip that sent three wolves in the direction of the disturbance. Bardolf stood braced in front of Axel's horse, his hackles up and head low. The rest of the wolves joined him in surrounding the humans. Several more howls, growls, and yips were heard before a loud whimper. An uneasy stillness followed. Gunnar began to increase the flame of the lantern he carried.

"No, put it down!" Bardolf sharply rebuked.

Gunnar lowered the light while Bardolf sniff the air and ground.

When the three wolves returned, Bardolf asked, "Well?"

"Two jackals. Advance scouts. They won't be reporting anything," replied one.

"Any injuries?" asked Axel.

"No. These jackals must have been young ones, and inexperienced in fighting."

Axel stared into the darkness ahead of them. "The enemy knows I'm coming. Summoning Black Jackals and harpys is just the beginning."

"We will remain alert for whatever he tries," assured Bardolf.

Gunnar looked east. "Not much time before dawn. I see a thin line of gray on the horizon."

"The rear gate of Sener is only two miles," said Bardolf.

Nollen picked up the reins to move when Axel said, "Wait!" Nollen paused, expectant of the reason why.

Axel lowered his head and took a loud audible breath.

"Highness?" asked Nollen, concerned.

Even in low light, the angst on Axel's face was visible. "What we are about to undertake, may Gott give us the strength to endure till the end." He moved his horse beside Nollen. The clear hazel eyes heightened by the reflection of lantern light. For a long moment, he held Nollen's gaze. "Gott's choice brought you here, for this time, for this purpose. When we arrive in Sener, obey everything Gunnar tells you without questions or doubt."

Sight of Axel's somber sobriety cause Nollen's voice to barely rise above a whisper. "What about you?"

With hard urgency, Axel seized Nollen's arm. "No questions. Please. Remember your promise. I depend upon it."

Words failed, so Nollen just nodded.

Axel turned his horse to continue the trek to Sener.

In passing, Gunnar said, "Courage, lad, and trust Gott."

In Sener, everyone from the butler, jailers, servants, nobles, soldiers, Dolus, and Javan prepared for the Fealty Ceremony. Throughout the night, servants transformed the Great Hall from a banquet to a high state affair devoid of all furniture save the throne. Even the festive decorations were replaced by banners representing Javan's family and the Six Territories.

Morning sun shone through the stained-glass windows of the Great hall. Two large fires filled the massive hearths on either side of the hall. A half-dozen braziers scattered about the room, also provided warmth on the cold morning. Pages manned the hearths and braziers for the sole task of keeping the fires burning.

Soldiers in dress uniforms fashioned after Javan's family livery stood guard around the Hall. Nobles, and other important guests, began to gather for the ceremony. Each of the Six Territories had assigned places, though no one expected the Eagles to appear. Not only did the mighty birds refuse to pay homage to Javan, they never sent human representatives from the Halvor Territory.

Javan made his way down the rear hallway behind the throne. Dolus and Beltran accompanied him. A small group of men followed at a discrete distance. This included Bernal, Hertz, and Sylvan.

"Elector, you can't be serious! Having him at the ceremony may incite some of the representatives," Beltran argued.

"Or subdue them," countered Dolus. "Especially when Tribute is presented. Just think, the last high priest forced to pay homage to the *new king*."

"Just before his execution," Javan said with a mocking huff. "Will that satisfy you?" he asked Beltran.

"It will have to," stressed Dolus. Narrow, threatening eyes locked on Beltran. For a brief moment, the second minister flinched in what appeared to be pain.

"As you say, Elector," Beltran demurely said. Javan's sneer made him correct his address. "I mean, *Sire*."

Javan laughed with haunter. Upon reaching the door to the antechamber, he gave Sylvan instructions about Bernal, Beltran, and Hertz. "Escort them to a place by the platform." He then spoke to Dolus. "I will make my entrance when *everyone* is present."

Ronan, Cormac, and Irwin waited in the Ganel section of the Great Hall. Cormac and Irwin tried to curb any signs of uneasiness or anxiety. Ronan held an ornate box. Fingers gently drummed the box, which betrayed his nervousness. He made several glances up to the gallery that circled the Hall. Timing was everything.

"They'll make it," Irwin whispered to Ronan.

"Gott willing," added Cormac.

Ronan took a breath to steady his anxiety. He noticed Jabid and Ebert arrive. Ebert carried a rectangular box with gold gilding around the edges. They exchanged the barest of acknowledgements when The Doane men took their places.

Ronan saw Mather escort Gorman to the Freeland area. Gorman appeared pale, while the captain stoic. Gorman bore a long box with gold filigree and intricate carvings.

The Ha'tar caught attention in the fact that they were more highly decorated than normal. Emeralds and onyx embellished their polished dragon-scale armor. Fod carried a narrow-bejeweled box.

Entrance of the Nefal proved hard to miss, as the giants made an elaborate display of their arrival. Lord Argus carried a tall wide box made of tooled leather and wood decorated with turquoise.

The rattling of chains caught everyone's attention. Soldiers herded a group of prisoners into the Hall. All wore arm shackles. Ronan's eyes grew wide at sight of Arctander. Along with him came Jarred, Ida, Sharla, Abe, and Bart. Soldiers marched them to the front of the Hall and off to one side of the platform. Although informed of Arctander's capture, he didn't expect to see him and the others. Ronan managed to make eye contact with Arctander. Despite the circumstances, the old priest appeared calm. Ronan stopped drumming his finger, took a deep breath, and faced the throne.

Barely a moment passed when another prisoner joined the others. He came in from a side entrance. Ronan recognized Jonas due to his frequenting the inn at Gilroy when he traveled to The Doane. Jarred maliciously regarded Jonas. The animosity didn't surprise Ronan considering what Nollen told them about Heddwyn.

The herald pounded a staff and signaled to the trumpeters. The sounding call had the desired effect, as all turned to the throne. Dolus emerged first from the anteroom, followed by Javan. On his way to the throne, Javan flash a conceited smile to Lady Johana, who stood to the right side of the platform. When he sat, the trumpets ceased.

Outside, at the rear gate of Sener, Nollen, Gunnar, and Axel gained entry to the city. Although an affair of state happened at the castle, the day's activity continued as usual for the rest of the population. They weaved through traffic en route to the upper castle level. Soldiers guarded the gate, so Axel pulled off into a side street. Once dismounted, his regard of Gunnar made words difficult.

"This is where we part company, my dear friend," he said.

Against a tide of emotion, Gunnar gripped the hilt of his sword. "I'm going with you inside."

"No! You and Nollen are to proceed together. Nothing can change now," Axel practically pleaded.

Gunnar's jowls flexed with angry sorrow. He briskly took the horn from Nollen's saddlebag and held it out to the young man. "To your duty be true."

Nollen placed the strap over his shoulder. He took the lantern off his saddle bow. Even in daylight, he didn't extinguish the flame.

With a last agonizing look at Axel, Gunnar nudged Nollen to leave the side street. Instead of proceeding to the main castle gate, they dashed down an adjoining alley.

"How many times have you done this?" Gunnar harshly whispered.

"Once, which is why I recognized the baron's directions. Hopefully nothing has changed since the last time."

Gunnar pulled Nollen to a halt to ask, "When was that?"

"Five years ago. Father tanned my hide, but I wanted to see inside." At Gunnar's annoyance, he added with a tone of confidence, "I have a head for remembering directions. We wouldn't have made here, it if I didn't."

Gunnar again followed Nollen into the darkest part of the alley.

"Hold the lantern, but don't turn up the flame yet," Nollen said. He used his hands to feel along the damp wall. He tossed a grin to Gunnar when he found it. He paused at the sound of scraping of stone. He waited for any signs of response to the noise. None. "Help with the last bit," he whispered.

Together they made the opening wide enough to pass. Gunnar grabbed the lantern to follow Nollen inside.

"How will you close it?"

"That's easy." Nollen felt for the handle to crank the door back into place. He took the lantern from Gunnar and increased the light. Half power illuminated the dark passage.

"Where does this lead?"

"To a gallery that circles the Great Hall. It was under repair last time," Nollen casually replied.

Gunnar stopped Nollen from proceeding. "Do you know how to go from the Hall to the parapet?"

"Aye. The view is fantastic—"

"Never mind the view!" Gunnar raised the horn in front of Nollen's face. "That is where you must go to sound the horn."

"Very well."

"Let's continue."

Nollen proceeded down the passage before making a sharp right turn. A long, winding stairway led to a higher level. After another short passage, they ascended a second stairway. This one was straighter, and shorter. Finally, after a third set of stairs, Nollen stopped at a wall. Light filtered under the panel from the other side. Muffled voices and activity could also be heard. He lowered the light to a bare flicker before he placed it aside. With a finger to his lips for silence, he carefully slid back a small opening to peek out. The voices grew louder, then became muffled when Nollen closed the peephole.

"The gallery seems clear," he whispered to Gunnar. "To avoid being seen, crouch and crawl out when I open the panel. Stay below the rail and wait for me."

Gunnar made ready while Nollen slowly opened the panel. He quickly squeezed through followed swiftly by Nollen. From his knees, Nollen shut the panel. The ornate stone rail was mostly solid with occasionally carved openings in the pattern. Gunnar took up position behind a large column capable of hiding a man. He could see part of the Great Hall without being visible. Nollen joined him.

"Now we wait," Gunnar quietly said.

"Why?"

"Ganel archers, remember?" Gunnar then motioned to the floor.

For several moments they listened. Fod made a grandiose speech that ended with the Ha'tar presenting Shevet to Javan.

"The Treasures!" Nollen gasped, only to have Gunnar cover his mouth. Annoyed, he wrestled Gunnar's hand away. "We're too late."

"No. Now be still. We can't be discovered before ..." He couldn't finish. Nollen's quizzical expression made him say, "Just wait—quietly."

Chapter 40

JAVAN SMILED WITH GREAT SATISFACTION WHEN FOD CONCLUDED his presentation. Five of the Six Treasures were magnificently displayed on the platform before him. He smugly taunted Arctander. "Now, this isn't so hard to watch, is it?"

Despite his early calmness, the ceremony wore on Arctander. His placid expression turned grave.

At his silence, Javan laughed with haunter. "It appears the last priest has nothing to say," he commented to Dolus.

"He is witnessing the end of hope," said Dolus.

Arctander's eyes narrowed in righteous anger. "Beware, creature of darkness, lest you speak your doom."

Dolus approached Arctander, and violently slapped him. Chains rattled when Arctander fell sideways. Jarred caught him.

"Bring him here!" Javan ordered.

Guards jerked Arctander from Jarred.

"Grandfather!" Ida cried. When she moved forward, a guard shoved her back. She stumbled and fell to her knees.

At hearing Ida, Nollen hurried from behind the pillar to the rail. He kept low to view what was happening through a carved opening. He angrily sneered when guards brought Arctander to the base of the platform. His intense focus didn't change when Gunnar arrived.

"At least they are alive," Gunnar harshly whispered.

Javan rose. He walked among the Treasures to inspect them. He picked up the Book of Kings. "You think I am unaware of your pitiful attempt to claim that the Son of Eldar is here? To usurp me? Without these, he is nothing!" He tried to open the book, but the clasp wouldn't yield. "What's wrong with this? Dolus!"

Dolus came alongside. "It requires a key."

"Ebert! The key!" Javan snapped.

Ebert balked. "We don't have it, Elector."

"Then where is it?"

Ebert shrugged, and looked at Jabid with uncertainty. "We don't know. We only newly discovered the book."

Jabid hurried to add, "We didn't have time to learn key's whereabouts or miss the deadline."

"Your dagger," Javan ordered Dolus.

"You risk marring the book." At Javan's staunch glare, Dolus yielded his weapon.

Javan tried to pry the lock with the tip. When that didn't work, he fought to cut the thick leather binding. It finally snapped. Javan breathed hard from the effort. He gave Dolus back his dagger before he opened the book. His eyes grew wide with outrage.

"Blank!" He flipped several pages. "All blank! How is this possible?" he demanded of Ebert.

"Don't ask him." Dolus scowled at Arctander. He picked up the crown. He used the tip of his dagger to scratch the gold. It flecked off to reveal nickel underneath. "Fool's gold!" he said to Javan.

Argus straightened in surprise and spoke in hasty defense. "Not by our doing! We recently took possession of it from a turncoat." With rancor, he pointed at Arctander. "A secret follower of this corruptor!"

Dolus pried off the Star from the center of the crown. He held it up to confront Arctander. "If glass, it will shatter." He hurled it down to the floor where it smashed into pieces. "I don't believe I need to test rest of them, do I?"

"The Ha'tar have been possession of Shevet for years. It must be real," Fod said with prideful insistence.

Dolus dropped the crown to pick up the scepter. Again, he used the dagger to scratch the surface. "Only plated." He tossed the scepter to the Ha'tar.

Fod swallowed back anxiety at the discovery. He flashed an anxious glance to Gan.

"We didn't know! By our alliance, we swear!" Gan boldly lied.

Fod followed Argus' example to point at Arctander. "He's responsible for this dishonor!"

"No doubt they are all fake, and by his order," chided Dolus.

"Take him out and execute him! Execute them all, prisoners and representatives for this outrage!" Javan ordered.

Ronan, and all the Territorial representatives, prepared for defense when soldiers started to seize the prisoners.

Over the din of fearful cries and melee came a loud voice, "You will not kill them!" As the crowd began to hush in effort to determine the direction of the voice, the words were repeated. "You will not kill them!"

Javan and Dolus scanned the crowd to see a man approach with his hood raised. Once the path became clear, he removed his hood.

Bart seized Sharla to hurriedly say, "It's him!"

"Gott, have mercy," she murmured.

"Axel!" Nollen murmured in surprise.

"Be quiet," Gunnar harshly hissed a scolding.

"What is he doing?"

Gunnar again covered Nollen's mouth. His tone and expression showed conflict of sorrow and determination. "This is why he came." He shook his head. "No questions, remember?" He turned Nollen's attention back to the scene.

"Who are you?" demanded Javan.

"Axel, heir of Oleg," he loud stated.

"Son of Eldar." Dolus' announcement brought murmurings of astonishment from those assembled.

"Seize him!" Javan ordered.

Axel didn't resist when soldiers roughly grabbed him.

"Bring me the horn!" said Dolus.

One soldier took the horn off Axel's belt and brought it to Dolus. The First minister examined it.

"Is this real or fake like the others?"

Axel didn't reply.

Dolus descended the steps to confront Axel. "I only have to blow it to discover which."

Axel didn't react, rather kept his eyes straight ahead.

Dolus stepped into his line of sight. "Why are you here?"

This time Axel looked at Dolus. "You know why."

Dolus tried to curb a mocking smile. "Is it fear I see in your eyes, hear in your voice, Son of Eldar?"

Axel stared past Dolus.

The First Minister glanced to Javan and gave a knowing nod. He issued orders regarding Axel. "Strip him and bind him between the columns!"

In the gallery, Nollen struggled against Gunnar's hold, as he watched the mistreatment of Axel. Finally, he got free and tried to crawl away. Gunnar seized him and used his body to pin Nollen against the rail out of view.

"You swore to obey what I tell you," Gunnar hissed in Nollen's ear. Distress on the young man's face pricked Gunnar. "I don't want to witness this either, but we must trust Gott. If not, then what he is doing is for naught." His voice cracked in earnest plea.

Arms stretched to the limit, Axel stood bound between the column, his torso bare. Occasionally, he caught glances from Arctander, Ida, Jarred, and Ronan. Each time, he had to look away lest his lose his resolve. For their salvation from evil is why he came.

"Gott, give me strength," he whispered in desperate urgency.

"What say you now, Son of Eldar?" Javan questioned.

Axel lifted his head. Javan held a dagger in front of his face. He took a hard breath to contain his emotions.

"Do you fear the Blood Oath?"

Axel didn't reply.

"This will make me *king forever*," he spoke so only Axel heard.

Axel felt a surge of peace to say, "Only if Gott allows."

"You and your Gott are hardly in a position to decide." Javan turned to address the crowd. "Any of you know prophecy concerning the Blood Oath?" When no one replied, he continued. "A hasty, sad oath made by Oleg with my ancestor in the belief it would save his people. Only in the end, did Oleg realize the Blood Oath meant his death, and that of his descendant. The Son of Eldar!"

As he spoke the prophetic title, Javan plunged the dagger through Axel's heart. The end came so swift, Axel made no sound. His limp body hung from the bounds.

Women screamed, some fainted, while others smiled in sadistic triumph. Ida buried her head against Jarred. Sharla sank to her knees and covered her mouth, sobbing. Abe and Bart recoiled in shock. Even Jonas, gasped in horror.

Arctander looked to the ceiling, and prayed aloud, "Gott, honor his sacrifice as you promised! Keep your covenant with Oleg."

Dolus grabbed Sylvan by the arm. "Go! Put an end to all hope. Kill Othniel!" He shoved Sylvan toward the door.

Stunned to the core, Nollen sagged against the rail. His eyes immediately filled with tears.

Gunner screwed his eyes shut. Hearing nearby noise, alerted him to trouble. "Get to the parapet and blow until you can't blow anymore!"

"What?" murmured Nollen, confused.

Gunnar pulled him to his feet. "Run! Quickly!" He shoved Nollen away. "He depends up you!" Soldiers ran towards them. Gunnar drew his sword. "Go! I'll hold them off."

Despite tears blurring his vision, Nollen ran down the gallery toward the front of the hall. From there, he entered an upper hallway. Soldiers spied him, and he changed course. He ignored orders to stop. He ended out on a balcony where he quickly searched for a way up. The only means was to climb the downspout.

Nollen made it halfway up to the next floor when two soldiers appeared on the balcony. He heard order for archers. He kicked open a window to escape back inside. Not certain where to go exactly, he just knew he had to continue upwards.

He dodged soldiers at almost every turn, and at one point, was forced onto the roof. He managed to balance his way across the apex to a connecting archway. He navigated the archway to a turret. He flattened himself against the wall to hide, as soldiers ran past without seeing him.

Stepping out, he made a quick survey of where he was. It wouldn't be easy to reach the parapet, as soldiers scrambled to find him. The turret would have to do. Nollen raised the horn to his lips yet paused when sudden grief consumed him. He shut his eyes against the pain, and lamented, "Why did you make me promise? Why bring me here? Oh, Gott, help us!"

Nollen's eyes snapped opened at hearing what sounded like Axel's voice. "I depend upon you. No one can do what you must!"

Taking a deep breath, Nollen sounded the Horn of Kolyn. Gasps of sorrow interrupted each sound of the horn. With a clear, almost unearthly strength, the sound reverberated across the city.

Seven times Nollen sounded the horn. After the completion of the seventh reverberation, the horn shattered in his hands! Dumbfounded, he stared at the fallen pieces. What now? Had he failed?

Cries of birds overhead drew his attention. "Harpys!" More birds, only these calls deeper and majestic. "Eagles!"

He then heard the *thump-thud* of dragon wings. Ha'tar! Nefal warriors rode dire-buffalo. All drew near to Sener. "Gott, it can't end like this!"

Nollen swayed into unconsciousness when cold-cocked by a soldier.

Sylvan burst into Dolus' study when the first sound of the horn shook the room. Despite orders, he had no intention of killing Othniel, rather to prevent anyone from harming the Great White Lion.

He heard a grunting moan come from Othniel. With each successive horn sound, the Great White Lion seemed to come alive. After the seventh sound ended, Othniel jumped down from the mounted platform. The majestic head turned to Sylvan.

"By Gott," cheered Sylvan in triumph. "Othniel lives!" He knelt and bowed to the Great Lion. "In the King's service."

"The Son of Eldar?" asked Othniel in a deep baritone.

Sylvan raised his head, his face filled with regret. "Dead. The Blood Oath fulfilled."

Othniel's intense growl made Sylvan recoil. "Where is he?"

"The Great Hall."

The mighty lion smashed through the study door. Startled by the sight of the massive beast, soldiers and servants scattered. In bounding strides, Othniel ran through the castle. None dared to get in his way.

In the Great Hall, everyone looked about to determine the direction of the sounding call.

"What is that?" Javan shouted.

"The Horn of Kolyn!" Dolus replied. "Another fake!" He took the one Axel wore and threw it on the floor where it smashed.

Soldiers roughly brought in a wounded Gunnar. He bled from serious wound in his side; not life-threatening, but painfully debilitating.

"Who are you?" Dolus demanded of Gunnar

"I am a Freelander," Gunnar proudly announced.

Dolus surveyed the uniform. "No. You're not Eldarian. Where do you come from?"

Gunnar looked away in a refusal to answer. He winced at sight of Axel's body now lying on the cold floor. The fatal wound visible. Exactly what he saw in his nightmare!

Dolus jerked Gunnar's head around. "Did you come with him?"

More soldiers arrived. They dragged in a groggy Nollen. The young man staggered, as he still recovered from the head blow. He fell to his knees upon release.

"Nollen!" said Ida in distress.

He blinked to focus.

"Your foul companion?" Javan chided to Gunnar.

"He is Nollen of Far Point!" Hertz loudly spoke.

"Arctander's grandson," Dolus further clarified for Javan.

"My lord, we found him on the turret with this." A soldier held fragments of the horn.

Dolus recognized it. "So, you blew the horn." He jerked Nollen to his feet. "Too late." He roughly turned the young man to see Axel's body. Dolus flashed a smile, as he listened to commotion outside the hall. "Hear that? Our forces will destroy those foolish enough to follow the Son of Eldar." He shoved Nollen hard. The young man swayed in an effort to regain his balance.

Loud disturbance came from the hallway followed by the abrupt opening of doors. Othniel leapt into the room.

"It's supposed to be dead!" Javan angrily exclaimed.

"Sylvan failed!" Dolus picked up the fake Sword of Emet. "The Son of Eldar is dead! The Blood Oath satisfied. Oleg's line is ended!" He charged Othniel.

Nollen rushed to divert Dolus. He tried to tackle the First Minister, but in his woozy state, only knocked Dolus off stride. Nollen fell to his knees where he tried to shake off dizziness. Dolus' kicked Nollen in the abdomen, which made the young man collapse to the floor in pain. Dolus continued to his attack path.

Nollen's effort prompted Gunnar to act. Ignoring his wound, he landed a hard elbow jab to the face of one soldier and tripped another. He gritted his teeth at the throbbing pain movement caused. Before he could aid Nollen, other soldiers attacked him. One landed a hard blow squarely to his wound. Gunnar staggered back in agony. He fell to his knees beside a pillar. "Gott, help us!" he groaned.

With a rising shout, Dolus swung the blade at Othniel. Quicker than anticipated by his size, Othniel avoided the assault. A massive paw knocked Dolus sideways. Undeterred, Dolus launched other attack. The force of Othniel's roar rocked Dolus on his heels and rendered him unable to defend against the Great White Lion's leap. The sword clanged as it fell from Dolus' grasp before he hit the floor with Othniel on top of him. Powerful jaws clamped down on Dolus' throat, and quickly resulted in his death.

Enraged, Javan shouted, "Nefal! Ha'tar! Kill the lion."

During the panic, Ronan noticed Ganel archers arrived in the gallery. He called up a command, "Ganel, shoot anyone who moves!"

It took multiple arrows to strike down two Nefal warriors when they responded to Javan's command.

An arrow flew passed Javan's face when he started to flee. He yelled "Guards—" only to find Cormac's blade level at his face.

Fod suffered minor injury when an arrow clipped him in the shoulder. The Ha'tar were more suited for aerial combat than land warfare.

Shackles prevented participation, so Jarred, Arctander, and the boys shielded Ida and Sharla in a far corner. Jonas tried to dodge the fighting to join them. He became knocked aside.

Unable to fight any more due to his wound, Gunnar protected Axel's body from the melee. He sat back on his heels to guardedly watch the lion's approach. "Othniel?"

"Fear not. I intend no harm, quite the opposite," said Othniel.

The calm reassurance in the lion's gaze made Gunnar relax and allow total access to Axel.

Othniel nudged Axel's face and licked his cheek. He placed a massive paw on Axel's chest. Othniel lifted his head and let out a roar that shook the hall like an earthquake. People huddled to avoid any falling debris from the ceiling, or toppling lampstand, and brazier.

Gunnar scrambled backwards in fear, yet anxious in regard of Axel. Nollen managed to join him, also apprehensive.

Othniel lowered his head to huff on Axel's face. Axel gasped with an intake of air. His eyes snapped open. Othniel removed his paw to reveal no chest wound. Axel breathed hard for several seconds of confusion.

"Be at ease, Son of Eldar."

Axel blinked, as he focused on the speaker. "Othniel?" his voice hoarse with recovery.

"Aye, Son of Eldar.

Axel gingerly rose to his elbows. Audible gasps came from all around. Slightly confused, he tried to discern his location. "Where am I?" Startled, he jerked when someone quickly came alongside him.

"The Great Hall of Sener," Gunnar said a bit weak, but smiling.

"Gunnar. You're wounded."

"At least I'm alive. And now, so are you." He laughed with a few sobs of relief. "I don't ever want to see that again."

"That makes two of us," Nollen added his emotional agreement.

"I don't want to feel it again." Axel touched his chest.

"Rise, Son of Elder," said Othniel. "Take up Emet!"

Mather came forward. He drew what appeared to be a plain sword from his scabbard. "My liege." He held it out with both hands.

When Axel took hold, the plain sword transformed into a magnificent blade of silver with a gold hilt. Ancient Eldarian was engraved in the blade.

"Now meet the enemy!" This time when Othniel breathed on Axel, he became engulfed in light. When the light faded, Axel wore kingly armor of gold and silver.

Axel held the pummel before his face in salute of Othniel. "Gott's will be done." He grinned at Gunnar and Nollen.

"I'm coming. No wound will stop me!" Gunnar declared.

Axel looked expectant to Othniel. The lion breathed upon Gunnar. A quick brilliance of light enveloped Gunnar, and quickly faded to reveal his wound healed and clothed in knightly armor.

"Go, faithful warrior," said Othniel.

At Nollen's expectation, Axel kindly said, "Your task is complete. Stay and protect them," he said of Arctander and the others.

In determination, Axel walked the length of the Hall to the main entrance with Gunnar at his side. Ronan, Cormac, Irwin, Gorman, Mather, Ebert, and Jabid followed.

Othniel let out another roar, more thunderous one than before. It reverberated from the Hall, to sound all across Sener.

On the plain outside the city, Bardolf and Alfgar heard the roar.

"Othniel lives!" shouted Alfgar in exultation. The lord of the unicorn let out an ear-piercing bray of summons.

Bardolf added his ferocious howl. Overhead, Artair's cry echoed across the sky. The deafening sounds caused havoc among the flocks of harpys, packs of jackals, and flight of dragons.

The call to battle summoned both men and beasts!

Chapter 41

THE SHAKING OF GREAT HALL SUBSIDED WHEN OTHNIEL'S ROAR ceased. The agitation of those present was slow to ebb, caused by momentary confusion of what to do next.

A Nefal warrior chided to Argus, "We can't stay here like cowards!"

The proud Nefal lord shouted a war cry, "To your vow be true!" He drew his sword. "Kill the lion!"

The moment Argus and his comrades moved, a hail of arrows flew from the gallery. The powerful giants were not so easily felled.

The Ha'tar repeated the war cry and reinforced their allies. Javan, and those loyal to him, joined the fight against Othniel and those for the Son of Eldar. The Great Lion swatted aside all assailants.

Nollen took up the spear of a fallen guard. Although unskilled in formal combat, he used the spear like a quarterstaff. Being made of stronger wood reinforced by metal bindings, the spear took the impact of swords without shattering.

Jarred managed to waylay the guard who possessed the shackle keys. He took cover behind a pillar to unlock his shackles. He then freed Abe and Bart, Arctander, and the women.

"Now me!" Jonas thrust out his hands.

"Why? For more treachery?" Jarred gave the keys to Arctander then moved to join Nollen in fighting. Abe and Bart went with Jarred. Each of them became armed with whatever weapon that found, sword or spear.

"Arctander, please!" Jonas begged. At the hesitation, he pleaded with Sharla. "Don't let me die shackled."

Pricked, Sharla took the keys from Arctander and released Jonas. "Go. Leave."

Instead of doing as she bade, Jonas joined the fight.

"Cower or join Javan and avenge Dolus!" Hertz challenged Bernal and Udell.

"Out there. It's too dangerous in here," Udell said. The captain managed to usher them out of the Hall. They dodged more fighting when the struggle spilled out into the rest of the castle.

Javan's soldiers attempted to prevent Axel, Gunnar, and the others from leaving the main courtyard. An attack of harpys became intercepted by eagles. When Othniel arrived, the soldiers briefly recoiled at sight of the lion. His added strength made short work of those opposing Axel.

Ronan, and the others, commandeered horses waiting in the courtyard. Gunnar made two short whistles when he and Axel reached the main gate. Their horses galloped over to meet. Gilen came with them.

Axel spoke to Gilen. "Not this time, noble pony. Wait for Nollen."

Gilen snorted, tossed his head and stomped.

Axel and Gunnar led the group in a gallop through the streets of Sener. Citizens cleared out of the way of racing horses. Some ran from their homes with weapons in hand to follow Axel. Sounds of victory, freedom, and encouragement of all kinds called to others along the way.

At the rear gate, guards waved them to halt. When it became apparent, they weren't going to stop, the soldiers dove out of the way of being trampled.

Axel raised his sword and shouted, "For Gott! For Eldar!

Those with him repeated the battle cry. Axel and Gunnar headed for the center of the field. Jabid and Ebert broke off to head for the trees. In fact, each representative, went to their troops.

Jabid and Ebert took command of the army, which secretly followed them from The Doane. They managed to transport and assemble two ballistas, one for water, and the other for arrows. Partially shielded by the treeline, the ballistas worked in providing cover fire. Jabid shouted commands for the water team. Ebert led those targeting the dragons with poisoned arrows. While reloading the water ballista, two dragons converged on their position.

"Look out!" came a warning shout.

In haste, they attempted to launch the water ball. Not being at full tension, it only rose halfway where it met dragon fire. The ball disintegrated from the intense heat. The second dragon's scorching flame exploded thirty feet from the ballista. The impact sent men flying and pushed the ballista back off its pad.

"Jabid!" Ebert cried in alarm. "Fire!" he commanded the arrow team.

He didn't wait to see the results of his order, more concerned for Jabid. He raced over but stopped short at seeing Jabid suffered scorching of his clothes, with some burns on his neck near his chin. "Gott, no!" He fell to his knees. "Jabid?"

There came a low groan in response to Ebert's urgent shake. He coaxed Jabid with a second shake. Jabid's eyes slowly opened. "Thank Gott," said Ebert. "How bad are you hurt?"

Jabid shook his head, unable to speak.

"I'll take you to the surgeon." Ebert carefully lifted Jabid and retreated under the cover of trees.

Gorman and Mather rallied the Freelanders. Being a forest region, Freelanders were renowned hunters. Most of the three thousand troops consisted of archers using either longbows or crossbows. One thousand were foot soldiers. Mather commanded the infantry, while Gorman shouted commands to the archers.

Mather led the infantry in support of the east flank against a joint troop of Nefal and Javan's infantry. For being outnumber almost four to one, the Freelanders proved triumphant in more close quarter combat than suffered defeat.

Gorman divided the archers by weapons. Those armed with longbows targeted harpys, while those with crossbows, supported the land-based troops.

Othniel's roar nearly drowned out the noise of battle. Dragons shrieked and fought against the riders' commands. Harpys flew as if injured, which made them easy targets for the eagles. Since the harpy numbers began to dwindle, the eagles flew in formation against the dragons. Some successfully avoided flames while others, not so fortunate.

The lion's roar also made the Black Jackals suddenly whimpered in pain. Bardolf sent a large pack of Halvor wolves to take down the jackals. Several smaller packs of wolves attacked a Nefal troop of dire-buffalo riders. Alfgar dispatched fifty unicorns to help the wolves bring down the massive beasts. The unicorns used their horns to inflict wounds, along with mighty hooves to kick and knock down the enemy.

The Nefal drew spears from the weapons' harness to try and thwart the attack. However, coordinated efforts of unicorns and wolves proved more effective than a single Nefal warrior could repel.

Ronan, Cormac, and Irwin split their command into three companies. Cormac engaged the Nefal on the west flank, while Irwin went east to aid The Doane against the Ha'tar. Ronan rode in support of Axel and Gunnar in the thick of battle. They faced Javan's seasoned troops.

The talons of a harpy knocked Ronan from his horse, and right into the path of a charging dire-buffalo rider. He attempted to roll away when a back hoof of the dire-buffalo clipped him in the lower back and sent him sliding some twenty feet along the ground. Injured, he couldn't rise when the Nefal turned the dire-buffalo for a second charge. Ronan held his sword ready to make any defense.

The Nefal heard the vicious growl a second before Bardolf leapt at his face. The Nefal and Bardolf fell to the ground where the alpha landed on the warrior. Riderless, the dire-buffalo ran off, away from Ronan. Unable to breathe due to Bardolf's powerful jaws around his throat, the Nefal gurgled and grew still.

Ronan managed to rise to his knees. "My thanks," he painful grunted to Bardolf.

"You're wounded?"

"Kicked in the small of the back by one of those beasts." He pushed himself to rise but bent over with an annoyed scowl of pain. "I don't think anything broken, but …"

"Retire and tend your wound."

"No!" Ronan bit back a groan to stand. "I've been kicked before. It will not stop me this day."

Irwin rode over. He led Ronan's horse by the reins. "Did you lose something?"

Ronan didn't reply. It took great effort to silence any verbal expression of agony when he mounted. Irwin noticed. "Not a word," Ronan chided before he rode back into battle.

Bardolf moved in front of Irwin's horse to delay pursuit. "Watch him closely. A dire-buffalo's kick is dangerous."

Irwin nodded, and hastened after Ronan.

The citizens who followed Axel, flooded out of the gate to join the fray. Many shouted: "In the King's service!"

Other citizens joined the Ha'tar and Nefal in defense of Javan. A scruffy man hurried to Bernal to aid him in battle against a Ganel. The added strength ended with the Ganel wounded and forced to withdraw.

"My thanks …" Bernal blinked in astonishment. "Destry?"

"You don't need an explanation, remember?"

"You're alive. That's all that matters." Bernal embraced Destry.

"Let's both stay that way." He raised his sword. "Death to the traitors!"

They raced back into battle.

Though exhausted from effort, Axel emerged triumphant against a Nefal warrior on a dire-buffalo. The *thump-thud* of a dragon alerted him to the enemy's approach. He turned his horse in time to see a dragon poised to breathed fire. He snapped the reins for the horse to bolt just as the flame reached them. The exploding force of dragon fire striking the ground knocked Axel off his horse.

Stunned, he barely recognized the charging Ha'tar foot soldier. He raised his sword in defense when the Ha'tar suddenly pitched forward, seriously wounded. Curious, he noticed Nollen mounted on Gilen, and armed with a sword.

"My task isn't finished until you're crowned," Nollen said.

Axel grinned and stood. "What about the others?"

"The Hall is secured, and Javan in custody."

Axel whistled for his horse. Once mounted, he said to Nollen, "Stay close to me, since I still need your help." They returned to battle.

For not having battle experience, Nollen threw himself into the conflict. Most of his encounters happened with Javan's soldiers, and a few Ha'tar infantrymen.

The swift passing of a retreating, riderless dire-buffalo startled Gilen. The pony reared and threw Nollen. Not accustomed to the noise and confusion of battle, Gilen bolted.

Nollen scrambled to his feet. "Gilen! Come back here!"

A rising war cry from behind, alerted him to danger. He moved in time to see a battle-scarred Ha'tar race towards him with a raised spear.

"Gan!" Nollen exclaimed in surprise recognition.

Gan never reached Nollen. Gunnar intercepted the Ha'tar and cut him down.

"Not good to fight on foot in this fracas."

Nollen stared at Gan, stunned, then angry. "He plagued us for years."

"Now it's over. At least, that part is. There is more to do this day. Where is Gilen?" Gunnar stood in the stirrups to look for the pony.

"He doesn't like battle and bolted." Nollen grimly looked about at the devastation. "Can't say I like it either."

Gunnar made the same whistle as earlier to summon the horses. A distant whinny came followed by hooves. Gilen returned. The pony breathed heavy, covered in sweat, and pawned the ground.

"Courage, noble pony, and you'll both survive this day," said Gunnar.

Nollen took hold of the reins. "Let's listen to him. I do," he said to Gilen before he mounted.

By mid-afternoon the battle ended. No harpys remained while the two surviving dragons awkwardly flew away. One ballista lay in burning ruin from dragon fire, while the other broken, but salvageable.

Weary and battle-soiled, Axel surveyed the field littered with dead from men and beasts. Gunnar and Nollen waited behind him. They too appeared exhausted, sweaty, and stained from fighting.

Othniel, Alfgar, and Bardolf arrived. Alfgar and Bardolf suffering some minor wounds. Their hides and fur splattered and blemished. Only Othniel remained unscathed of personal injury.

"The day is won, Son of Eldar," announced Othniel.

"At a high cost." Axel motioned to the plain.

"Your sacrifice among them."

Axel leaned on the saddle bow, his studious gaze directed at the Great Lion. "I didn't expect to survive the Blood Oath."

Othniel grinned. "Unknown to Ottar, Javan's ancestor, Gott made a covenant with Oleg when he assumed the throne. For his faithfulness, Gott promised his line would not end."

"Oleg's foolishness almost undid the covenant," Gunnar groused.

"No," said Othniel, who then quoted, *"Yet my covenant with Oleg will remain. I do not deal foolishly like men. My word is forever.* The covenant was never in jeopardy.

"I never doubted that Gott would keep his covenant," began Axel in humble dispute. "It's been my prayer since I began this undertaking. I just didn't expect to survive."

"Your unselfish obedience satisfied Gott. And since you are Oleg's last offspring, it was up to me to keep you safe."

"That is why we mourned when Othniel was captured," said Alfgar. "If he died ..."

"I would not have survived," Axel concluded.

"Why didn't Dolus kill you instead of imprisonment?" Nollen asked Othniel.

"Ego. Daily, he gloated about his superiority in thwarting Gott's plan. Little did he realize, he actually helped fulfill prophecy by allowing me to be present when it happened." He then said to Axel, "When you are crowned, Sener will return to the glory it once had, and peace restored to Eldar."

"Peace," Axel repeated, his sober gaze again drawn to the dead.

Othniel nudged Axel's leg to get attention. "Come. Alfgar and Bardolf will tend to this task."

Axel sheathed Emet to follow Othniel back to Sener.

Chapter 42

BY NIGHTFALL, THE WOUNDED HAD BEEN TENDED, THE DEAD buried, and citizens celebrated liberation. For those who served Javan, the atmosphere proved more subdued, as they faced an uncertain future.

Cleaned, and arrayed in royal attire, Axel stood before the hearth in what had been Dolus' study. He learned from an old chamberlain that King Oleg used the room as his private study. Axel ordered all trophies cleared and properly buried. He heard the knock a moment before Gunnar entered with another man.

"This is Sylvan. The agent," Gunnar introduced him.

"My liege." Sylvan bowed.

For a moment, Axel regarded Sylvan. His eyes contained neither condemning nor commendation. Even his voice remained neutral. "Arctander tells me you were chosen because we are related."

Sylvan produced his medallion. "From the line Oleg's sister, Gerta."

Axel examined the medallion. "Cousin then."

"Aye, my liege."

Axel returned the medallion. "Are there any more relatives?"

"Sadly, none that I am aware of."

Axel pursed his lips in consideration. "What reward would ask of me?"

Sylvan became slightly offended. "I did not undertake my assignment for any reward. It is my duty to you, as liege kinsman, and before Gott by my Oath."

Pleased, Axel smiled. "Arctander told me you would say as much."

At the change of demeanor, Sylvan, asked, "This was a test?"

"I would be remiss not to examine everyone. Will you hold that against me?"

"No! I—"

Axel lightly laughed and clapped Sylvan's shoulder. "Be at ease. Though you do not ask, you shall be rewarded. A baronet, as befitting your royal rank."

"I … I don't know what to say," Sylvan stammered.

"Thank you is usually in order." Gunnar winked at Sylvan.

"Aye. Thank you, my liege."

"Until tomorrow." Axel dismissed Sylvan.

Gunnar shut the door on Sylvan's departure. "What plans do you have for our wily young trader, and pathfinder extraordinaire?"

Axel warmly smiled. "To be honest, I'm sure yet. Would he even accept a position at court, or will he return to Far Point?"

"You might ask him. He's waiting outside."

The statement surprised Axel. "Why didn't he come in with you?"

"Because, *you* are to be crowned tomorrow. There is new protocol with *the king*."

"Not for Nollen." Axel opened the door to see Nollen waited across the hall. "Come in, my friend." When Nollen did as beckoned, Axel shut the door. With great affection, he smiled at Nollen. "I don't know what we would have done if Gott had not directed us to you."

"I just led you around," Nollen modestly replied. "You," his voice became choked, "sacrificed everything."

"Don't diminish your contribution, my friend." Axel held Nollen by both shoulders. "You went from a skeptic to a seasoned man of faith. One, whose steadfast heart, carried him through the darkness time. You do your parents proud. And honor your king. How does one repay such a man?"

Nollen swallowed back emotions at the compliment. He shrugged with embarrassed uncertainty. "Hearing you call me *friend* is nice."

Axel heartily laughed. "Always! As such, you never need permission to come into my presence. I could also give you an appointment at court in charge of all commodities. Or have Far Point rebuilt. Both, perhaps."

Nollen flashed a sly smile. "Commodities, uhm."

Gunnar laughed. "The trader finally emerges."

"Done!" cheered Axel. "For tonight, rest. Tomorrow begins a new day for Eldar."

Bells of the castle cathedral rang in the rising of the sun. For the first time since Oleg's reign, the clear melody resonated. Shutters and windows opened, curious of the sound none had heard in their lifetime.

Servants, who once held their faith in secret, now served joyfully. With a song of praise on their lips, and hearts overflowing, they prepared the Great Hall for a coronation.

Nobles, commoners, tradesman, and farmers began to arrive. Among the mass of humanity, mingled unicorns, wolves, eagles, and a Great Lion. Some were wary of Othniel, but the lion patiently waited near the platform. To one side, stood Nollen with Ida, Jarred, Sharla, and the boys.

Ida's smile quivered. "What would Papi and Marmie say if they had lived to see this?"

Nollen comforted his sister. "They made this possible." He flashed a mischievous grin to Jarred. "Though I think Marmie would have been more pleased to see you two finally married."

"Oh, you!" Ida playfully punched his shoulder.

Humble, and uncertain, Jonas approached. He wore shackles and escorted by two guards.

"I … I'm not sure where to begin. I have so much to apologize for. Most of all, to you," Jonas said to Sharla. "I utterly failed as husband, and father." He nodded toward the boys. His sheepish gaze found Nollen. "I held great bitterness towards you. Anger propelled me to act in ways I never thought I could. Including … killing a man. Though not on purpose, but it happened. Now, I will pay for that crime." He blinked back tears of sorrow and regret. "I hope that someday, all of you can forgive me."

Ida comforted Sharla, who wept at Jonas' confession. Even the boys grew misty-eyed.

Gunnar appeared on the platform. He signaled up to the gallery where trumpeters waited. They played a regal anthem. Gunnar took his place to stand just left of the throne.

From the back room, Arctander appeared first, all bedecked in high priestly robes. Axel followed, dressed in white and gold, with purple accents. When Axel sat upon the throne, the trumpets ceased.

"Let us pray!" Arctander lifted his arms.

"Wait!" Sharla rushed to the platform. "Mercy, my liege."

Axel cast a knowing glance to Arctander before he spoke to Sharla. "For whom do you seek mercy?"

"My husband." She pointed back to Jonas.

Axel barely looked where she pointed. "Jonas' crimes are many."

"You know about him?" she asked with confusion.

"I sent him to seek your forgiveness, on Arctander's advice."

Sharla gaped curiously at Jonas, who nodded. Axel's voice brought her focus back to him.

"Do you forgive him?"

"Aye." She wiped her eyes. "It is for his crime of killing that I ask mercy for his life to be spared. Prison, but not death."

Axel motioned to Gunnar, who briefly disappeared from the platform while he continued to speak to Sharla. "It appears his crime was greatly exaggerated. Is that not so, Master Destry?" he asked without turning, since he heard the footsteps of return.

"Destry?" Jonas shouted in surprise. "How?"

"He was discovered among the captives loyal to Javan," Gunnar began in explanation. "A guard sent word and brought him to me."

"Explain to him why you faked your death," Axel commanded Destry.

Stubbornly reluctant to reply, Gunnar jerked on Destry's arm for compliance. "Revenge!" spat Destry.

"What for? I never did anything to you!" Jonas rebuffed.

"Revenge against those of the Faith!" Destry vehemently declared.

Axel's eyes narrowed in wrath. His raised voice almost echoed in the hall. "Javan was executed before dawn. Those who fought with him, will share his fate. Divine punishment for offensives against Gott and his people." He made a curt wave to Gunnar, who in turned, handed Destry to soldiers.

In the time it took for Destry to be taken from the Hall, Axel regained his composure. Compassion replaced wrath, as he once again addressed Jonas. "You are not guilty of murder. Your other misdeeds are not crimes in the legal sense. Morally, well, it is between you and those you wronged to deal with. Release, him," he instructed the guards.

Sharla shed joyful tears, as they removed Jonas' shackles. In chastened gratitude, he knelt almost prostrate before the platform. His voice contrite, and eyes filled with shameful tears.

"Such mercy is undeserved, as my foolish misdeeds sought to bring you harm. I cannot express the depth of my sorrow. When I saw your sacrifice … forgive me, my king!"

"I do. Now, rise, Jonas of Gilroy."

Wracked by sobs of relief Jonas needed Sharla's help to stand.

"Take him over with others," Arctander quietly told Sharla. Once they joined the group, Arctander began the ceremony.

"Let us pray." He raised his hands. "Almighty Gott, we give you thanks this day for restoring that which was lost. With each of these Treasures, we ask you to bless Axel, the Son of Eldar, the True King of your choosing."

He picked up the Book of Kings. "With this book, is established the True King's right to reign." He approached Axel. "Do you swear upon the book that you are Gott's chosen?"

Axel placed his hand on the cover. "I so swear."

Arctander handed the book to an attendant. He then took Emet. "With this sword, do you swear to defend the honor of Gott and protect Eldar from all enemies?"

Axel stood to place his hand on the hilt. "I so swear". When Arctander yielded Emet, Axel placed it in the sheath he wore, and sat.

Arctander next took the scepter. "With this scepter, do you swear to rule justly and rightly?"

Axel took hold of Shevet. "I so swear."

Arctander released hold to Axel. He held out the Star of Conant. "With this stone, do you swear to rule using wisdom?"

Axel reached out to touch the diamond. "I so swear."

Arctander placed the diamond firmly in its place on Sadok. He lifted the crown over Axel's head. "With this crown, do you swear to reign as Gott's representative in Eldar? To submit to Gott's precepts and laws for as long as you live? To teach them to your descendant not to stray from them?"

"Before Gott, I so swear."

"Then by the power granted me as high priest, I crown you, Axel, True King of Eldar. May Gott bless your reign."

The moment Arctander placed the crown on Axel's head, a heavenly brightness filled the Hall. The walls, columns, floors, and windows wondrously transformed to a magnificence lost. The metamorphosis spread from the Hall to the rest of the castle, out into the streets, down each level of the city until finally, Sener shined as it once did hundreds of years earlier. Thus, the reign of the True King began.

About the Author

Shawn Lamb is a multi-award-winning author of Christian fiction ranging from age 8 to adult. She is also an event speaker. Since 2010, Shawn has participated in homeschool conventions, book fairs, comic cons, and festivals throughout the Southeast, Midwest and Mid-Atlantic regions.

As a former screenwriter for children's television, and author of numerous books, she brings over 30 years' experience dealing with publishing and Hollywood to her speaking engagements.

For more information about Shawn's books and possible speaking engagements, visit www.allonbooks.com.

Made in the USA
Middletown, DE
14 August 2022